OMNIBUS

- **An Elongated Shadow**
- **Baying at the Moon**
- **Dream Peddlers**

OMNIBUS

- **An Elongated Shadow**
- **Baying at the Moon**
- **Dream Peddlers**

Dr. Lalit Kumar Singh Babu

BLACK EAGLE BOOKS
Dublin, USA

 BLACK EAGLE BOOKS

USA address:
7464 Wisdom Lane
Dublin, OH 43016

India address:
E/312, Trident Galaxy, Kalinga Nagar,
Bhubaneswar-751003, Odisha, India

E-mail: info@blackeaglebooks.org
Website: www.blackeaglebooks.org

First International Edition Published by
BLACK EAGLE BOOKS, 2024

OMNIBUS
An Elongated Shadow | Baying at the Moon | Dream Peddlers
by Dr. Lalit Kumar Singh Babu

Cover & Interior Design: Ezy's Publication

ISBN- 978-1-64560-083-1 (Paperback)
Library of Congress Control Number: 2024939364

Printed in the United States of America

CONTENTS

AN ELONGATED SHADOW

by

Dr L.K. Singh Babu

FOREWORD

Forty five years back Lalit Kumar Singh Babu was a student of M.P.C. College, Baripada, a premier higher educational institution of the state. I had the privilege to be his teacher. Those were the halcyon years of the college. A band of selfless, brilliant and dedicated teachers, disciplined and curious knowledge seekers, the students built up the rich tradition of the college. Lalit was soft spoken, respectful, unassuming but always determined to achieve something in life. He had a sense of purpose in life. Singh Babu was a voracious reader. He had encyclopaedic knowledge in many subjects. His finer sensibility and taste for literature impressed me most. A teacher by profession, he is mainly a creative literary artist, i.e., poet and novelist. Even in his student days he stood for excellence and rejected mediocrity in every walk of life. Lalit subsequently developed interest in Homoeopathy.

I had the good fortune to go through the manuscript of his novel 'An Elongated shadow'. I read it time and again with interest. Subhas is the central character of the novel. Like all human beings he too had ambitions in life, hopes and aspirations. But coming as he did from a middle class family which suffered from financial crunch, Subhas had to make compromise at every stage. As a result he could not become what he wanted to be in life. That is the tragedy. But caught in the midst of adverse circumstances, he never lost his cool. And this is the brighter part of his character. Lalit has brought in many subplots to make the novel more interesting. Many of them are imaginary. But much of the theme is real. He is a deeply religious person and believes in total surrender to God. And that is why he is sometimes unsparing and critical in relation to persons masquerading as litterateurs and poets. Incidents drawn from the contemporary society wrapped in the prevailing social fabric have been woven into the grand mosaic of 'An Elongated Shadow'. The language is simple, vivid and crisp.

The novel is small but beautiful, slender but sweet. I commend the book to the present generation, and the generations to come.

I hope and trust that Lalit will keep on writing, and give us still richer literary products in future.

I wish to live to see him achieve greater laurels.

Buddha Purnima   **Prof. Dipak Kumar Sarangi**
The 2nd May 2007,   *Retd. Principal,*
                         Kalpana BhavanM.P.C. College, Baripada.

PREFACE

During my college days I had gone through a book "Lust for life" by Irving Stone where he delineated the grim struggle of Vincent Van Gogh to be a renowned painter and how this obsession brought his tragic end in the most deplorable way.

It was so much impressive that it has left an almost indelible imprint in my mind since that day. Time passed. Again I read it after a long lapse of time. But this time I started with a tangible vision, with a subtle and discriminating analytical mind and towards the end a tacit compassion for the widely acclaimed Dutch artist streamed in the deepest core of my heart.

This inspired me so much so that a few days later, moved by a sudden impulse, I wrote this biographical novel in which most part of the main character, though not a proto type, as I know most intimately, has some analogy with the ill-fated Dutch artist although their ways of living and modes of thinking are poles apart. I don't know why the man of this tribe takes birth time and again in different names and in different places.

Subhas, the pivotal character of this novel observes life at very close quarters. To him the most amazing thing is this human being with whom he interacts. The gradual deterioration of human values, the bizarre society where only money counts so much and the duplicity of the socalled educated drives him distraught. He feels himself drifted away, almost marooned and the sum of life he has been working out so far proved a huge miscalculation leaving him in the lurch, but there is no going back.

Life, a sobriquet of an enigma, is like an inscrutable territory where many things remain concealed and a much deeper aspect is still to be revealed. Strange…strange are the ways of life.

While writing this novel, I have been spurred on by a host of friends like Mr. Bijay Kumar Barik, Dr. Pranab Ranjan Bhuyan, Mr. Ganeswar Sahu, Mr. Satyabrat Barik, Mr. Pradeep Kumar Pattanaik and this impetus dogged me through the drudgery of domestic work till its completion.

S. Radhakrishnan, the former President of India and a great philosopher of his times has once aptly said, "Through suffering we come to understand."

Let this suffering be our driving force to tide over all the encumbrances to fulfil our assigned mission.

Dr L.K. Singh Babu
Janardanpur, Baripada
September 5, 2005

ONE

The child ever so much fond of groundnut, clamoured for it. The parents tried to console him by patting him on the back but the obstinate child was inconsolable. It was late evening and all the shopkeepers had downed their shutters and had returned to their respective homes. It was a time when Baripada town had not expanded to its present limits. The grocery, stationery and drapery shops were very few in number and the Marwari community was the prominent merchant class which had a commanding control over the market. The roads were rugged, uneven and full of ruts and ridges and specially so in the rainy season. The rain water got accumulated here and there preventing people from walking along the road with ease. Sometimes due to sudden rush of vehicles, the splash of muddy water would stain the trousers and shirts of the passers-by making them fling filthy language at the driver. The rickshaw-pullers pedalled laboriously with heavy load straining their calf muscles drenched in profuse perspiration. There was no facility of electricity everywhere and most parts were submerged in massive darkness. Only the commercial areas where there was transaction of business were faintly lighted. The people were still conservative and they would not allow their ladies to go to market. Though the vegetables and other provisions of life were damn cheap, the people had no monetary stability to purchase them. To be the owner of a thousand rupees was a remote dream for them. One "seer" of meat would cost hardly two rupees. The price of fish was even cheaper than that. During winter, when all types of vegetables were available in plenty in the market, people would trudge to the market place to buy vegetables. In the late hours of the night the vegetables would sell dirt cheap, even four 'seers' an anna. Specially the brinjals were comparatively cheap and people would carry their bags overloaded with brinjals. The ladies of the house would roast them in fire, peel the outer coarse surface, mash the heat-softened brinjals inside a flat plate and then they would lace it with chopped onion and green pepper. Ginger paste ground on curry stone would be an add-on. Then this appetising fare would be thoroughly mixed with fried rice, a very tasty and palatable food for the inhabitants of the area. Young and old alike would take this to their hearts' content.

Though we got independence in 1947, the Britishers had not quitted this land fully. There were churches, schools and colleges organized by missionaries and the authorities had been receiving a heavy amount in donation for the management of these institutions. Very often the nuns of the churches would visit families aquainted with them and they would offer biscuits and chocolates to the children. They would not come to them but when they were lured by these tasty things, they would come to take those things from their hands.

The nuns often recited in chorus the song of Jesus Christ, the meaning being like this:

O my sinners ! Why do you go to the path of sin,
Don't you understand this...........

Their English tone in local language was, no doubt, very pleasant to hear. Some children burst into laughter by hearing their accent of local language. The division of the sub- continent was a bone of contention but at length it was severed into two parts, India and Pakistan. A greater part of Punjab was annexed to this territory of Pakistan. The great historical exodus began. A large number of Sikhs and Hindus whatever belongings they could manage to carry were forced to flee their native land. They lost their property, lost their relatives and above all their social position. Communal riots took a very violent form all over the country. Everywhere there was a hue and cry. At this opportune moment, hoodlums and hooligans looted property, set fire to houses, shops and committed all manner of heinous deeds. The whole country seemed to be on a burning cauldron.

But this town was an exception to that. It remained undisturbed and untumultuous by any type of communal atrocities. The two communities went hand in hand. Although they were not at loggerheads, the police were alert day and night taking all types of measures preventing upheaval of any chaotic situation. Still the minority community remained in constant fear and anxieties lest they should be retaliated at dead of night. The unruly and turbulent boys of the minority community reading in schools and colleges remained in unknown hush-hush trepidation, as if their parents, brothers and sisters would be dragged to the bare street at some unearthly hour of night and hacked to pieces; the muddy roads being reddened and spilled over by human blood. But to their utter dismay, no such thing happened.

When the town was overcast by the clouds of such fear and doubts, Subhas came out of his house to observe the situation. A poor boy as he was, he wanted to be tutored by his class teacher. Akhil Babu was not a greedy man although he tutored thirty to forty students in his first coaching class in the morning. Five to six students had been spared from the tuition fees. A very meagre amount of money like Rs.10/- per month was charged to each student. Even then the poverty-ridden parents heaved a deep sigh as they were incapable of paying such a paltry amount. A larger percentage of the parents could not afford to meet the expenditure of students as one rupee was also a big amount for them.

They could purchase neither their text books nor pens.

A rough note book was sufficient for them . They would roam hither and thither rummaging about the drain and gutters which ran just near the court and Government offices of the town. The rejected papers, one side written and blank the other, were scattered in these drains and they would collect them for preparing their rough note books. They could be utilized for two times, first time in pencil and second time in ink, as the writing in pencil was not so bold and prominent, overlaying it one could write on that paper in ink.

"Navin, you look at this pile", said Subhas. "The major portion of it has already been burnt", his tone was desperate.

Navin and Subhas stepped down the gutter and picked up the unburnt ones. Navin held up a handful of papers, counted them one by one and told Subhas, "It will do the needful, no more of it. The other day my mother bought me a new note book.

I have preserved it for Mathematics. Do you know, Surendra sir made me stand up on the bench as I did not workout the sum in my Mathematics note book. That devil tweaked my ears so ruthlessly that I burst into tears. He has asked me to bring the note book next time, otherwise he will break my spine."

"Subhas, to speak the truth, we poor fellows should not continue our studies so miserably. You know that my widow mother fries rice and sells them in the market. She is to support my other two sisters and me. How long could she carry the burden of the whole family and feed us by breaking her bone? Sometimes her legs and hands would ache terribly and she would beat her legs on the floor out of intolerable pain. I had to massage her whole body with warm mustard oil".

"Yes Navin, more or less the case is the same with me also. My father could not purchase me History and Geography books. So I have to copy them out in my note book. You know if the books are not at hand, how confused you will be at the time of examination".

"You see Subhas, we are not born with a silver spoon in our mouth. Our lot is like that as providenced by God. We cannot be like Devendra and Gaura, the sons of those moneyed persons. We have one shirt and a pair of pants. We have to wear them for six days and wash them on Sundays. Ironing our shirt and pants is a luxury for us. If it is torn some where, we have to go to a seamster and get it mended. The only consolation is that most of the people of our country go unfed and unclad."

On their way home, they stopped near a large triangular field. It was a grassy land with big 'kendu' trees here and there, In the corner, a lot of wild plants and shrubs had sprouted. Bordering the field stood a large number of sitahar in a row and the blooming flowers had profusely carpeted the ground. The flowers had been thoroughly drenched in the morning dew and were icy-cold to the touch. On the eastern side of the field there was a slew of massive anthills. During rainy season mushrooms grew abundantly on the base and top of those anthills and people would collect them in their bags. Very often poisonous snakes like the cobra would crawl helter skelter in search of food and they would not come out of their hideouts by day when the wayward kids played football or hockey in that field. On the northern side, there were some drooping deodars standing like the watchmen of the field.

As the place was desolate and no habitations were there nearby excepting a royal family of the then Maharaja, various types of birds flocked there and twittered all day long. On the opposite side of the road in close vicinity, there is a live-stock hospital surrounded by a compound wall. Within a stone's throw of that, there resided the secretary of Maharaja with his family. A Bengali gentleman of short stature, bulky body and rotund face, generally possessive by nature, lived there with his three adult sons, daughters and a tender aged grandson and a grand daughter.

Gopal Ray, the name we came to know later, was very honest and upright and he was the sole man in charge of the estate of the then Maharaja. Parimal, his youngest son, happened to be our classmate and in that capacity, we frequently visited him. His friends always held his father in awe and they never ventured to go near him.

Navin collected some Sitahar flowers and pressing his two lips together blew them hard one by one. Just like a piper, he blew them imitating the style of a snake charmer for a while. Then he dropped them with sudden disgust and said to Subhas, "It is getting late, I have to reach home earlier because my mother would go to the pond to have her bath. I don't know why she becomes so much worried if I don't get home in time. Now you pack a bunch of flowers in your pants pocket and spread them on the study table. You must inhale its sweet scent for some hours till the flowers wither".

TWO

"Subhas ! are you not ready for school ? It is already nine, don't you see?"

"Yes, mother ! I am ready but the thing is that Nareshda has not yet finished his bathing."

"Finish early and get ready to have your lunch. And don't forget to take your library book before you leave for school."

It was 4.30p.m. when Subhas returned from school. His mother swept the whole house with a broom. They had occupied two rooms only. One was a room for relaxation and another was meant for studies as well as guest room. As they were living in a joint family, all the rooms and verandas were awfully stuffed with elderly members of the family and young children. The eldest of them lived in a separate quarters of that house with his wife and children. His wife, as the eldest of all the daughters-in-law, did no household chores. She did manage the expenditure of the joint family, receive the guests and hear the grievances of the other daughters-in-law with motherly affection. Everybody in the house paid their respects to her and bowed their heads in allegiance.

The maid servant of the house was an old woman of fifty years and she did ungrudgingly all the household work like clearing the garbages of the house, washing the utensils and shabby clothes of each member. Before evening, when the twilight was still glistening in the sky, she would remove the stain of the lantern glass covers by mopping it repeatedly with a rag and put them aside in the corner of the room. She would be always seen flying from one corner of the house to another to be at the beck and call of her mistress.

The children never showed their curiosity regarding her whereabouts. Gradually she became an integral part of the family sharing their weal and woes.

After washing his hands and feet, Subhas would roll a mat on the floor and sit for studies. He used to study for two to three hours, quite engrossed. But his studies would be interrupted in the middle if some body of the house would take the lantern away on some pretext or other. He would wait till the arrival of the lantern. If not, then long waiting would make him drowsy and he would fall asleep on the floor and snore heavily.

Subhas grumbled violently when one night the maid servant stumbled over his ink-pot.

"You have broken my ink-pot. I bought those ink-pills from the market but you blind woman spoiled my ink as your are most unaware of your foot steps. I won't listen to any of your excuses. Now you go to market and bring me the same.'

'Yes, my dear, it is really a great mistake of mine as I am unable to see your ink-pot owing to my dim vision. Tomorrow morning I must purchase it for you.'

The maid servant used to receive a very meagre amount of money as her monthly wages. Subhas had no inkling wherefrom she could compensate his invaluable ink.

There were various types of trees at the back of their garden like mango, jack fruit, tamarind, bael, berries etc. On the extreme side of the garden, there were lemon plants of hardly ten to twelve in number. Twice a year, the branches of those trees became overladen with lemons. A number of ripe lemons would be collected for making lemon pickles. When a gentle breeze passed through those branches, they swung to and fro and a sweet scent of ripe lemons filled the atmosphere. Behind the garden, a long stretch of boggy land was there where some hundred years ago, a fortress was built by the then Maharaja. Now no trace of that fortress was seen there as it had gradually crumbled into pieces by the ravages of time. A shallow pond with knee-deep water was in the middle of that marshy land, almost covered by lotus flowers, aquatic plants and creepers like 'kalamb'.

The soapnut, cactus, datepalm, bamboo and all sorts of thorny plants grew so luxuriantly that it made the land inaccessible. Only some local people were going inside for defecation. A large flock of wild geese was seen flapping their wings and swimming across the pond water. They would hover in the sky honking endlessly and then diving into the water with a splash. Some times the people of neighbouring areas would carry a deadbody and burn it there. It was an ideal place for the municipal authority to unload all filthy detritus. The scavenger would lit fire to the pile of that garbage, with column of smoke going up in curls and mingling in the air. The water hen, heron and golden oriole would appear suddenly there and then spreading their wings with a jerk would disappear behind the trees. The hooting of the owls splitting the stillness of the air was heard in the thicket and the heart throbbed in premonition of some unknown impending disaster.

It was a wintry morning and the fog was still hanging like a curtain in the air. Subhas hurried to his elder brother, Surendrada and awakened him from his bed. As it was biting cold outside and his brother fell into a deep sleep towards the last part of the night, he was not in a mood to leave his bed so early. However he exerted himself and went to the veranda to wash his sleep-swollen face. He poured some water from a pitcher into a glass, gurgled and sprinkled some on his face. "Why have you come so early?', his elder brother asked him while mopping his face with a dry towel."

"Brother, in winter the meat of wild goose is very much relishing. You please come out with your gun and see for yourself how a flock of wild geese is hovering just under our very nose" Subhas implored.

Without delay, his brother loaded the gun and went to the back of the garden. "Subhas ! hurry up and call our all bush-fighters. We should be all alert. If any goose would fall in the thicket without our notice, then it would be too difficult to trace it out. So we must be very vigilant" – warned Subhas's brother.

Subhas shoved them all to awaken from their night reverie. They immediately sprang to their feet and rushed out to rally round their elder brother.

"Do you need any camouflage, brother" – Subhas murmured, "I must bring you your striped blanket."

"No, not necessary," He shrugged his shoulder." I must lie in ambush beneath the lemon grove and take aim. Rather you tell the others to hide themselves behind that green fence, over there."

The wild-geese were flying in flocks, gay and mirthful, one after another like numerous specks in the vast open blue sky. All of a sudden the gun boomed and from the cartridge a volley of tiny bullets were shot up in their direction. Seven or eight of them descended on the earth; flapped violently and after a while lay motionless.

"Haria ! collect them in a basket", Subhas's tone sounded imperative. "I have to look for other birds fallen unnoticed". He jumped over a hedge, crawled under some matted creepers and emerged into the open space. There lay two birds on the rugged sandy bed of a thin stream. Hurrah ! Subhas stood on the trunk of a fallen tree and lifting the two birds by their legs swung them before their eyes. Then he came in a round about way and joined them.

"Today our elder brother will cook the meat"- Subhas declared. "Of course I must assist him. If some fried arum could be added to that, it would taste excellent. The potato rather spoils the taste, you know."

Three cheers for the bush-fighters. All were in a jovial mood.

One Saturday afternoon in the month of April when Subhas felt terribly restless and was lying on a mat with the door and windows of his room slammed shut, he overheard a crackling sound of fire. To ascertain himself, he opened the windows and his doubts came true. The clump of bamboos was on a blazing fire.

As usual, as on other days, after setting fire to the garbage, the sweeper had left for his home. The fire coursed its way through the thick pad of dry bamboo leaves and gradually it passed its tongue over the adjacent bamboo clump and so was the bonfire.

The conflagration left nothing of its surrounding areas. It extended its sinister tongue upto Subhas's house and within less than one hour, the whole thatched house was wrapped in flames and reduced to ashes. It was a raging inferno. Only the mud walls stood lamenting, carrying the charred straw on their shoulders. The neighbouring people tried their utmost to save the house from the all engulfing hunger of the fire but it was of no avail. During this pandemonium, all the valuables and belongings of the house were kept scattered in a nearby field. When the members of the house ran about here and there in a confused state, the pilferers took advantage of this unguarded moment and looted some articles.

As the evening approached, a makeshift hearth was made to prepare food for the supper. A curtain was drawn to shield it from the gust of the wind. Night deepened and the inmates of the house lay here and there under the star-studded sky. Intermittent howling of jackals accompanied by the hooting of owls was heard from a distance. The soul of the night groaned, groaned in agonizing pain. The moon, overcast by flakes of clouds, cast her eerie beams every where and the burnt house stood like a ghost in deep silence.

The days rolled on. Results came out and the school

was closed for summer vacation. Subhas made himself busy to have a visit to his maternal grand-father's house. He alighted from the bus, walked briskly to his destination, resting a while under some shady trees.

"When did you start, my dear?" enquired his grandmother. "You should have informed us beforehand so that we could have sent a person to carry you back on a bicycle" Her pale face beamed with a smile.

"No, grandma, I did not face any trouble on the way. Besides, this distance is nothing for me. Do you know I used to go on a morning walk every day."

"I know, my dear, still… now you stand here and I will wash your dusted feet with tepid water." She brought a torn towel from somewhere and rubbed his feet a bit forcefully to remove the stain of the dust.

"Your mother never takes care of you all, she is always like that" she resented, knitting her forehead. "Can't she see what a world of dust has accumulated on your feet, how lazy she is, being a daughter of mine. Where is Panchu"? She asked her maidservant. "When you need him, he will be found mucking about, to my lot what a pack of shirkers I have". She shouted.

Panchu suddenly appeared on the scene. "Where have you been, you potbellied fellow ? Subhas has just arrived at our home and you people are nowhere to be found in the time of need. Don't you know he is very fond of fowl and you are to kill one for him ?"

"Yes aunty, I am just going to make necessary arrangements." His tone was apologetic.

It was a small village surrounded by cultivable land on all sides. On the eastern side of the village, flowed a rivulet which merges with the Haldia reservoir.

The village was definitely the gift of this river. All types of crops grew abundantly on its alluvial soil. The village and its neighbouring areas were always evergreen with various types of crops like paddy, wheat, sugar cane, all kinds of pulses and vegetables. As the river abounded with fish, local people only need a pinch of salt and a drop of oil to have a cherishing dish.

Last year, the river was full to its brim because of flood and to a large extent, the left bank of the river had been corroded. The forest starts from this bank and gradually becomes denser towards the interior. A narrow road stretches across the midst of the forest to some remote village. On both sides of the road, the Kurchi plants with flowers would be nodding their heads in rhythm with the tune of gentle breeze. The woodpecker, wagtail, black drongo, partridge, kite and tattler bird would be seen dancing behind the thick branches of the trees.

"Hi, Subhas, you did arrive yesterday. I came to know from Panchu on my returning from the river. Now tell me about your results this year" Satish asked.

"Not upto expectation. Besides you know what a mishap had befallen us," Subhas replied.

"Yes I learnt all about you from my uncle who had been to your place after two days of that accident. Now listen to me, have you had your breakfast ?"

"Don't bother about it. My grandma has just finished her morning ablution and after that she must feed me on curd and flattened rice."

"All right, you must be waiting for me till I return from home with a fishing net. This year the river abounds in fish. Do you know the reason?"

"Not exactly"- Subhas stared at Satish with ignorance.

The embankment gave way on the upper part of the stream. So hardly an hour's of netting will yield you a haul of fish, no doubt."

Both went downstream slightly far out of the bathing ghat. Satish was quite adept in netting fish. The scorching heat of the sun grew sharper but they were fully oblivious of that while busy netting. Some branches of the trees that stood by the brink of the river leaned downwards to the water and their sodden leaves and intertwined creepers became a safe haven for the fishes.

Satish knew the titbits. So he threw the net tirelessly over those places and within one and half an hour, he caught about two seers of a variety of fishes like minnow, gudgeon, shrimp, gilthead, eel, grig etc. After dressing them well, Subhas put them in a narrow-necked basket.

"This much today, Subhas. Let us bathe ourselves at the bathing-ghat as it is already getting late."

"How pleasant and soothing it would be to have a daily dip in the river"-Subhas said while bathing in breast-deep water. " In the town we don't have such a chance. We pour only tap water over our heads which,in my opinion, is no bathing at all."

Satish laughed. " Now my dear crocodile. Please come out of the water because the sooner you get home, the better, otherwise I shall be held responsible for this delay."- spoke Satish while squeezing the towel to drain out the water.

"Subhas, you take the major share of the fish. I don't need much. Hardly a day goes by without fish curry. Give them to your grandmother and she will fry them for you. She will lay by the excess to be used as dried fish"- Satish said caressing his hand very gently.

In the late afternoon, the two friends sat on a big flat stone and went on gossiping, telling the untold things that had been stored in their hearts since long. The sun was setting behind the distant hillocks casting its spells on the treetops.

"That school house near the mango grove is going to crumble; neither the public nor the government do take any heed of that matter, that straw thatched house where once we had started our early schooling"- Satish grumbled pointing in that direction.

"That really reminds us of our early schooling days"- Subhas said with a note of disappointment in his tone.

"Do you remember Satish when my mother told "Galai didi' to carry me in her arms to school, how peevish and unruly I was then. Most hardened and stubborn soul that I was, I would scratch with my nail her whole body but that affectionate heart never showed me any cruelty in return. She could have loosened her grip and let me fall on the ground to teach me a lesson but she would do nothing of that sort instead, what a sort of soft and forgiving heart she had"- Subhas's tone choked with emotion.

"Yes brother, my eldest sister is really a woman of very mild disposition. I have just forgotten to tell you very auspicious news regarding her marriage. Everything has been settled. There remains scarcely twenty days for the marriage to come off."

" Very good news, indeed. I shall be here to join her marriage ceremony"- Subhas's heart danced in exceeding pleasure.

"Subhas, you will be rather glad to know she learnt by heart those parting songs of marriage and has been doing recitation time and again."

"How strange and peculiar our social tradition is !"- Subhas remarked. "There is nothing strange in it, brother, it is obligatory and a bride is required to sing those songs in a wailing tone. Otherwise the relation and neighbours might think that the bride has no soft corner for any one and hence she would be taken amiss"- Satish said analytically.

"May God shower blessings on her"- Subhas saluted with folded hands.

The marriage day drew nearer. Hand written invitations were distributed among all the invitees seeking their gracious presence on that auspicious occasion. Satish's father was meticulous about arrangements. He bought all the necessary things from the market before a week of the marriage.

He remarked, "You see, the bride groom's party will visit our house only for one night. If we fail to feed them to their satisfaction, then it would definitely bring disgrace to our whole village.

Slightest negligence on your part will be seriously viewed, I warn you all to be utmost careful"- he seemed visibly worried.

At last the festive occasion came. Two forerunners arrived just before evening. Satish's father ushered them in to his house and offered them refreshments. They told him the probable time of the arrival of the bride groom's party.

At about 10 p.m., the party arrived in a grand procession. The bridegroom was the centre of all attraction. The altar where marriage was to take place, was thronged with a large number of people, trampling one another. The bridegroom was a stout young man of medium stature and he always bore a smiling face as if kindness and sympathy were writ large on his countenance.

Through sacred incantation of 'mantras' uttered by Brahmin, the marriage ceremony came to an end. Now came the time of departure. When the sacred fire was kept burning at one corner of the altar 'Galai didi' was as immovable as a rock and she was always guided by the barber's wife how to sit on her respective 'asan'. The red flame of fire brightened her face so much so that her exact condition of mind remained undetected. Perhaps she was wiping her tears off and on by the hem of her sari. At the time of departure, she hugged all, reciting that parting song in the most plaintive manner. The whole village felt as if their own daughter was going to take leave of them. The purport of that mournful song may be summed up like this,- "I married beyond that seven hills and across fourteen highlands, 'O' loving mother! Shall I be able to see my native land once again?"

She cried incessantly as if to lighten her heart from long stored anguish. A stream of tears began to roll down her cheek.

The palanquin-bearers carrying the bride and bridegroom disappeared while tottering along that winding course. As the party retreated to a distance the receding tune of 'shehnai' got lost in the murky night leaving an indelible scar of wound in Subhas's heart.

Her marriage, no doubt, created a void in the heart- nay in the soul, never to be fulfilled for a long time. Subhas grew restless- as restless as a bird flapping its wings helplessly inside a barred cage. The memory which he had fostered so far in the sanctuary of his heart, the unalloyed affection that he had received in his childhood days was snatched away so ruthlessly- he could not think further.

Two days later he went to meet Satish. He too felt the same, that same void inundating the whole atmosphere of the house. Satish was found sleeping on a cot staring vacantly at the ceiling with hands criss-crossing his chest. Seeing Subhas, he sat up on the bed and slowly reclined his back on a pillow, his voice inarticulate and hollow, he tried to mutter something as if in soliloquy and with eyes not all there, he finally uttered in a muffled tone as if he had just been roused from a nightmare.

"Must we go to the forest to inhale fresh air and rejuvenate our dull spirits. The lap of nature will help heal our mental wounds"- Satish suggested.

Subhas immediately acceded to this proposal and said, "Well, that sounds right, let us have a stroll in that wooded serenity to relieve us from pent-up agony".

They hiked up their trousers upto the knee and crossed the river. The forest starts from there. There was a day when the wild bears would frequently visit this place and cause a massive destruction of the sugarcane field. Roughly two decades ago, it was a hunting ground for the tigers. People say they could not venture into the interior to answer the call of nature for fear of these wild beasts.

Satish suddenly stopped on the way and pointing to a

deforested area, said, "You must have remembered the bright sunny days of our childhood when we played here together. We would thrust a long reed of grass in the tail end of dragon flies and enjoy their flight, clapping our hands in cruel pleasure. Once I frantically chased a dragon fly, stumbled against a tether and received serious injury on the toe. The nail turned livid and I spent that night sleeplessly tossing on the bed. I thought I was justly penalized for my sinful act and from that day onwards I never trod upon that forbidden path."

They went to the interior, crossed a few barren field and came to a clearing. The air was really very bracing.It pepped them up. A few yards away to their left, a bulky bull was bellowing while pawing the ground with its hooves.

"Some years ago I came upon an infant python behind that earthen mound. It was about twelve feet long and while gliding forward on dry leaves, it was quite unconcerned with my presence. I shuddered from head to foot, blood curdled within for some moments and when it slithered away out of sight, I came to my sense. I retreated a few yards and made a detour to meet my people, busy collecting 'mahul' flowers".

"How strange !, Subhas, I have never seen such a big snake in my life".

This is a rare chance. You won't come across such rock snakes all the time. They come out when they are extremely hungry, otherwise they remain coiled up in the hole".

On their way back home, they waded through the river, ascended the slope and came to a place where the presiding deity of the village had been installed. A number of clay- images of horses and elephants were also worshipped with her. They were well- protected underneath a bower at a little distance from the village. When there was sudden outbreak of any epidemic, the village dehuri would prostrate himself at the feet of the deity and elaborate arrangement would be made for the sacrifice of some black fowls to appease the deity and her associates.

"Hello brother Subhas ! Where had you been ? I had just been to your house to see you. Your grand-mother told me that you and brother Satish might be seen some where near the bank of the river. I just came to inform you that a dance is going to be staged to- night. 'chadeha- chadehani" (fowler and fowler's wife), a merry making so to say"- a village youth reported.

Subhas laughed and nodded his head "yes, I do take keen interest in all these rejoicings. But let me know who is going to act in the role of "chadeha and chadehani".- Subhas enquired.

"You know Trilochan Babu, a teacher of Naupal U.P. school, a veteran indeed. He has been acting in this role for so many years and that Kulamani, who acts chadehani, a real gliding swan, must keep the dace beat through out"- the youth exploded into a peal of laughter.

"All right, we must arrive in time. What do you say Satish ?"

"Yes, yes, I must accompany you to this entertainment show. After dinner, come to our house and from there both of us will go to a place near Chandicharan Babu's house, a village square, where all forms of entertainment are usually staged."

The night sky was overcast with threatening clouds. Only a few stars were blinking behind the veil of some stray clouds overladen with moisture. The air was warm and the earth was still radiating heat before it reached the coolness zone.

"Satish, if it rains tonight, all arrangements will be mucked up."- Subhas's tone was apprehensive.

"No, it may drizzle, but no prospect of continuous rainfall"- Satish assured.

It was an open pandal, lighted by a few petromax lights. Within earshot, there was a green room where a lantern was casting its flickering light. The players were busy doing their make-up.

All around the pandal, there was a large assemblage of people coming from far and near, all village folk, majority of them were cultivators. After the day's toil, they had come to unburden their suffering.

Satish and Subhas were jostled by the crowd and seeing their pitiable condition, some volunteers turned up and escorted them on to the seats meant for the respected persons. They sat down awaiting eagerly the beginning of the show. Along with festoons, some balloons were also hung up on bamboo poles. In the mean time some burst out into a huge uproar. The organiser immediately came on stage requesting them to calm down. He declared that the play would begin in a very short while.

Some whistled, Some hurled abusive language at the organisers for being unpunctual in the commencement of the show.

The play began. First came 'Banku bhai'- the comedian who gave a brief report on the daily activities of the chadeha- the fowler. The tune of music soared high heralding the arrival of the chadeha, and his consort chadehani. They were all in an elated mood eulogizing each others love-lorn heart and quality. In the middle, some misgivings crept into their lives and caused estrangement. Banku bhai became instrumental in bringing about an amicable settlement between them and at last the chadehani yielded to the steady and sincere courtship of the chadeha. Above all the dance of the chadehani was really laudable. Her amorous rolling of eyes and her graceful gait were as nimble as those of a frolicsome gazelle.

Satish whispered in Subhas's ear." I know this boy since long. He always acts in a female role and his voice is also feminine- a real nincompoop-quite befitting to act the role of a chadehani."

Then signalling with his eyes to the audience, he told, "You see Subhas how the people are enjoying the play. Some, here and there, have fallen asleep on the bare ground almost like the dead. I don't understand why they have come instead of sleeping at home?"

The crowd dispersed and when it thinned out Satish asked Subhas, "Have you kept my torch carefully? Hand it over to me and I will lead you out of here safe and sound".

THREE

Having alighted from the bus, Subhas went home straight. He recalled the days when his father could not provide him with the money to purchase the bus ticket. So he was compelled to cover such a long distance on foot. His tender feet ached but their miserable plight impelled him to do so. It is a tyranny, no doubt, on his body and soul, he thought to himself. Do these people come to this world only to increase the number of population ? A person who is not persevering from the beginning suffers like this. He cannot provide his family with food, clothes and shelter, the bare necessities of life. His life is a total failure- a failure which closes all the doors to success for other members too. So they cease to exist. General poverty may not be despicable but Subhas despises abject poverty from his very core. It nips the bud of ambition on its way to flowering. That is why a revolutionary idea sometimes sprouts in his mind to wage an incessant war against this ogre of poverty, a vampire which sucks the blood of an individual rendering him or her quite helpless.

Subhas's mother saw him open the wooden gate through the window. She came to the doorway. Subhas entered the room and kept the bag on the table. He was already wet with profuse sweating. He flung the shirt and banian carelessly on the cot and sat silent. His mother looked askance. Subhas looked up at her and smiled slowly.

"That old and worn out bus could not speed along smoothly for which it took more than an hour to reach the stand. Here is some vegetables and cakes in that bag your mother has packed before my departure."

Subhas rose to his feet and unpacked the bag.

"How are my parents and others? Did you say to them that I could not go as I am preoccupied with some urgent work."

"Yes, I have told them everything, nothing to be worried about. Your mother suffers from backache, that old trouble, you know."

"What can she do? Doing all the drudgery of the house without respite from dawn to midnight, no son or daughter-in-law to help them"- Subhas's mother heaved a deep sigh.

"They can come to our place but they won't. It is not so easy to cut off the tie of one's native place. Your parents will suffer like this. That is their lot"- Subhas became little irritated.

"Subhas, you wash your hands and feet. Then eat something and after that meet your paternal uncle. He returned from Anugul two days back".

"Why has he been there?" Subhas looked up with surprise in his eyes.

"O! you don't know. Your uncle is a chronic asthma patient. He heard from a lot of people that one 'Rantalai Baba' of Anugul is working miracles. He gives some nostrum to the patient. After some days it is expected to bring total cure. He has been to that place with some of our neighbours. God knows whether it is true or false- may be a floating rumour".

"No mother, it is not a farrago of lies. when costly medicine cannot do anything, a herbal root can prove itself extraordinary"- Subhas's tone sounded wise.

"Yes, it can be effective. Your uncle came back hurriedly, because the situation of that place is now something different. As there is no provision to shelter such a large number of people, they are compelled to remain in open space. Moreover there is terrific scarcity of pure drinking water. Where from would they get it ? They drank even the polluted water of the tank. So cholera broke out in that area and took a heavy toll of life. Your uncle narrowly escaped and by the grace of God came back hale and hearty." Subhas's mother was panting with apprehension.

"Mother, I feel terribly hungry. You do one thing. Take one brinjal I have brought from your parent's house. It would be nice to take roasted brinjal with fried rice. You know I am very fond of it." Subhas said while washing his face with tap water.

She disappeared into the kitchen. After half an hour she came back with a plate full of things to eat. Subhas could smell its aroma from a distance and it whetted his appetite on the double.

He began to gulp down the food.

"Where is father? I don't see him any where near?"

"No, he has been to his friend's house. Your father told me the other day that you face a lot of troubles as there is no separate room for your studies. So at present the veranda can be utilized by making it into a small room with the help of a bamboo curtain."

"Don't bother. I can manage it as it is."

"But the only trouble is that it is difficult to manage in the winter as there is no protection. Severity of cold may tell upon your health."

"No mother, I care little whether it is winter or summer"- said Subhas brimmed with confidence.

"Any way you should come out successful. That is our dream"- She picked up the remains on a plate and began to wash it.

"Had my father not come to our help, the situation would have been quite different. He always gives us this and that, specially your admission fees and the cost of books that we are incapable to afford."

That was the only weakest and vulnerable point in the character of Subhas's father. He was an educated person of his times. If willing, he could hold a Govt. job but his independent mind prevented him from doing so, a service holder under an alien power. He became a teacher of some private institution and managed the family with a meagre amount of salary, quite inadequate to make both ends meet. His father-in-law had also resented this. He had given his daughter in marriage to this educated person with a lofty hope that one day his son-in-law would be a promising man in society earning for a comfortable life. But all his expectation became topsy turvy when this gentleman did not like the thraldom under British Govt. He wanted to live in his own way, quite reluctant to eat a humble pie.

It was too difficult to meet the expenditure of a joint family. At last the situation came to a head. Subhas'a father was called for to hold discussion on this matter. It was unanimously decided that it was high time for separation. Everybody should have their separate establishments. Subhas's father was unable to ventilate his feelings before his elder brother before hand. Being the youngest, he had no guts to open his mouth but his eldest brother, of his own accord, told them all that it was not wise to drag on like this any longer. Moreover their nephews' incomes were also spent on the maintenance of the joint family. So let them have their own hearth."

Subhas also felt some imposed prerogative, some sort of high-handedness of his cousins. That was due to his father- a man of low income. For this reason, he was always looked down upon-an object of mercy- a man whom one should take pity on. No, they have to estrange themselves from this family ties to lead an independent life of their own- an entity of its own grandeur and no more to be a parasite on the others.

Over days Subhas remained extremely reticent. He was determined to mould his own future, shape his own destiny, come what may. Spreading a mat on the floor, he began to read his text books.

"Is Radhamohan Babu at home?"

Subhas could know from the tone of voice that his maternal uncle, Jayi Babu had come to their house. He rushed to the door and opened it.

Seeing Subhas, his uncle smiled broadly. Fishing out a handkerchief from his pocket, he began to wipe his spectacles.

"Uncle, please be seated, father will come back from the toilet in a couple of minutes." – Subhas dusted the surface of a chair with a worn out towel.

"Where is your mother, tell her that I have come".

"Yes uncle, she is just washing her clothes in the bathroom"

"Hello Jayi Babu, missing for a longtime. What's the matter?"

Subhas's father asked while putting on a lungi.

"Brother, I had been to my father-in-law's house with my wife for a few days, a ripe old man at the fag end of his life"- Jayi Babu said reporting the cause of his absence.

"Definitely, they are always agog to see their daughter and son-in-law. Apart from this we too have some bounden duty".

In the meantime Subhas's mother came in and touched the feet of her elder brother reverently.

"Why did you not come with our sister-in-law brother? I have not seen her for a long time".

"Yes, I told her to come with me to your house. But you know, she always takes pleas, she is so homesick" –Jayi Babu laughed innocently.

"How is your father-in-law? I heard that he was bedridden". Subhas's mother enquired.

"Yes, he has come round any way at present. But who knows what will be the next in such a worn out condition".

"That is true, of course, five years back I had seen your father-in-law for the first time. What sound health he had!"

"This time he told us that he cannot come to our place any more, so shrivelled and emaciated he is".

Radhamohan Babu came and sat by the side of Jayi Babu. "What is your future plan, brother ?" Radhamohan Babu asked while fanning his brother-in-law.

"Nothing definite at present. But I have diverted my attention to pisciculture. If I can rear little fishes the size of your fingers in our pond, then after a year it would weigh nearly one and a half or two seers each. Breeding fish and carp in our pond is a winning proposition. A very profitable business" – Jay Babu's eyes glistened with future possibilities.

"But what about your potato business ? You made it big in that line".

"It brings you profit no doubt. You have to bear the loss too. If the potatoes in your store once started rotting, all your business goes phut. I incurred losses for the last two years. It did not flourish well in my hand. I left that business with sheer disgust"- Jayi Babu's face seemed clouded with disappointment.

"I don't oppose you brother. But I fear, can you manage this pisciculture? You are single and there is none to help you."

"No, I have in mind to keep one to assist me. Let him take some money on the basis of wages. Deducting all the expenditure, you must get a handful of profit- say, three to four thousand net profit annually".

Jayi Babu gave a rough estimate of the investment and expenditure involved in that business.

"Now what about my maternal father-in-law? Is he pulling well?" Asked Radhamohan Babu while chewing a betel.

"O, my father, he is in fine fettle. The only trouble is that the distillery is not running well. To be frank it is not the business of gentlemen like us. Besides, the workers you have held in complete trust may throw dust in your eyes and whisk away the profit clandestinely."

"Why don't you help your father ? He may need you at times."- Subhas's father suggested."

"It's a fact that I can't tolerate the pungent smell of liquor. Last year we have had a loss of twenty five thousand approximately."

"Then why did your father still continue that business." Subhas's father asked in surprise.

"Money, brother, money. It was a growing concern but when he did get a huge profit, he hoped for more. But he has not the least idea as to what extent it will sweep you away. Once liquidated, you will be reduced to a pauper"- Jayi Babu mopped his face with the handkerchief.

"What is your source of income then?"

"Nothing, my father-in-law has given me a portion of his estate as dowry. You know he was a great landlord of his times. After independence, the govt. liquidated all immovable property lowering the position of kings and zamindars to a street beggar. When his position is so miserable, how do you expect him to give me any help? Any way I used to receive a very small amount of money per annum-not worth mentioning."

Subhas's mother stood over the chair and handed her brother a plate with some cakes made of rice and molasses.

"Subhas had brought these cakes from my parents' house. Mother knows my children are very fond of cakes. She prepared them in spite of her severe backache. She always does like that."

"It tastes excellent. My aunty is an expert in preparation of cakes. She knows a whole host of things. She does prepare curry with a very little amount of spices but its taste still remains in my mouth to this day. Once she prepared stuffed cakes, sandwich and rice pudding for me when I had been to her house. I ate my fill and came back with a package of various things." – Jayi Babu was full of praise for his aunty.

"Brother, there is a chance of my going to parents' house

only for a few days, about two weeks or more. What I am going to say is our Subhas will have his meals in your house in my absence. His father may also accompany me. When my mother is suffering how can I remain here"- said Subhas's mother with tears in her eyes.

"All right, is it a matter to think about ? He can dine as long as he can." Jayi Babu assured her.

One Sunday morning, they all left for the busstand. Subhas got into the bus and reserved seats for them. His mother warned him repeatedly to keep a watchful eye on their house. He nodded his head in response. Then he saw them off.

Back home, Subhas lay flat on his cot. He could hear the conversation of his relations on the other side of the wall. He tossed in the bed for a long time. The home seemed bleak and cheerless and took on a forlorn look. Only the chirping of the sparrows was heard breaking the silence of the house. They were hopping on the thatched roof and then frightened by some unknown reason, flew to perch on the branches of other trees.

Subhas gazed at them for a little while. How free and unbridled life they have! Are the birds afflicted by sorrow ? Is there any soft corner in their heart like human beings ? Does the mother bird pine for her cheeper?" – Subhas thought to himself.

With a long yawning, he stretched his hands upwards and rose from his cot. He finished his bathing and started for his uncle's house.

It was a quarter to 12 noon, when he reached there. He was a bit shy while entering their house. But the warm welcome of the aunt removed his shyness instantly.

As his uncle had no steady income, some how or other they were managing things. His failure in business put him in a very depressed condition. Still aunt did not lose her sang-froid in adverse situations. Being a daughter of a well-to-do family, she never budged an inch from her duty. Pleasures and afflictions were almost the same with her. That is why uncle was, to a certain extent, happy in the midst of miseries as aunt was a woman of very amiable disposition.

Subhas had never heard any grumbling or complaint of his aunty against anybody else in their house. Subhas had heard from his mother when the newly-wed aunt came to her father-in-law's house, she had worn heavy gold ornaments from her head to foot. With her came eight boxes, all packed with silk sarees. The neighbours gazed at her jewellery with open-mouthed astonishment.

Subhas's aunt served rice, dal and curry added with some fried potato chips- Subhas squatted on the floor and started eating. Close to him sat his aunt awaiting if he needed something more. "This is enough, I don't need more"- Subhas said gulping a glass of water at a draught.

He felt sluggish and belched two to three times and then came to the open court-yard. He cast his eyes towards the well where his uncle's father, Hari Babu was washing his feet.

"Hello Subhas, have you had your lunch ? your grandmother has just told me that you have come. You vagrant not showing up for donkey's years."

"No grandfather, I don't exactly find time to come to your house. Other wise…."

"Yes, yes, I know you are a busy student. How can you spare time to meet your grandfather. Go inside, your grandmother calls you."

"Be seated my gentleman. Jayi told me this morning that your parents went to seek a bride for you" – the old lady was bantering.

Subhas blushed and said, "No grandmother, she went to see her ailing mother. Being the only child of her parents, they could not keep her out of sight for long."

"Yes, that is true of course. Besides, she is the apple of

her parents' eye. How can they rest satisfied without seeing their daughter?" – her tone was tinged with sympathy.

Hari Babu was a man of middle stature having a corpulent body. Because of his obesity and bulging belly, he always wears a leather belt round his waist, so that his 'dhoti' would not slip off.

"Dear Subhas, you know everything about us. My money-lending business has also come to a set back. Time has changed a lot. The people who have taken something on credit, only know how to dilly-dally, or not in a mood to refund. How far can you carry on in such a degenerated time."- His tone choked with chagrin.

"Why are you running after money? Your sons being there to look after the business.... why ever do you invite unnecessary worries in this old age?"- Subhas chastened him with sympathy.

"Sons ! What do you say Subhas- a pack of good-for-nothing fellows. If they are so helpful and competent, why do I bother about things day and night ? All foppish Subhas… all foolhardy… too much mollycoddling by your grand mother has addled them all."

"This is your one-track view. I don't find any wrong with her"- Subhas protested.

"Time has reversed, A person, once my beneficiary, has now turned on me. I have my own means to live on. I don't need any one's help"- the old man seemed oversensitive.

"Partiality on the part of parents is also a contributing factor to cause discontentment among sons"- Subhas tried to defy.

"What partiality? Have I begotten them in a spirit of discrimination? Jayi must have told you this thing in your house. He now goes on blaming me being my eldest son"- the old man was visibly angry.

"He may be your extension, else…" Subhas mumbled.

"What? Who else has the bone in his tongue to defile

me like this ? Have I not done anything for them. Guts I have seen many. Let us have a confrontation. Let him swear in the name of God that his father has sacrificed nothing for him. Let him come if he is a real progeny of mine"- he flared up by degrees.

Subhas's grand mother intervened to assuage his anger.

"Jayi has never told you this thing. You have turned mad. Why will he blame his father? When you are off your chump, you just prattle without rhyme or reason."

"What ? Do you see Subhas ? I Just babble nonsense… but your grand mother? Doesn't she ever come wielding a sword in her hand against the daughters-in-law?"

Subhas stood up in between them trying to bring about a reconciliation. "Grandfather, you just blame your son without justification. He has never confided this trifling matter in anybody else or attempted to defame you either."

Subhas sought to fill in his emptiness. But in this conjugal row, he felt himself falling out of the frying pan into the fire.

Subhas never liked having meals in other's house however intimate one may be. When his mother would visit her parents' house and remain there for months together, he would cook his own meals. Going to market, purchasing vegetables, fire wood and all sorts of house work he would do without any hesitation. He was not an expert rather a probationer in cooking. There were days when his father would tell him with an air of correcting culinary errors. Subhas, you have dropped a bit excess salt or turmeric or you have overboiled the rice being unmindful."

His tender hands ached when he would have to fetch bucketful of water from a distant tap. While the rice was boiling, he would sit near the fire place and start reading. Rice, dal and mashed potato were enough for them. In the early morning, when he would eat simple fried rice with a dry pepper, he was never seen grumbling.

That day was really inauspicious for Subhas in the class room. Paresh Babu, their teacher in English, suddenly got furious in his after-noon class. The fact was that somebody handed a love-letter to his classmate who happened to be the brother of that girl. The boy went through the letter and started crying. It was a positive humiliation for him in the class. He stood up in rage, went near the chair and showed the letter to Paresh Babu. Subhas saw his teacher's face turning red being incited to violent anger. He thoroughly scrutinized the written note books of the whole class to match handwriting of the wily culprit. At last Jogeswar, the real offender, was found out. After a watchful scrutiny, Paresh Babu was convinced that the culprit was no other than Jogeswar. He enjoined a student to bring him a cane.

Paresh Babu stood vis-à-vis Jogeswar and abused him like anything. Jogeswar's face was painted red with betel-juice dribbling from his mouth. Then he went on caning him ruthlessly from head to foot. Jogeswar rolled down crying, "Don't beat me, I will die sir." Still Paresh Babu did not stop beating. There prevailed a reign of terror in the whole class.

That evening Jogeswar fell seriously ill. His body became warm with high temperature. Fever made him delirious, "No sir, no sir, I am not a culprit." Intermittent ravings went on like this. His mother administered a strip of wet cloth on his forehead to bring the temperature down. Towards the last part of the night, his body sweated all over and the surge of fever abated.

The next day Jogeswar's father rushed to the school, going berserk with anger. He was holding a stick in his hand and from the gateway he shouted, "who is that Paresh Babu? Is he a teacher or a brute ? Today I shall beat him black and blue for caning my child to death."

Seeing his violent appearance some teachers ran to him and made him understand the actual fact. Paresh Babu stepped out crestfallen and begged apology for his faults.

Paresh Babu was an expert in English grammar. He was a terror-incarnate to the delinquents, specially to those who were unmindful of his subject. For this reason the dull-witted students lacking fondness for English grammar, remained absent from his class deliberately. Moreover he was always held in awe by the truants. But those who were attentive in his class, rarely if ever committed any mistakes , scored good marks in English grammar.

At home, everybody kept a safe distance from him because of his hard-core heart and short temper. He used to scold his cousin in group coaching classes in a very filthy language. "You damn fool, has anybody got education in your fourteen generations?" Even his wife was not spared from his abuse.

His intense love for teaching made him say so. A brook of love and affection was streaming under his apparent sternness. The whole school could realize his quality. That is why they silently brooked his kicking, pinching and such other inflictions.

FOUR

Saturday classes were scheduled to be taken in the morning. So at 11.30 A.M. the school was over and the boys ran out in a cheerful mood dangling their bags on the shoulder. Subhas and some of his close friends sat together under a tree and held a discussion to undertake an adventure. 'Rani Bagan', the orchard of the then Maharani, was full of fruitbearing trees. Specially the mango grove was overburdened with juicy fruits. Choicest classes of mango sapling were planted in that garden. A number of care takers were also employed to look after it. Although it was surrounded by a hedge, some openings were made here and there by the mango burglars.

With permission, Subhas and his friends entered the garden. The care taker did not have iota of doubt that they had come with an ulterior motive. The mango grove was on the extreme side of the garden near the bank of a rivulet. On the other side of it, there was a temple of Lord Shiva. The boys strolled about inside the garden praising its beautiful sight. The mango grove drew their attention. When they reached there, they found it unguarded and there was no one to watch their activities. The mangoes by their long stems were hanging over their heads. Some were within their reach. They touched them with their hands and felt the warmth passing through their veins. Then in the twinkling of an eye, they stripped off the branches and ran recklessly towards the bank of the river. The gardener saw their nuisance from a distance and gave chase. But they descended on the sandy bed and went out of sight. All laughed at the foolishness of the gardener. Sitting on the verandah of the temple, they sliced the mangoes into pieces with the help of a blade, smeared them with red pepper and salt, then started chewing.

Next Monday, the gardener went to the school and reported everything to the headmaster. Having heard the activities of his students, he was very much infuriated. He took the gardener with him to identify the mango thieves. They could not escape. The peon herded them into the headmaster's office. They were compelled to wear 'donkey caps' on their heads and made to go-round the school as a punishment for their wicked activities.

Subhas was repentant of his follies. He stepped out with caution debating in his mind whether this news had been circulated in the town or not. He came upon a friend near the Cinema Hall.

"Hello Subhas, what's the matter with you, looking sullen?"- Arun accosted.

"No, it is nothing, I just slept a sound sleep this after noon"- Subhas made an excuse.

Have you not seen this picture, "Jay Hanuman", it is so entertaining!" He picked up some stubs of cigarettes from the ground and fished out a match box from his pocket; puffed two to three times, took the smoke in and blew them through the nostrils. He giggled and said, "Don't know why I like these butts of cigarettes. I got fond of it as I am an inveterate smoker."

Subhas stared at him in amazement.

"Why don't you puff fresh ones?" You may contract some disease through this," advised Subhas.

"No brother, it won't harm me any way. I am going to see the picture for the second time. Will you go with me? What should I do sitting idle at home? Rather, this is the best way to while away the time."

He dragged Subhas to the gateway of the cinema hall. He held one hand of Subhas and said, "Do you know I have just slipped into the hall surreptitiously avoiding the notice of the gate keeper, no payment". Ha... Ha..." Arun laughed for his cunning.

"No Arun, I can't do like that. One of my uncles serves here. Let me approach him."

It was drizzling with sun shine in the intervals. The morning breeze full of water particles, went past him. Subhas crossed the king's palace and the temple of goddess Shitala and turned right to enter an alley.

"Jogi, are you in ? Subhas knocked at the door.

After some time the door opened and Jogeswar came out.

"When did you come?"

"Just now."

"Please wait, let me put on my dress."

They went together to a confectionery shop not far from their house.

"Let us have some refreshment here"- Jogeswar said.

A few people were sitting in the shop, busy eating breakfast, some sipping steaming tea.

"There are some seats left vacant, let us sit there",- Jogeswar directed.

"Would you like to have some 'luchi' or something else"- Jogeswar asked.

"No, fried rice and a cup of peas soup".

"Why not luchi? It is quite fresh."

"It won't agree with me, this luchi, it is so rich in oil."

"Whatever you take, you always think that it will upset your stomach."- Jogeswar said while nibbling the luchi.

"From the beginning, my system is defective"- Subhas grinned.

"Why did you not bring along Deben?" – Jogeswar asked after washing his mouth.

"He was not at home, I asked his mother and she told me that he went to the Jail quarters to see his uncle."

"O, then let us go back home. We will gossip there."

It was still dripping. They pulled out their handkerchief from their shorts pocket to cover their heads.

No sooner did they reach home, than it rained heavily.

"If we had stayed longer there, we could not have reached home"- Jogeswar said pulling a chair for Subhas.

"Yes, we had not taken our umbrella along."

Jogeswar picked up a towel kept on his bedsheet and began to rub his head to dry it up.

"Will you Subhas?"

Subhas ran his hand through his hair. "Not necessary," he mumbled.

"What about your parents and brother ? When will they return?"

"I don't know exactly. Perhaps after a week or so".

"Why do they stay so long ? It must hamper your studies", his tone was a bit indignant.

"What could they do? You know my mother is the only heir of her parents. Their intention is different."

"What's their intention?" Jogeswar asked while reclining his back on a pillow.

"They want us to settle there".

"Then what will become of your studies."?

"They don't attach any importance to education."

"Why?"

"Because they are illiterate and their world is limited".

"But they should know that prime importance is now being given to education."- Jogeswar was irritated.

"They are least concerned with education. They want my father to settle there with his family instead of serving here unnecessarily."

"What's your father's opinion"?

"Are you mad?" He won't go there, not the sort to seek refuge under any one's roof".

"And your mother"?

"She somewhat likes to. But never ventures to ventilate it because my father will gnash his teeth if he hears this absurd thing."

"Yes, I know, he is a great lover of education."

"I heard that Paresh sir realized his mistake later on"- Subhas reminded him of the past.

"It is his gross mistake. Lalmohan had written that letter. But Paresh Sir was mistaken just because my handwriting is quite similar to his. I could have uttered his name but to save him, I took the risk."

"That day your father was in high dudgeon. When I saw him entering our school compound, I thought that Paresh Sir would be taken to task."

"My father is very short-tempered. When he saw my suffering for no fault of my own, he turned dare-devil and rushed to avenge."

"Really Jogi, I could not sleep that night as I had seen that rigorous punishment with my own eyes."

"Still I have a satisfaction; I saved my friend from utter humiliation."

"All right, Now you take rest. I am going to meet Prasanta."- Subhas was on his feet.

"Will you not come in the evening?"

"If I find time, I may."

Jogeswar banged the door from behind. The rain had ceased. The clouds floating in the vast expanse of the sky had changed from black to grayish when they poured sufficient water on the ground. Other clouds were racing behind to take up their position.

In the twilight hour Subhas met Deben at his place.

"Your mother told me that you had been to your uncle's."

"Exactly, I returned only this afternoon." Deben came outside and both of them sat down on a cement bench.

"Yes, when I did not find you, I went straight to Jogi. I told him about your absence."

"I remind you that we will start vigorous preparation for the ensuing examination from today"- a resoluteness sparkled in his eyes. He was always so particular as to his studies.

"We can't study indoors. The grassy field in front of our house is a suitable place for this"- Subhas looked up at Deben seeking response.

"It is definitely a good place. What we need at present is a large mat to sit on."

"I have an old one. It will make do," Subhas gave him the assurance. Deben's mother came out and stood at the door.

"Your parents returned Subhas?"

"Yes, aunty, they came back yesterday."

"Very well, there was none to cook for you. Where did you have your meals during their absence?"

"In my maternal uncle's house" – Subhas replied looking down at the ground.

"Now come in and have some refreshment. I have brought potato curry for both of you."

They went upstairs. There were two spacious rooms. One was used as a bed room by Deben's father and in another, many gods and goddesses were installed in a shrine to be worshipped. In the early morning, Deben's mother would finish her bathing and sit on an asan to worship the gods. She would offer some sweets at the altar and recite some lines from the holy scriptures .

She was just literate. Her parents did not allow her to go for higher studies. They thought it sufficient if their daughter could write a letter. She had committed many lines of the sacred books to her memory-a devout lady in a true sense.

Deben's mother brought a cup off the table and poured the curry on a plate. The two friends sat together and started eating.

"There is a petty shopkeeper at the back of our house

who prepares a variety of curries. If I require some, I send him word and he does my bidding."

"It is very tasteful, aunty. But I don't know why the curry prepared by my mother in the kitchen is not so delicious."- Subhas asked foolishly.

"It is tasteful because the shopkeeper prepares it with overmuch oil, spices and pepper. But it does harm to your digestive system. We don't use such a heavy dose spices. This is the difference."

"Come with your towel Subhas. We will take a bath in the tank before we sit for studies. It will refresh your body as well as mind."

"Bathing at night! All right, I will come back within a minute."

They rolled the mat on the ground. Keeping a lantern just in the middle, they started reading.

The flickering of the light became fainter as the oil was going to be exhausted. Deben began to doze.

"Take care Deben. Your eye-lids are beginning to droop and you are bending down over the lantern."- Subhas warned.

"Bathing made me drowsy, you see," he tried to straighten his body and rubbed his eyes with one hand.

After a week, Subhas suffered from fever. His mother sat on his bedstead and attended upon him. She could not know the reason of the sudden onset of the fever. Deben was called in. He stood over his bed and stared at him. When his mother was unmindful, Subhas slowly waved his hand giving a sign to Deben that their night bathing should not be leaked out.

Although the fever subsided and he began to recover, he became very much feeble. Somebody shook the chain of the front door from outside. He dragged his feet in a staggering gait to open the door. There stood Nrusingha, all mute and silent.

"How are you Subhas ? You remained absent from the

class for a number of days." -Nrusingha said going to sit on a chair.

"I caught a cold and suffered from fever" – Subhas sneezed twice when he leaned his back against the wall.

"Now the fever is over but the chill remains, doesn't it?"

"Yes, it will prolong for some days"

"I came to know that you are studying collectively, I mean Deben and yourself" – Nrusingha said while opening a book and running his eyes on its pages.

"We started a few days back, don't know what would be the outcome."

"Why? You must fare well in the final exam. Besides, you are endowed with a sharp memory"

"Memory can't help me in any way. Regular studies with perseverance is required for that" – Subhas stretched his body, moved his buttock to the edge of the bedstead to let his legs down in suspension.

"I am quite ardent to join you but coming from such a long distance…" Nrusingha seemed to be in a fix.

"No worries my dear. Is there any disadvantages if you remain here, with me?"

"Nothing of that sort. So I shall come with my books in the evening"

"Without fail".

The evening sky was purple with the parting glow of the setting sun, A flock of vultures were hovering in the high slicing the air hilariously. Gradually the evening deepened and the sky was faintly lighted, decked with innumerable stars.

Nrusingha got down from a rickshaw, lifted a bag and placed it on the ground. Subhas came to his help.

"So you told your parents regarding your temporary settlement here, didn't Nrusingha?"

"Yes, I can't study alone at home. I do get an incentive in a group. I am distracted if I stay single."

"That is true, we can discuss with each other."

"Will not Deben come here?"

"Yes, it is now time for his arrival."

"Let him come. We will sit together for studies."

"I admire your one quality Nrusingha, that is very special and distinctive- your unflinching devotion to studies."

"Do you know Subhas? All my relatives view my studies with contemptuous eyes – rather envious of my enterprising zeal."

"Why ?"

"Because very rare people are educated in the barber caste."

"What is that to your relations ?"

"I don't know. My father always keeps mum in the house.

Even my elder brothers have no moral support for my education."

"Then who is defraying the expenses of your studies ?"

"why , my father... my mother is no more. Were she there..."

"Don't bother. Now keep your books on my table and laugh away the problems of life with gusto."

Nrusingha was an early riser. He shook Subhas to rouse him from sleep. The darkness of the night was still there to be expelled.

Subhas got up and rubbed his eyes.

"What the hell drives you to get up so early" – Subhas shouted, "I had not a wink of sleep last night."

"Then how were you snoring so loudly? It amply says that you had enjoyed a sound sleep"- Nrusingha began to think himself guilty.

"I don't mind brother, to speak the truth, I just slept fitfully towards the last part of the night."

"Tell me one thing Subhas. You see how I am striving hard to grasp the subject matter to store it in my mind but I fail inspite of my best efforts to memorise a thing. It is surely due to my weak memory power. Isn't it ?"

"Yes, memory cannot be ignored but one thing is vitally important, that is concentration. You have to pull your mind away from all things and converge at a point. Then everything will get printed in your consciousness. But you have to practise it with single-minded devotion."

"But how do you come to know all these things, I wonder."

"Brooding… dive into the matter, if you cogitate over a subject very deeply, then it begins to crystallize in your memory-cell. It is beyond your knowledge as to how and when it gets implanted in your brain. When you need it, it comes out without any effort like the web of a spider."

"Shall I be successful if I concentrate like that."

"Undoubtedly. Meditation is necessary. You have to increase the time of meditation by degrees. It has extraordinary power. Go on striving and you will come to know its truth at length."

"Subhas, I feel the urge of nature call. I will go to that embankment "Jhinjri Bandh" for defecation. You know that I reside on the outskirts of the town in a rural atmosphere. We people look for a place where we can freely empty our bowels."

"That depends upon one's habit"

"Will you give me company?" – Nrusingha requested Subhas

"No, I am waiting for Deben."

"Why ?"

"Because Deben and I will go to a banyan tree to prepare some medicine."

"Will you tell me about its utility ?"

"Why not ? It helps one to maintain one's celibacy."

"What are its ingredients ?"

"Nothing special, the succulent stems of the offshoots of the banyan and sugar. You have to extract the juice and mix it thoroughly with sugar and then gulp it down on an empty stomach."

After lunch, Subhas was going to take rest in his bed. Like a sudden gust of wind, Abhay came with a note book in his pocket.

"What are you doing Subhas?" his eyes were blinking. He had worn a striped shirt and the hair on his head was trimmed. His father was once a landlord. They were three brothers and the eldest of them was practising law in the town. After his father's death, Abhay and his mother came to the town to settle permanently with the eldest brother. His brother had a roaring practice and earned a lot.

Abhay got admission in the same class of Subhas and came closer to him as the days rolled by. He was of silent nature and a little bit introvert.

"Please see my poems, written a month ago," Abhay spread his note book before Subhas.

Subhas saw the title of the first poem and flicked through it.

"Yes, it is beautiful but the thing is that your ideas have been jumbled and some lines are abstruse and unfamiliar."

"Have I written some rubbish, Subhas?" – his tone sounded injured.

"No, no, I can't ignore its merit. What you are writing should be in an orderly form having inter se coherence. Don't be disheartened. If you maintain continuity, it will be refined. Go ahead", - Subhas said giving him an impetus.

"What happened Subhas, one day my poems fell in the hands of my sister-in-law and she told this thing to my brother. He came to the study table and picked up my notebook. He read it for a while and then stared at me with blood-red eyes, full of wrath. You scoundrel, the final exam is at hand and you are writing trash, no conscious at all."

"My body was then quivering, I thought I might be

driven out of the house. But he silenced himself because of my mother."

Subhas gave him back his note book.

"Let me sleep Abhay. Go to your house and sit for studies"- Subhas said while dusting his bedsheet with hands."

"I don't want to disturb you Subhas, Goodbye"- He tottered on his feet, opened the gate and disappeared.

Two days later, he was informed by some neighbouring boy that Abhay's eldest brother wanted him.

Subhas entered their drawing room. Abhay's sister-in-law and mother were sitting there in a gloomy mood.

Abhay's sister-in-law blurted out, " Look Subhas, what your friend has done this morning."

Subhas could not realize at first. He looked around the room and in a corner caught sight of some broken pieces of a T.V. set.

"What's the matter, sister-in-law! I can't make out anything"

– he spoke out his ignorance.

"Your brother was seething inwardly for some days on account of utter negligence of studies by Abhay. Many a time he had also rebuked him for this. Abhay was always seen scribbling something in his note-book. We thought perhaps he was jotting down some notes. But yesterday, he was caught redhanded. 'A rising poet, indeed' – his brother tweaked his ears and gave him some slaps. Then he snatched away the notebook from his hand. This morning Abhay came to me and asked for his notebook. I told him that his brother had kept it somewhere, let him come. He stood grim, rushed to the T.V. table and in a moment tumbled it down. The T.V. set fell on the ground with a thud and was broken into pieces. I have swept those shattered pieces to that corner of the room."

"Where is Abhay?"

"His brother dragged him to the doctor".

"But why?" – Subhas looked at her in surprise.

"Because we saw some signs of his incipient madness ".

"But I don't see any abnormality in him."

"No, he does his thing in a normal way. But in a month or so, he behaved with us in a different way. If I serve him meals, he would sit mute for a long time as if he is musing over something. If he is alone, he mutters to himself. He would sit in the restroom for hours. If he is in the bathing room, he would not come out in less than an hour," so we perceived a change in his behaviour ." Tears stood in the corner of her eyes.

She wiped them with the hem of her sari and said. "We are unlucky Subhas, his brother brought him from the village with a high hope. My father-in-law, before his death, told your brother to rear Abhay with utmost care. We did so to our level best. We have never dreamt he will go to such an extent. So simple and innocent boy he was...."

"But we cannot say until the doctor confirms us."

Subhas came to his protection-

"No, let your brother come."

Abhay and Ashis Babu got down from a rickshaw. Holding one hand of Abhay, Ashis Babu led him to the drawing room. The eyes of Abhay had been sunken in the socket and hair dishevelled. He looked quite pale and evading us, disappeared into the house.

Ashis Babu flopped down into a chair as if he was extremely tired. Abhay's sister-in-law stood close to him and asked with a thumping heart, "What did the doctor say?"

"Our apprehension is true to a great extent. He has prescribed some medicine to soothe his irritation. He also told us, after taking medicine, he will fall into a stupor. There is nothing to be afraid of. If the medicines are not effective or do not produce any expected result, we have to take him to a specialist."

"Then will the medicine prove effective?" – Abhay's sister-in-law questioned in a doubtful tone."

"Let's see. You know that there is no specialist or psychiatrist in this town. If it fails, I will take him to Ranchi."

"Why don't you take him to Ranchi earlier?" –she suggested.

"Yes, wait for a month, we will see how best we can do for him."- Ashis Babu was seen irritated.

He turned his face to Subhas and said, "What is your opinion Subhas?"

"I fully agree with you brother, I could not think the thing would shape this way".

"That is our lot Subhas, tried best... left no stones unturned to boost him up. But you see what fortune he brings me."

"You should not lose hope, let us see what will happen in the long run. Time will take care of itself."

"Your final examination is drawing nigh." He muttered. "Time wasted, life wasted, your friend can't make amends for this loss of time once again in his life."

FIVE

There was the scourge of cold out side. The bamboo curtain dangling on the edge of the veranda from a bamboo pole was not adequate to shield the severe cold. It was like a sand-embankment braving the strong current of water. Subhas curled up under a thick blanket. Towards the last part of the night, his sleep was interrupted by the long drawn crowing of the cocks. He overheard the sound of the opening of the gate and then somebody tip-toed towards their house.

"Radhamohan Babu" the person called out.

Subhas flung aside his blanket and groped around in the dark for the torch light kept by the side of the pillow. It had been displaced during sleep. He felt the cold-touch of the torch and switched it on.

"O! Dibakar Sir, please come in." –Subhas stood up to greet him.

Bending his head, he stepped up on the veranda and sat on the cot.

"How do you sleep in this open veranda Subhas, in such biting cold?" he said as if he saw the seven wonders for the first time in his life.

"I am habituated Sir, I care little," his voice sounds resonant with self confidence.

"And what about your studies?" –his interest began to grow concerning Subhas."

"I am well up in other subjects, except Mathematics."

"Why?"

"Because I could not clear up my doubts. Moreover tuition is necessary for that subject as I am weak from the beginning" –Subhas unfolded his mind.

Dibakar Sir remained silent. Perhaps he knew their financial position.

"Intimate your father that I have come."

Standing outside the door, Subhas called out his father. After a few minutes, Subhas's father opened the door and came out with a lantern in hand.

"Well, Dibakar Babu, you have come in the nick of time. Please wait, till the medicine is prepared"

He kept the lantern on the ground and went in.

"What is the medicine for, Sir ?" Subhas enquired.

"I have a four-month –old-child. There are some reddish rashes all over its body. I came to know from your father that your mother knows a very efficacious herbal medicine for that."

"Yes sir, many infants have been cured by this medicine. This will work without fail." – He said as if he gives guarantee on behalf of his parents.

"Would not your mother come out? I want to discuss with her."

"She won't Sir, because she has given this medicine without washing her face and mouth. She is to obey the principles" – Subhas explained.

After washing his face, Subhas went on his usual morning walk. He liked to inhale the fresh air when the town had fallen asleep in its deep slumber. The birds drenched in the morning mist began to twitter. Some women getting up from bed in the early morning were seen sprinkling water in the court-yard.

On his way home, he plucked some flowers from the shrubs growing wild by the side of the road. When he neared the cinema hall, he saw water seeping from the cracked pipe and flowing out into the gutter. It had not been taken into account as it was not a concern of anybody else. He felt himself rejuvenated when he passed through lush green regions of the town. Some places were shimmering by the slanting rays of the morning sun as they filtered through clouds. Subhas looked up at the sky. Some gray-white lines had been drawn here and there in its expansive arena. Morning- a bountiful gift of nature! infuses life anew in the body, mind and spirit. He sensed its celestial beauty pervading the whole atmosphere. The tranquillity mingling in its air stirs one with new vigour and energy. The inner soul, lying dormant within, unfolds, awakening the inaction to activity by the magic spell of the morning.

Back from the morning walk. Subhas went to the latrine. After half an hour, he came back to his study room and sank into a chair. He closed his eyes in order to chalk out a plan regarding Mathematics. He wanted to consult the watch but it was missing. He was sure that he had kept it on the table. Flabbergasted, he saw worms before his eyes.

"Mother, who came to my room?" – Subhas asked worriedly.

"Why? Your friend Sobhakar came to see you. I told him to wait in your room."

"Then where is my wrist watch? I could not trace it anywhere."

"I have warned you repeatedly not to keep any expensive thing in your room. But you did not pay any heed to my word."

Intuition ! strong intuition prompted Subhas that it was Sobhakar who had taken away his watch and no one else.

Without wasting any time, he hastened to his house. When Sobhakar came to know of his presence, he was scared and did not come out.

Subhas knew that he had no moral courage to face him.

After sometime Sobhakar came but he was quite indifferent to his presence.

"Is my wrist watch necessary for you Sobhakar?"

"Who has taken your wrist watch?" – He asked in mock-astonishment."

"Why, my mother saw you taking my watch." – Subhas said with confirmation."

Then fumbling for a moment, he pulled out the watch from his pocket and handed it to Subhas.

"I did not know your mother had seen me.

All right, you have come in time, other wise I would have sold it to somebody else."

Mathematics was Latin for Subhas. He could not delve deep into it. When he worked out the sum, he felt himself lost in wilderness, no way to emerge. Algebra and Geometry seemed more impregnable. He felt himself feverish if he was to practise them.

Rabi, one of his class-mates, had agreed to rescue a drowning Subhas from this deluge. He found an avid learner in him and brought the subject home to his pupil. Gradually Subhas's interest grew and he understood the intricacies of that subject.

One day Subhas told him "Rabi, you helped me a lot. I shall remain ever obliged to you."

"But you coward pissed in your pant at the beginning. Now it became as easy as Sanskrit. As to Sanskrit if you sprinkle drops of ink here and there from your pen, then it definitely brings you pass marks. You chicken-hearted…" Rabi said in his humorous style.

When they were sitting in the evening hour to practise Mathematics, Rabi's father came from the treasury and handed him a packet of groundnuts.

"Rabi, bring me my tobacco-box. I will sit here to brush my teeth." He uttered in a feeble voice as if he has gone famished for a few days and sitting on the edge of the veranda he began to rub his teeth with a tobacco-smeared finger. He spat the spittle of tobacco out from time to time.

He was a slender person of amiable nature, very affectionate to Rabi and that much avuncular to his friends. He had four sons, Guru Charan Babu being the eldest of all.

Gura bhai always bore a smiling face. Subhas came to know from Rabi that he was now practising Tantra in a cremation ground. He would go to that place at the witching hour of the night unbeknownst to his family. The female dead body being his asan, he would sit there for hours reciting some occult mantras. Then he would come back home in the early morning after finishing his morning ablution in the river. Everybody knew him as a 'sadhak' and saluted him from a distance. He wore a rosary of holy basil round his neck which evoked reverence for him. Once his wife said to Subhas "I was blessed with a son. But I could not bear a child for the second time because of your brother. As he was a devotee of 'Mother Kali', the goddess would not allow me to be so."

Though Gura bhai was a service holder, he continued worshipping "Mother Kali" all through his life. His mind always stuck to the feet of the goddess in the midst of worldly life. In course of time, a heavenly power descended upon him. He could foretell many things with perfect accuracy. Subhas began to worship him in his heart.

One day a well-to-do Marwari came to him for some help in his family affairs. On request he went to that Marwari's house accompanied by Subhas. The other members of his family were sitting in a spacious room awaiting their arrival. A large white sheet had been spread on a thick cushion. Gura bhai entered the room and sat comfortably in the middle of the mattress. Everybody stared with dilated pupils at his august appearance. The dot of red vermilion painted in the middle of his forehead seemed to cast a magic spell on the people.

Gura bhai sat for a while in complete silence. He raised

his right hand, drew some lines in the air by his fore finger, and finally uttered, his eyes still closed, "Your son is now in a terrible disaster. He has just been discharged from the hospital being poisoned by his wife. He would have died but by virtue of your good luck, he had a hair's breadth escape." Then he opened his eyes and looking unwinkingly to the old Marwari, he said, "If you want to save your son, you have to cut off all relations with your daughter-in-law. She had a liaison with some local youth, a paramour before this marriage. But she married your son under duress by her parents."

Everybody was in total silence. The Marwari gentleman stood up and prayed with folded hands," Guruji, what are the possible means to set right the matter, if you…"

Gura bhai signalled him to be silent and said, "Come to my residence at night. I shall do the needful to pacify everything."

The old man drove them to their house in his own car. After he left. Subhas gazed at Gura bhai as if he saw something supernatural in his face.

Astonishment writ large on Subhas's face, he became almost tongue-tied. Gurabhai observed that and said smilingly,

"You are thinking how Gurabhai could tell the past of that Marwari youth and the tangled affairs of his wife with unerring accuracy."

Subhas could not say anything for a moment. "Is he a mind reader?" –he thought to himself.

Then drawing his attention, Gurabhai said, "This evening you must accompany me to a temple of Shiva. I have one bicycle, arrange another for yourself. I shall tell you everything regarding my will-power later on."

Riding on bicycles, they reached a suburb of the town. A small temple of Lord Shiva had been built there. A renowned 'Sadhak' from Bengal was residing in a cottage in the vicinity of that temple. That 'sadhak' had his own hermitage near the bank of the river Subarnarekha. There was a day when chanting of sacred name of Radhakrishna would go on for days together in an open space by the hermitage. People from remote places would gather there to share the veneration. There would be a number of volunteers to feed them in a company. All the devotees would give their offerings at the feet of the revered 'Sadhak' seated on an altar.

The daily activities of the hermitage went on unhampered. A young lady of vivacious beauty once visited that hermitage. Her arrival was greeted by all the ashramites. She told the sadhak she had an intention to settle there as one of the ashramites. With the passage of time, a clandestine relation grew up between that lady and one inmate of the hermitage. After some months a son was born to her. But that stained the image of the sadhak. Everybody thought him to be the putative father of that ill-begotten child. The sadhak could not blame any one for that. He accepted this unwanted fatherhood without opposition. Nobody could venture to raise a voice against him. Whispering had its affect. His previous fame gradually dwindled away. When the sadhak saw things were all unfavourable, he took the lady with him and came to this cottage built by some of his faithful devotees. They praised him inwardly as they knew the sadhak to be quite guiltless and irreproachable.

Gurabhai entered the sanctum of the temple with Subhas. The sadhak was already there, engrossed in deep meditation. Gurabhai muttered some incantations which drew the attention of the sadhak.

He beckoned Gurabhai to be seated near him. He stared at his face for a while as if reading something from his face and then finally uttered, "You are not an ordinary person but a great soul of a higher plane. Come tomorrow to imbibe something more from me."

So saying the sadhak abruptly stood up and went to his cottage.

It was circulated among the friends that Gurabhai had possessed an extraordinary power to read one's mind. Whenever they discussed anything, they talked in a very low tone.

Gurabhai was a diabetic patient. But he did not care a fig for his health. Thinking that this negligence might worsen his condition in days to come, Subhas forced him to get him examined by a doctor. They went together to the clinic of Dr Jena. Subhas gave his identity and proclaimed him to be man of extraordinary quality.

Leaving the clinic in the care of an assistant, the doctor led them to show his newly constructed building.

When they reached there, Gurabhai suddenly stood in a stand still position before the building, closed his eyes for a short span of time and said, "Dear doctor, why did you install that image on the top of the building? It is surely an ominous sign and if you do not remove it within a few days, great distress would befall you."

His forecast came true. A few days later, Dr Jena's mother fell ill without any premonition and breathed her last.

When Rabi was at Bhubaneswar, residing in a hired house, he developed a suicidal tendency, a fatal mental disease which rendered him helpless. He attempted many a time to strangle him to death. He felt as if some supernatural power prompted him to commit suicide. One night when he stood on the table and made a noose to strangle himself, Gurabhai suddenly burst into the room in the nick of time and saved him from inevitable death.

He knew the art of 'planchette call'. Like a professional planchette caller, he could exhibit it before others to the utter amazement of the onlookers.

Perhaps just like two parallel lines, agony and ecstasy go together, they keep a gulf of difference and never converge at a point. When one tosses in the throes of grim struggle for existence, another is exhilarated rolling in the lap of abundance. When meeting ends, parting begins. Those affectionate, kindly hearts that pour sweetness of love without any self-interest disappeared suddenly unknown and unseen. They left only an irreparable loss, a void in us which could not be adequately compensated.

Subhas felt himself isolated as though he drifted towards the deep sea, far away from the shore, a marooned state, no island was there to give him a refuge. The more he endeavoured to touch the land, the further he was swept away by the surging waves.

Headmaster Gaurishankar Babu was a man of principle. He was quite upright and gave much emphasis on character-building. The slightest slackness was seriously viewed by him. He often narrated in class how he strived hard to educate himself in his early schooling days. His son Hiralal posed a problem for him. His frittering away time in the company of errant boys became intolerable to him and one day he exploded, "You rascal, you are always unmindful of your studies. I won't allow you to have meals any longer in my house, going astray and dining in father's inn, be off this red-hot minute from my sight."

That day the school was full of commotion. Subhas entered the school compound but he could not understand the reason of that tumult. One of his classmates came to Subhas and whispered, "Our examination will be postponed sine die."

"Why?" Subhas exclaimed.

"Don't you know our English question has leaked out."

"How?" Subhas dropped from the blue.

"Hiralal was instrumental in leaking the English paper. Last night he distributed them among his cronies." – he divulged the secret.

"Where is Hiralal?"

"Found nowhere, might have absconded."

Chaitanya Sir was standing under a 'neem' tree. Seeing Subhas he grinned, "That delinquent dare-devil spoiled everything. What the headmaster could do, a rotten, a weed indeed."

Chaitanya Sir lowered his tone and said, "Come closer Subhas, I would tell you a very interesting episode. The day before the question leak out, Hiralal had gone to see a picture. As he had no money, he sold his shirt to a betel-shop keeper and came home barebodied. His father planted a heavy slap right on his cheek. He turned virulent and while his father had fallen asleep, he whisked away the keys of the almirah and now you see the outcome for yourself."

That night Subhas went to Rabi's house to bring a note book of English as he was badly in need of it. The building near their house was brilliantly lighted. Rabi's sisters-in-law giggled and said, "Showing up after a long time Subhas."

"I was busy. Where is Rabi?"

"Busy for your marriage? You have to hunt no more. Here is a bevy of beauties, you choose one of them," –they cackled in impish delight.

"Where?" Subhas pleaded ignorance.

"Look there, how that dancing girl throws her hair to a bun and her eyelashes have been tinted sea-blue. Her coiffure really entices, look another, a fawn-eyed with braided hair"-

"But why have they gathered here?" – Subhas asked as if he could not grip an intricate clue of mathematics.

"A mid-night revelry – a junk-show" –they giggled again.

"But what is that to us" –Subhas grew stoic.

"Look Kamini Babu attired flamboyantly in super fine dhoti and gilt Punjabi, is mimicking the famous dancer Gopikrishna. A long chain of gold is dangling over his Punjabi-a real Krishna of our age."

"Why Kamini Ranjan Babu is so much enthusiastic on this occasion?"

"You don't know, he teaches those girls the art of dancing. You see how that girl is nestling against Kamini

Babu. Why simply nestling? Hug him tightly. Their mother came out, said something with a grin to Kamini Babu. See her hair style and sari. She thinks herself much younger than her daughter."

"Why Bholi Babu, her husband is so much lenient towards this matter? Subhas's tone was distasteful."

"He is too much uxorious, a hen-pecked husband, so to say.

He keeps mum as if he does not know how to fry a fish."

"His wife?"

"Pooh – pooh ! she cares a little, She thinks, if somebody elopes with her daughter, the danger will be over, saving from unnecessary dowry. Even she herself is ready for elopement."

"How would they be benefitted by dancing?"

"Name, fame, they would have shows in all the cosmopolitan cities."

"Who will go with those girls?"

"Why? Bholi Babu's wife and Kamini Babu. You now mark how Kamini Babu touches the body of that girl, head, cheek, belly and… Rabi's sister-in-law made a grimace as if she relished the scene with an absorbing interest. Subhas withdrew himself thinking him an eavesdropper.

Rabi appeared.

"Where have you been?" Subhas asked.

"I just strolled towards the market"

"Rabi, Subhas already enjoyed the drama, now it is your turn." Rabi's sister-in-law gave him a gentle nudge.

"I used to observe daily. Let Subhas witness "Radhakrishna' drama without any payment. – a fringe benefit."

Next morning Rabi came to Subhas with a sunken face, appearance being anaemic.

"Subhas, you have to come with me. I have been embroiled and drawn to a perplexed situation. You know that poulterer who resides next to our house. I had a verbal combat with him this morning."

"What's the matter with you?" Subhas was obviously surprised."

"He blamed me that I have eaten up his fowl last night."

Subhas immediately slipped into his dress and said, "Let us go."

There was a poultry farm to the right side of Rabi's house. Before that a tiled house was there where some high school students were residing, naming it "Bapuji Mess."

S. Krishna, a middleaged man, was the sole proprietor of that poultry. He earned his livelihood by selling eggs and fowls. The students of the mess were also his occasional customers. Very often the unruly, stray fowls would encroach upon the area of the mess, even into the kitchen and peck at the food kept near the hearth. They were so clever that they would remove the lid of the food container and peck at it quite defiantly. If the door of the kitchen was open for negligence of the cook, they would create havoc inside the room.

One evening some students designed a plan. They were vexed and exhausted by continuous trespassing and oppression of the fowls. They scattered some shreds of dried fishes inside a room in order to lure fowls into their trap. They remained vigilant as to the movements of the fowls. At last they caught a big one and twisted its neck to death.

That was a festive night for them. They invited the gentleman to their dinner. He praised the cook's art of cooking and went home late at night.

Next morning as usual he counted the number of fowls. Then he found one missing. Rabi once snubbed the gentleman as they were the victims of the same tyranny. He was let off with a warning.

So. S. Krishna smelled a rat and charged Rabi with this theft. Rabi firmly protested against this accusation.

Rabi and Subhas pushed his front door. S. Krishna had sat on a stool covering his face with his palms. He looked up in a very sorrowful mood. He came to Rabi and held his hand.

"Rabi Babu, you are quite innocent. I just guessed you to be the thief because of your previous threat. Please, don't misunderstand me."

'Who is then the culprit?' Rabi asked sympathetically.

"The students of the mess" –he replied lowering his head to the ground.

"Krishna Babu, I know your condition. You toil day and night in nurturing those fowls. Even a rogue would think twice before committing this nuisance."

SIX

Subhas appeared at the final examination. He raised his head to look at the fellow - examinees. All were absorbed in writing answers bending their heads. He looked up at the ceiling. The fan was hovering over his head. Complete silence all through the room. One could even hear a pin drop. He had answered only three out of ten. Some were easy but most of them were stiff and beyond his knowledge. He consulted his watch. Time ticked away. There was still one and half an hour in his hand. He was now in a tear up hurry. The last bell rang. Lo! He had answered only six questions. He was confounded. The invigilator snatched away the answer book from his hand. He perspired profusely. His head reeled. A cold sweat streamed down from head to feet. Subhas tossed restlessly in his bed muttering something in his sleep. He woke up, his whole body moist with sweating. He came to his composure. He consoled himself – it was simply a dreadful dream.

"Subhas , have you got up?" whose tone is this?

"O! Deben, please come in."

"Where is aunty? you have passed in the examination'- Deben announced.

"Is it ? I don't know the results are out."

"I have been keeping information. Our clerk Sudhir Babu returned from Cuttack with the results last night."

"Then?"

"I rushed to our school. There was a huge gathering, all anxious to know their results. After one hour, jostling through the crowd, I went closer to Sudhir Babu.

I told him my roll number and yours" Deben said with a gasp.

"What is the success rate of our school this year?'

"Up to the expectation. Gourisankar Babu was exulted seeing the result.

"So we have been rewarded" – Subhas said heaving a sigh of relief.

They were beaming with satisfaction at their performance. Subhas filled up the form and got admitted into the college.

"Father this time I can't go to the college wearing this pair of shorts' – Subhas felt ashamed.

"Yes, you go to a tailor and give your measurement, for one bush shirt and a pair of trousers."

"One shirt and a pair of trousers are not sufficient father. I have to change them from time to time" – Subhas objected.

"You know my pecuniary position. How do you press for that?" His father said with an agitated tone.

"All right, then give me money. I shall go to market with Deben to select the cloth."

Their classes were held in the morning in the high school. There were no adequate number of rooms in the college to accommodate such a large body of students.

Subhas was very fond of Arts subjects like History, Economics and Oriya literature. He embarked on a greater perspective. A new vista opened up for him. The rustling of green foliage, the soothing beam of the moon, the murmuring of a rivulet, the fragrance of flowers, the crimson rays of the setting sun – all conveyed a message, a new meaning to his life.

A feeling of loneliness, a void, a lack of complacence crept into his mind. He brooded over the moonlight when it percolated through the slender off-shoots of the coconut trees. He went on staring at the western sky when the sun dipped down below the remote horizon and the earth was gradually enveloped in darkness. He mused on the plaintive note of Lata, the renowned singer, which was haunting and that accentuated his feeling of pining – an infinite quest – which stretched out to an unknown world.

"Subhas, you told me your admission fee is Rs. 60.00 but Jogi said it is Rs. 52.00. Where is the rest of the amount?" – his father demanded an explanation.

"Yes father, it is …" Subhas faltered.

"All right, you go now."

Subhas knew the reason. Jogi and he himself had had refreshment after admission. He had given him word that he would not reveal this matter to his father.

How could he refund the rest of the amount ?

How treacherous he is! His father might have taken him amiss. He could not remonstrate owing to this minor folly.

"Would you lend me your English and History books for a few days, Deben? I have to note down some points?" requested Subhas.

"Why not? There are my books on the shelf – keep them with you so long as you like."

"Mr. T. Jayaraman taught us 'A Mid-summer Night's Dream to day. It is too difficult to follow him, specially his pronunciations."

"Yes, he hails from Madras. When he teaches, his words come out pressed through his lips. It seemed difficult to all of us. That afternoon we went in a body to meet our principal Mr. Jagatananda"

"Do you want to know what did he say?"

"Yes"

"He said, how many teachers are there like Mr. Jayaraman. You are lucky that you have got such a teacher in English."

"Yes, I do admit it. He has profound knowledge in English literature. Besides, he is a widower, quite lonely at home, except his daughter." Subhas praised him inwardly. Taking a pause he said, "We have got another born-teacher, he is Mr Rath… a voracious reader.

That day he taught us a short story of R.N. Tagore. You know 'Kabuliwallah' – an excellent story. Perhaps you were absent on that day. The way he taught us was admirable as if he infused the feeling in us. Towards the last part of the story, tears welled up in my eyes." Subhas was full of praise.

"And our Mr Baral, a veteran in Oriya literature…

When he teaches, it seems as if a spider is weaving its web – a spontaneous overflow of powerful feelings… there is no end there. We listen to him spell- bound" – Deben became emotional. Subhas was physically as well as mentally tired. He was sound asleep after his dinner. At midnight, he dreamt a dream.

The hall was full of teachers, Mr. Ray, Mr. Sarangi, Mr. Mishra , Mr. Rath – all were present and Subhas was the only student listening to them. They were laughing and discoursing on their respective subject. He could not make head or tail of their utterances.

The cat mewed and the rats went squeaking and scurrying about in the room. He woke up suddenly from his sleep, his throat became desiccated.

The dream still flashed across his inward eyes. They are living at present and will disappear after some years just like this dream. Subhas is selfish out and out. When the teachers will be retired from their service and living with their respective families in different places, Subhas will still remain selfish and ungrateful, no desire to see them once a year. When he will come upon them in the way, he will bow his head with folded hands, "I was your student Sir." They will stare at his face. ' I can't recognise you son, please tell me your name.' He will say his name then. They will say, 'O yes, you are…'

Subhas was a bit hesitant to borrow books from his friends. So he resorted to tutoring some students privately in order to purchase some necessary books.

At last he got a student, the nephew of a close friend. He tutored him in the morning for at least one and half an hour and came back home for his own studies. He was a goodnatured pupil; did his home work very promptly to the satisfaction of Subhas. He never noticed any disobedience or disloyalty in him. After some months, he came to a tank to take bath. His parents waited at home in a state of feverish anxiety for his return but to no avail. At last both husband and wife frantically looked for their son. When they came to the tank, they saw his bloated body floating on the water. Only the bust had been exposed; the rest was still immersed in deep water. They caressed the dead body to their bosom and wailed heartrendingly. The neighbouring people and passers-by gathered there out of curiosity. They moved to tears seeing their lamentable condition. Nobody could comfort the distraught parents.His mother went on raving, "My son cannot die, he is still alive. let us take him to the hospital." Time passed but she could not forget his son. Eventually she turned mad and did not take a bite of food. She became bed-ridden and passed away pining for her son.

Subhas lost one shelter.

"Sangita, Why do you doze so early?"

Subhas tapped her fingers with a pencil.

"I had a dance lesson in the school sir, I have become tired."

"You are quite lethargic. You have not poured heart and soul to studies."

"I do Sir."

"Your handwriting is illegible… you have crammed your note book with some grievous mistakes in spelling some words also."

"Yes Sir."

"If you are not conscious from the beginning, you can't build your career. Besides, if your results are unsatisfactory, I shall be blamed. Where have you been before my arrival?"

"I have been to the temple of goddess Ambika with my mother."

"Why?"

"To invoke the blessings of mother for yourself and me."

"Why are you so keen on me?"

"Because I always have your good at heart."

Do perseverance, truthfulness and honesty bear any value? The sages of yore wrote in eulogy of these things in right earnest. If they have not, he will tear those pages where those baseless, absurd things have been written. It may be these qualities cultivated in his life, that have been stored for his future use. One day they will germinate and fructify to his benefit.

"Why do you talk so loudly Subhas?" – his mother asked him in obvious surprise.

"I talked with a stone-deaf guy on the way. I could not withdraw myself fully from that thought. So I feel I still talk with a person hard of hearing."

"Take care; you fondle a lot your younger brother Chandra. You are always giving him this and that."

"I love him from the core of my heart mother."

"No, he may go astray right at the beginning of his formative years."

"I don't think so."

"Where are you going Subhas?"

"I have kept a dish of meat under Chandra's care; see how he has sat near it.I want to observe his reactions through the window."

"What do you see?"

"I see, he is quite indifferent to the dish of meat. He is awaiting me so that we will eat together."

"Nonsense."

"Mother, you see how Bablu is throwing stones at me."

"Why?"

"Because I told him to be mindful of his studies and read vigorously."

"Mind your own business."

"Mother! He would be spoiled."

"Let him."

"Would he keep a tea-stall in future?"

"What is that to you?"

"O God, I had been dreaming all through the night." With a start, Subhas rose up.

Subhas had sat with Deben on the terrace of their building. Deben winked at him and whispered,

"Have you ever heard the cry of the soul, Subhas?"

"No"

"Why?"

"Because I always hear the cry of death"

"Why death?"

"It holds a greater meaning for me."

"How?"

"Death is the beginning of birth. The mission starts from there."

"I can't really make out."

"Worldly people fear death because they think, here ends all their pleasure. They roll in luxury and lead a cosy life till death. They don't know the stark naked truth of life. They indulge in momentary revelry. But pain and suffering remain in an embryonic state unnoticed, lurking in a very subtle form in that transient pleasure. We value its outward appearance but never delve deep to explore its intrinsic quality, its real hue. Crude materialism saps their lives and renders them too insensate to understand the mechanism of life. But wise people are always awake while the world falls asleep. They are never scared of death, rather invite it with a smiling face."

"How do you know all these things Subhas?"

"Contemplation…inward consciousness. If you are once endowed with that divine insight, you can know anything before hand – past, present and future. You have to develop this rare quality after years of austerity. For this reason, a sannyasi or a sage living in an obscure cave knows everything of this world. But common people do not want to take the pain of this austerity. What is the value of taking pain? Let us enjoy life to its fullest brim – they think in that way."

"But I pine for the Love of that girl reading in our class. My soul cries for her."

"It is not your soul, Deben but a body cries for another body. Listen to me, you are passing through a very delicate and dangerous period. There is every chance of distraction and derangement. You are still in your teens. If you are not conscious of your footsteps, You will go astray."

"But her tantalising, enticing beauty…"

"Don't speak of beauty. You don't know its definition. You speak of beauty from biological point of view. That is why there are so many home - breaking disasters in this society. Try to find out one's inner beauty - if you have found it, you will in no way be beguiled by the tinsel glory of the world."

"What should I do at present?"

"Nothing, you ask your conscience, dwell on that matter for a long time. then decide and do according to its dictations."

"But I am in a fix, perplexed to take a direction."

"We are standing at a cross roads, Deben, from where a number of routes stretch out. We are confounded because we don't see the lie of the land. When misguided into a wrong route we freely fall into an abyss only to flounder there pathetically. You are bewitched because impelled by youthful fancies you are being attracted by her illusory appearance but not by her realself. So long as you are under the spell of love, you cannot come to a decisive conclusion. It is just like a stuporous condition, no control over yourself."

Subhas could not stir out from hall as the English period was not yet over. He was bored through the grinding drudgery of classes. The ebullient noisy uproar, ascending and descending of the steps, wrangling over politics, all worsened his mental state. He felt like a young bird about to fly up but not capable to flap its wings in a narrow cage. The incessant twittering of birds had a meaning for him. He abandoned the idea of lingering any longer on the college campus and slipped away to his uncle's house.

His uncle's father Jadu Nandan Babu was bed-ridden for a long time. When he was an earning member, he had kept a maid servant exclusively for his wife, waiting at the dining table, washing utensils and marketing, all sorts of house-hold chores. Despite his old age, he was a voracious eater. Meat-dishes were his favourite food which he craved for. Successive drought, cyclone, flood and labour problem brought declivity in his social standing. The two sons owing to a pampered upbringing became foppish and depended upon the landed property. Being neglected, the oldman would prattle in disparagement his sons and wife. But they would harangue others blowing their own trumpet.

Subhas drew a chair to sit beside the old man. His grand – son came gasping and declared "Here comes the Maharaja."

All the inmates of the house became immediately alert and the best chair was placed near his bed. Subhas stood in a corner and was eager to see the Maharaja as he had not seen him before. The Maharaja came smiling, stepped on to the veranda and sat down on the chair comfortably.

Seeing Jadu's ailing condition, he said, "You know it very well that I am now residing in Delhi. You could have dropped me a letter stating your sickness."

"I could, Your Highness, but the fact is that nobody heeds to bring me a card to write on."

"Why?"

"Because all are preoccupied with some work and remain busy."

"Remain busy for nothing. It is their obligatory duty to take care of you which should be given prime importance. Where is your son Maniklal?"

"Pranam, Your Highness?" Manik promptly came and genuflected.

"Manik, you have not done your duty to your father. Do you know how he was worried about all of you? Had he been indifferent to his family, he could have spent his time with me in the palace. But he never did that because of his strong sense of duty. As a dutiful father, he brought you all up with utmost care."

"I know Your Highness."

"What to speak of your father, I too have been utterly neglected by my family, birds of a feather. I remain alone in my parlour. Adjacent to it, there is a kitchen. I have kept necessary things like rice, dal, potato, spices in an almirah. I usually do my own cooking without any assistance. After eating meals, I throw away the plates and dishes of leaves through a window – No botheration of cleaning utensils."

"And Her Highness?"

"I stopped keeping any relation with her since that disastrous episode. I had just a narrow escape from death being poisoned. I am dead so far as she is concerned.

I equally divided all my property between my two sons. I now reside in the upper storey. After my death, I don't know what they will do with their property. Jadu, drop me letters from time to time."

Thus saying he stood up and set right his dishevelled dhoti and started towards his car.

Subhas knew during the monarchical regime the common people demanded honesty and integrity from their rulers and they in turn fulfilled the demand by sacrificing time, money and energy. Specially the Maharaja and his forefathers set a bench mark in their high ideals and they never browbeat the people into subjugation. So peace and happiness reigned supreme every where during their rule. After merger too, the dynasty was still held in high esteem as the noble descents of this lineage had never besmirched their stature like other rulers sunk in luxury. Life has a significance of it own. Some are boosted from rags to riches and some reduced from a potentate to a pauper. It is the irresistible power of time which carves a person into its own shape in spite of his power and pelf.

SEVEN

Subhas's grandfather was habituated to the cultivation of sugar canes. The soil by the bank of the river was suitable for their luxuriant growth. They were huddled together like a crowd in a fair and waggled their heads when the wind passed through them with a rustling sound. The twittering tiny birds would play with their shaggy dishevelled hair hopping and gliding on their slender branches. The reaper women, young and old alike, would strip off their bark, cut them into long pieces and keep them in pile near the crushing machine.

The old man required Subhas to supervise their work. The woman daily wagers would hide some sugar cane stacks underneath the leaves for their children. If by chance they were caught, while stealing, they would say, "little master! we have nurtured them under scorching heat, heavy downpour and piercing cold. Have not our tiny tots the little bit right to chew them?"

Subhas would remain silent. He could not debar them from such a trifling petition.

The preparation of molasses was in full swing.

A mammoth hearth was made, the pit being waist-deep. A big iron cauldron was placed over it. Like a canopy, a long thatched roof was drawn on bamboo poles to protect it from rain and cold. Subhas's grandfather finished the puja and lit the hearth with his own hands. Then a man thrust a bundle of fire woods through the mouth of the hearth and soon it blazed to a flame. The machine went on crushing and tins filled with sugarcane juice were collected and poured on the heated cauldron. The process continued for some hours. The water portion evaporated and now it began to condense.

Subhas was sleeping on a bamboo cot at a little distance from the cauldron. He could inhale its sweet, rich aroma when it gradually formed into treacle. A person churned it from time to time with a skimmer. After the final preparation, he filled the earthen jars with treacle with the help of a ladle.

It was a moonlit night. Everything looked hazy from a distance. The grass was moist with the constant falling of dew drops. Silence all around, save the crushing sound of the machine. When the moon tilted to the other side of the horizon, Subhas rose from his bamboo charpoy and came outside. He heard clearly the chorus of rustic women accompanied by a rhythmic beating of drum. It came floating in the air:

"With jingling, comes the gentle shower
Hold an umbrella over,
O! my younger brother-in-law,
My sari as delicate as betel-leaf gets wet.
Here blows the north breeze
in a gentle way,
I feel ashamed of,
O! my younger brother-in-law,
My veil of head flies away being blown.
The fragrance of jasmine and champak flowers
Comes wafting in the air,
"O! my younger brother-in-law,
be on the way, it will enchant your mind."

He came back to his cot. The chorus went on ringing in his ears. He could not sleep .He lay still with his eyes shut. Dawn stepped in.

Subhas brushed his teeth and drank a glass of sugarcane juice with lemon. His attention was directed to Shiva Babu, his maternal grand father's younger brother, busy in plucking green peppers in his kitchen-garden. He slowly walked towards his garden.

"Hello Subhas, please have breakfast with me."Shiva Babu requested with glowing warmth.

"Yes, let us sit on your front veranda. I like green pepper with fried rice." complied Subhas.

Shiva Babu was a middleaged man, short-statured having an oval face with a pigtail on his head. When he recited a 'bhajan', his tone would become suddenly feminine but it was very amusing to hear.

Shiva Babu came with two plates of fried rice. Some chopped peppers had been scattered on it, with some drops of mustard oil.

Subhas was about to jump from his seat.

"Can I digest them grandfather, such a great quantity of raw pepper."

"All right, all right, I transfer some to my plate but brother, my usual food is like this", he laughed a hearty laugh. In front of them, there were some rows of green pepper plants, all laden with peppers, some ripe, some curved and some straight. On the other side, there were a number of brinjal plants and to its left, a clump of banana with a few bunches. Some branches of china rose with serrated leaves had extended up to one bunch, nestling against it wind-blown.

"From this morning the sway of unbroken chanting of God's name will continue for three days. It is very good of you that you have stayed here this time." Shiva Babu announced with a laughing voice.

"Thanks!" Subhas smiled back.

The ground for chanting 'bhajan' was made consecrated, bedaubed as it was with cowdung with a broom. The mango leaves were hanging from strings fastened with one bamboo peg to another. In the centre, around the place of installation of Lord Krishna, four curved gateways of bamboo pole had been erected, all decorated with sacred mango leaves and paper festoons. The organisers ran helter-skelter to arrange some petromax light for the night.

The procession started from the bathing-ghat. The leading man with a pitcher full of water on his head was in the centre of the front line. Younger boys and girls were dancing with branches in their hands, keeping steps with the tune of the beating of the 'Mridanga' and cymbals. After the installation of the propitious 'kalasa' in its proper place, all shouted in one voice, 'Haribol' (Sing the name of God).

Then the chanting of sacred name of Lord Krishna began in a chorus. They went round the makeshift shrine with their heart overflowing with devotion. Their faces had been dotted with sandal paste and they wagged their heads to and fro, lost in reverence to God. The two 'mridango' players were ahead of the devotional congregation.

Shiva Babu was one of the devotees. He went in a circle, with the chanters of sacred name, throwing a yellow towel on his shoulders. After some time the chant reached a crescendo. Right then, Shiva Babu, suddenly caught with devotional frenzy, began to roll on the ground. He smeared his forehead with sacred dust. Then he jumped to his feet and waved his head vigorously still chanting the name of God. His pigtail also swirled according to his devotional stepping. At last he foamed at the mouth and fell unconscious.

The day the 'bhajan' came to a consummation, Subhas started for home. He remained absent for several days. The pupil he tutored was awaiting his arrival. Over and above, his own studies also had been neglected.

Two days after his arrival, all the educational institution went on sympathetic strike. The students of Revenshaw college, Cuttack demanded some legitimate rights to be fulfilled and they put forward their ultimatum to the government. The Chief Minister did not consider their demands to be so important and remained indifferent to the students' unrest. The agitation took a violent form. The students being united resorted to revolutionary steps, burned trucks and buses, shut the doors and windows of government offices preventing officials from doing any official work. They shouted before the Assembly house, barricaded the main roads, removed fish – plates of the railway lines, as an aftermath, the government came to a dead-lock. Every day the students held procession waving their hands and shouting defiantly. "Down, down, the Janata Party – Let our demands be fulfilled – victory to students' union." The Chief Minister ordered the police to suppress the students' strike. In order to rout the mob, the police burst some tear-gas shells. They kicked the students mercilessly with boots, struck them blindly with sticks, even innocent people were also not spared the brutal atrocity of the police.

"Subhas Babu, do you hear me ? Subhas….."

Some body thumped on the door in the late hours of the night.

Subhas was just going into the stupor of sleep. He sprang to his feet and taking a lantern in hand opened the door.

Lo! Gauranga Babu was standing there. He had wrapped his body with a plain sheet. and some portion of it had veiled his face. His eyes shimmered when the light fell flickering on them.

Subhas dragged his hand and said, "Please come in Gauranga Babu, you must not stay out."

Subhas knew that a search warrant had been issued and the police were now searching every nook and cranny of the town to apprehend him. He was the key man of the students' agitation and they were mad after him. But he managed to elude the police for three days.

Subhas led him to the bath room and told him to wash his feet. Gauranga Babu's body was quivering when he sat on the bed. Subhas could not know whether the quivering was due to fear of the police or severity of cold.

"Please eat some thing Gauranga Babu" – Subhas said in a compassionate tone.

"I went famished for the last two days Subhas Babu as I could not come out from my hiding place" – Gauranga Babu's voice was too feeble to utter these words.

"There are flattened as well as fried rice for you. You can have either of them," so saying Subhas went in to tell his mother to serve food to Gauranga Babu.

"Please remove the lantern from this room", Gauranga Babu said in a trembling voice."

"Why?"

"I feel awkward, please......" Gauranga Babu was obviously alarmed as though the police knew his new hiding place.

"Go to your bed, I will put out the light", Subhas went near his bed and spread the mosquito-net.

The next morning Subhas went to Himanshu, a convivial friend and narrated to him everything. His father was deputy superintendent in the police department and his official residence was at a short distance from Subhas's. He was hard of hearing and because of this physical handicap, he was not promoted to the rank of Superintendent.

"Is Gauranga hiding at your home, Subhas?" Himanshu's mother asked in utter surprise. D.S.P Saheb was present then. Subhas signalled her not to disclose the secret.

Himanshu's mother burst into laughter and said,

"You know your uncle is hard of hearing. He can't hear a word of our discussion. The police are searching frantically to find him but see, he is snoring at your home."

Then pausing for a moment, she said simperingly, "The place beneath the lamp is always dark Subhas."

Once Subhas tried to find out an English word. He consulted the dictionary. Read other books one by one. Rummaged about the shelves. He thought about it in the latrine. In the study room. In the bed room.

He was not a thinker. Not a philosopher. Not a scientist. He was not a mathematician and inventor like Archimedes to utter 'Eureka'.

He could not catch a word. A purpose. A gory purpose. A purpose of gory history.

One student and two civilians were shot dead. The police dealt indiscriminately. A vulture, carrying a dense shadow of sorrow on its expansive wings, swooped over the town.

"Come this way, Gauranga Babu. Be careful, stepping down the slope. Left side brother, there is a deep pit there."

A curtain of thick mist was hanging from the sky. The night droned in the prolonged drone of a cricket. The two shadows under cover of darkness plunged into the night. The night had spread its tentacles from all sides to constrict their necks like an octopus.

They were now on the sandy bed of the river Budhabalanga. The light of a torch blinked twice; the shaft pierced through the shrill darkness of the night.

They came to a rendezvous.

"Are you all here?" whispered Gauranga Babu.

"We have come all at appointed time, Gauranga Babu."

"What is the latest news by this time?"

"The oppression of the police has crossed all limits, Gauranga Babu. Today the police forced Malay Babu to drink their urine.

Gadadhar's nose bled profusely as they gave a heavy blow on it. Sitanath received a serious head injury as a brute beat him with a staff. He has been hospitalized with an oxygen cylinder by his side. Jadu's condition is so deplorable that he is now struggling with death."

"Any information by pen and paper from the secretary of the students' union?"

"Yes, the secretary had given a memorandum to the chief minister. He has now given his consent to fulfil some of our important demands. News received so far from reliable sources is the strike will be called off within a very short time. The public are so annoyed that if the government will not take any amicable steps for settlement of the dissension, they will come out to openly support the students".

Gauranga Babu was crestfallen. He could not know the consequence of students' strike if the authority would not come to a conclusive decision. Finally he let out a deep breath.

Over a period of two weeks, Subhas was quite inattentive to his studies. He tried to recover his mental strength. Spending no more time on twaddle, he went that evening to Sangita's house.

Sangita, a lot of valuable time has been spent caused by the present chaotic situation," Subhas's tone was remorseful. "Yes sir, I have to concentrate my mind upon studies. That strike acted as the dropping of a stone in still water. It disrupted all our plans."

"Absolutely correct. Our country has lost its value after independence. Anarchy or total lawlessness is now pandemic and the order of the day. The elected Government, the representatives of the people are heedless to the complaints of the general public. The common people resort to violence if they fail to achieve their desired goal. During the tenure of ministership, a minister with a thin veneer of people's welfare tries endlessly to amass wealth for his next generation. So what will be the future   of this country, one can visualise easily."

"What are the possible measures to set right the government machinery, sir?" Sangita asked to know the situation.

"Selflessness. If the people's representatives are unselfish and sacrificing, they can do a lot for the uplift of the country. But they become self-centred, corrupt to the core. They don't feel any shame to take bribes. As a result corruption gets the upperhand over the pro bono publics feelings. The government employees and others concerned learn this art from them. "Scatter with one hand, gather with two" has become the 'catch word' of their lives".

"Why don't they think things through concerning the progress of their own country?"

"Those who know the value of dedication, honesty and truthfulness, never retrace their steps under any unfavourable circumstances. But I regret to say they are very few in number. For the rest, these qualities are simply meaningless having no base at all. The maxim of their lives is 'eat, drink and be merry'. Those pseudo-moralists pose a menace to one's country. They are, no doubt, detrimental to one's progress. Moral vacuity has reduced them to hollow men. So how can they contemplate the progress of their own country? If we try to remove all the socio- economic evils, it would be like cleaning the Augean stables."

"If one cogitates on these problems, one will be hopeless sir"- Sangita said with wounded feelings.

"Yes, if such a situation prolongs for decades, the country will go to the dogs, no doubt"- Subhas sounded prophetic.

Subhas was returning home after tuition. Suddenly a man on a bicycle emerged from shadow and hauled his hands.

"You fool, examination is at hand and you are still engaged in tuition" – Jogeswar roared.

"I have no way out Jogi, I can't neglect my duty" – Subhas explained helplessly.

"All right, let us go to them and state your present inconveniences."

Sangita's mother was sauntering in the corridor after dinner.

"What's the matter Subhas Babu, you came back again"? - Sangita's mother asked while advancing towards them.

Jogeswar blurted out, "Your sir" is very dutiful, his examination starts hardly in twenty days but still he is engaged in tuition. I admonished him for that."

"Why did you not tell us Subhas Babu? That is really

more important than this." -She was helpful.

"If I see you some other day like this, I shall definitely crack your head" – Jogeswar warned Subhas on the way.

Subhas was ambitious. He was on his mettle to pass through many difficulties. Three weeks' time was too short for a good preparation. Although he passed for a good student, his success in the final degree examination was not so remarkable.

The conferring of degrees by the Utkal University was held at Bhubaneswar. He attended the convocation with full zest. A confluence of intellectuals delighted him. That animated his spirit to do post-graduation under any hardship. After his return, he stayed for two days in 'Kishore Bhavan' where one of his intimate friends Kripasindhu was doing higher studies in Mathematics. He advanced him some money to reserve a seat for him in that mess.

The return journey by train was too tedious. All the compartments were spilling over with passengers. Subhas could not get a ticket. Some of his co-passengers also encountered the same adverse situation. The compartment he got into was so jam-packed that there was no room even to stretch out his legs. He felt himself sandwiched between two very stout men in the train. He was compelled to journey the whole distance in a virtual vice-grip. Towards the last part of the night the train arrived at Balasore railway station. His co-passengers advised him to linger for some time on the platform as he journeyed W.T. Subhas knew he might face an embarrassing situation if the T.T.C. demanded his ticket for verification at the gate. Seeking an opportune moment, he sneaked away from the railway station. The helper of the bus bound for Baripada was shouting to draw the attention of the passengers. Subhas sprawled on a seat and felt himself relieved as if he sank into his mother's lap.

EIGHT

The relentless pursuit for Oriya literature became an obsession with Subhas. Dr Basudev, his teacher, also advised him to do post-graduation in that subject either in Utkal University or at Shantiniketan.

But the pecuniary position of his family was not at all sound. His father expressed unequivocally that he could not afford even Rs.50/- per month. It posed an insurmountable problem for him.

Vicissitudes of life are erratic by nature. One of his distant relatives arrived to take him to his native village.

Haldigarh, situated on a steep high land, presents an enduring picturesque sight. A stony slope meandering through a thin bush peters out to the river Subarnarekha. Some ancient banyan and tamarind trees, huddled together on both sides of the stony path, signal the passersby invitingly to take rest under their cool sheltering shade. Squirrels are seen scampering with nuts and wild roots in their mouth. At a distance, there lies a small patch of marshy land where the domesticated pigs nuzzle their snouts in the mud. If somebody passes by them they raise their heads as if they are trying to recognize him. That boggy-land never goes dry all through the year.

There are a number of flat stones, five feet long and three feet wide, in the bosom of the river. The edges of those stones are mossy and quite slippery to step on. They are seen like small islands in the lap of the river from a distance. The village youth, after massaging their bodies with oil, would lie on those stones for a long time before their bath. They would wave their legs playfully with ripples and enjoy its soothing effect. The long steep slope ends at the common bathing-ghat of the river. The rustic girls and women would take bath for hours in waist-deep water chattering endlessly about their household affairs and that is the suitable time for them for the reciprocation of day-to-day small matters with each other. Some would be seen rinsing their clothes after washing and some changing their saris holding a corner of them between the teeth. The small children would splash water swinging their hands and feet like expert swimmers to the annoyance of their mothers. They would drag them naked along the village path with a shower of abuses.

"Subhas Babu, your parents told me a very important matter on the eve of my departure from Baripada". Maheswar Babu said while Subhas was changing his dress after bath.

He looked up at the old man with growing anxiety. Maheswar Babu loitered a little while in the room and broached the subject slowly.

"You are ambitious for higher studies. That is, of course, very good. I have paved a way to materialize it."

He went to the dining room and came back after some moment with a glass of sherbet in his hand. He looked into Subhas's eyes thoughtfully and said "one of my relatives has a marriageable daughter. If you marry her, her parents are agreed to back you with financial help for your higher studies."

Subhas remained silent. His ego had been injured. So here in this place also, some people came to know of their miserable condition. He felt a plug stuck in his throat. After a while, he said without demur "Well, I have no objection. But let me see the girl first."

Maheswar Babu coughed covering his mouth with hands and then said, "I told them the previous evening regarding this matter and they are prepared to show you their daughter this afternoon."

Subhas was neither remorseful nor delighted about this matter. He was just thinking the strange way of life which turns in its own way, in its own rhythmic manner to tune a gamut with staccato beats.

It was an 'L'-shaped tiled house. In front of the verandah, there was a holy basil plant with slightly curled leaves. A rugged muddy path went past their house. Before the doorway of the cowshed, a pair of bullocks were masticating hay from a trough. To the right of the cowshed, there was a cow-dung pit. A foul scent was emitting from it. Seeing the strangers, the bullocks wagged their horns.

Maheswar Babu and Subhas crossed the front door. To their left, there was a drawing-cum-bed room where sitting arrangements had been made for them. It was for the first time in his life that Subhas was ever going to see a bride. He looked around the room. Some bags of rice were kept in one corner of the room. Some framed photographs of gods and goddesses were hanging on the wall. He looked through the window. On the other side of the back verandah, a pucca well was there with a hook and rope hanging from a horizontal iron bar raised on pillars.

A middle aged woman entered the room, holding two plates of sweets in her hand. She kept them on a table and gestured some one to place glasses and a jar of drinking water by their side. Drawing the veil over her head, she said with a bit coy tone, "My daughter has prepared these sweets. She does all the house hold works alone, also knows embroidery work very well".

After pouring some water in the glass of Subhas, she said, "She keeps the account of our monthly household expenditure; but there is no scope for higher education in our village. We also don't want her to be highly educated. What is the need for imparting higher education ? This is enough for her."

She pulled her face as though she despised higher education like she did to a foul pig.

She was going to drop a stuffed cake on Subhas's plate. He held his hand over the plate and said, "No, no aunty, this is enough for me. I can't eat any more."

"Are the sweets palatable son?"

"Yes, aunty, but I am a temperate eater, please…" Subhas shrank within.

"Maheswar Babu, you take some" the lady turned to his side and dropped three stuffed cakes on his plate.

In his old age also, Maheswar Babu was a voracious eater. While chewing he said "Subhas Babu, you will be surprised to know in my youthful days, I used to eat one seer of flattened rice with curd every day as my morning meal. But my quantity of food is gradually diminishing for old age."

"That is quite natural. But usually I don't take more. I am aware of the capacity of my digestive system from the beginning."

Maheswar Babu washed his hand and made a sign to the lady to bring her daughter before them.

After half an hour, the girl came with a small plate in her hand. There were some betels and cloves kept separately. She had worn a printed sari and prostrated herself at the feet of Maheswar Babu and then Subhas's. She kept staring at the ground drawing lines with her toe.

Subhas was too embarrassed to look directly at her face. He stole a covert glance at her. The girl was of sickly physique with an emaciated long neck. Her face was somewhat oval, cheeks a bit sunken and some sort of helplessness was there in her eyes.

"What is your name, please?" Subhas asked the girl.

The girl remained mute and twisted one skirt of her sari with her fingers trying to rid herself of growing nervousness.

"May I know your education?" Subhas grew suddenly sympathetic to that girl. He saw clearly the beads of sweat glistening on her forehead as she could not get over her shyness. To save her from this ordeal, Subhas said to Maheswar Babu, "All right, let her go inside. No more of this."

The girl's father came half-way with them. During conversation, he gave them sufficient hints that his daughter had also personal savings and would give financial help to Subhas if such a situation occurs. Maheswar Babu had a daughter of marriageable age. As her complexion of body was not so appreciable, he could not venture to propose for her. She was a girl of medium height and possessed a very sound health. Her eloquent eyes seemed to tell more things than her mouth. She often cast her look in an inviting way as though binding some one in a snare. She would sometimes hum a tune of some folk-songs and loiter on the open verandah from one corner to another stuffing some flowers in her chignon.

It was the early hour of the night and the sky was studded with a whole constellation of stars. Subhas was strolling about in the garden thinking over the girl he met that afternoon. Though the girl was of average beauty, he was to sacrifice himself for the sake of higher studies. Otherwise his aspiration, his lofty dreams will remain unfulfilled. The fragrance of some unknown flowers came floating on gentle breeze. Some yards away a frog was croaking pitifully, devoured by a snake. Subhas turned his direction homeward and entered the bedroom. The penetrating smell of burnt joss-sticks was still there.

Subhas was hesitant to enter the room. Maheswar Babu's daughter was busy in spreading a bed-sheet over a mattress. While keeping a lamp on a small table, she sensed the presence of Subhas.

"Please come in Subhas Babu. Why do you feel shy? Treat this house as your own." She dragged a chair for Subhas.

Subhas sat down and let out a deep sigh.

"What's the matter Subhas Babu? Do you appreciate that girl? A bosom friend of mine, body to a certain extent is thin but after marriage" She giggled and rolled on the wooden cot She winked at Subhas. There were some strange erotic hints in her eyes. She threw him a sultry glance and said in a sing-song manner, "A slim body, modern youth likes that. Is it not Subhas Babu?" Again she giggled pressing the border of the sari to her mouth.

"Why are you keeping mum? Please say yes or no", She curved her lips to one side, her bewitching eyes still smiling at him. Her flirtatious gestures sent a horny tremor down his spine.

"Yes, it is..." Subhas could not answer back. His tone muffled half way.

"Subhas Babu !" Maheswar Babu called him from back. "Here in the village, we have our dinner at an early hour of the night. Please come to the dining room."

Subhas followed him with a sigh of relief.

Subhas felt himself a purchaseable commodity in the marrige market. He had come to bid him for a certain amount of money. If the bidding holds a considerable amount, he would be accepted otherwise rejected outright. Is it mandatory to him?

Is it not like sending him to a gaol with fetters on his feet? He is permitted to move in a confined area like a tethered cow, a diabolic servitude to drag on.

He felt suffocation. A wave of abomination surged up impetuously in his heart, the last man was he to withstand the slump of educational stature. A sharp rebuff came from their side after a week. Their denials reeked of hypocrisy.

Subhas applied for the post of teacher in Jhariadihi High School set up on the outskirts of his town. It was a private institution established by some generous persons of that locality. Most of the students, who could not shine in other educational institutions, came to this high school to get themselves admitted.

Though it was a thinly populated area, tiled houses

and thatched huts were littered here and there. Not far from the school, there was a grave yard of Christians, encompassed by a low compound wall. A large number of wild trees grew on the campus of the burial ground as it was left unattended for decades. One cannot conjecture some years back the area was a dense forest. Only a narrow winding path ran through the forest where one dared to go with a thumping heart. While going along that route one could hear the long droning sound of the cicadas accentuating the dread of the forest. There was a time when a notorious thief and burglar Dhanapana by name had wreaked havoc in that forest area. That was the usual way for the milk-maids and flattened-rice sellers to come to the town from neighbouring villages. Dhanapana would suddenly emerge from his hiding place to the amazement of the milk maids and snatch away the milk pitchers from their helpless hands. The flattened-rice sellers were also in dread of him and their blood came to a freezing point when Dhanapana would leap over them and unleash a shrill cry like a demon. At night he would break into the kitchen of some householder, gulp the water rice with some remaining curry kept for the next morning and then he would empty his bowels sitting over the hearth to remind the householder that he had visited the previous night to consecrate it.

Subhas was in the good book of Paramananda Babu, the secretary of the management body of Jhariadihi high school. By profession, he was a petition writer of the local court. But basically he was a poet- a born-poet par excellence who spent most of his time composing poems. His poetic talent excelled all the contemporary poets of his district. He was quite indifferent to the household management being deeply engrossed in the world of poetry. As a poet he derived maximum pleasure from poetic fantasy. On Saturday afternoons, both Subhas and Paramananda Babu would sit together discussing various aspects of Oriya literature. He would read out his recently composed poems in a very melodious tone finding in Subhas a patient and appreciative listener.

One day he said to him, "Subhas Babu, this school is an integral part of your life. You must remain in this institution after your teachers' training course is completed. You can't tear yourself away from this school so long as I am alive."

Subhas stared at him for a while and remained silent.

Paramananda Babu took his taciturnity as an oath-taking and smiled broadly.

"My headache is over Subhas Babu, I want teachers of your tribe, fully dedicated in dignifying the name of our school. I admit that the managing committee has no capacity to give your prescribed salary. But you have to brave the storm, stride ahead to overcome all the difficulties that stand in your way."

When Paramananda Babu became emotional, his voice would be choked and he would not be able to find out an outlet to vent his feelings.

During recess, he went to a restaurant owned by Jagannath with some of his colleagues. After he came back to the teachers' common room, he chastised Bhupen Babu, the science teacher of that school.

"Bhupen Babu, you have passed only intermediate science, what will you do with this much education ? If you don't try for higher studies, then your future is sealed. Be mindful of your future career."

Bhupen Babu was not in an inviting mood to brook this chastisement. He burst out, "Why do you bother if I don't go for higher studies. It is my pleasure whether I do it or not. Why do you unnecessarily scratch your head for my future?"

Subhas got suddenly scared. He remained restrained without any reaction. Perhaps it was his unfulfilled desire which prompted him to say so to a colleague, to a person whom he thought as his own younger brother. The world is like that. The person should not be blamed. Any uncalled- for advice may be viewed differently in this self-centred world. Why did he go to show commiseration to him?

Two dates had been fixed for collection of the tuition fees. It was the duty of the class teachers to collect fees on 15th or the last date of the current month. They would get each twenty five to thirty rupees, a trivial amount every month and the rest of the amount after the school received a grant-in-aid from the government.

Subhas lost himself in boyish uproar of the school students. He could see in them his own boyhood- always exuberant and juvenile in their own ways. He forgot his own trials and tribulations, his turmoil of life being completely oblivious of the irony of fate.

Days rolled by. After a written test he was selected to undergo teachers' training course at Sambalpur.

He was predestined to be a teacher.

NINE

Subhas did not want to be a mediocre, an average man to lose his discriminating identity among teeming millions like Tom, Dick and Harry.

There was none to see him off at the time of departure for Sambalpur, although there were other members of the family enjoying their midday nap. The house looked desolate, he too forlorn and discarded by the world. He was alone, simply alone.

Subhas had only two hundred and fifty rupees in his purse when he came from home. After he got admission in the Govt. Training College, Sambalpur, he could not rely upon the remaining amount to meet his monthly expenditure. He waited till he received the stipend from his college. His cousin happened to be the assistant jailor of sadar jail, Sambalpur with whom he stayed at insistence. He was senior to him in age only by one and half a year. By that time he had no children and his wife was the only companion of him in that set of Govt. quarters. Seeing Subhas he was highly delighted and his loneliness in that alien land was lessened to some extent.

One day he said to Subhas, "Your college is far away from our quarters. It is not easy to cover such a long distance on foot. Let us see about a second hand bicycle. That will rather ease your trouble."

"Brother, I have a very small amount of money, say, one hundred and fifty only. I am at the beam ends." Subhas said in a tone of helplessness.

"A colleague of mine is going to Lucknow to undergo a training course. He is now in need of money. By the by he told me that he will dispose of the bicycle if it sells at a reasonable price. It is as good as a new one. I have seen it."

After the duty was over, his brother came home riding on that bicycle. The condition of that bicycle was really very good and his sister-in-law also appreciated it.

A month later a bouncing male child as beautiful as a cherub was born to them. Subhas was in a mood to shift to some mess but his brother precluded him from doing so and told him to wait till the twenty first day of the child.

In the mean time, an unexpected transfer order reached his office. As the assistant jailor of Balangir jail fell suddenly ill and he was put in Burla medical hospital on the ground of hepato cellular jaundice, Subhas's cousin was transferred on deputation in his place.

So handing over the keys of the quarters, his brother went to the nearby railway station with his wife and newly born child. Subhas too went with them to bid them good bye. The train gradually picked up speed and soon they disappeared from his sight.

Subhas used to receive forty rupees as stipend from his college every month. The hotel 'Pravat' where he usually had his lunch and dinner also charged forty rupees a month. So there was not a single pie left with him for refreshments. Some months ago, when there was a little amount of money in his purse, he was regularly having his breakfast in a restaurant near 'Gaiety Talkies.' His favourite food then was 'masala dosa.' The waiter would drop a dosa on his plate stuffed with sufficient onion and fried pepper. After he finished it, the waiter would come to his table and ask, "Any thing more, Babu?"

"No, this is sufficient," Subhas would nod his head. After washing his hands in the basin he would ask the restaurant owner, "how much, brother?"

"Twenty five paisa," the owner would cut short his reply and view Subhas from head to foot thoughtfully, a poverty-ridden student cannot pay more than that.

In the hotel, a big chunk of fried fish would cost hardly thirty paisa. But Subhas would take fried fish two to three times a month practising frugality as he would not be able to give such a big amount at the end of the month.

The owner of 'Hotel Prabhat' was a kind-hearted man. When Subhas handed him forty rupees coming straight from the college, he looked over the account. The number of meals had been recorded there.

He raised his head and said, "You remained absent for eight days. Where had you been Subhas Babu?"

"A friend of mine is a student of Burla Engineering College. Every Saturday I slip to his place and come back on Monday morning to attend college here," –Subhas said in an apologetic tone.

"O yes, I see, all right, you please take ten rupees from me the money you deserve." The hotel owner pushed a ten-rupee note in his pocket.

Subhas stood for a moment thinking the hotel owner perhaps gave him a little amount more.

He read his face and said, "No, no, Subhas Babu, I have deducted the actual amount and refunded you the rest. No worries, please." His face brightened with a compassionate smile.

It was a sombre afternoon and the lightning flashed cris-crossing the vast arena of the sky. After a moment, the rumbling of thunder flitted from one corner to another. The black clouds began to gather in the sky. It drizzled for some minutes but stopped all of a sudden as a strong gale swept them away to the east. The sky began to clear and there was no possibility of recrudescence.

After the college hours, Subhas descended the steps. That day Subhas could not eat his lunch to his heart's content as the curry was not at all tasty. A new cook had been appointed in place of the old one. So he stopped eating in the middle, washed his hands hurriedly and took his bicycle to college. At mid-day he felt the terrible pangs of hunger. He glanced at his watch, there was yet one hour to go. The bell chimed out the closing time of the college.

Subhas's legs trembled. Subhas knew that it was due to his excessive hunger. The empty stomach revolted. Drop something edible, then it is appeased. Subhas wanted to pacify the beast within but he had no money in his pocket.

He pedalled his bicycle towards Burla. He went past some hillocks, looked several times at the green munificence of nature and was amused. The cattle-stock were returning from pasture with jingling-bells on their neck. The cow-herd boy had caught a tune of some folk-song on his pipe while holding a stick to spur the cattle homeward. The western sky was smudged blood-red and a few nest-bound birds were seen flying towards that crimson effulgence.

Himanshu was in his hostel room, busy in dressing himself to go for a walk to the sadar bazaar of Burla town.

Subhas kept the bicycle in a corner and entered his room. Himanshu looked straight at his face and asked him "Why are you looking so sunken Subhas? Is not your health going well?"

Subhas sat down on his bed and relaxed himself. His sweating body began to dry up. He could not give an instant answer.

Himanshu observed him and said,"You look dead beat, must you have some troubles, otherwise..."

"Nothing, I am half-fed today. Besides....", Subhas tried to explain his real condition.

"Now you wash your face and be ready to go to bazaar with me. I know your actual disease". Himanshu surveyed him with the eyes of a mother.

They both went to the market. Himanshu led him to a

restaurant. It was flamboyantly lighted by multi-coloured lights, perhaps to attract the customers. All the restaurants were pullng well because of the students of medical and engineering colleges. Particularly in the evening hours, the roads were choked with traffic. Not a single seat was lying vacant in that restaurant. So they had to wait outside for half an hour.

After they had finished refreshments, Himanshu said, "Let us go to Sobhakar. I have some important matter to discuss with him.

They turned to the left and went through the dazzling array of neon lights on both sides of the metalled road.

Sobhakar was reading a news paper and an oscillating fan on a stool faced his bed. He welcomed them warmly and requested them to sit on two plastic chairs.

It was Subhas's first meeting with him after a long gap of six years. After a chitchat for some time, Subhas asked him,

"Brother, after some years you will be a promising doctor, no doubt. I have some indisposition to explain to you. That I have been suffering from a dry spasmodic cough for some months, now, please prescribe me some efficacious medicine for that."

Sobhakar soon picked up his stethoscope and auscultated his chest thoroughly. Then he sighed and uttered, "NAD."

Subhas looked at him agape. Then Sobhakar made him understand that NAD means "Nothing abnormal detected."

"You have no special disease, Subhas. It is most probably due to your empty stomach. What I mean to say is that you have kept your stomach empty for a long time. This is the root cause of your dry cough."

Subhas looked at Himanshu with a cryptic distress in his eyes.

On their way back, Himanshu chastened him, "Why do you go on an empty stomach, Subhas?"

Subhas suddenly stopped on the way and held his hand. A moment later he replied with reluctance.

"It is as clear as a crystal, Himanshu. My monthly hotel expenditure is forty rupees. I receive exactly that amount as stipend. There are people who squander money to gratify their senses. But I have no extra money to spend on victuals."

Himanshu blinked at his face vacantly trying to find a meaning of it, all.

Mr Muralidhar Patnaik was the Revenue divisional Commissioner of Northern Division, Orissa. He was a tall, stout, middle aged person with a pleasing appearance. Some portion of the hair on his head specially on the temporal areas had turned gray which rather heightened his gravity. He was a man of the spiritual school of thought, an ingenuous and serious devotee of Srimaa and Sri Aurobindo. His wife had tamed two Alsatian dogs to watch the house. Although they were tied to a peg with an iron chain during the day, nobody could venture to enter the house because of their ferocious appearance.

Subhas had been acquainted with that family through his elder brother. The rapport had continued since that time. Whenever
there was some festive occasion, Subhas must be invited to their house. On other occasions also, Mr. Patnaik's wife would send him some palatable dishes through an orderly or a bearer of the house.

Subhas passed for a pupil teacher of their eldest son Anil who spent most of his time in his company. Very often he would come to Subhas to clarify his doubts. He was reading in Sambalpur Zilla School and going to appear at the final High School Certificate examination that year.

One evening Mr. Muralidhar entrusted Subhas with a responsibility to set questions for the clerical examination. He handed him the question paper of the previous year and gave some suggestions how neatly it could be set.

With much caution Subhas prepared the question paper that night and soon he fell into sleep in his bed. Towards the last part of the night he dreamt a very awe-inspiring dream.

He had gone on a picnic with some of his friends. When all were busy in preparation of food, Subhas went to a nearby tank to take bath. While bathing, he grew eager to swim across the tank. He plunged into the water but his hands and legs became suddenly paralysed. Gradually he drowned in the water and his legs were stuck to the mud underneath. The process of respiration stopped and he died a hapless death there. He slowly came awake from his sleep but was startled by a loud calling of somebody from outside.

"Subhas, are you at home?"

He flung open the window and looked through it. He was no other than his cousin Naresh who seated on a rickshaw, was calling him loudly. He did not get down. A large airbag was there at his feet. He signalled Subhas to go closer to him.

"You are alone brother ! Where is our sister-in-law?" Subhas queried.

"She is now staying in her parents' house at Bhubaneswar. Listen, yesterday Bapi died of measles" – His brother informed him coolly being bowed down with grief by sudden death of his first born child.

"What!" Subhas's heart began to thump violently. He fumbled, "But how?"

"We take measles lightly. But I know it is a killer disease. Doctors also say that. If it is suppressed, its prognosis is very bad."

"Please rest a while."

"No, I am going straight to the bus stand to catch a bus plying between Sambalpur and Bhubaneswar. I should not delay a minute."

He directed the rickshaw puller to turn round and went

straight without looking behind. Subhas remained standing as though his legs had been glued to the ground.

All day long overpowered with grief, Subhas could not do any thing. He did not attend college on that day and brooded over the days gone by. At the approach of the evening, he grew more restless. So he went to the public library to be absorbed in reading. There he unexpectedly met his old friend Satish. He intercepted him when he was going to leave the place to have his dinner. He had heard Satish had been transferred to Sambalpur but he did not know his whereabouts. On being asked he told Subhas that he was now residing in a hired house with his family at Christian para. During conversation Subhas noticed that he was talking in a desultory manner and a bit reluctant to tell him to visit his house once. Perhaps he wanted to keep him at arm's length. Subhas thought pensively whether time changes or a person changes under circumstances. After a long lapse of time, Satish seemed to him a quite stranger.

"Where the hell did you disappear to? Must be in hibernation", Subhas fondly smacked him on the back.

"Hm, I got a job in the Distrcit veterinary office. Working for two years in a clerical post but have not yet received my increment as my attempt did not fructify into success in the departmental examination."

Satish's disappointing look moved him.

"That examination as I know starts day after tomorrow. Would you please come with me?"

Where ?

"To my room."

"Why?"

"To know the questions set for the ensuing examination."

"What? How did you know all about that?" Satish stared at him sceptically. He was thunder struck.

"I offer you fish, don't ask me the exact location of the tank."

They went together to the commissioner's colony. Subhas unlocked his room. "Please get in."

Subhas switched on the light.

Satish looked all around the room and sat on a chair timidly. His eyes looked lack-lustre and pale as those of a dead fish.

Subhas pulled out the question paper from the drawer of a table and pushed it towards Satish.

"How it came to your hand?" Satish still surmised that he was lying.

"I myself have set all those questions. Here is a pad of paper, copy them all and don't leak out." Subhas grinned,

With a trembling hand, Satish copied them from beginning to end.

"One day's gap is sufficient to prepare the answers well. What do you say?"

"Why not? Of course… " Then he hastened out of the room and disappeared into the darkness.

TEN

"Himanshu, here in your place, a banian is sufficient to protect one from cold. But at Sambalpur town, it is terribly biting. Why this difference?" Subhas asked.

"Don't you know this simple geographical reason?" Himanshu laughed at his ignorance.

"I don't know actually," Subhas retorted.

"It is due to the vast sheet of water of Hirakud dam. It helps keep the climate temperate," Himanshu explained.

"O, I see", Subhas looked at Himanshu enjoying his ignorance.

Lying in a supine position on his bed, Himanshu confided to him, " One thing you must remember Subhas, here in our hostel the manager thinks you to be a student of engineering. You should not reveal your real identity to any body else."

"Why?"

"Because you can have your meals here so long as you like. The manager knows a few students, who are closely associated with him. He has taken charge of this huge hostel on a contract basis. It is too difficult for him to keep an account of all the students. He is least concerned if any outsider eats meals without his knowledge".

"Is it? In the medical college hostel also, the manager thinks me like that," Subhas wondered.

The bell went on ringing for some seconds announcing dinner time. Both of them went to the dining hall.

There were some oval tables in the hall with chairs

encircling them. Food had been kept at the centre of each table. Self-serving system had been introduced in those hostels since a long time ago. One could eat meals according to one's option. There were no taboos whether he or she was vegetarian or non-vegetarian. When they were eating meals and busy in conversation, one student suddenly got up from his chair and went straight to the manager with some hot 'chapatis' in his hand. He pressed them on both sides of his cheek and said, "You blind wretch, should I eat these half burnt chapatis? You see for yourself their condition, kept in that basket."

Then he raised his hand to slap the manager. But some how he controlled his anger and came back to his seat.

He shouted, "We pay money but you servile do not supervise the work of your cook. I won't pay a single pie if it goes on like this."

The young student went on grumbling.

Many a time the manager had to drink such a bitter cup of humiliation. Perhaps he was seasoned to all these daily barbarities and assaults,otherwise one could not pocket such an insult in the presence of all. That looked quite unusual to Subhas.

Back to Sambalpur; Subhas ate his lunch hastily and went to the college. After the recess, Mr Gaurishyam, the Principal, sent for him to his office. Subhas could not know why he was called upon. With palpitation, he entered and saluted him.

The principal flicked the ash from his cigarette with the tip his finger into an ash-tray and looked at him through curling smoke. Then he asked, "Do you know Sriramchandrapur Subhas? Where is it located at Baripada ?"

Actually Subhas had no idea. He told him extempore, "It might be near Krishnachandrapur Sir."

"What? I know Krishnachandrapur, it is not far away from Baripada town. You are supposed to know as a permanent inhabitant of that place and you do not know

Sriramchandrapur. How is that ? Why do you come to undergo teachers' training course with this much of knowledge?"

Subhas stared foolishly at him.

Mr. Gaurishyam put the stub of the cigarette in the ash-tray and said, "Will you go to Burla next Saturday, Subhas?"

Subhas shook his head.

The Principal pulled a bundle of notes from his pocket and handed it to Subhas over the table.

"I gave two hundred and fifty rupees to Manas, count it and tell him to see me sometime."

"Yes sir."

Subhas was returning after finishing his nocturnal meal in the hotel. There was a sharp nip in the air and he shivered from head to foot. Even his hands got numb while holding the cycle handles in that freezing cold.

He unlocked the door and kept his bicycle aside. He washed his feet with tap water but there was no provision of fire to warm his body. Suddenly a feeling of helplessness crept into his mind. The blanket was also icy-cold and he shivered under it.

There was a programme chalked out for the study tour to south India. The government was ready to provide all the expenditure necessary for it. The Principal had served a notice to enlist the names of the willing students.They were to start their journey in the ensuing Xmas holidays.

Subash knew it was a rare chance. But he was in a fix whether to accept it or not. At last he resolved to go on a study –tour. He had no warm garments.He thought if he asked Himanshu; he might lend him his coat for a few days.

Their itinerary was fixed. After a long tour all over South India, they returned by train and halted at Jharsuguda en route to Sambalpur.Subhas got down the train with his belongings and directed a rickshaw puller to get him to Mahanadi vihar.

The next morning Subhas went to Mr.Muralidhar's residence. After saluting him with reverence, he offered him two oil portraits of Srimaa and Sri Aurobindo and one white banian that he had brought from the Aurobindo Ashram, Pondicherry. He looked at them minutely and smiled, overjoyed.

"Excellent, where from did you get these portraits Subhas?" His innocuous look sparkled with rare ecstasy.

"At Pondicherry, Sir."

"I have some, but this is simply superb, a rare picture of its kind."

His wife came out from the bed room and sat down on the sofa.

"Yes, let me see those pictures."

Mr. Muralidhar held them up before her eyes.

"Lively pictures indeed, looks like Maa staring at us with a meaningful message, doesn't it ? She looked at her husband expecting from him an unquestioning support.

Mr. Muralidhar closed his eyes and uttered as though in a trance. "I am really glad, Subhas, I hold them above all my earthly possessions. It is no other than the blessings of Maa. She sent me a morsel of her mercy through your hands. Strange are the ways of heavenly benediction." He cleared his throat as his voice choked half-way.

Mr. Muralidhar slowly leaned against the panel of the sofa, closed his eyes contemplating. For a period silence surged.

Mr. Muralidhar's wife lowered her tone and said," Why don't you approach him for a better service, Subhas? He is in the rank of a commissioner. He can find a way out for you, if he wills."

"No, aunty, I don't like other services. I shall stick to this profession unto my last. It is preordained and I have that inalienable right to decide my own future."

"But do you know Subhas, the life of a teacher is full of hardships. Particularly from the financial point of view."

Subash laughed benignly, caring least about his murky future.

Late in the afternoon, Himanshu pushed open the door.

"Hi, Himanshu, you appeared unexpectedly. Please be seated on that chair."

"Why unexpectedly? Two days ago I came to know of your returning from the South India trip. Now tell me how did you enjoy yourself ?"

"Thrilling…Very exciting I could not dream of that, I mean some worth-seeing places, that is why it is said, what is not in India, is no where in the world."

"Any mishap or casualty on the way?"

"No, by the grace of God, But at Nagpur railway platform, I was going to lose your coat."

"How?"

"I went to a railway restaurant requesting Bhagirathi sir to keep my coat in his safe custody. The moment I left, a drunkard came tottering to him and tried to whisk away the coat from his lap. A tug of war for a moment and admitting his defeat, the man disappeared in the crowd."

"O'thank God, then?"

"When I came back, sir narrated to me this humorous story."

"What have you brought for me?"

"Yes, I bought two pieces of terylene cloth at Dadar Sadar market, Bombay, one for me and another for you. You will be surprised if you know about the lack of their geographical knowledge. When the shop owner learnt that we were from Sambalpur, Orissa he kept on staring at us. Then sensing his ignorance, we asked him if he knew Jagannath Dham. A smile of familiarity began to play on his face and he said. "O'God ! are you all from Jagannath Dham? I have already visited that holy place two times in my life."

We paid him the price of the cloth and at the moment of parting, he gave us some steel rings as gifts to remember him."

"It is so interesting ! What about other places?"

"In the Muir market, Madras, sir warned us all not to buy any thing as the place is full of swindlers. I moved around the market alone and caught sight of some old books in a book store. I bought two books from that store, one is complete works of Shakespeare and another 'Gulliver's Travels" by Jonathan Swift at an incredibly low price."

Any other remarkable place that you highly appreciate?

"Yes, Bombay is quite distinguishable from all other places. Situated on the western shore of the Arabian sea,. It is "the gate way of India' in the true sense of the phrase. Its marine drive, long stretches of five-star hotels, Flora fountain, Botanical garden, all are there to astound you. If you see its posh area where only elites walk the earth, an idea will grow in you how living in an ivory tower, they try to reach the zenith of luxury. A multistoried sky-kissing hotel 'Oberoi Sheraton' is now under construction and we sought permission to have a dekko inside. An access to 'Hotel Taj' is inviolable to a commoner. On the whole, the tinsel world of Bombay has been purely westernized and people like us will be lost like country yokel in the midst of din and bustle."

"Well, will you go to see a movie to-night at Gaiety talkies?"

"Please excuse me. I want to take rest for a few days" implored Subhas.

The next day Subhas went to Patna house-a boarding house under Government Training college. He was empty-handed as he had not yet received his monthly stipend.

"Sarat, would you please lend me five rupees? I badly need it."

"Yes, why not?" Sarat opened his box and pushed a five rupee note into his hand.

"Sarat, this hotel food will not suit me any longer."
"Why?"
"Because I feel drowsy, right from the first hour of teaching."

"The reason …"

"The reason is that the hotel boy is doing some mischief, a foul play, mixing stale rice with fresh one."

"How did you know?"

"Just a hunch. A doubt has been lurking in me for long. When I pressed the boy to extract the truth, it came to light."

"O, what will you do then?"

I will approach Dologovind. He is now staying on the upper floor of zilla school-making a miniature mess, so to say."

"Yes, you try your best to adjust yourself there. I hope the thing will come to your favour."

Subhas took his meals in zilla school mess hardly for three weeks. But the reason best known to others, a misunderstanding grew among them and in course of time they left the mess one after another.

Francis Tirky and Purnananda were staying in a veranda protecting it by bamboo curtains from all sides. They had to pay Rs12/- as rent every month. Subhas saw their wretched state. He invited them to stay with him.

Francis Tirky, a man of Sundargarh district, was a Christian by faith. A picture of mother Mary, a suckling Jesus Christ in her lap was hanging on the wall. A tender, filial affection had been reflected in her eyes. It was really superb and Francis looked at it at the first entrance of the house.

"Why did you hang this picture Subhas? Any special liking?"

Francis asked turning to him.

"Yes, definitely, I view mother Mary as an embodiment of universal motherhood."

"Any more…"

"A streaming rivulet embellished with serenity…a honey sweet tenderness piercing through all barriers, a pulsating sylvan calmness has suffused her appearance-only a connoisseur of art can realise this."

"Do you know, Subhas? I was Dinabandhu Tirky before my proselytisation, but after conversion, my name changed and now I pass for Francis….Francis Tirky."

From that day cooking had been done unitedly. They distributed the work among themselves and the days passed smoothly.

Once Francis took him to the church and introduced him to the Church Father. Subhas used to attend the church on Sundays. Francis would carry him on the back seat of his bicycle. The tranquil atmosphere, their steady devotion and discipline drew him and it began to seek a place in the niche of his heart.

"Subhas, I will go to my native place the next Saturday. Pure ghee sells at cheaper rates there. If you are willing, you will get two seers of ghee on payment of twenty rupees. My mother also prepares ghee at home; I need not look else where. As it is home made, there is no question of adulteration."

Francis came back after five days with four seers of ghee in an earthen jar. When he removed its lid, the whole room was filled with its sweet scent.

"If you drop one spoonful of ghee on boiled or flattened rice, it will taste excellent," while speaking, saliva shimmered in Francis's mouth.

After the final examination, the college remained closed. 18th May was a red letter day in Subhas's life. Francis and Purnananda hugged him on the day of departure. They left for home with a lump rising in their throat. It was for the last time, Subhas saw them waving their hands to bid him goodbye. "We will miss you Subhas, even may not get a chance to meet you once again in our life time" they uttered letting out a deep breath.

During journey by train, a cycle might be a great inconvenience. So Subhas decided to sell it to Kamal Krishna, an employee of the postal department. He agreed to pay the cost of the cycle in two instalments.

Subhas went to the jailor sahib to hand over the keys of the Govt. quarters and started for the railway station. He booked the ticket and got into a compartment. Before the train began to pick up its speed, he cast a last lingering glance at the town through the window.

A gloomy western sky was going darker heralding the advent of monsoon.

ELEVEN

Learning from reliable sources Narahari Babu, the headmaster of Kanchanpur high school, came unexpectedly to Subhas's house. Subhas ushered him into his study room and asked the purpose of his sudden visit.

"We are in search of a trained graduate teacher. I learnt that you have passed teachers' training course this year. Our school has been accredited and it would not be entitled to receive grant- in- aid unless we fulfil the terms and conditions laid down by the government from time to time. I, on behalf of the managing committee, request you to join us within a week"

With a brief smile, Subhas came to an assent.

Kanchanpur was a growing village. A narrow gauge railways passes by this small station touching the western tip of the village, where the dwelling houses were very few in number. Most of the passengers would journey without paying a single pie to the railway department. The ticket checker also connived at their free journey and scarcely paid any importance whether it ran with profit or loss. The station master, a Bengali gentleman, wearing a loose spectacle would wink at the passengers with dilated eyes as though he was disgusted with this tedious job, eyes seeming to bulge out of their sockets.

A betel shopkeeper had opened a shop outside the platform where there would be always a small gathering chewing betels, puffing biris and cigarettes.

If some important familiar face went past his shop, he would call him, "Babu, please take a betel. What can I offer, poor man as I am. It is with your blessings Babu that I am running this shop through thick and thin."

The children wearing buttonless half pants and tattered shirts on their back would squeal with delight near his shop, throwing rubble at each other.

"You cheeky little devils, stop that infernal noise and go to your house. Your parents are awfully slack in leaving you all carefree like stray bulls. Is it some play-ground ? Don't go on chattering here, if you all hail from good families," the shopkeeper would suddenly shout in anger.

Then the errant boys would flee making a face at the shopkeeper.

Subhas was given a separate room as the superintendent of the hostel. The cook Bhavataran and his assistant Nitai went to the village market with two sacks on bicycle to bring vegetables. Nearly fifty students were residing in that hostel. The kitchen was at a little distance from the hostel. A deep well surrounded by a small grassy field lay between them.

Three assistant teachers were the occupants of the adjacent room next to the superintendent's.

It was late evening. The hostel and its surrounding areas seemed to be flooded with moonlight. An owl was hooting intermittently behind a thick bamboo grove. The feeble cry of bats perched on the nearby trees was being heard as they skirmished among themselves. Miss Shipra suddenly burst into Subhas's room.

"Sir, how do you remain in your room when there is a flood of moon light every where? Come outside and enjoy it," she said with a peal of laughter.

"You see I am reading a book. I don't have any desire to go out side" Subhas said with a withdrawn mood.

"This is not the time for reading sir. Please come with me," Miss Shipra whined like a child.

"Listen Miss Shipra, this is a rural area, not your town. Here the people will think us brazen- faced if they see us together. Don't insist on my going with you. "Subhas tried to make her understand.

"I don't care, people may say but what rights they have to obstruct my way. I never bother myself with their malicious remarks." Miss Shipra straightened her body as if to challenge the backbiters.

"But I do care as I am completely new to your area. What impression would they carry if I roam in this way" Subhas said, slightly irritated.

"As you wish sir, but I have some important discussion with you. I may come tomorrow evening."

Miss Shipra wore her high heels and walked away in a languid gait.

Some one pushed the door.

It was Amiya Babu, assistant teacher of that high school.

"Dreadfully sorry, Subhas Babu as I disturbed your reading."

He came near his cot and sat down on a small stool. There was some suppressed mystery in his eyes.

Subhas looked at him and asked, "What is the night halting for Amiya Babu? I have requested you many a time but you have not stayed once."

"No, I have to attend the obsequies of my uncle's father." He drew the stool closer and looked at the door cautiously.

Lowering his tone he said," I saw Miss Shipra emerging from your room. What is the matter, Subhas Babu?"

"It is not so important. She just requested me to have a stroll with her on this moonlit night. But Amiya Babu,I don't expect such guts from a newly acquainted lady."

Many things are to be seen Subhas Babu if you stay in this place for a few months. The witches are wandering, if they find you unguarded, they will definitely suck you dry."

Amiya Babu dropped his tone almost to a whispering

and said, "But more gruesome witch is Miss Shipra Banerjee, the head mistress of M.E. School here."

"Is it? I don't think so."

"I just made you aware of these things because I know, you are a simpleton. Whenever you put your steps here, do it prudently, not to fall in some pitfalls," his tone sounded intimate.

" I am conscious from the beginning Amiya Babu. Besides, my philosophy is totally different from others."

Amiya Babu glanced at his watch and said, "It is getting late, my uncle might be looking for me."

He was on his feet and said, "I have a lot of things to do. So I must be off."

Miss Shipra grew anxious to meet Subhas. She was temporarily residing in 'Mahila Samitee' close to a grocery shop. Subhas came to the shop with the cook to purchase some grocery articles. Miss Shipra saw him through her window. She came near the shop and requested Subhas to step into her room.

"I have some grievous objection to put forth to Subhas Babu, because I hope it is you who can solve this problem I face at present "Miss Shipra said while directing Subhas to sit on a chair.

"May I know your problem?"

"Although the matter is not so serious, I am nonplussed at the conduct of your student," Miss Shipra knitted her brow

"Tell me the name of that student."

"You know Bipin, a Peeping Tom who came deliberately to my bed room window to sneak a look through it."

"But why?"

"I don't understand his intention," Miss Shipra glanced at Subhas as if he knew the motive of his student.

"Why do you keep the window open?

"What can I do Subhas Babu? You see for yourself I stay single in this cubby-hole. It serves as my kitchen as well as my bedroom. Am I not coerced to be cooped up inside a room shutting its doors and windows in this sweltering heat? "Miss Shipra was exasperated.

She went to one dark corner of her room and took out an egg from a paper carton.

She lit the oven to fry it on a pan. While frying; she turned to Subhas and said,

"I don't have any objection if he simply peeps through the window . But he says some filthy things like…"Miss Shipra blushed and kept staring at the frying pan to avoid his look.

'Why are you so tense and twitchy, please speak out." Subhas pressed her to know the fact.

"It has become an all night's affair Subhas Babu. Wielding a sharp knife he would push his hand through the window and implore:

"Why are you so hard-hearted didi, killing me in such a cruel way? Please take this knife and do as you like. If I must die, I will die with a smile in your delicate hands."

Subhas suppressed his laugh and said,"Miss Shipra, man always falls victim to the bewitching beauty of a lady. We have heard it and will hear the same for ages to come. One cannot cut off the snare of enticement so easily."

Subhas began his discourse but Miss Shipra interrupted him and said, "Please take this omelette, Subhas Babu.You know a good confectionery or a restaurant here is a distant dream, a god-forsaken place indeed."

"No, no, you should not worry. This is sufficient."

Miss Shipra washed her hands and asked, "Well Subhas Babu, would you lend me your Bengali novels for some days. You cannot deny. You must have some as you are a regular reader of Bengali novels and all sorts of magazines."

"How did you know this ?"

"Madhusmita, your favourite girl student, told me the other day that you highly appreciate Bengali literature, Don't you, Subhas Babu?

"Yes, I will give you a few books tomorrow that I have got at the moment. And I will try my best to solve your present problem, I assure you".

Subhas rose up from his bed when the sun was yet to rise. The cook Bhavataran handed him a cup of steaming tea. He began to sip it gingerly. Soon the courtyard of the hostel grew radiant with the mellowed light of the sun.

Rasik Babu, a teacher of Elementary Training School, came to Subhas and said "Subhas Babu, please tell your cook to keep the gruel in this tin-container. I have kept two milch cows. Now it has become a problem for me to feed them daily."

"Why do you tether them day and night? Let them move freely in the nearby forest," Subhas advised him.

"Yes, I did it a few days ago. But while grazing on the border of the forest, one cow went deep into the forest and after a thorough searching, I found it three miles away, asleep beneath a 'Sal' tree."

"All right, what about the studies of your daughter?"

"Yes, she is well up in other subjects except English. Subhas Babu, it is my request to you to guide her, otherwise her performance would be far from satisfactory."

"You see, in the evening I tutor a girl student at her home. I can at best spare the morning hours to guide her."

"Yes, that time would be suitable for her to come to your place. Let her be taught at least one hour."

Dhiren, the bursar and copper-bottomed boy of the hostel, came to Subhas and showed him the account of the meals. Two students were found to be defaulters as they had not paid their hostel dues. As per rule, a notice was served to them debarring them from eating meals from that day. At night the cook came to serve him his dinner. But Subhas refused saying that he could not eat his meals when two students went to bed on empty stomach. The next morning when they heard this from the cook they went to their houses to urge their parents to clear up the outstanding dues of the hostel. That day Subhas felt a satisfaction which he had not experienced in his life. Winning the heart of others by a bit of sacrifice he assayed for the first time and a little suffering brought him a savour of untold pleasure. He knew it well how much difficult it would have been to afford the expenditure of studies specially to keep a pupil in a hostel on the part of a poor tiller.

The ringing of bells and sound of cymbals from some distant temple was heard long after the sunset. He did not know why he could smell a sweet aroma redolent of incense in this moth-hour of evening, although he was far away from a temple. He felt an urge to sit some hours crosslegged in complete silence in a temple to be lost in deep meditation.

Subhas stepped into the study room of Madhusmita. A joss stick was half-burnt and it had filled the air of the room with a pious sweetness.

She was writing something. Well acquainted with the sound of foot steps, she raised her head being quite sure of his presence.

She was sitting just on the other side of the table placing a lantern in the middle with her face towards the doorway of the room.

Subhas found her to be thoughtful to some extent. What could be the reason? He began to think. He sat down and saw the English book lying on the table. When he was about to pick it up, suddenly Madhusmita pressed it with her right hand. She did not allow Subhas to take it away from her custody.

Subhas was shaken by a spasm of anger and asked, "What is this madness for Madhu? I don't understand,"

Subhas stared at her face with certain sternness. But she neither looked up nor responded to him, Instead she began to scribble with her pen carelessly on a scrap of paper.

"So I am going. You keep reading as you like," Subhas

stood up, dragged the chair to one side and made a dart for the door.

But he was startled when he heard," why did you not come yesterday, Sir?" With a distinct edge to her voice she looked straight to Subhas,a shadow of sadness still clinging to her face.

"Why? I had some urgent work in my hand." Subhas felt as if she demanded an explanation for his absence. He could not put up with her impertinence.

Madhusmita gave a sardonic smile and said,

"How could you sir? You could not come because you could not say 'no' when Sharmila herself came to your room to invite you. Of course who am I to raise an objection?"

"No, Madhu, try to understand me. Actually I had no desire, but her father came that afternoon to take me with him."Subhas seemed to enjoy the outburst of her anger.

"So you had a good chit chat with her that night, isn't It.?"

She eyed him from a corner to read his expression.

"No, I did not have time to talk with her."

"But you will find time to talk for many nights henceforward," she chuckled and said,"Her father will give you that opportunity; you should not bother about it."

Subhas's head reeled for a moment. He defied her blue jokes and vagaries.

"Do you think I am that cheap, Madhu, don't belittle me in such a mean way."

"No, I don't think so. But Sharmila is a bait and her father has been waiting with a fishing-rod to hook you at any time. And I apprehend she will soon find her way into your heart."

Madhusmita smiled at him and said, "Sir, to-night I don't have any mood to study. You please wait here till the dinner is ready."

"Why? I can't tolerate the wastage of food there, I mean our hostel."

"Let it be wasted,"Madhusmita said while going out of the study room.

"No, No, I am going."

Subhas was about to put his steps but Madhusmita came back with the speed of the wind and stood at the doorway blocking it by outstretching her hands. "No Sir, you can't. go. What will my mother say if you run away like this."- She stood there defiantly like a block of stone.

"All right, as you wish."

Various items had been served elaborately on a big plate like stuffed cake, rice pudding and luchi, all prepared with fresh buffalo ghee. Three to four big chunks of fish with a little juice in a dish drew his attention. Subhas looked around the dining room, everything was in apple pie order.

"Can I take such a big amount of food, Madhusmita?" Subhas said with raised eyebrows.

"Tell your sir, Madhu, not to leave anything on the plate"- a veiled woman murmured behind a wall.

Madhusmita turned her face from her mother and grinned, "What did Sharmila serve you that night, sir, your touch-me- not blushing creeper?"

Madhusmita poured some water in his glass, smiling.

"No, No, you don't have to wash your hands any where. You please wash on that plate."

Madhusmita tried to save him from an embarrassing

situation. Subhas stood up and pushed his left hand in the trouser pocket. Now he remembered he had forgotten to bring his handkerchief.

Madhusmita could realise his helplessness. She immediately extended the skirt of the sari.

Subhas looked at her face puzzled.

"No, don't hesitate. Please take it." Madhusmita said leaning towards him.

"Henceforth if you don't eat food with your hand, I shall feed you, no doubt" –she giggled.

After coming to the study room, she handed him a cup of steaming tea and said, "It has been prepared with pure milk, no water."

"But you know, I never take tea,"-Subhas retrieved himself.

"This time only, sir," Madhusmita insisted while playing with her rippling braided hair.

Subhas wrinkled his forehead and said, "How much sugar you have added Madhu? Is it tea or sherbet?"

"I have poured only two spoonfuls of love in that cup, Sir."

Her sensuously curving lips seemed to devour him.

Subhas could clearly hear the thumping of his heart. His legs too were slightly quivering. When he tried to calm himself down, he heard, "Must you accompany me to see a movie the next evening" she exhorted Subhas.

It sounded imperative and Subhas could not reply in the negative. He disappeared stealthily into the night like a ghost.

TWELVE

Mr. Jagat Narayan had passed civil engineering with brilliant academic achievement from Benaras Hindu University. But on account of acute unemployment problem and lack of god father's knacking, he could not get a job although the State Government had given extravagant promises many a time to create thousands of posts for the unemployed engineers. However he struggled hard to get through the tough competiton to secure a job, but all his efforts fizzled out. The people of Kanchanpur had high regards for this Brahmin family. He happened to be an alter ego of one of the cousins of Subhas's. His clear-heart, straightforwardness of character appealed to Subhas and both of them killed time weighing heavily on them, specially after the school was over. He would wander with this boon companion into the interior region of the forest, gossip on various topics and enjoy the calm beauty of nature.

One afternoon, they stuffed their trouser pockets with fried maize and went to a thicket surrounded by 'Sal and 'Asan' trees. Mr. Panda sat down on a flat stone and said, "Subhas Babu, you must have heard for the first time as a rhyme goes here concerning a bevy of beautiful girls, all trying to surpass each other in different aspects."

Mr. Panda looked with twinkle in his eyes.

"Please tell me, really it goes beyond my knowledge"- said Subhas innocently.

Mr. Panda did not want to keep Subhas any longer in mystery. He straightened his legs and recited:

"Living in this domain of fairies,
fed on juicy grapes
On moon-lit nights roam carefree
Play the harp and go on a drinking spree."
He recited it again.

Subhas could not help laughing.

"I don't still understand Mr. Panda, what does this couplet mean?"

"Does it seem to be a riddle?", he convulsed with a funny laughter, "but if you had known the clues beforehand, it would have been as clear as day light."

Mr. Panda shrugged his shoulders.

"But I don't know the girls or the relative context of your cited couplet either," Subhas said with eagerness to know its inner meaning

"I would tell you some other day, Subhas Babu. Let us go to your hostel."

"Why are you in a hurry Mr Panda, this time?"

"No, my elder brother has come from his service place today. I have some urgent discussion with him regarding my job prospects. He will have to leave for his office the next morning at the earliest, So…"

"O, very well, let us go."

Subhas heard the bell ringing from a distance; a mass prayer would begin and after some minutes, another bell announcing the hour of studies.

Back to hostel, Subhas discussed with the cook as to the preparation of curries and advised him to thoroughly wash the rice. He rested half an hour on his bed and as it was Sunday, he was not occupied with any other work. He thought of having a visit to his friend's house, not so distant from the hostel. To the left side of the village, there was a long row of houses, some clustered together and some were at a little distance from each other. His was in the middle of the row, just close to the kacha road.

Gananath's father was a cultivator, a man of the middle income group and because of old age, he had now abandoned his previous occupation as his eldest son had opened a grocery shop in his own house. Gananath, his second son, was an assistant teacher of Kanchanpur High School, married two years ago and blessed with a son of one and half a year. Gananath had lost his mother when he was a two-year-old child. His father remained a widower for some years but the management of household affairs posed a big problem. So he married, for the second time, a woman many years junior to him in age.

Both of his sons received better treatment from their step-mother. Even after a son was born to her, she remained as sympathetic and kind-hearted as before. Subhas opened the front door and got into the drawing room. He looked around and found Gananath asleep on a wooden cot, his face facing the wall, without any motion. He stood for a while in grim silence. Then he went near his cot and shook his shoulder to rouse him from sleep. Gananath slowly opened his eyes, twisted his body and gestured him indicating that his wife was sleeping on the other side of the room. Subhas could inhale the aroma of prepared curry coming from the kitchen. He tip-toed to the bed room. His wife, draped in a bed-sheet from head to foot, was lying motionless on a cot. In the corner, a lamp was burning casting its yellowish light, not sufficient to brighten the room. He called her aloud. Gananath's wife woke-up and rubbed her eyes with the back of her hand and said in an indistinct voice,

"When did you come Subhas Babu? I am just taking rest after cooking." Her tone sounded lifeless.

"But answer me first of all why you, husband and wife, are sleeping in this way?"

"Nothing of that sort, Subhas Babu," she tried to avoid a reply.

Subhas came back to Gananath. He was then sitting

on his cot, suspending his legs and trying to overhear their conversation.

"What is the matter Gananath? You all suddenly became dumb. I hope you must tell me the fact."

Gananath stood up, went to a pitcher and poured water into a steel glass and drank it. He placed it below his cot and said, "You see these two saris that I have bought today from the market, eighteen rupees each at Basudev Store. Do you think those saris are below standard, not befitting a lady to wear them?"

Gananath pulled them from a horizontal bar of a wooden rack.

Subhas saw them and ran his hand on their smooth surface.

"No, no, it is quite good. It has been woven by thread of eighty count, as smooth as a paper, even one can write with a pen on it. Who says that it is not fit to wear?" Subhas chastised.

Subhas could not know that Gana's wife had already stood at his back. She looked over his shoulder and said, "I never rejected them nor did I tell that I won't wear them. I simply said that one better and finer sari instead of two will be preferable."

A moment later she forced a smile on her face and said, "Our dinner is ready, Subhas Babu. Please have at least two to three pieces bread and dal."

"No, I won't unless you two sign the armistice and come to sit together."

Both husband and wife smiled their conflicts away and said, "All right, here we sit together," Gananath directed his wife to serve food.

Subhas sat by the side of Gananath, his wife at a little distance. While eating, Gana's wife looked at her husband from a corner and said smiling to Subhas, "Well, Subhas Babu, how do you like Madhusmita?

"Why? She is a good girl."

"No, no, my question is regarding her behaviour and appearance..."

"Yes, her appearance is incredibly remarkable and above all she is quite well-behaved"

"Even her enemy cannot deny that fact," she stopped eating and said emphatically to impress him, "Subhas Babu, make hay while the sun shines; otherwise you will steadily lose your ground."

"But what is that to me? It does not depend on my appreciation whether she is beautiful or ugly, healthy or sick- in no way am I related to that."

"No, Subhas Babu, you can't avoid. What I am going to say is that she looks like a million-dollar babe so far as her beauty is concerned. She is endowed with both: behaviour and appearance which must be reckoned."

"But I don't understand what you actually intend to say" – Subhas was a bit nervous and in a fix.

"You understand everything Subhas Babu. I am well acquainted with masculine scruples. The fact is that you don't venture to go to such an extent but if somebody does explore your heart, he will find out only the picture of Madhusmita and nobody else. Am I correct Subhas Babu?"

"You are correct a hundred percent. That is why you two have a child of one year and a half within the married life of at best two years." Subhas retaliated.

Gana's wife immediately became grim. Gananath came to her rescue and said, "Our summary of conversation is that she completely banks upon you to be your life partner."

"Is it as easy as you think Gananath? Moreover caste-differences are there which would be given prime importance. Besides I cannot overrule my conservative parents nor their age-old ideas."

"Of course, a great hindrance is there as I know about

the "this far-and-no further" taboos of your parents'"- Gananath said thoughtfully.

"I am really sympathetic seeing you on the horns of dilemma, Subhas Babu. Now the parents of three girls are anxious to give their daughters in marriage to you," said Gana's wife.

"I really wonder at your knowledge, the information you gather from various sources. Can you give me the name of other two girls?"

"Yes, definitely," Gana's wife came closer to Subhas and said, "Shipra Banerjee is now mad after you. Very often she comes to our house and lays her heart bare as she knows our relation with you. She has some inhibitions about saying to you what she really desires."

"Is it? I don't know the water has flowed to such an extent." Subhas grew alarmed.

"Then take the case of Sharmila. Her father is a low-paid government servant. He knows that he cannot give the demand if his daughter marries in some other places. The dowry has become a fear-factor in our society."

"But I didn't know all these facts till now. Why did you not confide in me Gananath?" Subhas was greatly pesky.

Gananath laughed and said, "Brother, don't be sore at me. I came to know about this matter only the other day."

Then for a minute silence fell.

"Subhas Babu, you are now being drawn from three sides", Gana's wife said while removing the utensils to one side of the bedroom.

"You are now swimming in a sea of dilemma, Subhas," – Gananath remarked.

"But I know how to keep myself afloat in the water" – Subhas said, defensively.

"There is every chance to slip side ways, however conscious a man may be," said Gananath to unnerve him.

"Don't joke Gananath. People may consider me mad as

I have chosen the by ways and do not walk along the main road of life. It is safest to go along the pavements to avoid all sorts of impending disasters."

"Why do you demur to marry Madhusmita that charming girl? After some months she will be admitted into a college. Then you will be alone in your father-in-law's house and look after the property as your brother-in-law is a minor one."

"You always build castles in the air Gananath. Do you know Delhi is far way from Daulatavad? I don't day dream like you do."

"But I see ages of innumerable dreams have been stored in your eyes." Gananath said rhetorically.

"Do you remember Gananath? All our friends had reminded you of not deceiving the girl you loved before your marriage. If we had known your foul play with her, we would have abandoned your friendship. But luckily you had not done that. Many thanks to you for your sincerity in love affair" –said Subhas admiringly.

Subhas always tried to remain aloof and not to be involved in these tangled affairs. He could not be thick skinned inviting all sorts of innuendoes defiling his image. There was a set of persons trying to nag at him for no fault of his own. Should he remain always in a state of panic ? What do they want – those girls' father? Do they want him to be truncated like a bald tree leaving him in the lurch? He could have waged a crusade against those insinuators. But he waited… waited to observe the turn of the situation until it was in his favour. His confidence told him he would come out unscathed… triumphant without the least trauma. Not to squabble with anybody to present him standoffish. He would not wince rather stand pat hurling defiance at the inimical forces. A valiant dies once-he said to himself. He swore to keep his chin up.

Shipra Banerjee would come to his bedroom during school hours, sleep on his cot so long as she liked during his absence. He could not understand her intention, why did she keep on sleeping in that way? She would expose herself almost to a vulnerable point, not caring the least to burn the moths hovering round the flame of her beauty day and night. When she was in some other. M.E. School, she was made pregnant by the young secretary and that hapless youth was strongarmed by some local goons to pay a handsome ransom for his past follies. A past mistress of seduction. Wherever she goes, she spreads the net of her enticing beauty to ensnare the simpletons who come in her way. They fall willy nilly in her trap and she fully exploits their simplicity and helplessness. That sultry siren once more hatched a hideous plot to overpower Subhas. She sent an intermediary with an appealing message to meet her. But Subhas was inexorably stubborn not to proceed any further. With discerning eyes he could envisage the consequences, a celibate never depraves himself to such a level. That aberration would be unpardonable. A sudden precipitous fall from a respectable height would be viewed disdainfully.

A week later, Miss Shipra waited to meet Subhas on the verandah of her school. Subhas was returning to the hostel. She stepped down and said, "Subhas Babu, you did not turn up inspite of my repeated request,"

She was wearing light blue goggles and a matching cotton sari.

"You won't get back those Bengali novels unless you come to my room," she said following him. Luckily she did not frown at his utter callousness.

"I don't have time Miss Shipra. You please come with those books or send them through a messenger. I am really awfully busy these days."

"I won't if you don't turn up," she gave an alluring smile.

"I will never mind if you keep them to read at your leisure"

Subhas wanted to put an end to that chapter. ■

THIRTEEN

It was late evening by the time Subhas got to Madhusmita's house. Her elder sister had arrived two days ago from Kusum Pur, a thickly populated village under the jurisdiction of Gopiballavpur, West Bengal. Her husband, a revenue inspector, under the State Government of Bengal, had been working for ten years. They had two children, a son and a girl. Her husband stayed back for official pressure and he could not come to his father-in-law's house although his wife insisted that he accompany her to her parental house. She advised him to take leave for some days on medical grounds but he took up some alibis and she frowned at her husband and came alone with her two younger children.

When she came to the front courtyard to inhale some fresh air, she saw Subhas opening the gate. She drew her veil over her head and stood aside. She had not seen Subhas before but she could conjecture that he was no other than the tutor of Madhusmita. She called out her younger sister and Madhu came out with a lantern.

"Charu didi, he is our Subhas Sir. You have not seen him before."

"Yes, but I guessed him to be so. Madhu, it is extremely warm inside the room, better sit outside, here on this verandah."

"Yes didi, I also think so." Madhu went to her study room, brought a mat and spread it on the verandah.

In the mean time the two children came and babbled near them.

"Charu didi take them in, else I can't study"

"Yes, yes, that is true. They usually disturb their father like this when he does some official work at home. Don't worry Madhu, I am taking them inside."

Charu held the hands of her two children and dragged them to the interior of the house.

"Sir, you are a bit late today. What is the reason?" Madhusmita asked while writing.

"No, I just went to Narahari Babu to discuss the Annual day of our school to celebrate it successfully."

"O, yes, may I ask you sir, how do you like Narahari Babu?"

She raised her face smiling.

"No, he is quite jovial and cooperative, why did you ask me such an unusual thing, swayed by momentary frenzy?"

"No, I am just"… she stopped half way and said,

"A man is like an iceberg, three fourth of it cannot be seen as it is immersed below the water."

"You have read it from Geography book haven't you?"

"Yes, but tell me whether my comparison of man to an iceberg is appropriate or not?"

"It is the real Mc Coy. But I could not understand your purpose."

"Our headmaster Narahari Babu, you have seen his tip portion only."

Madhusmita's eyes sparkled with a new discovery.

"How"?

"A great womanizer! As good luck would have it, I escaped from his clutch one afternoon." Madhusmita drew the skirt of her sari to cover the body as if trying to keep herself safe from his amorous hug.

"What did he do? Did you not oppose him?" Subhas said excitedly.

"Yes I did, otherwise….

"What otherwise?"

"Otherwise, I would have been captured and…"

"And?"

"And raped," she almost whispered towards the end.

"Is it ? But how?"

"I had been to meet his wife to learn embroidery. But she had gone to a neighbouring house. Narahari Babu had a cat nap after lunch in his bedroom. When he heard the sound of my footsteps, he sat on his bed and told me to fetch a glass of water from the kitchen. I did so. When I handed him the glass, he grabbed my hand and drew forcefully towards him. The water fell all over his bed but he did not loosen his grip. Finding no other way, I applied the last trick…"

"What last trick?" echoed Subhas being gobsmacked.

"I feigned to fall on his body but before he could understand any thing, I bit his right hand with all my might. He shrieked with pain and the moment he loosened his grip I ran out of his room"

She trembled a little when she recalled that horrible afternoon. Now Subhas remembered the day when Narahari Babu had told him about the beauty of her mother. She hails from Bankura district. So far as her health and beauty is concerned, she happens to be the most beautiful woman in their village. Madhusmita is a facsimile of that most charming woman, a perfect similitude rather more beautiful than her mother.

Charu came carrying her daughter in her arms and told Madhusmita, "Madhu, tell your Subhas sir to wait for some minutes after the tuition is over."

"Yes didi, please prepare some food for sir."

"Don't worry." Charu disappeared into the house with her sleeping daughter.

Subhas could not avoid Charu's request. He started eating but some portion still remained on the plate. Madhusmita pressed him not to leave anything on the plate.

"I can't eat my dinner tonight in the hostel Madhu, no

room in my stomach," Subhas said while drinking a glass of water after the meal.

"Don't take anything excess, rather it may upset your stomach," –Madhusmita said in a repartee.

Madhusmita collected the utensils and went inside.

Charu appeared and made him sit in the study room.

She fell silent for a while and said, "Subhas Babu, I have something urgent to say which my parents did not venture to ventilate.

Do you like our Madhu? If it is so, how do you like to accept her as your life partner?"

Subhas anticipated this type of thing since a long time. He mulled over it for some moments and said, "Charu, the question of rejection need not arise in this matter provided my parents accede but I don't have courage to put forth this matter before them. Don't take me amiss."

"No, no, I do understand. My uncle, a big shot, can have a break through however intricate and insurmountable the problem may be."

"You see I don't have objection if you all desire this. But who would untie this Gordian- knot ?" retorted Subhas.

"We have to proceed cautiously. I would discuss it with our uncle and have recourse accordingly. He will do the needful deftly to ease off this matter, such a far-sighted man as he is!

"All right, you do sedately what you all think proper"- said Subhas in anticipation of some good fruition.

Her daughter cried aloud. Charu suddenly became alert.

"I made her sleep just one hour before but now you see, she again woke up just to spoil my night sleep," she said in an irritated tone. "I am just coming Subhas Babu, let me see what she is doing?" She flitted to her daughter.

Madhusmita entered and touched his shoulder.

"Sir, would you accept a humble gift from me?" She said in an imploring tone. She fished out a gold ring from her purse and handed it carefully to Subhas. She eyed him curiously and asked, "Do you like it Sir? A signet-ring, my name being embossed on it."

"But why are you bent on giving it to me?

"To remember me for ever, Sir."

"What?" Does it count much to remember you?

"No, but whenever you see this signet-ring, you will recall me, no doubt. It is not a mere appellation without worth but I have given my heart and soul with that." Her eyes brimmed with tears.

"Is it? But if I fail to keep its worth?"

"Then I will know that actually there was no sincerity in my love."

"God forbid. Suppose my parents would not accede to the proposal."

"Then I shall remain unmarried for the rest of my life. I dislike

cupboard-love. I cannot reoffer myself to some other person" – She tried to remove tears with the skirt of her sari.

Subhas laughed benignly and said, "Don't be so emotional Madhu. God seldom fulfils one's desire one cherishes most. So wait for the suitable time and it will take care of itself. I have seen and observed vicissitudes of life. To materialize a thing and become verbose are two aspects of which I prefer the first. So let us hope for the best."

Subhas accepted the ring not to give her any mental shock. But he knew what looked most important today may not look so tomorrow. Everything comes according to God's dispensation. Neither he nor others can do anything.

FOURTEEN

The national highway passes at a distance of two miles from Kanchanpur. The buses bound for Midnapur or Kharagpur stop for some minutes at Kanchanpur bus stand, a desolate place where there was no shop, restaurant or human habitation within a radius of half a mile. Only there was a defunct sugar factory which became a deserted place where some stray cattle and dogs took rest in the shade of those dilapidated buildings. The cattle were seen ruminating with closed eyes, deep in meditation like a Sannyasi and the dogs gasping protruding their tongues.

Subhas got down from the bus. He consulted his watch. It was a quarter past eight. So it took him about one hour to reach Kanchanpur from Baripada busstand. A narrow unmetalled road passes through the forest which leads to Kanchanpur. He accelerated his speed but he knew that it would take sharply forty five minutes to reach the hostel. He used to visit his Baripada home weekly once to remove the restlessness of his mind.

He unlocked his room and placed the bag on a chair. He wanted to wash his hands and feet by the well. In the meanwhile Dhiren came into his room and reported to him a sad matter, handing over to him a joint application of the inmates of the hostel. Subhas held up the application and ran his eyes from beginning to end. Subhas forced him to narrate everything.

"Have you seen that girl?" Subhas asked.

"Yes Sir."

"Is Panda here?"

"No Sir, five minutes ago he went to meet somebody."

"Will he return or not?"

"I can't exactly say but most probably he will come back."

"But why did you not all dissuade him from going to do that nuisance."

"We all turned against him but he bullied to deal with us severely if this matter comes to light."

"Do you know his father?"

"Yes Sir."

"How far is his village?"

"Eight to nine miles from here. It will take hardly forty minutes on a bicycle to reach there."

"All right, you do one thing. Go to his father and tell him that the superintendent of the hostel wants his presence on some urgent matter."

"Yes Sir."

In the mean time Subhas took his bath by the well and came to his room to have some snacks. He opened the wrapper of the biscuit packet and chewed them one by one. It was 11.30 AM. when Panda's father arrived there riding on a bicycle.

Subhas took him to his own room and advised him to take rest. He was in his mid forties with a muscular body and swarthy complexion. Panda was his only son who would appear at the final H.S.C. exam. that year. Subhas told him about the misconduct of his son and his involvement with a prostitute last night. By that time Panda had already returned to the hostel. He was panic-stricken when he heard about the sudden arrival of his father.

Though infuriated, Panda's father said calmly, "Sir, I slogged all my life as a poor tiller, I am trying my best to educate my son to bring name and fame to our family but you see how accursed I am to have such a debased son, a licentious boy that I never dreamt of. Let him die prematurely, I won't have any sorrow for that." The sweat was pouring off him due to intemperate outburst.

He went wild with rage and gripped a lathi from a corner. Then he dragged his son outside and beat him mercilessly from head to foot. The lathi was shattered into several pieces. But Panda neither cried nor shrieked. He stood covering his face with two hands; his robust body trembling like banana leaves.

His father made him take an oath that very day not to commit such a sinful act once again in his life.

The eastern side of Kanchanpur was surrounded by a deep forest. Supply of fire wood by local wood-cutters had been fulfilling the requirement of the people for a long time. But during the harvesting season or festive occasions, the supply would be cut off for a long period of time. The people generally faced a great disadvantage on such occasions. The hostel usually needed a huge amount of fire wood for its daily use. The guards or foresters allowed the hostel boys to chop off the dry tree tops to use those as fuel.

One Sunday night when the superintendent was absent from the hostel, a group of boys went to the reserved forest and felled five 'sal' trees. They cut them into small logs and carried them to the back of the hostel. The whole night they were engaged in cutting them into small pieces. The sound was heard from a long distance in the stillness of night. The guards of the forest department became alert and they caught them red-handed. A tussle and altercation continued for some time. The obscene language of the guards provoked them too much. They beat them severely and carried one guard on their shoulders and locked him in the superintendent's room.

Subhas returned that morning from Baripada. He did not have the least idea regarding this incident. When he opened the door, the guard suddenly prostrated at his feet and began howling. A foul smell of urine was coming as the guard had urinated there, being imprisoned in the room. The guard narrated him everything. The other guards had lodged a first information report in the local thana against the boys of the hostel. The Officer in-Charge of the thana with a group of constables raided the hostel from all sides to arrest the offenders. Subhas, remaining inside the room, was observing the situation.

A constable entered his room and saluted him.

"Sir, thana Babu wants you to meet him."

Subhas was quite enraged by that time.

"What?" Let him come to meet me if he so wants."

"He won't come Sir."

"I also won't go."

Subhas came out to the verandah. He saw the police lining up outside the campus of the hostel. While pacing on the verandah he declared that he won't allow any police to trespass upon the campus of the hostel, if so he would be hung on the nearby 'Mahul' tree. The thana officer knew any trespassing would be taken seriously and then political involvement, so on and so forth. So he thought it wise to inform the headmaster regarding this matter and let it end there. By that time a large number of villagers had gathered there to see the ongoing appalling situation. When the police left the place, they also went to their own homes.

An hour later, Narahari Babu came to the hostel and fined the boys five rupees each for their offence. He also admonished Subhas as he was supposed to watch the activities of the inmates of the hostel. Subhas explained some of his practical disadvantages to him. But he was not a man to listen to any pleas or alibis. Deeply mortified Subhas refused to remain in charge of the hostel any longer. So later on one assistant teacher was entrusted with that duty to maintain peace and order in the hostel.

FIFTEEN

Madhusmita's uncle came back disappointed. The age-old hierarchy had divided the society creating an impervious wall between high and low, and the inferior ones had always been looked down upon. Subhas, being the first born, his father humbly rejected the marriage proposal on the solid ground that he would be the rightful heir to perform all the funeral rites after his death and if he would marry a girl of some other caste, his fourteen generations would not get water although it might be regarded as mumbo jumbo in the eyes of the rational society. That straight-cut refusal upset the apple cart.

Although the proposal was rejected outright. Madhusmita's parents did not shun their hopes. Affronted by that repudiation Madhusmita groaned inwardly. A cold war persisted for several days.

One day she exploded before Subhas, "My elder sister has rightly said. A modern youth loves one but ultimately marries some other. They don't keep their fidelity up to the last."

Subhas could not tide over the present crisis. He found himself in a whirlpool. If he married disregarding social taboos, his parents would be unhappy. He appealed to his conscience and waited to act according to its dictation.

So long as man is under the spell of a vicious propensity, his sight is blurred and sharpness of wit blunted. In that semi-unconscious state, deciphering a thing and taking a conclusive step may be injudicious and would be a wild goose chase.

Error once committed is sufficient to make one weep throughout his life. It is a mistake which can neither be rectified nor can it be obliterated under any circumstances.

Fire wood became a burning problem for the hostel. The wood cutters who usually came with loads of fire wood on their heads, kept themselves busy in some other work to earn more than they did from this tedious work. Some went to the distant places as the land-owners there decoyed them to give more wages in addition to food. The condition grew worse day by day. The number of students in the hostel gradually tapered off as the guardians thought it wise to send their children to school on bicycle. They could no longer afford the expenditure of the hostel.

Good natured and honest as the secretary was, he never harassed any teacher regarding the prescribed scale and dearness allowance. Even the science and Sanskrit teachers received some amount more than their prescribed scale. But the aid from Government was not sufficient to pay them monthly wages throughout the year. The deficit increased every month. A day came when the management incurred a heavy loan from money lenders to clear up the outstanding dues.

That year the boy appeared at the final H.S.C. examination at Jhariadihi High School Centre. Subhas, as the supervisor, had gone with them. After it was over, he came by train to Kanchanpur. On the way, in the same compartment, a gentleman of nearly thirty-five years of age was sitting with a news paper in his hand, engrossed in reading.

Subhas could not see his face as the gentleman had held the news paper just in front of his face. When he removed it, Subhas at once recognized him. He was Mr. Baradakanta, Lecturer in English of Baripada College. An Anthology of poetry written by him had been widely appreciated. Subhas had read it and eulogised the elegance of the poems before others.

"What a great surprise Sir ! you are coming on this train?" asked Subhas.

Baradakanta Babu looked up and smiled. Then he held one hand of Subhas and indicated him to sit by his side. He lit a cigarette and said, "I also didn't expect to see you in this compartment. Where are you going ?"

"Of course you don't know sir, I am serving as an assistant teacher of Kanchanpur High School."

"All right, all right, my father-in-law's house is at Kanchanpur. I am going to bring my family back to Baripada."

"I did not know it. May I ask you your latest contribution to English literature?"

"I am not writing anything at present because of some domestic troubles. Subhas Babu, do you know one cannot repair one's house in a hurricane as the proverbial saying goes.

"Definitely Sir, but if I ask you about your domestic affairs, it would certainly be deemed as discourtesy."

"No, no, I treat you as my younger brother. Besides I always like to be informal. A decade ago, I fell in love and married a girl whom I was teaching English. At that time I did not have any idea that she was eccentric to such an extent. Her elder brother who was also of queer nature, recently gave up his law practice for this lunacy. Any way she gave birth to two children. So far as I have been observing, she is becoming more abnormal day by day. One day she was so turbulent and oppressive that I had to keep her inside a room under lock and key. She tore my shirt into pieces and bit my shoulder with her sharp teeth. She flung her sari and rebuked me in a filthy language, an implacable maniac. As I saw that she was completely out of control, I locked her in a room. She remained there for two days. I consulted a psychiatrist. He advised me to leave her in her parental house for some days. You see, what can you do in such a confusing situation?" Baradakanta Babu sighed deeply in penitence.

Subhas was obviously compassionate towards that gentleman. He left him at the Kanchanpur railway station and went to the hostel on foot. It seemed deserted. He knocked at the door where the Sanskrit teacher had slept. Panditji opened the door and asked him about the performance of the students.

"Have you eaten your lunch Panditji?" Subhas asked.

"Yes, Dhiren invited me to take meals at his home. But for your information, Bhavataran has not returned yet."

"Then what will we do at night?" Subhas's tone was full of distress.

"We can manage with a snack dinner. Not a single student in the hostel. Everybody has left for home."

"Is it? But Panditji, anyhow we have to arrange firewood for the next day. Otherwise we will perish."

"Yes, yes, let us go to Dhiren's house. He told me today that he would offer some bundles of fire wood to the hostel as a makeshift."

"He is always sympathetic to his teachers. May God bless him." Subhas uttered out of his own accord.

"So let us go to Dhiren's house. Shall we ?"

Panditji closed the door and went outside.

"Wait a bit Panditji. I am just coming."

Subhas opened his box and took out the gold ring. He thought it unnecessary to keep it so long with him.

"Yes, let us go now," Subhas said to Panditji.

The sun had already set but the air was very hot. It was almost burning. Subhas saw at a distance a whirlwind moving upwards rolling with dust particles. Then it went past them.

He wiped off the dust from his face with a handkerchief.

Dhiren entertained them with two glasses of cold 'sherbet'. Subhas drank it to his great relief and said, "Dhiren, let Panditji sit here. I will come back within an hour."

When Subhas got to Madhusmita's house, she was

sweeping her study room. She kept the broomstick in a corner and welcomed him to sit on a chair.

Subhas could not say anything at the beginning. Though not at fault, he felt himself guilty. Even the study room seemed to him unfamiliar that evening. Madhusmita always looked more beautiful in her sullen mood. Both of them knew the unexpected turn of their destiny. If his father had acceded, everything would have been settled. Madhusmita broke the silence and asked,

"Did you come back this afternoon, Sir?"

"Yes, it is terribly hot at Jhariadihi, an arid atmosphere, specially to remain for a number of days in a drab tiled house."

"You must have grown impatient to stay a long period, didn't you ?"

The thing has turned worse for me. It is almost the same here too," Subhas said in disappointment. Madhusmita smiled forcefully.

"How?"

"You see, the cook of our hostel has not come back. We can't say what we will do the tomorrow morning"

"You should not be worried about it. What would be the harm if you have your meals here for some days?"

"No, no Madhu, better to starve there. So long I was the superintendent of the hostel, I had managed everything without any hindrance. But this new one, a good-for-nothing fellow is so careless…" Subhas could not complete in anger.

"Have some snacks Sir," Madhusmita handed him some biscuits and mixture on a plate.

"No, I won't. Let me have a glass of plain water. Dhiren gave me a glass of sherbet which increased my thirst." Subhas waved his hand, denying snack. In the meantime, the maid servant of the house brought the lantern and kept it on a small table.

Somebody blew the conch-shell in the back yard, perhaps her mother.

Subhas signalled Madhusmita to sit closer to him. She was twisting the skirt of her sari with fingers unwittingly.

Subhas took out the gold ring from his pocket and said, "Don't mind Madhu, this evening I want to give back your gold ring, here it is."

Subhas stretched his hand while looking at her bewildered mien. Madhusmita suddenly stepped back as if she saw a snake in his hand. Madhusmita fondly held his two hands in hers and said weeping, "Don't say to me like that Sir. I had given it just to remember me. Our marriage seems impossible in this birth, but I shall be waiting for you." Her voice trembled.

"But Madhu, this is quite indecent. I can't keep it any longer. I kept it not to give you any mental shock. For the last few days, I have been constantly thinking to give you back your keepsake. So don't insist on my keeping it any more."

Subhas kept the ring carefully in her palm and shook it a little to cheer her up. Two drops of tears glittered in the light of the lantern and rolled down her glossy cheeks.

The maid servant again appeared with a steaming cup of tea.

"Why tea, Madhu? You know I am quite averse to it."

Madhusmita took the cup from her maid servant and implored,

"Take it Sir, it won't do any harm."

"I will take it if you do one thing," Subhas gave a sad smile.

"Please tell me."

"I recall that night when you said that you had poured two spoonfuls of love in the tea-cup. Now you just pour two spoonfuls of tears in it. I want to know how it tastes."

Both of them smiled benignly.

Subhas came back to Dhiren's house to take Panditji and both of them went to the hostel.

Back in his room, Subhas felt the heat waxing beyond the limit of endurance. He did not like to dine on anything tonight. They dragged their cots outside and slept on the open verandah.

The next morning, Subhas was surprised to see his shirt missing. Somebody had taken it away with the help of a stick through the window. After an hour, Bipin arrived there riding on a bicycle.

"Sir, Haren had taken away your shirt, I am sure."

"How did you know Bipin?" Subhas asked anxiously.

"I have seen you wearing that shirt. Besides O.T. has been printed on its collar. I observed it going close to him."

"Yes, yes, O.T. means Orissa Tailors. Your are quite right, What is he doing now?"

"Sir, he is loafing around the railway station wearing that shirt."

"All right, let him take it. But can you tell me why he did like that."

"He was a bit revengeful Sir. He thought that it was you who were mainly responsible for his failure in the last Test Examination. He had not been sent up to appear at the final."

"O, I see. But he did not know that I was absent from the consideration meeting. As a teacher, I never bear a grudge against any student."

"He is a fool, a useless fellow Sir, who does not understand anything." Bipin was furious.

"Keep quiet Bipin. He will be paid back in his own coins."

A fortnight later, Bipin came gasping and said, "Sir, do you know Haren died of heart failure last night ?"

"No, I don't. How could it be? He was so strong and stout."

Subhas could not believe in such an untimely death.

"It is possible Sir, how could he escape your curse? He

was as bold as brass, so very soon he reaped such unexpected consequences." Bipin was in a state of bewilderment.

"I never curse anybody Bipin. You are quite wrong. It is purely accidental."

"That may be Sir, but so far as I know a miscreant never goes unpunished. A teacher is always respectable. If anybody disregards or humiliates him, he must be penalized some day or other, that is my strong conviction."

Subhas was out of his bearings owing to pecuniary instability. He had to run the family on a shoe-string budget. A moderate amount of money every month was necessary to maintain it. Here in this school he had to wait for months together to receive his salary. He was easily annoyed for this hangdog financial position. Finally he decided to serve in some other school to strengthen it. After a week he went to Narahari Babu and told him about his wretched condition. Narahari Babu was sympathetic but he knew that he could not help him in this matter. Subhas resolved not to stay there any longer. Lotus may bloom on the top of the mountain but he would not flinch from his decision. He neither met the secretary nor tendered his resignation. That afternoon he left Kanchanpur bag and baggage.

■

SIXTEEN

Subhas's mother was illiterate and conservative. For some reasons she disliked educated girls. In her estimation, they pay respects to neither their in-laws nor their husbands. Secondly, they are to some extent aggressive. They argue with their elders caring little for their superior position. Thirdly, they take greater care of their beauty than their duty.

A marriage proposal for a girl with a post graduate degree in Economics came but it was rejected point blank for these obvious reasons. She had seen many newly wedded brides of her neighbouring houses who had come with a big amount of dowry. She had been fostering a dream like that since long, but had no guts to speak out as her husband was quite opposed to such a social evil.

Subhas's father was a man of a different temperament and ideas. He had been nurturing a good impression and high regards for educated girls. He strongly denounced the dowry system as a curse on the society. No member of the family ever dared utter a pro-dowry word in his presence.

A marriage proposal came through one of their relatives. The mediator also accompanied them to the bride's house. It was in the remotest corner of West Bengal in the district of Purulia. The bride's father, an octogenarian, was once the Zamindar of that area. He was highly regarded as 'Raja Babu' by the local people. But his hey-days were gone and now he had been reduced to an ordinary peasant.

Subhas's parents stayed one day more to finalize the

matter. Specially they liked the etiquette of the bride's father. Back home, they informed Subhas of every thing in minute details. The only impediment was that the girl was less educated. But his mother overruled him professing the same theory because of her preconceived ideas regarding highly educated girls. She was still steeped in unreasonable prejudices and denied him to visit his future father-in-law's house to have a glance at the bride. Finally, he yielded to his parents' choice.

The miserable pittance posed a problem for Subhas. He borrowed some money from Deben's mother to repay her in due course. The date of marriage had already been fixed. He racked his brains to get over the problem but saw sparks in his eyes. His brother-in-law, Gopal Babu, pacing up and down his Electricity. Department, at last requisitioned a hackneyed, threadbare motor van to carry the bridegroom's party. The last leg of their gruelling journey was an ordeal of fire. Any how, as the driver was very skillful, he managed to drive the van as cautiously as possible. By late afternoon, they got to a broken bridge where the driver stopped the van and got down to inspect the condition. He shook his head and refused to drive further as it would be a risk to cross the bridge. They halted there to refresh themselves while they sent a messenger to inform them as to their arrival. The place not being far away, they soon got the news and immediately responded. Two villagers along with the bride's elder brother came with a bullock cart. Subhas and the priest rode on the bullock cart and the bride groom's party followed them on foot. A thatched school house had been arranged as their resting place.

Late at night, the procession started from that place. With some fire works and ear-rending explosions, they took a circuitous way to get to the wedding venue. At the hour of the auspicious look, Subhas could not see the bride's face clearly as the veil had been drawn over but he could guess the bride's appearance was not that bad. The sacred fire was still burning when the marriage was over. After an hour, dawn broke.

At the departure hour, howling and wailing went on for sometimes while the bridegroom's party left the place with uproarious laughter. The marriage day was memorable not only in the life of Subhas but also in the history of mankind. On that auspicious day man for the first time put his steps on the surface of the moon unfurling the flag of his victory over nature.

Subhas's father was serving in an educational institution but as it was a private one, he retired miserably with no pension. After Subhas's marriage, a new member had been added to his family and the household expenditure grew day by day. Subhas was the only earning member and he had to shoulder all the responsibility but some how or other he tried to carry on. At times his mother got exasperated and shrieked.

"Subhas, you give only two hundred rupees to meet all sorts of expenditure, how can I manage with such a meagre amount of money?"

Subhas responded to her with a subdued tone," Mother, you know I am serving in a private high school. Had I had post-graduation, I would have been placed in some higher post with better facility but as I could not do that for you people, I rot and don't have the capacity to give more. In such a situation how do you expect to live a decent life? Don't you see I bristle with difficulties?"

Subhas's mother flared up and said, "Better tell it to your father.Don't complain to me. It is I who fought on your behalf for your higher education. I have run the gauntlet of misfortunes in life only to give you a boost. Being an only child of my parents how unfortunately I am decaying here. Your father, a useless man, spoiled my life and here I am no better than a maid servant."

"I too have been discharging my onerous duty without the least grumbling."

Subhas said trying to mollify her. "Have patience mother, don't blame others. Time and tide will sure come to favour us at long last."

"I must warn you about one thing Subhas. Your wife is a little bit extravagant, not restrained in using oil and spices, while cooking. Have I not been doing that thing with much frugality?"

"I do admit. But as a mother-in-law, is it not your duty to make her conscious of that? I need not hear that petty objection."

Subhas took out some money from his box and went to Deben's mother to repay the loan which he had incurred for his marriage.

She welcomed him warmly and asked him all about his home affairs. Subhas briefly reported to her and said, "Aunty, you please make my mother understand not to meddle unnecessarily to make things worse. I don't like constant bickering."

"Subhas, do you think I have not tried to make your mother understand? But she is incorrigible by nature. Try your best to adjust when there is no other way for you."

Subhas came back soon as he had to eat his lunch sharp at nine to reach his school in time. It was difficult to cover twenty-two kilometres on bicycle particularly on a full stomach. The village Laxmipur, where the school was situated, was only one kilometre away from the river Jambhira. The water usually remained waistdeep but it was very difficult to cross the river specially in the rainy season. Nobody could guess how turbulent it used to be in that season. Two to three death cases had been reported as the consequence of an audacious attempt to cross it. Some boys were always at the river side to help the passers-by in crossing it. If there was some bicycle, they lifted it up on their shoulders and handed it over to its owner after reaching the other side. They charged a very trivial amount for their work.

On his way back, his cycle got punctured and he got it repaired at a way side cycle repairing shop. He reached home when it was evening. Dog-tired, he wanted to take rest for a while.

His mother abruptly entered his room and said, "your wife vomits three to four times a day. Whatever she eats is vomited out. How is it that she became pregnant so soon?"

Subhas was wiping his face with a towel. He stared at his mother trying to find out its meaning. He could not welcome the sudden onrush of her frowning.

"There is nothing unusual mother," he explained, "It is but natural during first trimester of pregnancy, so what?"

"No, I don't expect her pregnancy so hurriedly, going to brew all sorts of troubles." Her voice was full of strange discontentment.

"You should not bother about as it happens in thousands of cases. Don't leap when the river is a long way away."

Subhas was exhausted and had no patience for such rigmarole.

That night he had invited Deben to have dinner with him. He brought two dishes of meat from a nearby stall and kept it in the kitchen. When his wife served them, Deben tasted it and said, "Why it is so distasteful Subhas, not at all relishing?" Subhas too declared the same thing. After dinner, Deben left for his home.

Subhas was smarting inwardly. He was dubious of some foul play. He immediately called his wife and asked her the reason. She innocently told him that she had to serve some portion of the meat curry to others. So she mixed the meat that she had prepared for lunch with that of the shop. This amalgamation might have spoiled its taste.

The value of sincerity in every work was dinned into her ears but it was all useless. That made him disgusted.

"You foolish woman, you are always liable to commit some mistakes now and then. Why did you do that? Don't you know it would spoil its taste. In addition to your abnormality, your affected ignorance is unpardonable." His blood rushed to his brain and he began to think in his indignation that it was due to ill -assorted match and her utter lack of education. He slept on his cot and began to doze while blaming his parents.

One hour later, he was suddenly aroused from his sleep. "Brother," his cousin cried out, "Go and look how our Surama bhavi is vomiting."

"So what? It is natural."

"No, brother, she has taken something poisonous in anger."

"She is only shamming.How could she do that at the time of pregnancy?"

All the members ran about in some sort of hullabaloo. A doctor, well acquainted with the family, was called in. As it was not possible to wash her stomach, she was made to gulp down some glasses of saline water to make her vomit out the poisonous substances. Then she was advised to take rest comfortably without any disturbances.

His teaching staff had arranged a feast at school. Although Subhas was in a sad mood, he had to cooperate with them. But his mind was wandering far away from that revelry. Before lunch he received a letter from his cousin where he mentioned that Surama bhavi had been admitted in the hospital the previous day and a stillborn female child was born to her. Some how she was now in a better condition. It was like a bombshell to him. The letter dropped from his hand. He knew fortune had not all along been smiling on him. In such an adverse situation, he prepared himself to bear up well against all these mishaps. He could not expect such a bolt from the blue. Everybody enquired about the matter but in that dazed state, he could not answer anything. He fumbled and without losing any moment he started for Baripada. Some of his colleagues requested him to eat his lunch before departure. But he was in no mood to eat even a morsel of food. He just waved his hand in denial and rode away on a bicycle.

On reaching home he saw his wife sleeping in a separate room. He went near her bed and placed his hand on her forehead. Surama slowly opened her eyes and stared at him vacantly.

Subhas dragged a chair and sat on it looking towards the ashen face of his wife. He did not rebuke or console her. In that state he thought it wise to remain silent. But he could not forgive her utter foolishness. In a momentary rage what she had done could not be restituted at any time. Rather he blamed his lot. He was an all time sufferer. How could he hope for a good fruition? The situation at home was tense. He rebuked her for a little fault. It acted just like adding fuel to flames. The misfortune always lolled its tongue like this. Whom did he blame ? His mother could not adjust herself to the situation and the wife remained always inflammable. They could bury the hatchet but remained like sleeping volcanoes. It was just like sitting on a crater. Nobody could have a presentiment how and when it would have a volcanic eruption. Nobody could pacify it. But an innocent child who could not see the light of day paid a price for it. He could not excuse himself nor could he excuse anybody in the house. The mental storm that he suffered from made him dumb for a number of days. He was shell-shocked.

After her convalescence, she expressed her desire to go to her parental house and Subhas did not waver to keep that humble request. While staying in her parents' house, he did receive a letter where his wife mentioned that she was now suffering from post-partum haemorrhage. A friend who happened to be a gynaecologist at the Primary Health Centre, Laxmipur, came to his rescue. Subhas consulted him and according to his prescription, he despatched those medicines to his wife. His wife gradually recovered her previous health.

But after recovery she became peevish and could not tolerate anything harsh.

Back to her father-in-law's house, although she was in a snit , she did all the household work with mute resignation. Subhas consoled her; they must get back their lost child. Subhas had sworn in the name of the departed soul of his child that some day or other he must write her story with his own tears.

SEVENTEEN

Subhas's mother was unable to know one's true worth. In spite of this recent mishap, she did not make any attempt to iron out differences. Subhas kept his finger crossed but could not see anything to have grown better. Whenever he came to his house, he saw the thing in a disorderly form. Although there were four younger brothers, nobody cared to shoulder any responsibility of the house. Subhas had to purchase grocery, firewood and all the bare necessities from the market. He did not get any one to lend a helping hand. If, on certain occasion, one was entrusted with some duty, he would shift his responsibility to some one else. Subhas was completely fed up and he could not cope with those bone lazy fellows. Apart from this, his mother at times burst into altercation on some petty matters which vitiated the whole atmosphere. Subhas felt suffocation and at length decided to take his wife to his place of service where he could spend his days at least in peace.

He went to Deben's mother to request her to lend him their car. She immediately agreed and even accompanied him upto Laxmipur. When she departed, tears welled up in her eyes. With parting advice, she left for Baripada. Subhas rented a house and began to settle there.

Mr. Mohanty, a livestock inspector, was a great lover of drama. He had appeared in leading roles in many a drama in the past and now he grew enthusiastic to stage a drama based on the great epic 'The Mahabharat'. The name of the drama was 'Karnarjuna' which had been written by one of the eminent play-wrights. A meeting was held on this occasion. The employees of the local Primary Health Centre, teachers of High School and M.E. school and other interested persons joined this meeting. All were unanimous but to stage a drama was not an easy matter. Financial strength, a director, some professional lady artistes, gaudy dresses for the actors, all were indispensable. They raised donation among them. Some ticket-books were also printed. Umesh Babu, a veteran director, was chosen to direct the drama.

Two lady artistes from outside were brought on payment to play the role of Kunti and Draupadi. The casting of roles was done under the direct supervision of the director. The rehearsal went on in full alacrity at night. All were in a flurry of excitement.

The director Umesh Babu was a diabetic patient. He was a man of sixty-five years but when he directed, he surged up with youthful virility. He could not tolerate any mispronunciation while somebody was delivering a dialogue. Once he was about to slap a person acting in the vital role of 'Karna'.

At night before the rehearsal started, he would eat two to three chapaties with a little amount of milk without sugar. He kept himself under strict dietary regimen.

To raise money, push-sale had started. They divided them into different groups and approached the moneyed persons of the neighbouring villages to book tickets one month before the drama.

The two lady artistes Pratima and Vaijayanti who had been playing the role of Draupadi and Kunti respectively were put up in a separate room, a few steps away from the school.

One morning while they were taking "lemon sherbet", an old woman of that locality came to them and saw them drinking 'sherbet'. She approached them for a lemon. They refused to give her one as they had no extra lemon. The old woman muttered something discontentedly and went away. That evening because of intolerable heat they went to the river Jambhira for bathing. Just after coming back Pratima went on raving in the language of that old woman. She began to say repeatedly. 'Why did you not offer me a lemon?' Practically, Pratima had no capacity to utter a single word in that language, spoken by the local tribe. It was an amazing thing for all. Somebody remarked that she had been possessed by some evil spirits.

So an exorcist was called in. He came and began the incantation of some obscure 'mantra' to expel the evil effect.

He threw a fistful of mustard at her body while muttering 'mantras'.

He asked her in a resonant voice.

"Who are you?"

"I am Haru's mother, Sir."

"Why did you cast your evil spell over her?"

"I requested her to give me a lemon but she did not."

"Will you now leave her or not ?"

"I will go Sir, I will go."

"Then do go, you rascal woman."

The exorcist again hurled some mustard at her body. Pratima began to doze and at last sank to the ground.

The rehearsal was postponed on that night.

Subhas was curious to know more about the livelihood of the professional artistes. But he did not find time to talk with them freely. He knew that his wife had an aversion to them as they used to lead an unbridled life which she thought was simply vulgar. So that afternoon he took a plea and told his wife that he was going to a place to review the balance-sheet concerning the drama. On the way to school he turned left and entered the room where Pratima was gossiping with the other lady artiste. As on other days, there were no fans or admirers to crowd the room. Subhas was warmly welcomed and seated on a chair.

"When did you start your acting career Pratima?" asked Subhas.

"Since five years ago, Sir."

"What about the views of your parents regarding this career?"

"Acting is a passion with me. When I expressed my desire to be an artiste, they did not object in the least. Particularly my father encouraged me a lot to be a renowned artiste in future. Acting is a higher sort of art which should be mastered with great skill and perseverance. So nobody was a barrier to my progress."

"Well Pratima, you don't know the language of those tribal people but how could you speak so fluently?"

"It is really strange. I am amazed when you all told me that I did babble in that language although I did not have that capacity, it might be due to the spell of that black magic."

"I don't believe in all those baseless things."

"After the spell was over, I felt myself extremely weak Sir," Pratima admitted.

Subhas began to laugh defying her statement. He felt somebody halt by the window to overhear their conversation. He cast his glance through the open window. It was his wife Surama who was looking at them with unblinking eyes, a fierce gleam of anger sparkling in them. She stood for a few minutes, muttered something, throwing a contemptuous glance at him and bolted away.

An unknown tremor ran through his body; his throat began to go dry. He could not know what he uttered to them. He was almost in a semi-conscious state.

Subhas knew the anger of his wife. Surama was in the kitchen. She could sense the sound of languid footsteps of Subhas. When he came to her sight, she hissed like a fanged cobra.

"Look at my innocent husband . He has come back reviewing the accounts. Don't fib, I want to know my dear what accounts were you doing with those ladies? You pillow talker, don't you find pleasure having a tete -a-tete with your own wife?"

She came out of the kitchen with a skimmer in her hand. Now she found out the vulnerable spot in Subhas and seized upon it with the savagery of a wild tigress.

Apprehending that this domestic storm might assume a severe form, Subhas tried to soothe her.

"Please, listen to me Surama. Don't shriek like that. One of my colleagues is living just on the opposite side of the wall. Think over it, what would they think if you shout in this way? Don't degrade me in the eyes of others. I warn you."

Subhas was inwardly a peace loving man. He could not put up with such bickering in an uncivilized way. There was a limit to everything. But Surama had neither pity nor remorse in her heart.

She started howling. "Why did you come back from that brothel? How joyously you were talking with those vulgar women! I don't know you have ever talked with me in that cheerful manner.

Fuck off at once from my sight."

Surama was about to slam the door but Subhas kept it open by applying force and said, "Don't put me into a ludicrous position, Surama, please be quiet and listen to the whole fact."

"No, no, I don't want to listen to any of your excuses," Surama shook her head violently and her eyes burned like embers.

"Have pity on me Surama. Have you gone out of your head?"

He besought her to salvage some dignity . In his frenzied efforts to simmer her down, he gripped her hands but she wrenched herself free with a jerk. She recoiled from his touch and fell like a log on the cot and wrapped herself from head to foot with a bed-sheet .

Subhas stared at her motionless body for a while and asked,

"Would you not do your cooking to-night Surama?"

But she did not respond. She was lying still in bed.

Subhas shoved her to rouse from sleep but she did not make any move and lay like an inanimate object as she was indisposed to do anything.

He knew that he was to go without meal that night. So he changed his dress and slept on a mat pondering over this baptism of fire that God ordained for him a moment ago to test his capacity to bear and forbear.

EIGHTEEN

The next morning when Dhrubendra Babu, one of the assistant teachers of Laxmipur High School, was returning from Baripada, Subhas accosted him regarding pushing-sale.

"Uncle, we came back with a broken heart."

"Why?" Subhas asked.

"Somebody had run away with Mohanty Babu's bicycle."

"How did it happen?"

"Mohanty Babu and myself had been to the court premises to meet Bishnu Babu. We left the bicycle outside the office and after a brief discussion with him we came back within a few minutes. To our utter surprise, the cycle was found nowhere as if it disappeared into the air."

"No, there are a number of cycle-thieves prowling around in search of prey here and there in Baripada. The hospital area and court premises are two strategic places for them. Did you lock the bicycle?"

"No."

"I didn't know you are so careless !"

"Because we did not expect it would be stolen away so soon."

"No, no, it should not be. Whenever you go somewhere, you must keep it under lock."

"Uncle, now we have been put into further trouble."

"How?" Subhas looked at him with gaped mouth.

"Mohanty Babu demands the price of his cycle. He says that it has been used for the work of the drama. So let us raise a subscription to buy him a second hand bicycle. If it is not compensated, he would not take part in the drama."

"All right. I don't have any objection. But we have to discuss it among our members to make a decision."

"Definitely."

At the meeting, some members vehemently protested against that decision. They said that those two, who had gone to Baripada town, should bear the cost of the bicycle as they lost it through their utter carelessness. They were quite reluctant to shoulder that responsibility. However, five to six members agreed to share the amount among themselves and they raised the money to offer him.

One night Kundu Babu who played the role of Bhima, the second Pandava, was furious when he saw some young players hang about the retiring room of Pratima even after the rehearsal was over. As he despised those sycophants and their evil motive, he hounded them out. She was like a queen-bee and the drones were buzzing around her even in the dead hours of the night.

On the day of the presentation, a troupe of make-up men and decorators with screens, wings and canopies arrived at Laxmipur. The decoration went through the day. As there was no facility of electricity, a generator had been hired. An announcement as to the staging of the play had been made on the public address system at the village market. Before evening, the stage and its surrounding areas were magnificently lighted and it presented a phenomenal spectacle.

Sitting arrangements had been made carefully. The chairs being numbered, the spectators did not find any difficulty in finding their seats. A responsible person was entrusted with that duty to usher them to their respective seats.

In the green-room, the players one by one began to

gather. All the necessary things according to scene were kept
in order. The make-up men were really good at their job. They
asked the players their roles and painted them accordingly.
After it was over, they found it difficult to recognise each other.
All were in an elated mood. Pratima, in the gaudy dress and
make-up of Draupadi, was wandering about the commodious
green room like a fleeting fawn.She was the cynosure of the
fans who were waiting eagerly to see her on the stage.

It was preplanned to stage the drama consecutively for
two days. One confectioner, a fat, middle aged person with a
bulging belly and another, a manager of distillery with a pock-
marked face, were very eager to play the role of Lord Shiva,
the destroyer. In that scene Lord Shiva would condescend a
boon to a young girl and the dialogue was:

"I am highly pleased with your austerity, O young girl!
Now you ask me for a boon to fulfil your desire."

That was the only dialogue of Lord Shiva in the whole
drama but a tug of war started between the two. At last the
director Umesh Babu vouchsafed them the boon that both of
them would play the role one after another on two subsequent
days.

But he was not at all satisfied with the dialogue-delivery
of Jhungu Nana, the local priest. His pronunciation was
always jumbled which he condemned most. "You wretch of a
Brahmin!" He exploded, "you are not able to pronounce a
word correctly."

Some local teachers identified him as their village priest.
Umesh Babu cast a stern look at him for a moment and fell
silent.

The fight between Karna and Arjun captured the
attention of the audience the most. The wheel of Karna's
chariot went deep into the earth and he struggled hard to
pull it out. When he was thus unarmed, Arjun was about to
shoot a sharp arrow at him. Karna reminded him that it was
quite unbecoming on the part of a Kshatriya like him when

an opponent was unguarded and in a disadvantageous position. Arjun wreaked vengeance and asked him where his wisdom was when the seven charioteers jointly attacked tender Abhimanyu and killed him in a helpless condition. He defied him and in a trice shot an arrow which immediately put him to death.

In another scene Bhima ran with a mace to attack Duhsasan, the second brother of Duryadhana. His dreadful appearance sent a terror in the heart of the enemies. The two were engaged in a mortal combat brandishing their clubs to strike each other. At last Bhim pinned him to the ground and with a demonic fury landed a concussive blow on his abdomen. Disembowelled, blood welled out and as a dipsomaniac long deprived of the sip of wine he drank it with his palms. The whole battle field resounded with his deafening roars. Blood splashed in all directions and with gory fingers Bhima staggered out to smear Duhsasan's blood on Draupadi's flowing tresses. The audience gave Bhima a thunderous ovation.

Harihar Babu fell into a very disappointing position. His mustachio glued on the upper lip accidently slipped to his mouth. In consequence he could not deliver his dialogue clearly. His dialogue was, "Who was that rogue, condemned soul, who had no fear for thieving cow-stock." It sounded something ridiculous and it swept away the whole audience in a tsunami of side-splitting laughter. Being nervous, Harihar Babu darted away from the stage.

On the second night, there was a mad rush and people began to gather in the auditorium in the evening hours. Many were turned away for lack of seats. A large number of persons broke through the tent openings, pushing and shoving the crowd, to witness the exciting play. Umesh Babu, stationing him in the corner of the stage always encouraged the players with his enthusiastic smile.

The night came to an end. Gaura, the head of the troupe,

came to Sarat Babu, the headmaster, to receive his dues. The subscription collected from the participants fell short as the expenditure mounted high and Sarat Babu being compelled handed him the money bag, the dearness allowance arrears of the teachers, received somedays' ago from the office. Although it was a sad event, nobody did care on that festive occasion.

Over some days, the focal point of their discussion was only the enacted play. For some, the departure of Pratima was very painful and they pined for her for several months. A few enthusiastic teachers even proposed to stage another play inspite of the unforgettable financial body-blow inflicted recently upon them.

NINETEEN

It was late winter. The flour bought at the nearest grocery was not at all good. Surama felt irritated when she sieved them to separate the bran and it was, no doubt, a tedious job.

She suggested to Subhas to grow wheat in their own field. He thought over the suggestion and decided to go to his maternal grandfather to take an initiative in this. His grand-father nodded his head in assent but he told him that he had already handed over that piece of land to his nephew, as he was not able to cultivate that land at present. It was just by the bank of the river, most suitable for growing wheat. Subhas approached his uncle and revealed his plan. He did not discourage him but told him that he had to seek quality seed at first. Besides, four to five times irrigation of land was necessary to have a good harvest. Subhas agreed to take risks as he was sufficiently delighted to undertake a painstaking job for the first time in his life. The work continued. The pumping machine to water the land was brought on his grand-father's bullock-cart from far away. Subhas even cajoled the labourers into agreeing to do the work promising them to reward blankets if his wheat field would bring him a bumper crop. Subhas worked the whole night with the labourers to irrigate the field, shivering in the cold. Later on the luxuriant growth of wheat removed all pains from his mind. He ran his eyes from one end to another. The long spikes of wheat filled him with unending pleasure. Sure enough, he became a real cultivator.

At the time of harvest, his wife came to help him. Subhas had thought in his mind to offer some bags of wheat to his grand- father as he was the real owner of the land. He engaged two labourers to weigh the wheat and pack them in sacks but his grand father obstructed him in the middle. He handed Subhas a lengthy list of expenditure concerning manuring of land and its fencing, the rent of bullock-cart and some miscellaneous items too had been added to that. Subhas saw that even if he sold the whole sacks of wheat, he would not be able to repay the amount he owed to his grandfather. He thought for a while and went to his uncle to show him the list of expenditure. His uncle scrutinised the list and gave an ironic smile. He could understand how Subhas had been hoodwinked by his grand-father. When he was engaged in conversation with his uncle, somebody hid himself behind a door to overhear their talk. But knowingly Subhas remained unconcerned with the Peeping-Tom role of his grandfather. So far, he had been thinking his grand parents to be his own and the land too. Once the old man had been hospitalized and he and his wife attended upon him day and night sparing their food and sleep. The true colours of a man get revealed when his self-interest is hampered. Such are the ways of life. When he recovered from nostalgia, his grandmother consoled him.

"Subhas, why are you so much worried? It is almost the same whether we keep it in our house or you carry those to yours."

"I don't have any greed for this trifling thing, grand-mother," Subhas was in the grip of emotion, "And I have decided to leave it all in your house. What difference does it make?"

Subhas smiled sadly as he was forced to swallow a bitter pill.

His wife intervened dreading that he might create a scene. She tried to pacify his anger. But Subhas rebuked her as she poked her nose into this matter.

Subhas bit his lips and signalled her to pack their things and started for the bus-stand, two miles away from that place.

His grand parents did not come out of their house to see them off.

All through the way, Subhas was pensive. Was it a dream or harsh realities of life? He could not imagine a rustic old man could be so much shrewd and greedy.

When he reached home, he was in a downcast mood. He narrated to his parents all about the incident. But his mother served an antithesis, "You may have done something wrong or have some lacuna, if not why had he gone back on his word?" Then she said, "It is only for me you are related to them otherwise are they your kith and kin?"

Subhas expected something consoling from his mother. But her cutting words worsened his mental state. His father also chided, 'Have I not warned you not to grow wheat in somebody's field? But you did not attach any value to my word and now you are paid in the right manner."

Their words pierced through his heart and made him crestfallen. He was at the end of his tether. He staggered to his feet and burst out,

"I don't want to keep any relation with filthy minded people. From this day on I severe all the ties with you when you people count them as being more intimate than me. Well, I won't rely on you too henceforth."

To him the piercing words of his mother were like a red rag to a bull. Subhas's whole body was trembling in anger. Now the horizon of life held a different colour for him. Life was not as he thought it to be. This incident, an eye opener, would make him aware of the coming days. This would hold deeper meaning and prompt still more cautious steps in the days ahead.

On to the right side of his bed room, on the small veranda, there was a husking tool. Keeping it as it was, he blocked its two sides with bamboo curtains and converted it into his kitchen. Though it was narrow and not so convenient, still cooking continued in the midst of all inconveniences.

Surama was again in the advanced stage of her pregnancy and could not do work comfortably. She and her mother-in-law were at cross purposes over some trivial matters. So there was no one to bear a hand in her difficulties. She poured her all discontentment on Subhas for she was uncompromising while her husband strove utmost to have peace-at-any price at home.

Subhas's mother often threatened her, "I will see who helps you at the time of delivery. Mind it, I would not go to hospital with you."

Surama remained quiet. She told this fact to Subhas but he did not want to snap back, instead he maintained a sullen silence. Whatever distress might come his way; he would not yield to injustice.

The next morning fell the New Year's day. It was a holiday and all the teachers were busy arranging a grand feast. On the other side of the river Jambhira, under an old tamarind tree, a hearth was made and the cooking started there. Gagan Babu, a man of facetious nature, opposed the cook when the latter cut the meat into small pieces as in his opinion, the big chunks would taste something different. Everybody enjoyed the picnic and returned to the hostel in high spirits.

Subhas had kept his wrist watch above a tin box. He was taken aback when it was found nowhere. He searched every nook and cranny of the room but it was of no avail. Somebody had stolen the watch. He could not think he would be robbed of on such a gala day. Two of the teaching staff went to a village to call in an exorcist reputed far and wide in catching a thief. He spread some 'sal' leaves anointing them with mustard oil on the ground, closed his eyes for a little while and said, "The thief cannot keep your watch any longer.

He will be compelled to throw it through the window this night. You need not worry. I have done what is needed." He chuckled and assured Subhas. It was simply hocus-pocus to console him.

A week passed by but nobody threw the watch through the window. Subhas decided to go to his cousin who had earned a good name in the art of catching thief by practising exorcism in his life. But his method was totally different. Two pieces of slender bamboo poles, eight to ten feet in length, were required for that. A tender boy would hold them under his arm pit and advance in step with the chanting of 'mantras' by the exorcist. The suspected culprits would stand in a row and the two ends of bamboo pole would grip the neck of the real culprit like a vice.

That famous exorcist who had several certificates to his credit for his stupendous work came with Subhas and stayed in the hostel. At night, he regaled the teachers by telling some incredulous stories of his experiences and all took him to be a wonderful man. The news spread like bush fire all around the village.

Within a few hours, the whole village and its surrounding areas were in a state of excitement over his presence.

The next morning the school campus was congested with a large number of people to witness this wonder, unprecedented in their area.

After the 'puja' was done with all the elaborate rituals, the boy selected for the purpose, advanced equipped underarm with two bamboo poles and the exorcist accompanied him step by step muttering his 'mantras'.

"Somebody has stolen Subhas Babu's watch, catch him," he uttered several times between mantras. He paused for a while and repeated the order. At last the bamboo poles turned their direction and gripped the neck of Manmohan Babu, a respectable man of that locality. He had come, out of curiosity, to see the wonderful work of the exorcist. Standing at a corner, he was observing the progress of the thief-catching endeavour of the exorcist.

When his neck was caught by two ends of bamboo poles, he was stunned. For some moments, he could not say anything. But his face went red in anger and he was going to slap the exorcist. When he came to know that the exorcist was related to Subhas Babu, he controlled his anger and forgave him.

The thief remained undetected and after this ludicrous incident, Subhas did not make any attempt to trace out the missing wrist watch.

TWENTY

Jayi Babu's father was in a miserable plight. His distillery business ran down and he incurred a heavy loss. His debtors did not turn up to repay the loan. His four sons remained indifferent and callous to their parents' woes. Even he could not clear up the electricity dues. The authority concerned disconnected the line and both husband and wife suffered a lot. His tide of life was really at an ebb. He was living in squalor. The youngest son favoured him a little by lending a connection of electricity only at night time and they had to tolerate many harsh words for this. Though his old wife could not see clearly, she would fry fishes and cook different curries to appease her husband. At last she died and the old man was left alone to pine for the happy days of life. The eldest son grew sympathetic and took the responsibility to feed him thinking that his debt as a son would be lessened to an inordinate limit. He knew it well that the decrepit old man would not survive for long.

It was around lunch that Subhas reached their home. He crossed the front room, a long corridor and at last reached a back room where Jayi Babu's father had sat on an 'asan' to take his lunch. He sat down on a chair and observed him. Some rice on a plate, dal and a curry of boiled potato with some poppy seed had been served to him. While eating he said, "Subhas, have you ever seen me taking such substandard diet in my life?" The old man started grumbling.

"It was a different matter grand-father," Subhas became compassionate, "but now you are living with your sons and grand- sons. You have to remain satisfied whatever they offer you according to their capacity."

The grand daughter-in-law was standing at a distance. She was waiting to serve if the old man would ask her for anything more.

"Is not there any tomato in the house?" The man shouted at his grand daughter-in-law.

"Do you know the price of tomato in the market? Always wants this and that", the grand daughter-in-law suddenly scowled at him as she could not approve of the old man's whining in somebody's presence.

With an injured ego, the old man resumed eating in silence. His eyes seemed tearful but he did not utter anything.

Subhas left the place with some parting consolation.

Bijay Babu was the headmaster of Laxmipur M.E. School. The cook, Kalicharan was left alone in the hostel. After finishing his morning bath in the river, he returned following the narrow foot track which ran through the corn field. He sunned the towel and came back to his room to change the dress. Then he ferreted around for the wrist watch. He opend his box, but it was not there. He suspected the cook because he was the only person who had remained in the hostel when he left for the river.

But he could not venture to ask him directly as the people of that area might view it differently. Moreover he was an ex-military man and when the superintendent of the hostel found nobody to cook there, that person came voluntarily to help them in such an adverse situation.

Some teacher lodged a first information report at the police station on this theft. The officer in-charge with one of his constables arrived there riding on a motor-bike. All the teachers of high school and M.E. School had gathered on the school campus to discuss the matter among themselves. When they heard the sound of the motor bike, they became suddenly alert and led the officer to the hostel room where the watch had been kept. The officer heard the narration and asked one of the teachers to call the cook immediately. The cook was sitting in a corner of the hostel. Somebody told him that the police officer wanted to ask him some questions regarding this matter. Kalicharan thought himself innocent. He slowly approached the officer with folded hands.

"What's your name?" The officer asked him while thrusting his chest with a truncheon.

"Kalicharan, Sir."

"How long have you been working in this hostel as a cook?"

"Nearly two months, Sir."

"What were you doing before that?"

"I am an ex-military man, Sir."

"Why do you like to be a cook here?" The tone of the officer now became sharper and more strident, his assumed gravity was more impressive.

"I have no one to support me nor any physical strength to earn my daily bread, so…" Kalicharan's eyes were sparkling with tears.

"You are an ex-military, so undoubtedly a crafty man who knows the art of talking very well." He turned to the teachers and said,

"Don't underestimate him. You see how he talks wittily. You cannot judge an ex-military man so easily. I know these people as I often come into contact with them. I am cock-sure he has stolen the watch. I shall apply third degree methods in the thana unless he makes a clean breast of his guilt."

Though there was circumstantial evidence, still he treated this petty theft as a capital crime.

The officer stood up from the chair and ordered the constable to bind his hands with a rope and take him to the thana.

He went straight to his motor bike, started it and

vroomed away. His last quizzical look unnerved everybody and left a disheartening air of dire consequence.

After the officer left the place, all the teachers condemned Bijay Babu for his action. He started crying. He slapped his own cheeks not to commit such a grievous mistake once again in his life.

The next day Krushna Babu and Bijay Babu went together to the thana to persuade the officer in-charge to set Kalicharan scot-free. But the officer was a man who could catch fish in a dry ground. He put his foot down on all their arguments. At last Krushna Babu paid the officer sixty rupees as bribe for his acquittal.

After his release, Kalicharan went home and did not return to work as a cook in the hostel.

TWENTY ONE

After Subhas was blessed with two daughters, his mother expected the third pregnancy to bring her a grandson. When the hospital nurse came out of the labour room, she immediately rushed and asked her the gender of the child. The nurse looked at her face, paused a little and said, 'daughter' and then went away. That single word seemed to dash her hopes and she sat down on the floor and began to wail like a child.

After delivery, Surama was brought back to her bed on a stretcher and she lay there in a very feeble condition. Her face was ashen white as if all the blood had been drained out. After a while, a nurse came and put the child by the side of her mother which snuggled up to her lap. Subhas's two daughters had also been to the hospital to see their mother. On the way they had bought some toffees to offer those to the new born baby. Subhas warned them to stand away from their mother and not to touch the child with their filthy hands. Surama looked at her children with wistful eyes and tried to smile. The two daughters held her hands and urged her to come home immediately.

"Yes, my sweet girls." Surama caressed their back turning to them and consoled, "how much you will be glad by playing with your little sister."

The second daughter stamped her feet on the floor and whined, "No mother, I won't play with her. She is mischievous"

"Don't say like that my child. Won't you love your sweet little sister?" Surama dragged her second daughter to fondle her while the elder one kept on looking thoughtfully at the child. She could not know what to do at that point in time.

Although the nurse warned Surama not to feed the child anything other than the milk of her breast, Subhas's mother dropped two drops of honey in the child's mouth refuting the nurse that she knew nothing about child care. Surama had heard many times the altercation between the nurses and old mothers-in-law regarding this subject. So she smiled silently and did not oppose her mother-in-law.

When Subhas came out of the hospital gate, he came upon Dhrubendra Babu who was going along the road towards the market.

"Hello uncle, why did you come to the hospital?" Dhrubendra Babu asked coming closer to him.

Subhas gave a sad smile and said, "I am again blessed with a daughter, Dhrubendra Babu. We all expected a male child but…."

"So what! son or daughter, it is all the same", he smirked, "rather you should give us a grand feast for that." His lips curved with a wry smile.

Subhas had work at home. So he sat on a rickshaw with his two daughters to reach early.

His father, Radhamohan Babu had gone to supervise the work of his farm, a place which was some three miles away from Baripada. On his way back he felt an excruciating pain in his right knee and he sat down helplessly on the ground. Fortunately a rickshaw puller was going along that way. He shouted at him and narrated his helplessness. The rickshaw puller very sympathetically made him sit on his rickshaw and left him at his home. The condition of the old man became very grave.

He was taken to the doctor and after a thorough scrutiny and routine examination, it was found that he was suffering from diabetes. The doctor prescribed some medicines and he took them regularly. He was kept on a balanced diet. Previously he was not a shirker of physical work. Every day he would nurture the flower plants and kitchen garden in the backyard of his house. Post-retirement, he concentrated more on that work. Now he was ill, he felt like a fish out of water. Because of his ill health, he was not allowed to do any sort of physical labour. After his recovery to a certain extent, he resumed the same work inspite of all objections. His wife's warning fell flat on him. It was set in idyllic surroundings. Perhaps he felt a mental solace in the natural ambience of the growing things and green. His enthusiasm for work had not been depleted yet.

After returning from the hospital, Surama remained for certain days in confinement. A local nurse was engaged to take care of her. She was put on a simple diet. As she was extremely weak, her mother-in-law advised her to take some raw wine to rejuvenate the body. One night when Subhas entered her room, he saw her quaffing a bottle of wine. He was taken aback as he had never seen her wining. Surama smiled and said that it was invigorating and she would be all right within a few days.

Three weeks later, Surama began to cook and do some domestic work slowly. One morning when she was in the back yard basking in the sun shine, she overheard a remark, "I have no daughter to bother about, see I have two sons who are like two gold apples. Why should I care for anybody?" The woman flaunted and flicked a furtive glance at Surama and then disappeared into the interior of the house. She knew that the woman was pugnacious and the barbs were definitely shot at her but she remained quiet and did not want to pick quarrels with her.

Since her return from the hospital, Subhas's mother was thoughtful. She was dismayed that Subhas would not be able to dispose of his three daughters with such a poor income. In this society the dowry system had become a curse and the greed for dowry was increasing by leaps and bounds. The daughters were growing like coconut trees. After some years they would attain a marriageable age. The expenditure on their studies would be a considerable amount. After spending money on their education how much would be left for him to meet the expenditure of the marriage. God alone could help him.

Again the doctor advised Subhas's father to eat bread at night instead of rice. It involved another extra expenditure. When Subhas often failed to manage, he would get irritated and admonish his mother to sell rice and purchase flour with that amount. So a verbal combat would continue for a short time. In India, ten persons depend on one earning member. They are worse than parasites. How could a person be in clover, shouldering Atlas-like a huge responsibility, Subhas thought.

A number of teachers were tutoring students to earn more.

But Subhas despised that commercial mentality. He had often noticed the lack of sincerity of the teachers in the class. They taught the students perfunctorilly and   never thought about their future.They would just prattle to while away the time. A revolutionary idea often surged within him to bring a radical change. But he could not do anything single handedly. The government machinery and its responsible officials were callous to the extreme and self-centred out and out. A cohesive force was the need of the hour to wage an incessant war against them. Then only could one expect a drastic change in the society, otherwise all efforts would end in a fiasco.

TWENTY TWO

"You don't believe in ghosts or ghouls? If you think yourself lion-hearted and bold enough, then bring to-night the wooden mace of Surendra Sathua from the cremation ground which had been hung on the offshoot of a 'mahul' tree."

This challenge came from one of the colleagues of Subhas's. Surendra Babu all through his life was a freedom fighter. In his early youthful days, he was a voracious eater too. He could gobble up one kilo of flattened rice and half a kilo of ghee within a very short time. In the pre-Independence days, he had fed hundreds of freedom fighters off his own hearth. He had stood firm against many atrocities of the British police while championing the historic non-violence movement. Towards the last part of his life he grew obstinate and to some extent abnormal.

After his death, his dead-body was carried to the cremation ground in a grand procession. It was by the bank of the river Jambhira, his mortal body was reduced to ashes. His two huge maces were also carried along with the dead-body. But somebody had hung those on the branch of a tree and thus they escaped the omnivorous tongues of fire. When Subhas and his companions went along that way to the river to take bath, they noticed those maces and it reminded them of the unforgettable memory of that freedom fighter.

Although the cremation site was not far away from the hostel, it transformed to a gruesome place at night. Nobody ventured to go there specially during this unearthly hour.

Subhas accepted the challenge of his colleague without any hesitation.

"But what would you offer me if I did the work successfully?" Subhas asked. "We shall offer you a plump bullet if you show us one of the maces here in this hostel." All the colleagues present there said in a chorus.

"All right, but I fear snakes and nothing else. Would some one of you lend me his torch light?" Subhas prepared himself.

"Yes, here it is." The headmaster Sarat Babu handed him his torch.

With torch in one hand and a little amount of tobacco in another, Subhas hit the path to the cremation site.

He crossed the corn fields and briskly reached the bank of the river. He rinsed his mouth with river water and went to the 'mahul' tree under which the funeral pyre had burnt the deadman to ashes. The tree stood like a giant sentinel over looking the river, a thick darkness encircling it. Quite fearless at heart, Subhas focussed the beam of the torch on the leafy branches and in all directions. If some ghost appeared before him; he would definitely greet him in a friendly manner and talk with him. He would open his heart, his pathos and his problems of life. He had heard good ghosts often help a person in distress. But alas, he couldn't see anything. He unfastened one mace and dragged it along the ridge of the field till he reached the hostel. The teachers came out of their room when they heard that dragging sound. They were all astounded at his daring spirit.

"Subhas Babu, you have done splendidly. We did not think you could hit the jackpot." All clapped their hands in joy.

The sun was rising. Everybody had finished their toilet. Menai Nana, a vagrant priest of that locality, emerged from his hideout and was staggering on the way boozed with country liquor. He was gesticulating and raving at Haladia

Nana, another priest, a sworn enemy of his priestly profession. He was heading towards Chhaka Bazaar where he accidently met Haladia Nana. So a mock-battle in the line of priesthood started between them. A skeleton-like body with sunken belly, Menai nana was ready to pounce upon him. He glared at him rolling his drink- sodden eyes, pulled out his sacred thread with the right hand and shouted at him.

"You fool, know nothing of 'mantra', still you brag of your priesthood! I am a sincere celibate from my childhood days and never touch a woman. Do you want to see I can burn you to ashes by virtue of my celibacy"

Haladia Nana saw that Menai was trying to belittle him before the public. He also wanted to show his priestly prowess in counter-attack. He immediately somersaulted on the road and stood on his hands with his legs upwards, in an asanic posture of an acrobat.

Menai Nana was a man not to admit his defeat so easily. He picked up a fistful of dust and intoned some mantras and threw it at Haladia Nana. The number of people increased to enjoy the comedy. At last some persons separated them and they went their separate ways.

The next day Menai Nana resurfaced. This time he was limping and could not walk steadily. He entered the school campus and showed his bleeding leg to a teacher.

"Sir, I was once the cook of your hostel. I have learnt something from my revered teachers. But now you see my lot. The dogs that I have tamed snapped at my leg how cruelly, you see sir."

He raised his legs and showed them one after the other to the teachers. Blood was oozing out from the wounds. Some amount of blood had streamed down his ankle and dried up.

"Nana, you please consult a doctor immediately. They would give you antidote for dog bite. The sooner you go, the better. Otherwise you will contract hydrophobia which is, no doubt, potentially fatal." Some teacher advised him with utmost sympathy.

Menai Nana laughed heartily through his tears. When he laughed, it was seen that there were a few remaining teeth in his mouth. A stream of saliva with some froth came out of his mouth. He wiped them with his towel and hastened towards the primary health centre.

Menai Nana was born in a poverty-ridden Brahmin family. He had no hearth or home. His early schooling was neglected and there was none in his family to support him. He could not marry as nobody was willing to give his daughter to such a poor Brahmin. So he remained a confirmed bachelor. Ousted from his house, he could not find any shelter for him. At last he took up residence under a tree and kept all his belongings in its hollow. Although he did not know any mantra, he performed the marriage of tribals and low-born people as their priest. He would sell the dhotis at a throw-away price that he received from the bridal party as his fees. He would buy country-liquor with that money and remain boozed from morning to night under its intoxicating spell. No body knew whether he took any anti-dote for dog bite or not. A few days lapsed. In the calm hour of the morning, news reached the school that Menai Nana passed away last night. A passer-by saw him dead and cold beneath that tree that the poor priest had once made his sweet home.

TWENTY THREE

Panditji and Jagajjiban Dey, the teachers at Laxmipur High School were saint like persons and had forsaken the happiness of married life in spite of repeated persuasions. As the hostel diet was not suitable for them, they hired a house and started a mess there.

Panditji, a Sanskrit scholar, had bought a radio set to listen to news and various items and thus he spent his time merrily. He had kept some savings certificates in his box under lock and key. Every day he would eat his lunch at 9.30am and start for the school to reach before time. His punctuality and sincerity in teaching was above criticism and everybody admired him for his good qualities.

One afternoon when he returned from the school, he noticed that the lock of his bedroom door had been broken and there was a pandemonium inside the room, the things being at sixes and sevens. The burglar had taken away his radioset, a box where he had kept some amount of money and some valuable savings certificates. He was terribly hurt as he had a great liking for those things. When the students heard about this theft, they began to scour every nook and cranny of that locality. After a thorough combing operation, they found out the things in a ramshackle video hall. Though Panditji got back his things, the search for the culprit was on. Some witty students suspected Sanjay who was an ex-student. As a dropout he had been misguided and had gone astray. Some students caught him and dragged him to the school compound. After some kicks and sound thrashing, he confessed his guilt. A shower of merciless blows on his nose caused profuse bleeding and he was gasping for breath. He asked for a drink of water. He drank it and rested a while. Panditji was still sympathetic and finding him alone gave ten rupees to make him flee.

Seated on the last bench of the bus bound for Baripada, the recalcitrant Sanjay was looking in all directions cautiously to make his trip a successful escape. But the police could sense this stealthy escape from some where and he was dragged to the police station by two constables.

The next day Panditji was called for by the officer in-charge of the thana to present himself in the police station.

Panditji stood before the police officer. He was basically very mild and submissive by nature. The officer looked at him but remained quite indifferent to his presence. He seemed to be busy with his file work.

After a while he asked,

"Are you that Pandit of Laxmipur high school?"

Panditji coughed a little to clear his throat and said, "Yes, Sir."

"Tell me, you are an educated person but how did you do this thing in an uneducated way?"

"What do you mean Sir?" Panditji could not understand the real purport of his saying.

The police officer said patronisingly as a myrmidon of the law, "You have committed two grievous mistakes. First, you have not given any report or information to the police as to the theft. The second mistake was legally unforgivable that you helped a culprit to escape."

The tone of the police officer turned to certain sternness.

Panditji remained silent. But he knew that the result was ineffectual whether he informed the police station or not.

The police officer submitted the charge sheet and the legal procedure went on.

Panditji's room-mate Jagajjiban Babu and the secretary

of the managing committee of the school Satyaban Babu were summoned by the court to give their evidence.

At first Panditji stood in the witness-box. The magistrate asked him some questions. A nervous man as he was, he was almost sweating but somehow he stammered out his statement.

Then came the turn of Jagajjiban Babu. He answered in a vacillating way to save the culprit. The magistrate doubted his statement. He could know that this person did not want to reveal the whole truth.

When the trial was going on, Satyaban Babu unexpectedly felt the urge of the call of nature. He was a long sufferer of chronic amoebic dysentery. He pulled his dhoti above his knees and ran towards the 'Jhinjri' embankment. But fortunately he came back before time.

The trial ended. Sanjay was accused of theft. As he was not an adult, his punishment was extenuated and he was sentenced to remain several months in a Borstal.

Sanjay's conviction meted out by the court did not make Panditji happy. He could not imagine that an ex-student would turn a quisling and descend into a distressing and humiliating situation. He had been giving financial help to a lot of poor students. If somebody stood at his door expecting some help, he had never been turned out disappointed or empty handed. He would greet everybody with a warm heart and ask him his weal and woe. His magnetic personality won him an august position in the eyes of the students and teachers. A man of literature as he was, his mind was always roaming in that golden realm that always fills his mind with exquisite pleasure-galore.

Satyaban Babu, son of the freedom fighter Surendra Sathua, was a man of principle and never deviated from the path of truth although he underwent many trials and tribulations in his life. As a cultivator, he had often won prizes by putting on display vegetables of rare variety and size in the district exhibition organized by the government.

Surendra Sathua had possessed some good qualities. When he was offered a portfolio of a minister under the chief ministership of Sarat Das, he laughingly rejected that offer and planned to spend his life in serving the downtrodden of society. His selflessness set an example to the younger generation of that area.

TEWENTY FOUR

Subhas wanted to obtain admission into the law college. But Dr. Sahu advised him to study Homoeopathy, a science which would help him in many ways in future. So he got himself admitted into the Homoeopathic Medical College and Hospital on payment of some money as donation.

He could not follow osteology well although he studied it vigorously for two months. At last he sought the help of Dr. Dutta who helped him out by explaining the intricacies of anatomy in a simple manner. His coaching helped him a lot in scoring good marks in that subject in the final examination.

The condition of Subhas's father had worsened. His blood sugar level was very high and he developed gangrene in his toes. Previously a carbuncle on his back had been treated with utmost care. It took about three months in healing up.

As his diabetes was out of control and grew worse day by day, Subhas thought it wise to admit him in the hospital. There he received treatment with care. Dr. Birendra, one of the class-mates of Subhas, treated his case as his own. As the necrosis on his toes developed to an alarming degree inspite of the best treatment, that portion was to be amputated. One day Subhas asked his doctor friend about diabetic gangrene. Dr. Birendra smiled a little and said that he would know it vividly when he would be a sophomore of medical college. At that time he did not have any idea about ketogenesis or keton bodies formation. If sugar and acetone both are present in the urine, one may think of diabetes with Ketosis. The breath contains the smell of acetone which is very diagnostic of this condition. There is Kussmaul's air hunger with hissing respiration. The patient may be conscious initially but gradually drowsiness and hyperosmolar coma supervene. Before Subhas's father went to a state of coma, he always smiled through his agonizing pain. His eyes were upturned and a sweet smell was coming out with his expiration. Subhas lifted his father's head to his bosom and wailed like a small child. The next noon, his lamp of life extinguished for ever. Such a great soul would never come to their lives again.

The deadbody was brought home and all the members of the family squatted on the ground encompassing it. Some neighbours who adorned him as a dignified personality stood at a distance to offer their homage to the departed soul. Subhas's mother sobbed and cried bitterly till the deadbody was carried to the cremation ground. Subhas was at the forefront of the funeral procession, throwing some coins and fried grain on the road. Soon they reached the burial ground and the deadbody was placed on the funeral pyre. Subhas lit the fire and the flame rose high. Within one hour only ashes and some charred logs remained on the fading embers.

Towards the last part of the night when the eastern sky was yet to grow red he returned and bathed in a tank with water dripping from his dhoti. Subhas was about to cross the front verandah of his house, suddenly a shadowy figure stirred from one dark corner. Surama had sat there alone. She had wrapped her whole body with a thin blanket burying the head between her knees and was biding her time.

"Have you now realized the bereavement of a father's death?" She burst with a growl and her feud with him lying dormant suddenly escaped.

The arrow shot by her pierced straight into his soul and it started writhing within. He felt as if his body would be shattered into pieces. Her voice was bereft of sweetness and full of contempt. Subhas was stunned for some moments but tried to recover his calmness of mind. He had been totally exhausted and not in a mood to make a counter-attack on her. A gust of fury shook him but he lugubriously fell silent, entered his bed room and shut it from within.

Now he recalled the past days when Surama was suffering from threatened abortion. It was her first trimester of pregnancy and the doctor advised him not to allow his wife to go on a long journey in that condition. Her father expired and she had a great longing to attend his funeral ceremony. Subhas had no objection but he was apprehensive. So he reminded her of the doctor's advice and warned her not to take such a risk. Since that day she had been harbouring a grudge and now the long smouldering rage flamed into a blazing fire.

Over and above she was pregnant for the fourth time and he did not want to give her any mental shock. After three daughters were born to her, he wanted to put an end to a reproductory process. But his maternal grand mother kept on urging for a son to help perpetuate the progeny. As there was no certainty, he administered some medicines for termination of the pregnancy. It is difficult to uproot a tree which goes deep into the ground.

As a system, a bed of straw was made where Subhas went to sleep on at night. He went to the river Budhabalang accompanied by his younger brother with a burning lamp and there they made a deep pit in the sand to keep the burning lamp safe and not to be extinguished from the gust of the wind. A day came when all the near relatives gathered by the river side and a barber had been appointed to shave their heads. After bath, they discarded their old clothes and wore new ones. In the Bhagavad-Gita, the Lord says,

"As a man shedding worn-out garments, takes other new ones, likewise the embodied soul, casting of worn-out bodies, enters into others which are new" (Chapter II-22)

So this was quite symbolic. On the last day of the funeral

rites, all the invited guests were fed with delicacies. The Brahmins and Vaisnabas were offered their fees before their departure. They placed their hands on the head of Subhas, recited some 'mantra' and blessed him.

One by one all departed. The house seemed terribly dreary and desolate. On his shaven head Subhas had worn a cap to stave off the scorching heat of the sun. After his father's death, he felt a stab of insecurity in the world. He was like a main prop on which the whole burden of the family had rested securely. Subhas knew he had to keep memories of many near and dear ones in the niche of his heart in the coming future. Why do they come? Where do they go? Why do they nurture us and depart in a mysterious way? These questions remained unanswered to him.

After some days Subhas's mother revealed something which seemed very strange to him. She had gone to Dhangdisole to a quack, who had earned a reputation for curing patients from various ailments. She had brought some herbal medicines prepared from honey and other sweet things. She had repeatedly asked that quack if those concocted medicines had any untoward effects on a diabetic patient. The person assured her of its efficacy. To the contrary the medicine was pernicious and it exacerbated his condition soaring the blood sugar to a very high level. But she had not disclosed this matter before her husband's death. In other words the inevitability of one's death couldn't be resisted by human efforts. It was just a consolation. Man perpetually remains in this 'would have been' and unnecessarily blames others for no fault of theirs. Strange are the ways of life!

TWENTY FIVE

Sekhar Babu was teaching social studies in Laxmipur high school. After his wife's death he remained morose for several months. On account of some inconveniences, he couldn't bring his children from his village to his place of employment. He left them there under the care of his parents.

It was mid-day and the bell rang signalling recreation. Sekhar Babu and Subhas emerged from the school compound to have their lunch in the hotel. On the way they came across a small residential house where a forest ranger was staying with his family. Though a mother of two children, the ranger's wife Giribala had an enticing beauty.

"Would you not come to our house Sekhar Babu?" Giribala stepped down from her house and greeted him. Subhas did not know how and when Sekhar Babu had become so much familiar with that lady. She led them to her front room and requested them to sit on chairs.

"I am coming back with tea." Giribala gave a charming smile and hastened to the kitchen.

"No, no, I won't take tea at lunch time, please don't prepare." Sekhar Babu formally objected.

After a minute Giribala came back with two cups of tea and put them on a small tea-poy.

"No, only one cup, Subhas Babu never takes tea." Sekhar Babu said while lifting the cup to his lip.

"Is it?" Giribala said smiling, "but why do you dislike tea, Subhas Babu?"

"No, no, there is no specific reason, simply I am not habituated." Subhas said blushing.

"That is very good, of course. Once habituated you cannot give up that habit easily. From that point Subhas Babu has done a wise thing. A good boy really..." Giribala laughed loudly looking at Subhas in genuine admiration.

"May I know what other things you don't like?" she asked still laughing. Subhas fell silent .

Giribala chuckled and said, "Perhaps you don't like to talk freely with a newly acquainted lady. You are very shy, aren't you?" She looked at Sekhar Babu expecting support from him.

"But he likes old film songs very much," said Sekhar Babu. "Do you know Subhas Babu, Giribala Devi has a huge stock of cassettes and most of those are old film songs."

"Old is always gold, what do you say Subhas Babu?" she tittered and said, "I have already delayed your lunch, please excuse me but don't you ever forget to come next time."

On the way Subhas said to Sekhar Babu, "I admire your one quality brother, you can mix with others very easily. But tell me how did you come in contact with this lady?"

Sekhar Babu gave a meaningful smile and kept Subhas in a conundrum Since that time Sekhar Babu was seen laughing and talking with Giribala for hours in her house. A mysterious relations developed between them. One day Sekhar Babu showed a letter to Subhas where she had mentioned her deep love for him. When the love reached its pinnacle, they planned to elope to some distant place. Her fidelity in conjugal life was questionable. To Subhas, she was verily a strange woman. Finding Sekhar Babu alone, one evening Subhas tried to make him understand, "Sekhar Babu I don't like your heinous thought nor do I like her extramarital affairs with you. You are a widower and she is a married woman and moreover a mother of two children.

It would be inexpedient to proceed further . I could not think how both of you have become so shameless!"

Sekhar Babu went on listening head lowered in a downcast mood.

"Whatever you may think of me but I must chastise you like your elder brother for this deviant behaviour. Really Sekhar Babu. I am very much amazed when I start to think about your ways of life, your ways of thought. Does not your heart move a little when you recall the love and affections of your dead wife? And how shall I view that woman-a luminous example of Indian womanhood?"

"But she loves me so deeply…" His face did not register an iota of repentance.

"Do you call it love Sekhar Babu? Does a woman love another man who has already a husband and two innocent children? My head reels when I think of it. Is there any sincerity in her love? Simple debauchery and nothing else. A woman who can cheat her husband today, must kick your ass tomorrow. The character of those women is like that. You are too despicable in the sense you are also a father of three children, still you view your biological urge more important than anything else. Where is your rationality? You don't know what love does really mean. What does it purport? A real love does not mean your biological need, it is not at all confined to that. When you say that you love her, you love her body only, her physical beauty. So long it persists, you go on loving her. When it dwindles and fades, your love ends there. So when we speak of love, we don't have clear conception of it and for this reason we generally get confounded and thus stumble at every stage of life. Love is very very subtle and its aim and purpose is very transcendental. I am not saying it from textual learning nor regurgitating the sayings of some great men or saints. It is simply self-realisation. Once you realize a thing, see its real form, your illusions are gone."

"So what should I do under such circumstances, Subhas

Babu?" His tone was very depressive and imploring. "I am on a conveyor belt, the only way left for me is to move forward."

"Your explanation is patently ridiculous. Old habits die hard. Stop visiting her house. You are a very passionate man, I know. Forbidden fruit is always more attractive. You cannot resist yourself nor can you evade the bewitching spell of her beauty. Rather try to remove her thoughts from your mind and recall the happy and pleasant memories of your wife which would dispel all libidinous thoughts rooted deeply in your mind."

Sekhar Babu thought for some moments and said, "All right, I shall try my best to avoid her."

"You can do one more thing Sekhar Babu. I know your mental agony. You tell your relations to see a bride for you. It is better to marry once again and lead a sound conjugal life. Because somebody would be there to give you company in later life."

TWENTY SIX

r. Giri advised Subhas to practise medicines and start a clinic. Subhas was then doing his second year medical degree. He told him that he was not well-versed in medicines and did not want to take any risk. But for his repeated persuasion, he started an ordinary clinic on the outskirt of the town. He became a popular practitioner there and the number of the patients gradually increased. After a few months the land lady wanted to have a renovation of the building for which he was requested to shift his clinic for a short period. He brought all his things home and waited until the repairing work was over. His two-year old son was playing inside the room where he had kept both homoeopathic and allopathic medicines on a small table. As his mother saw him playing, she went to the bath room to take her morning bath. There she remained at least for half an hour. In the mean time the child unscrewed the lid of one bottle of medicine and put three to four tablets in his mouth. But as the medicines tasted very much bitter, he could not swallow them. His mother just returned to that room to change her dress. She noticed the child munching something. An obstinate child as he was, his mother suspected him and asked him to open his mouth. She then cast her glance at the unscrewed bottle. Now she realized that her son might have chewed them. She removed all the tiny particles of medicines from his mouth with the help of the skirt of her sari. Since that moment the child cried incessantly and vomited at regular intervals. Unfortunately Subhas was absent then. So Surama and her eldest daughter took him to the head quarters hospital to consult a doctor. Diagnosing his condition as something serious, the doctor immediately admitted him in the hospital. Oxygen and saline were given according to the advice of the doctor.

At Laxmipur, Subhas had gone to the Chhaka bazaar to buy some betels. When he turned to the left, he met Pultu who came from Baripada riding on a scooter. He got down and came closer to Subhas. He was panting hard.

"Subhas bhai, I have come to take you back to Baripada as your son is now in a critical condition."

"O God! What do you say Pultu? How did it happen and where is he now?" He was almost in a confused state and bowled over by that woeful news.

Without losing a second, they started for Baripada post haste. On the way Subhas drank water several times as his throat began to parch terribly.

When they reached the hospital, Surama was sitting by the bed of her son and she was just running her hands on his tender legs. Seeing Subhas, she started to sob. He saw the livid face of his son and his patience gave way. The lividity was prominently marked on the nails of his hands and legs also. Dr. Kar, a very good doctor, was in charge of that ward. Subhas ran to him and asked him as to the state of the patient. From him he learnt that the condition of his heart and kidneys was hopeless and God alone could save him from this danger.

In the evening Subhas was standing on the balcony. Some women were also there discussing the dangerous state of the child among themselves. They said that the survival of the child was least possible as the blood had already been poisoned by medicinal effects. They did not know that the father of the child was hearing their discussion. His head reeled and he felt as if he would fall down on the ground. With slow steps, he came back to the bed of his son and sat on a chair silently.

The bygone days flashed before his eyes. There were no

gods and goddesses to whom they had not devotionally appealed for a son. How exulted they were when a son was born to them after three daughters! He looked at the photograph of Lord Jagannath and said, "Merciful Lord! Why are you so much cruel to take back my only son whom you have given me once as the sign of your bountiful mercy."

Babar had circled three times the bed of his ailing son Humayun and prayed God fervently to take his life instead. He at last heard his appeal and saved his son from inevitable death. Similarly Subhas was, lost in trance, ejaculating fervent prayer to God.

The doctor was non-committal about his child's chances of recovery. He had been kept on tenterhooks in the hospital for three days. He neither slept nor did he take a morsel of food. He almost turned semi-mad. Dr. Kar had prescribed a medicine which had an efficacy to counter act the toxic affect. As it was not available in the local market, two persons went to Tata and Calcutta but they came back disheartened. Finding no other alternative, Dr. Kar began to give ascorbic acid with the drip to drain out the poison through urination. Seeing the mental state of Subhas, Dr. Kar became very much sympathetic and requested him to take bath at his residence and have some food to keep him fit for the incoming disaster.

Dr. Kar also remained watchful by the bed side of the patient for a few nights. He took it a challenge to save the life of his son. One night he suddenly stood up from the chair and said to him;

"Subhas Babu, I have never got the opportunity to witness the famous Chhau dance of your place since my transfer to this town. I will remain absent for a few hours only and then I will return. Please wait for me."

Thus saying he went away on his scooter.

Subhas had sat on a chair and was reading a text book of Pathology to prepare himself for the ensuing examination. His wife counselled him to drop the examination that year.

But Subhas was determined to appear and nobody could dissuade him.

Towards the last part of the night he fell into a deep slumber. He saw a very strange dream. Seated on a gold throne, Satya Sai Baba was looking at him with a beautiful smiling face and he was waving his right hand in a gesture assuring safety. Subhas cried and asked; "Why are you laughing Baba? Please explain. I am unable to interpret the meaning of your laughing as it is quite incomprehensible to me ."

But Baba did not say anything. He just went on laughing. That divine vision abruptly vanished. After one hour, an old lady with scanty hair on her head appeared at the door. She had held something in her fist. She came to the sick child, put a dot on his forehead, fed the child a little and exited through another door. Subhas observed the activities of the lady and did not say anything. Perhaps he was under some self delusion for which he could not correlate the dream with the sudden arrival of the old lady. After she exited, Subhas came to his senses and searched for her up and down and in every conceivable place within the hospital campus. But he could not find her as though she had disappeared into the air leaving him in an unending mystery.

When Dr. Kar came as usual to follow up the cases, he narrated to him the dream and the unexpected arrival of the old lady. Dr. Kar stared at him for a moment and said, "Subhas Babu, now I can say your crisis is over."

Those consoling words set his heart at rest. From that day his son gradually recovered and after a week the doctor declared him out of danger.

TWENTY SEVEN

As Subhas's maternal grand parents attained their ripe old age, they could not do hard work any longer. They were very independent minded people. They did not want to seek shelter under anybody's roof. But Subhas's mother pressed them to come to their house as there was no one to take care of them in their declining years. Since that misunderstanding, Subhas had not visited their house. After coming to Baripada town, they faced an embarrassing position. They could not talk freely with Subhas. He understood their awkwardness and behaved in a normal way.

One day he said to his grand-mother; "Grandma, whenever I talk to you, I notice that you don't talk to me as freely as before. I think the misunderstanding between us has not been completely removed. You are verily a fountain of love and affection. And I count those earthly things quite ignoble when I think over your noble qualities. If I have committed any mistake unknowingly, please forgive me. Take me into your lap grandma which I have been craving for since my childhood days."

The grand-mother could not say anything and remained silent. Perhaps she was ashamed of her past deeds. Subhas knew that a little earthly gain could make a person surprisingly selfish and mar his conscience.

His grand-parents remained for two years in their house and again decided to spend their last days in their ancestral home.

During her life time, whenever a palmist or an astrologer

visited their house, his grand-mother would ask him whether she would die with vermilion on the parting of her hair or not. She always wanted to die before her husband. One day she suffered from severe diarrhoea and passed away. She remained a devotional woman till her death. Subhas had never seen her frowning at her husband in any circumstances.

It was a winter morning. The harvested corn had been stacked in piles all around the farm yard. A patch of ground, in the middle, had been smeared with cowdung to keep it clean. Subhas's grand-father had sat there on a cot with his second grandson Bablu. His daughter handed him a glass of Horlicks and he drank it with pleasure. After some time the old man began to doze in the warmth of the pleasant sun shine. He tilted to his grandson and rested his head on his shoulder. Without any suffering how peacefully he died!

Numerous tragic incidents are occurring every moment in this world. It is a regular phenomenon, still ignorant and foolish man pines for a transient thing. As the days passed, the memories began to fade. Subhas rolled his sleeves up to construct a new house. The place was thinly populated and it was at a distance of two and a half kilometres from the old one. At first Surama did not like the place as it was not habitable for a civilized person. But the purse did not allow them to buy a better place somewhere in the heart of the town. He piled all the materials of construction and started the work wholeheartedly. The only difficulty he faced was scarcity of water. He had to bring water by the labourers from a distant well and the river. Moreover there was no helping hand to watch over the materials specially at night. Spreading a towel on the sand, he had to sleep and watch, still he could not save things from the hands of the pilferers. In the midst of thick darkness, he would patrol the construction site with a torch in hand. Sometimes, he would spend sleepless nights by sitting in a dark corner. Through financial stringencies he at last completed the work. When one problem was solved, a new one lurked its head.

His old friend Deben came after a long lapse of time. He was an officer in the commercial tax department. When he was in charge of Boriguma Check Gate, his compassionate nature won the heart of all. He always looked to the interest of his subordinates. The two friends sat together.

Deben opened a leather box and took out a gold biscuit. He passed it to Subhas and said.

"A gift of a rich man when I was transferred from Boriguma."

It was a bit heavy and its golden hue was really attractive.

"Gold biscuit is the business of the smugglers. I have read in the newspapers how the customs department hunts down the boxes of gold biscuits imported illegally from the Gulf countries," said Subhas, seized with excitement and fear.

Deben laughed and said, "If you want to be a proud owner of that biscuit, I am ready to sell it at a very low price – three thousand in toto."

"I don't have such an amount at present nor do I have any interest in it. However I have gained some knowledge when I now see it and feel it."

Subhas handed it back to Deben.

They went to Baidhar, a betel-shop keeper to buy some betels. He was very much delighted seeing Deben after a long period.

He prepared some betels and said, "Dear Deben Babu I am a poor man. Now I am unable to meet the expenditure of the family. Even I don't have money to purchase new dresses."

Deben took out his purse from the pocket and handed him three hundred rupees without any shilly-shallyings.

Baidhar accepted the money in a trembling hand.

"I shall remember you till I live Deben Babu." Baidhar said in overflowing pleasure and gratitude.

As it was the morning hour, the market place was not so crowded. He instructed a fruit-seller to load a rickshaw with some bunches of ripe bananas, oranges and apples. Then he took them to his house to distribute them among the neighbours.

During his sojourn at Baripada, both of them would go to a restaurant to have their supper, chapati and chicken roast being their favourite dish.

"Don't spend so lavishly Deben, better to take food at home," one night Subhas suggested.

"O, that does not matter. You don't know some amount of money also come to my pocket in an indirect way. I don't want to keep a pie of that ill-gotten money, better to spend it on merry making." He said with a tinge of carelessness.

On the way to their home they sat by the side of a well and there he said, "Subhas, money may come and go but you should do something for which people will remember your name. Your activity is the epitome of your life. That's why at Bajrangpur where I am serving at present I started the construction of Lord Jagannath temple with the contribution of a few munificent people. Ninety percent of the work has already been completed. I hope the temple will be ready before the car festival."

"A noble work indeed," Subhas said, "but why did you not bring your wife Sagarkanya this time Deben?"

"Yes, I had that desire. I pressed her to come with me but due to some family dissensions she frowned and told me in a huff that she would go to her parental house instead, that ancient ultimatum."

After some days Deben went to his work place and resumed his official duty. One day he felt a dull aching pain in the region of the liver. He swallowed some tablets but it could not mitigate the pain. A specialist examined him and suspected liver cirrhosis. After thorough scanning, it was confirmed and his family members decided to take him to Delhi to obtain better treatment at All India Institute of Medical Sciences. There they remained in a rented house for a few months. Some expensive injections prescribed by a specialist were given to him. The severity of the disease now slightly abated. The doctors kept him under minute observation and the medicines continued as usual.

After three months, the condition improved miraculously and he was discharged from the hospital. With advice to take some medicines regularly, he came back but did not join his office. He was strictly instructed to take absolute rest.

During this time he read the Bhagavat-Gita minutely and committed many lines to his memory. Whenever a friend or a colleague sat by him, he would discuss the quintessential meaning of those things with great pleasure. He gradually lost his interest in this materialistic world. A transformation came over him and at length he became a different man.

Then he was transferred to Puri, a coastal area which was very conducive to his health. There he stayed for several months. Although he was apparently recovered, his disease was lying dormant. One day when he was working in the office, he felt a queer restlessness. Soon he fainted and was immediately shifted to S.C.B. Medical College and Hospital, Cuttack by car. There he remained in the Intensive care unit and received treatment. Inspite of the best care and efforts, his sense could not be restored. The next afternoon, he exited his earthly abode leaving his dear and near ones to mourn over his death.

TWENTY EIGHT

It was in the month of October when the children and the adults were preparing themselves to rejoice and celebrate the auspicious Kumar Purnima, nature with all its fury loomed over the town. Before evening, the sky was overcast with black clouds. Nobody had expected such a heavy downpour. The children sat indoors with their sullen faces looking at the ceaseless rainfall. Then came violent lightning and ear-throbbing thunder. At every two to three seconds, there was a blazing lightning followed by a sky-splitting thunder. The lightning and rumbling continued all through the night. Although all the doors and windows were shut, a streak of lightning through the gap of closed door was sufficient to dazzle the room. Everybody thought it to be the Doom's-day. Towards the last part of the night, the fury abated but the sky was threatening and in the late morning also, the sun was still enveloped with dark clouds. No one could know what happened to the others. In the early hours of the morning when they came out, they saw the northern side of the town besieged with a deluge. The river Budhabalang was in spate. The areas near the Sadar Hospital and Jagannath temple were overflooded and the patients of the hospital were being shifted to the upper storey on a war footing.

Subhas went alone to see the situation. He saw the people wading through the water with something on their heads. The mud walls had been washed away leaving no trace of the house. The people of extreme old age were heard saying that they had never experienced such thunder nor had they seen such awesome flood in their lives. When the flood receded, the birds were seen dead, strewn all over the ground. Half of the live stock succumbed to death and their decayed bodies emitted a foul smell. The whole north-eastern side was totally disrupted.

Subhas could not have a wink on that night. He spent the dreadful night tossing on bed. Though the house had recently been thatched, the rain water trickled down here and there. At dead of night, the mud wall of western side collapsed and all were roused from their sleep. Nobody could utter a single word.

"Have I not warned you many a time to shift from this house? But you don't attach any importance to my word," Surama growled in the dark.

Subhas knew that his wife would assail him if he did not support the prophecy of her warning.

"Yes, this time I must shift," Subhas said, "I assure You," but there was no such determination in his voice.

"I know, you always speak like that. When the danger is over, you totally forget your word. If the wall had collapsed on my children what would not have happened to them? You think over it. If you so like you may remain in this house but I won't nor will my children."

Two days after on a sunny morning he accidently met his old friend Manu, the chief medical officer of the district.

"Have you not heard anything about the health of Jogi?" Manu suddenly asked.

"No," Subhas stared at him expecting something menacing.

"You know he is a diabetic patient and above all suffering from high blood pressure. His condition is not at all good. If you have time, let us visit him this afternoon."

"Definitely. I don't know his condition has become so critical. Please wait for me."

On the upper storey in the corner of a room, Jogi was

lying on a bedstead. In his youthful days, he had robust health. He was a ravenous eater and found pleasure in feeding others. But where was Jogeswar, that bulky mirthful man? A skeleton like body with skimpy hair on his head greeted them with a smiling face. Seeing two old friends his joys knew no bounds.

He invited them to sit on his own bedstead and himself got down to prepare betel for two friends.

"Yours?" Jogi asked looking at Manu.

"Plain, without tobacco," Manu warned.

"And yours?" He looked at Subhas and said, "I know your brand. Yes, I had forgotten."

"But I did not think your condition has aggravated to such an extent." Subhas said while tucking in a betel in his mouth.

"No, I have taken all types of measures, am even practising 'Yogasan' to keep my health normal but neither the medicine nor the 'Yogasan' proved efficacious." Jogeswar said hopelessly.

"I don't rely on your words unless I ask your wife about your activities. I know your nature," Subhas said.

"Yes, you may ask her," Jogeswar said in a guilty tone.

"Where is your wife?" Subhas found a servant boy and told him to call her.

Sabita appeared at the door and stood there. She was a little hesitant to come inside the room as she saw Manu for the first time in her life.

Jogi could understand.

"Don't feel shy. He is also my childhood friend like Subhas."

Sabita entered the room.

"May I ask you why Jogi's health has deteriorated so much? I think Sabita, you don't take his care properly," Subhas said in a tone filled with anguish.

"Brother, you blame me without my fault. If I divulge

the secret before his two friends, he would flare up. Come what may, I must tell you the whole thing." Sabita straightened her body to speak out the truth.

"As his wife I have taken every precautionary measures to keep him in sound health but he is pertinacious and craves for sweet things. When he sees me absent, he slips to the ground floor and takes 'Sandesh' or "Rasgullah' regularly without my knowledge. You now tell me if a diabetic patient takes sweets like this, how can the medicine work effectively?"

When Manu heard all these facts, he looked straight at Jogi. Jogi smiled a little and bent down his head.

"Please Jogi, don't try to convince me by your flimsy explanation. It is patently obvious that you are lying. You are not a small child. Here I am prescribing some medicines to keep you better. Listen to me mindfully and do according to my advice."

Jogi immediately nodded his head like an obedient student and promised not to commit any wrongful deeds henceforth.

After three days, the servant boy came to Subhas and informed him that his master had been hospitalized as his condition was distressing. Subhas ran to the hospital. But to his ill-luck, Jogi was in a semi-coma stage. His eyes were upturned and he was not in a position to recognize anybody. Subhas sat by him and asked him what he wanted to say. A streak of recognition sparked in his eyes and he pulled Subhas's head close to his mouth trying to whisper something in his ear. Only his lips trembled for a moment. Two streams of tears rolled down his cheeks showing his frailty to utter anything.

That night he exited this world.

TWENTY NINE

Time sped by: Subhas's three daughters Anindita, Suchismita and Nibedita attained their marriageable age. It is a Herculean task to find a suitable groom for the daughter in this modern society. If a groom is educated and well placed then he is rara avis. To fulfil their sky-kissing demands is beyond the capacity of a low income-earner. However Subhas left no place unexplored with an unbeatable zeal.

It was in the month of December when he wanted to visit a relative with his wife, the second daughter Suchismita expressed her eagerness to accompany them. He did not know an unexpected thing awaited him there. At noon, when the lunch was over, Subhas was taking rest on the terrace of the building. There the pleasant sun shine made him drowsy. The youngest daughter-in-law of that relative broached a marriage proposal for her uncle's son there.

"First come, first served. Although I had thought of my eldest daughter's wedding ceremony to be performed first, still I have no objection for the second," Subhas said quite innocently.

"I like Suchismita. They would also like her. This evening I would intimate them over phone to come to our place to see her," the daughter-in-law Chanchala assured him.

"You must also treat this as your sacred duty. Go with my wife to some telephone booth and inform them to come tomorrow as it is the sooner, the better," said Subhas.

The next day the groom and his cousin arrived on a

motorcycle. They expressed their choice and asked them to visit their place to discuss with the guardians.

Subhas went to their place and returned. Then the groom's father came to see the bride. The discussion went on to finalize the matter.

"As dowry you have to give one lakh and thirty thousand rupees excluding other accessories" the groom's father said gravely.

"You see, I have three daughters. I can't afford such a big amount. I can give at best a motorcycle according to your choice and other necessary things," Subhas said.

"You have financial capacity but no heart to give," the old man tried to injure the ego of Subhas.

Subhas called the mediator to the back of the verandah, "Tell that old man that I can't give more. He should rather go back," he said.

After much deliberation at last the demand was fixed at one lakh and the old man came to a final settlement.

The date was fixed and towards the last part of February, the wedding ceremony was performed.

After retirement from service, Subhas sat silent at home. Soon his Sisyphean labour started to dispose of other daughters. His eldest daughter was a meritorious student having a distinguished career. She came out successful in written examination and fared well in viva-voce. At last she got a good post under the Central Government and was posted in a distant place.

A retired sales supervisor of Hindustan Petroleum apprised him on phone to have a mutual discussion on marriage negotiation and promised to come within a week. Three days later, he arrived at the bus-stand. Subhas was waiting for him.

A middle aged person with a bulging belly got down from the bus. Subhas was in a confusion as he had not seen him before. On being asked he told his name and Subhas greeted him warmly. He hired a tempo and reached his house within a very short time. The moment he entered, he saw his old friend Pradeep seated in his drawing room. He was very much delighted and introduced him to that new guest.

"I am Kulamani Samantaray, a retired supervisor of Hindustan Petroleum Co." - The gentleman gave his self-introduction after sitting comfortably on the sofa.

"I have one son and one daughter.," the gentleman continued, "I have given the daughter in marriage to a well placed young-man. Before that I had to go to Deoghar to consult 'Barada' of Anukul Ashram. He gave his consent and now they are leading a happy, peaceful conjugal life."

"What is your son?" Pradeep perhaps grew impatient by his long introduction.

"I have already informed Subhas Babu that my son is now serving as Probationary Officer in the United Bank at Bareilly and he has come home on leave to see a girl of his choice."

"Five years back I had been initiated into that cult," Subhas said to be a kindred.

"May I know your 'Rittik'?," the gentleman asked.

"Tapodhan Panda," Subhas succinctly replied

In the mean time Gautam, Subhas's son appeared at the door and beckoned his father to come inside.

"Father, when you left for bus stand, the brother-in-law of this gentleman informed me on phone that this person has left his handbag in the carrier of the motor cycle in haste and now the problem is how he would go back without money."

Kulamani Babu glanced at his wrist watch and seemed quite impatient to wait any longer. He asked some formal questions to Subhas's daughter and stood up for the return journey.

Before departure Subhas inserted four hundred rupees in his shirt pocket and said, "I know your awkward situation as you have forgotten to bring your handbag with you. I think you can manage with this amount."

Kulamani Babu held the hand of Subhas and drew him to a corner.

"I have to attend the marriage ceremony of one of my relations at Baliapal. So befitting my social position I have to offer some valuable gifts to them," Kulamani Babu uttered in a low tone.

"How much amount is necessary at present?" Subhas asked.

"At least fifteen hundred rupees will ease my problem. The day after tomorrow I am coming with my mother and son. So I will repay your money at that time."

"All right, I have no such amount at home. I have to draw it from the bank. You please wait at the bus station." Subhas gave him assurance.

Subhas scribbled down on a withdrawal paper and handed it to his son to draw the amount and himself went to the bus stand to see off the gentleman.

But that benign person did not turn up on the appointed day. At night he phoned him, "Subhas Babu, regret to say that my mother expired the day I went to Baliapal to attend the marriage ceremony. During my absence suddenly her blood pressure increased to a severe state and my son admitted her in the Kalinga Hospital. There she breathed her last at dead of night."

"I too share your woes Kulamani Babu. Even I am ready to attend the funeral rites of your mother", Subhas told sympathetically.

"I will tell you later on. If possible, I may go to your place in a couple of days to discuss how to solve the problem for both of us."

"Yes, the last straw also slipped from my hand," said Subhas.

"No, no, don't be disappointed. My brother-in-law

assured me that if it is feasible he would adapt my son to his own 'gotra' and perform the marriage ceremony."

"I don't know what fate decrees for me," Subhas sighed.

Tepid response from the other side. Then the phone went dead.

When the gentleman remained silent for a few subsequent months, everybody suspected him to be a swindler.

One day Surama rebuked Subhas, "I had a hunch and warned you not to give such a big amount to a newly acquainted person. But you did not care. A pea-brained idiot you must be."

"You see Surama, when he introduced himself as my 'guru bhai' I did not hesitate to help a person in a tight corner. Moreover he who helps others is helped by God."

"You made a fool of yourself. So you paid the price of your tomfoolery. You could have given that humbug only the bus fare and not more than that as we are not responsible for his imprudence.

"Does that gentleman think that his problem of life will be solved with that petty amount of money?", Subhas was irritated.

"No, but how much would he have been glad to cheat a good Samaritan like you. Don't have horse sense." Surama supplied the fuel.

"Yes, I must have owed something to him in my previous birth. But the fact which pricks me most is that he must have thought me a damn fool or in the words of others he has emotionally blackmailed me."

"Yes definitely. Even a small child can outwit you. What a gentleman he is!"

"Don't harp on that, I took it as a mishap. While going on a journey, somebody picked my pocket in my unguarded moments and not more than that."

THIRTY

As Subhas thought the delivery would not be so convenient at their place, he brought his daughter Suchismita to his home in her advanced stage. A gynaecologist examined the foetal position and blood pressure and declared everything to be normal.

On a winter night the pain started when all the family members were at dinner. Half-fed they hurried to call an auto rickshaw from a neighbouring area to take her to the hospital as soon as possible. All through the night they paced up and down and towards the last part of the night, she gave birth to a female child.

Eyes closed, it remained silent on a cradle. After three hours it began to twist its body with closed fist. It was wrapped all over with a clean cloth except the face.

Surama carried the child to her lap and directed Subhas to call a tempo as she did not want to linger there. At home, the mother and child were kept in a separate room. A nurse was engaged to take care of the neonatal. When the child was four months old, Subhas's son-in-law Animesh came to take them. Although the child was suffering from a mild diarrhoea, his son-in-law was in a hurry to go back. Subhas advised him to stay two to three days till the recovery of its sickness. But he did not listen to him. When Subhas scanned paucity of manliness in that young man, he did not oppose him.

After their departure, he remained sulky for a few days. His grand daughter Papali inscribed many happy memories on his mind which could not be erased. Attachment to something gave always this type of mental afflictions.

"Hi Subhas! Not showing up for a long time," his friend Pradeep said while alighting from his scooter.

"Welcome my brother, of course I am a stay-at-home person for the present. You know my austerity. When I go deep into that contemplation. I never go outside lest my thoughts should be distracted."

"Yes I have gone through your poetry book 'My Own World' and do appreciate the poetic beauty but I don't like your last novel 'Jealousy' so much."

"Why?"

"That novel is full of characters and different stray incidents. I don't understand why you did depict them so elaborately?"

"Of course I do admit, it is a little bit descriptive. But the real beauty, the complexities of life is radiating through these characters. Many more things are there still to be explored specially man the abstruse is not yet articulated to us."

"But I don't find any uncommon or queer in those delineation…"

"Certainly. The real worth is their lack of uncommonness. I have never propounded any new theory nor tried to reveal any divinity or bestiality in them. I have showed how humanity is gradually declining in their being and its dire consequences and impact on the coming generation. Human being, the best creation of God, has been overpowered by a satanic force. The creator beholds his own creation gone morbid, shrivelled and melancholic. The shrine of the heart remains untidy, unholy, and abandoned. It is doubtlessly an awful evacuation of the spirit and the premonition of a certain dissolution."

"But you don't know most of the people are now hard of hearing. Your clarion call will not reach their ears. Moreover you are not a social reformer. Do you think it will bring some change?"

"Not, of course, at present. But surely it would have a result in the long run."

"You always dwell in a fool's paradise. Don't confuse your head as to what the world is heading towards. Cultivate your own garden."

"To be self-centred out and out, isn't it? But I must shout."

"Nobody will hear."

"I don't care. I won't cease until you all hear me with rapt attention."

"Listen to me. What has been said so far are all confusing and inconclusive."

"But the real is always permanent and unchanging. You cannot discolour or tarnish it by your antithesis or modern flattery."

"Definition or interpretation of something is changing fast now-a-days. What you call truthfulness or honesty may be viewed by somebody in a different hue. Strange is their way of thought."

"What Socrates said in those days has been accepted as truth to-day. Truth is always truth. You cannot distort it nor can you defy it."

"If you cling to that truth, you will be awfully defeated in this struggle for existence. Your ideas and modes of thoughts that you have fostered so far in your mind have become obsolete and you will find yourself incongruous with others, as you are going in the opposite direction. I fear you may be discarded for this incompatibility," Pradeep warned him.

It was late evening and they came out of the drawing room to witness a procession. Lord Ganesh was going to be immersed and a group of boys were dancing like lunatics before a truck. Perhaps they were under the spell of 'bhang' or charas' and break- dancing had started according to the tune of the music.

Pradeep drew his attention and said, "See Subhas, how spiritedly they are dancing. Do you see any devotion to Lord Ganesh through this hysterical dancing? I can't resist myself from kicking them on the buttocks, those shameless creatures."

"I have gone a step further. I call this dance as epileptic fits. They imitate those frantic dances of movies and find a wild and erotic pleasure in exhibiting them before the public. Even the parents think themselves glorious when they see their sons and daughters, showing their skill in such forms of dancing. Now the young ladies are dancing half naked, swinging their hips more provocatively and are applauded by all. For money they can go to any extent, no fault to dub them super prostitutes."

"Subhas, you are really old-fashioned. That is not nakedness. It all depends on the eyes of an observer. I don't want to cite those erotic sculptures of Khajuraho as you know all about that."

"Everything has been commercialized. Hectic race for money has spoiled the power of thinking. In the name of art you are quite independent to do anything. Is there any difficulty to have a plea in the garb of art? The minority of us have raised their voice but it has been curbed by the highhandedness of the other group. Although they have deviated from all the social norms and modesty, the feeble voice cannot resist them from moral lapses. You have to be a martyr if you really want to bring an awakening in society. They think we are blind and noodles. That is why they have become so daring to do all these diabolical things."

"We blame politicians and bureaucrats who are the upper crust of society but all are not the same. A few among them have polluted the water. They always remain in the background and patronize others. They are the kingmakers.

They hold the string in their hands and make us dance like puppets. They are the root of all provocations. You see how murderers and ruffians have come to the political arena through muscles power. If the crows and vultures would be doctors of a dead body, can it be resuscitated?"

Their discussion was interrupted. Surama called them to have tea in the drawing room. Pradeep came back and after sipping tea sank into a chair.

"What about the Cuttack party? Did they say anything about their appreciation regarding your daughter?", Pradeep asked.

"They are all treacherous and barren of humanity. I have no idea an educated person can be so much conceited and deceitful. They have received only some certificates of thick paper but they are awfully in dearth of real education," Subhas twisted his eyebrows with sudden vexation.

"What did they do?"

"They did nothing, simply following a Fabian policy to keep me in constant tension. The groom's elder brother handed me a photograph of his younger brother and told me of his appreciation before his departure. But the candidate did not turn up even after seven months. The groom's sister-in-law assured me on the phone that it would be finalized very soon and they were getting ready to perform the marriage ceremony in their newly constructed house. The marble work of the upper storey was now going on and it would take hardly two months to be completed. They were quite averse to hold this auspicious ceremony in a rented house.

After my seven months' patient waiting, the grooms elder brother informed me that his younger brother was now unwilling to marry and that unfeeling gentleman begged apology for his helplessness. The refusal had no cause or effect. You know, people who talk big seldom keep their word."

"Do you think his elder brother has some control over his family ?"

"Not at all. But I know they keep some brides wait-listed. They visit several houses under the plea of marriage negotiations. But they keep in view the financial status of the bride's father. How much they would get as dowry ? I have seen a number of fortune-hunters, nay, rich beggars like them in this society."

"But do you think somebody will take pity on you. You are bound to give dowry." Pradeep laughed to tease Subhas further.

"I despise this system very much. If you want to have a family tie through marriage negotiation, you may demand according to his capacity. There are thousands of cases of break down of negotiation because of their excessive craze for money."

"Good days are coming Subhas. Conscience must prevail one day. The new generation will come forward and bring a radical change in our society. Let us hope for a better future."

THIRTY ONE

It was before dinner when the night sky was enveloped with black clouds and a shaft of cold wind was blowing intermittently, Suchismita and her old father-in-law appeared at the gate of Subhas's house. They got down from a tempo and knocked at the door. Perhaps her father-in-law did not know where the call-bell was. Subhas immediately hastened to open the gate. The old man entered the drawing room and following him Suchismita and her daughter Papali. Both of them had caught cold and Papali was often sneezing from a head cold.

"My dear Papali." Surama extended her hand to take her to her lap. Lo! She threw her arms to come to her grandmother without any scruple.

"Maa, I thought she might have forgotten you", said Suchismita.

"No, no, she can't. I have nurtured her here in this bosom. How could it be? But Mita, your daughter has a slight fever, I feel it."

Surama pushed her hand below the dress to ascertain herself. "O God! There is a burning temperature. I could not feel it at first."

She grew pale and turned to Subhas, "You please bring some medicines for the child, without losing moment," and then she chided her daughter, "how wise you people are that you came in this cold weather. Your father-in-law is a block-head too."

The child was under the weather but still she was active.

When Surama spread a mat on the floor and threw some toys, she began to play with them. After some time she started crying. She got exhausted and wanted to be carried about in arms. By the time Surama lifted her to her lap, Subhas arrived with medicines. He gave the antibiotics and then one spoonful of paracetamol for remission of the fever. After one day all the symptoms subsided and she began to recover.

Mita's father-in-law stayed for three days and left.

When Papali came round completely, she toddled from one corner of the house to another. Subhas would often appear at the door with a bag full of vegetables from the market and the child would run to him with unsteady feet. She would grab one ear of the bag and come with Subhas upto the kitchen and then she would keep potato, brinjal and tomato etc. separately on the floor. Her grand mother would often utter in surprise, "Look, how intelligent the child is ! She must be a precocious one."

Subhas bought her an English doll whose eyes opened and shut. Down, its eyes would get shut, up, then its black eyes would open like petals. When Papali squeezed it at a certain place it emitted a squeaky noise and she jumped with pleasure. Subhas ran with her, danced with her. When her youngest aunt smeared her face with powder and preened herself sitting before the dressing mirror,she would also see every detail of her face. With her unaccustomed hand, she would smear her face with a thick coat of powder. Her aunt would snatch away the powder-puff from her hand and say, "Have you ever dabbed your face like this, you stupid child or seen it in your paternal race?"

Then the child would roll on the ground crying. Surama would come out from the kitchen, dust her body and say, "Did your aunty rebuke you my sweet? We will beat her later on." Thus saying she would carry her to the kitchen. Papali had long, glossy black hair. It was so long that sometimes it almost covered her face. So one day Subhas cropped it short with a pair of scissors.

Suchismita observed the hair-cutting and said, "Father, you made my daughter quite ugly."

"No, no, after some days it would be all right," said Subhas consoling his daughter.

One day her eldest aunt mockingly frowned at her. She could not stop her crying. Surama came running and patted her on the back and said, "Don't cry my sweet, you see how I beat your aunty." Then she raised her hand and the aunt began a mock-cry. The child stared at her aunt's face and suddenly stopped sobbing.

In the afternoon, Papali would stroll with Surama with her squeaking shoes on. She would run expanding her two hands and fall down on the meadow. Her grand-mother would remove the dust from her knees and thump the ground in mock-assault.

"You made our Papali fall down. I must beat you." Surama thumped the ground with her feet.

Her grand-mother put a mark of 'kaajal' on one side of her forehead to ward off the evil eye. In the evening she would make some small balls from kneaded flour and roll them to give a shape of 'chapati' imitating her grand-mother.

Subhas brought her some sweet grapes and she made a peculiar sound by thrusting her tongue on the soft palate while sipping the juice.

One day Mita, being annoyed pulled her daughter's hair a bit forcefully and the child began to yell rubbing her eyes with her palms. Subhas saw it from a distance. He walked to her and said, "You cruel hearted mother; why did you do like that?"

"She always sticks to me like a leech and has been pestering me for which I don't have a few minutes' rest, father, so unruly she is."

Mita left flinging a burning look at her snivelling child.

"Now you came to realize the hardship of rearing up a child. But here in this lap I have reared up four. How was that possible?"

Mita went back, lifted the child to her bosom and tried to soothe her.

One evening Mita said, "Maa, I can't tolerate my mother-in-law's abuse to my father in an uncivilized way. Even that old lady abuses my elder sister also. She would not mince her words although my father has never offended her."

"Why?"

"Because you could not find a suitable groom for her and that became a plea to abuse me in the name of my sister."

"Mita, I really regret that your mother-in-law does not think my daughters as her own. Let it be, as I am going through bad days," Surama sighed.

Subhas had sat cross legged on the floor. He heard their conversation.

"What a woman she is!" he said with honest surprise.

"She upbraided us for no fault but do you know Mita what Confucious has said: A woman with a long tongue is a flight of steps leading to calamity."

"Your mother-in-law is the only sister among eight brothers. All the brothers and sisters-in-law are quite sober, sociable and non-aggressive. But this lady is an exception, a cat among doves. I don't know why she emerges as a tigress from such a good family. Fie on your mother-in-law." Surama said in a fit of fury.

"I have committed many a catastrophic mistake in my life," notebly this precipitous marriage,"Subhas said in a tone of penitence. " But this is a colossal one. One should not be biased by anybody else. The biggest tragedy has come to my life for my own relatives. They have not only hurt my mind but also lacerated my soul. God alone knows what a terrible anguish I have experienced all these days."

"Is Subhas sir at home?" Somebody called out at the door.

"O, Pradeep! Please come in" Subhas warmly greeted his friend.

Pradeep plonked himself down on the sofa and straightened his legs.

"Please have a cup of tea," Subhas pleaded.

"No, I have just had tea at home. Now come to the point. What is your progress regarding marriage negotiation?"

"Not worth mentioning."

"Why?"

"Because they won't get an expected amount from a teacher."

"Baseless." Pradeep pressed his lips.

"In this materialistic world, nobody wants to recognize your real merit-your upstanding personality. The inner man remains perpetually obscure. Nobody tries to explore it."

"Why do you always prattle materialistic… materialistic? I think you are suffering from some complex."

"Not at all. I am telling you the fact as true as death. Most of the people like to plunge themselves into abysmal depth of ignorance due to their sheer foolishness. Although they rot, they think they are in a state of euphoria. Why should they toil to know your innerself? What is their necessity? They come with a commercial motive. Sell their goods at a higher price and then go back home. They won't even look back to observe your predicament-your doleful condition.

Time has changed. Your ideas, attitude, values of life and above all refined sentiments are viewed as a form of lunacy in this crude society. The friend you treat as most trustworthy and intimate today may turn sworn enemy tomorrow if his self-interest is slightly hampered. I don't blame any one. In this vicious atmosphere they have lost their humanity. Human form but no humanity. I feel shame to call myself a human being."

"Do you recognize me as a human being?" Pradeep said laughing.

"Of course. You are my only friend who can understand me well. There was a day when I was boastful of my friends. But some hopelessly despaired me. Because they are in a higher position and their social status is quite different from mine. They even feel shy to identify me as their friend."

"Don't be so much sentimental, Subhas." Pradeep suddenly appeared grave.

"This is not mere sentimentality, Pradeep. The wearer knows where the shoe pinches. I was once trying to expand. My target, my ultimate aim, was to reach the remote horizon. But some irresistible power has constricted my neck barring my steady progress –my elongation. My indomitable zeal began to decline. Perhaps I have been defeated though not totally. I want to cease my cycle of birth. I fervently pray to God not to send me back as a human being again. My mission of life has failed. I am groping in the dark. Standing at a square I am pondering on and on which route will lead me to my desired destination. My dreams have been shattered, my citadel of hopes and aspirations has crumbled into pieces. I have sacrificed everything which a human being aspires most in his life. But for whom? I won't say to anybody for whom. That chapter must remain untold. I am gradually losing confidence in man. This much I regret that nobody could understand me. Perhaps there is some incompatibility with 'my own world.'"

Pradeep stared for some moments at a metamorphosed Subhas trying to read him this time with utmost sincerity. An ocean of revolt was heaving and surging in his two sparkling eyes.

After four months, Animesh, Subhas's son-in-law, came like an untimely rain to take back his family. How delighted all were when they arrived before some months. Now the time of departure came. He stood at the gate way. The tempo skidded to a halt and they all got in. He saw the tender hand of his grand daughter waving to and fro bidding him goodbye. His elongated shadow ran after her but it got rarefied on the way and could not hold up which his soul yearned for.

He sat closing his eyes for a long time. The sun was going to dip down the western horizon scattering its last radiant glow on the kaleidoscopic earth. He saw enough of life. To sing the last requiem of life, he wielded his pen and began to write :

"The sky has been darkened
blurring the vision of horizon
No heaving, no surging of sky-kissing waves
On the bosom of the ocean.
Sepulchral gloom prevails,
No singing of birds, no fluttering of wing
No voyage piercing the breast
No lashing of ruthless waves
The hue crystallizes,
The rhythm modulated to high pitch
Shrill cries resound
From sky to sky
From ground to ground
From pole to pole.
A voice of rejection
A voice of repulsion
A voice of collision
Proclaiming a sanguinary battle
Bathed in pools of blood
Clad in crimson attire
The augur cast a lurid glare
In the guise of a tantalizing damsel
In the guise of loving apparel
Sworn to maim the image
Bent on assassinating
the veracity, the humanity, the magnanimity.
A smile changeth to guile

A brilliance changeth to extinction
A mirth changeth to moan
Appears, appears in virulent form

Uninvited, unexpected, unsolicited.
Full of spite, full of malignancy, full of vengeance
Vowed to reach a vile goal.
The ship of beauty to be blown up by torpedo
An abode to be turned down by tornado,
The altar of deity to be swept away by torrent.
No adoration,
No jubilation.
No coronation,
Aura fades away, divinity is exiled and it gives in
Satan holds the rein to reign
Dawn of prosperity remains shrouded
With fog,
With frost,
With drizzle
Beset by barricade.
The creator,
Full of elation,
Full of dejection,
Beheld
His own creation
Morbid, shrivelled, melancholic,
The shrine of the heart remains
Untidy, unholy, abandoned
An awful evacuation,
Nay, a certain dissolution.

The present day society became horrendously cankerous
and more suffocating and Subhas had enough patience for
another resurrection.

"Keep moving" – he heard a voice.

He stirred himself and gripped the brush to paint again.
For more than six decades, he had been painting a number of
portraits. One of them was a portrait of a web, of a mingled
yarn, good and ill together. He had been ensnared in that.
That was his self-portrait... a masterpiece and his ultimate
high. He saw him flopping and floundering there but exerting
himself to wriggle out to fling himself free.

THIRTY TWO

"Son or daughter, what's the difference ? After two daughters are born to you, you are fixated on begetting a male child. Do you think a daughter is a veritable curse to her parents ? Subhas grew irritated.

"No, father, I never think like that. A tree never denies to bear another fruit although it is overladen. Moreover a daughter is more helpful than a son. So I don't have any scruple if I shall be blessed with a daughter the next time. Smita remonstrated.

Why are you worried about this gestation then ? Subhas calmly asked his daughter.

"My husband desperately wants a son. He got scared and scanned this pregnancy to know the sex of the child. During my first trimester of preganancy, the doctor was equivocal and gave some unfavourable hints. I could not restrain my curiosity and debating so many times, finally I decided to come to your place for confirmation." Smita opened her mind.

"I am not in favour of that. Your husband is quite averse to female child. If his cherished dream will be shattered, he may go crazy to terminate it. I shall be happy if your child remains unscathed in the womb and I hope, you will not resort to any dastardly design to nip it in the bud. My youngest daughter and her husband were ecstatic when they were blessed with a daughter. They doled out sweets to the neighbours. Is it not a real eye-opener for you?" Subhas prodded the core of her heart.

For a few minutes Smita relapsed into silence and then said, "I don't know what life holds in store for me. I pray to God day and night to fulfil my yearning desire. She heaved a sigh of despair.

"O, don't be so much disappointed. If fortune favours. I shall name it Sandip, the name I conceive at the outset and in case of opposite, I shall name it Sonali keeping coherence with your other two daughters, Papali and Mamali."

"Father, are you a great fan of Sonali Bendre, the popular actress of Hindi Screen ?" asked Smita.

"You don't know the enormous charisma of your daughter. Sonali, the golden hue, will one day definitely dignify your home."

A fortnight later, she went back broken-hearted. The doctor gave her fair warning that it was, no doubt, risky to terminate the child during the second trimester of pregnancy. Her husband was not mentally prepared to welcome the fatherhood of third child and that too a female. Without rhyme or reason, he was found irascible. So at last Smita surrendered to her husband's caprices.

As there was no one to bear a helping hand, Subhas and his wife went there the next morning.

A lady gynaecologist, reputed far and wide for her skilful hand, agreed to terminate it with great hesitation. She gave a date of appointment and without undue delay, they rushed to the Nursing home.

Subhas looked fraught with incoming disaster. It had been gnawing at him for days. He feared the worst as the gestation period was about eighteen weeks.

In the evening when all the arrangements were made, medicines and injections were administered to her. Half an hour later an excruciating pain started. The fierce bout made her writhing and tossing in bed. Subhas tried to flinch away from that pitiable sight while he was consumed with fear.

In the mean time, the lady doctor entered the cabin and measured her blood pressure. Smita screamed and groaned like a beast as if her throat had been constricted by a vice.

"It is just the beginning, as the time speeds by, the more intense will be your pain", the doctor warned her.

Her limit of tolerance gave way.

'Mother, I am dying", her face contorted with agonising pain.

She started raving and sometimes became delirious. But there was no way to deaden her pain. Subhas, a silent spectator, had nothing to do except pacing up and down the room praying fervently to God.

The pain continued unabated. For a brief period, she was lying motionless. No groaning was heard. Perhaps his daughter was no more in this mortal world, thought Subhas. He felt his heart flip . After a few minutes, her body terribly convulsed. Beads of sweat trickled down profusely on her face and it was racked with pain. She clenched her teeth, creased her forehead to overcome the pain. At about 3.30 P.M. she gave birth to a steel-born child. It was aborted but the placenta retained. Subhas hysterically thumped the door where the nurse remained watchful lying on her bed. She immediately sprang up, left the door ajar and rushed to the cabin.

She managed to remove the retained placenta to the great relief of Subhas and his wife. The pain seeped away . The gale blowing all through the night now abated.

The lady doctor reappeared, measured the blood pressure and instructed a nurse to give her an intravenous injection. She sat in front of Subhas, closed her eyes for some moments and seemed to be lapsed into brooding silence. She slowly opened her eyes and said, "It was an intractable problem. Her frail body could not withstand such continuous pain. I tried my best to dissuade them from doing such inhuman act. Since your son-in-law is quite obstinate,I am being compelled to do such unpleasant thing."

Smita's husband stood like a statue and listened quietly what the lady doctor said to them.

The next morning they got ready for return journey. They reserved a van to avoid jolting and rattling over the rough road. Smita lay sprawled on the comfortable seat resting her head on the lap of her mother. The van shuddered to a halt near their residence. Surama held her daughter's hand and ushered her very carefully into the bed room.

The nurse had draped the aborted child with a white rag. It was blood-soaked and kept aside in a corner. They could not decide in their confused mind what to do with that. But Smita shrieked, "No mother, if we leave it here. they will bin it with some garbage and the stray dogs will savagely devour it. Let not the deadbody of my child be left here carelessly. What she said had a logic and they packed it in a bag to be buried.

Some relatives huddled together with considerable anxiety to see the dead child. They unfolded the bundle, and were taken aback when they saw a lump of flesh there. As it was laid crumpled inside the bundle, they fondly spread its hands and legs. The tiny head tilted to one side and its puffy eyes were seen closed as though in profound austerity. A delicate flower was lying there having been trampled under some ruthless feet. Its tender body was smudged red with blood which moved Subhas to tears.

"You did not allow me to survive. My gender is the root cause of my untimely death, let your wishes be fulfilled", the child seemed to whisper.

There was none to dig a pit to bury the dead body beneath the ground. Though worn out owing to night vigil, Subhas was ready to do it. He dug out the hard soil with a spade.

A neighbour came and took the spade from his hand.

He began to dig the pit deeper. The burial was completed. The man piled a few tufts of grass to cover the pit completely. When that harrowing sight flashed before Subhas's eyes, it made him dizzy. He had been in the doldrums ever since the child fell victim to barbarity.

Feelings of guilt seared him for several days . He too shared this unpardonable sin for he could have dissuaded them from doing such heinous deeds. Why did he keep mum? Why did he not forbid them to help flourish the child unhampered ? Could he deny the fact that he was not an accomplice in that crucifixion ?

While going to the toilet, Subhas cast a look in the direction of that site where the child had been buried. Suddenly he felt himself under the spell of some strange hallucination. The earth rent asunder and the child scrambled over the pit being resuscitated. It came toddling and uttered in a feeble voice, "Nana, would you not hug me to your bosom? Do you loathe me like my father ? What's the fault of mine that the path of my progress was impeded and I was forcibly put to death ?"

The silhouette of the child disappeared and he stood glued to that delusion. A number of days passed but he still had nightmares about it.

Man has become abysmally unscrupulous. His mental prostration has reached its culminating point. Refined sentiments and feelings have been all distorted and he has been demeaned to a hollow man. It seems as if evil has been embodied in him.

Subhas envisaged from a vantage ground where the world was heading for. He knew that in this humourless, brutal world he was to encounter fundamental good and fundamental evil. He was to wage ceaseless war against all perverted sensibilities, wipe out the primordial, predatory lust which has overpowered the whole human race.

Such are the tortuous ways of the mundane world .

Subhas fell lamentably on the thorns of life and bled, still for the fallen man, a prayer undulated in his heart :

"Let my life fall perpetually in the quagmire of hell but let this world be delivered."

It was the witching hour of mid night. Sleep came to him in brief snatches . There was a knock on the door. He awoke with a start .

"Would you please open the door ?'

The voice was too familiar and intimate . With a heaving heart he removed the latch. The door flung open. He peered into the pitch-dark.

'We are all here , Nana."

"Who are you my dear ?" he asked, eyes wide open with wonder.

"Don't you recognise us ? I am Mithu Nana, your loving grand-son."

"We are Papali, Mamali and Gehli, your loving grand-daughters."

"Where is Sonali?"

"She would not turn up. She is now in a shady retreat of an exotic land where one dare not trespass."

"Coming,Nana?"

"No,no,stay away, please."

"Why ?"

"I always keep memory of dear ones in the dark recesses of my mind. Your brief absence heightens my pain. I have been stoic from the beginning but your serene faces have a hypnotic spell which allures me and my mission of life fails there. You look precisely the same to me for which I am unable to discern that pretty difference . Your voices seem sometimes identical and I keep staring at your faces in utter amazement. All blended together-verily a bunch of delicate flowers of that family tree."

Then mingled in the air those voices as they came .

His eyes could penetrate the darkness. At a distance was

flickering the light of a hovel. A few glow-worms were blinking here and there. The houses enveloped in the dark looked like pre-historic mammoths. He shifted his gaze and looked at the vast arena of the sky . A lonely star was winking at him.

"Nana I am here,please look at me."

It was Sonali's -a voice of taciturnity.

He closed his eyes half . A shaft of soothing beam came instantly from that far-off star and merged with his gaze.

Then everything disappeared from his sight . He stooped to the ground and began to grope about in the dark to catch something from the air. Was it a lack of complacency or lust for life? he confused. He ran his hand vaguely through his hair. Inside him , he felt something struggling to well up- something repressed billowing to spurt out . He was to trace a secluded spot in some corner of this vast world where , without interruption , he would be able to shed tears to relieve himself from pent-up agonies. Perhaps he woud be woe- begone for the rest of his life.

He could not see anything for a moment. Before him , stood a lonesome ageless night leaning forward to pour something untold and unheard-of in his ears.

GLOSSARY

Baba -Saint

Babu -a respectful address, title of a Hindu gentleman equivalent to Mr.

Banku bhai - Comedian in the dance of Chadeha chadehani.

Barada -The eldest son of Thakur Anukul Chandra, a great devotee.

Bhai-a brother

Bhavi -Sister-in-law,

Bhang-hemp-leaves used as an intoxicating drug.

Chapati-a kind of bread.

Dehuri -a village priest.

Dhoti -a loose garment, long piece of cloth worn round the loins by males.

Didi -generally addressed to elder sister.

Da -contraction of "Dada' means Elder brother

Gotra -lineage

Guru bhai - co-disciple of the same guru or religious preceptor.

Jagannath Dham - a place of pilgrimage in the state of Orissa Where Lord Jagannath is worshipped.

Kalasa -water-jar, pitcher

Kendu -a fruit bearing tree.

Kalamb -an aquatic plant, bind weed

Kaajal -Collyrium.

Kurchi -a sweet scented flowering plant.

Luchi -Thin cake of flour fried in boiling ghee.

Lungi -a loose, long piece of cloth hanging from the waist.

Mridanga - an egg shaped drum

Mahul - Mahua tree.

Mantra -incantation, spell, hymn or verse in praise of some deity.

Nana -Priest, maternal grand -father

Pranam -obeisance, bend one's head to (as a token of respect)

Rittik -Priest, one who initiates (a disciple) into a form of religious practice.

Sitahar -a flowering tree.

Sadhak -a devotee, a worshipper.

Yogasan-Proper posture or position for abstract meditation.

BAYING AT THE MOON

by

Dr L.K. Singh Babu

"To
My Wife
Who Furnished Me
with
Materials To
Write This Novel"

AUTHOR'S NOTE

A time comes when a man thinks his days are numbered and his journey to the other world is drawing nigh. But God desires something else.

About a year ago, when I was in fine fettle, I had completed two-thirds of this novel. The irony is that when I volunteered to give something unasked to literature, my health broke down. Though I bust a gut to finish it on time, my body did not allow me to proceed. My condition became worse and it seemed to me an insuperable barrier. I was starved and tormented day and night in that intellectual deprivation. Though some nitpickers have been slugging me off, I am impervious to their harassment and criticism as I know damn well their inadequacies. I am not a man to acknowledge defeat. It is a personality trait bestowed upon me by God. In spite of impediments galore, I trudged along that murky path to get to my destination.

There are a few persons who are just figments and their contribution is no less significant to spruce up this novel. The other characters in this expose are real and it is based on the plain unvarnished truth. I have narrated all those incidents which actually happened in my life. I have changed their names on purpose not to besmirch their social stature.

Though some characters wilted and withered unexpectedly, their memory has been etched on my heart and that will remain unfading till my last breath.

This novel is a fusion of my bitter experiences and inner psychic reactions to sufferings and sufferers. From a vantage point when I observe the way of the world, very often I question myself, " Is everything we do is preordained ? The reply I receive is always equivocal. I think my conclusion (if I have come to) on this controversial issue still remains a moot point. Similar complicated questions, intriguing and relevant in this context, which sometimes jumble my mind, remain insoluble. Being inquisitive I fumble around looking for that open sesame. But I get completely lost in the maze, searching frantically for that much sought-after thing. Like many other mysterious things this too poses enigmatic and I have been hunting for the clues for its consummate solutions and the hunt is on. I am keen to keep my quest unhampered and unremitting.

Life itself is a novel. I discern no such glaring discrepancy between the two. As novel reveals a panoramic picture of day-to-day events of the world, it is inextricably linked with life or bound up with each other. It is a true mirror on which the harsh realities of life is reflected.

I have seen many hollow braggarts who are pleasure seekers and bone idle. But they jeer at the creative ideas of others.

This novel has not been created from my morbid imagination nor it is my momentary freak or frivolity, but it has evolved from my genuine emotion and nostalgia.

I am really obliged to those, who, by their concerted effort made all the factors conducive for the novel to see its dream come true.

ONE

Baripada bus-stand. After a tedious journey from Bhubaneswar to Baripada, ultimately the bus glided to a terminal point and shuddered to a halt. Chinmay always loathed a long journey. But under pressure he could not avoid. He was getting browned off with this delay.

It was evening and the surrounding areas were all illuminated by bright lights. The helper shouted to make the passengers alert to get down there. Chinmay rose up from his seat when all the passengers alighted with their belongings. He stepped down slinging his bag on his shoulder. He was a bit in a brown study while passing through the exit where vendors had spread out their wares to draw the attention of the customers. He just browsed through the little shops and came to a book-stall where he became enthusiastic to buy a worthreading book. There was no such book to appease his taste. But to kill time, he bought 'The Adventures of Robinhood'. He grew a trifle nostalgic when he recollected his salad days and started 'hero-worship' as it happens in almost all the cases of teen-aged boys and girls. In those days he was very fond of detective stories and especially the character of Robin and his younger brother Ratan, depicted in those stories influenced him most. His hero looted the property of well-heeled and doled them out among the poor. Although he was a wanted criminal in the eyes of law, he was note-worthy and the poor spoke highly of him. The impact of his commendable work found a niche in his young heart and he, with the help of a piece of chalk, wrote down 'This is Robin's house' on all the doors and walls of his house.

"Any other novel or fiction?" He asked the stall-keeper.

"No, sir, we don't keep those books as nobody is interested to read. Why should I invest money unprofitably on that?"

He was peeved when he thought about the mentality of such people and their ways of thinking. They spend pointlessly on unnecessary things but they won't spare a single pie to purchase a readable book. That galls him most.

Damn them. He was seething inwardly but could not articulate his thoughts or feelings. They don't know who are hooked on books, they derive exquisite pleasure. He takes pity on those pleasure-seekers who are averse to book-reading.

As he walked edging his way through the milling crowd lost in thought, somebody called him from behind. Jayram came out of a tea-stall spotting him from a distance. He stood there waiting for him.

"Hi, Chinmay ! Where have you been to ?" He stared at him with some sort of inquisitiveness.

" I had been to Bhubaneswar on some urgent matter. Just got down from the bus".

"Are you in a hurry ?" Jayram asked, "If not, come with me to that restaurant over there to have a cup of tea".

They entered the restaurant and occupied two seats. It was not so crowded. Jayram ordered for two cups of tea and looked at Chinmay's face thoughtfully. After a brief pause he said.

"I have been a little disconcerted for our family affairs. You know my elder brother, how work-shy he is ! He would always brush off his responsibility to somebody else. Takes more than one hour to shave and dress up himself, gobble up his food and goes out at full tilt. My sister-in-law too dawdles and follows suit, does something pressurized by my mother." Jayram's forehead furrowed with disappointment.

"Why do your mother keep mum when a daughter-in-law whiles away her time sitting indolent on a cozy bed ?" Chimay said. Then he continued, "Yours is a joint family. If you don't work unitedly, everything will be delayed. Moreover it is a collective responsibility of all."

"My younger sister is a service holder. She leaves briskly at 10.00a.m. to attend the office. Sometimes she goes without lunch as the food cannot be prepared on time". Jayram tried to hide his discomfiture.

From his early school days, Chinmay had been in close nexus with their family members. On every festive occasion, they would invite him and treat him indiscriminately as one of them. He used to be at all times informal in their unassuming company. They would ask him about the health of his wife and children and often implored him to visit their house with his family.

Jayram set the tea cup on the table and throwing a vacant look said, "There is a constant row over this issue which really vitiated the atmosphere of our home. I don't know how to set right the matter". He pressed his lower lip and said, "You please come to have a candid discussion to find a solution to our problem else I will go off my head if such turmoil continues for long". He clenched his fist in frustration.

Chinmay noticed clearly a gossamer of despair had enveloped his pallid face and at that moment, he looked older than he was. He feels drowsy whenever he begins to think anything seriously. In that besotted state he scrabbles about to find a solution, a conciliation which mediates opposite forces into one.

Time and again he had seen Jayram's Kins-folk come down on his sister-in-law with surly hostility. A fierce altercation swept the house for a brief period. They were unaware of the problem they had caused at home and were locked in stalemate. Nobody simmered down to bring a reconciliation. Jayram, with folded hand, would cringe before them to restore peace. Defeated in that slanging match, Jayram's sister-in-law would cry bitterly burying her head between her knees and start cursing her parents and inlaws while ranting and raving about their atrocity.

He thought them to be draconian and grew sympathetic to that woman having no prop there to support her. Her husband, slammed the door when this brawl would be going on. He had no patience to glean such absolute drivel. Of the three sisters, the eldest one got married in some distant place but after a few years, her husband died in a car accident and being tortured at her father-in-law's house came back to her parental house to have a safe haven. The other two remained unmarried upto their old age. Chinmay knew the grim situation of a daughter-in-law where inlaws made a pact to wage an unending war against a helpless one.

He boggled at the idea of spending so much time in their meaningless squabble and made an excuse to slip away from that place. He was held up for nothing as every one wanted him to be an eye-witness to prove his innocence. The less involvement, the better – he thought.

Chinmay was toying with the cup revolving it on the smooth surface of the table. His reverie broke up when Jayram gave him a friendly pat and shuffled across the room to boot the bill.

"You have had a long journey. You must be tired", he said. "But don't forget to see me the next evening". Then he turned, waved his hand and was lost in the milling crowd.

The whole afternoon Chinmay kept puttering around his house. His body was sore and he badly wanted a cup of steaming tea with ginger juice. His wife immediately responded and began to prepare it in the kitchen. The flavour of tea came wafting through the air. He yawned and sat up on his bed suspending his legs on the floor. He took the cup and sipped it comfortably. The curling smoke and its sweet fragrance filled his nostrils.

The evening deepened. Slipping into his dress he came out. There stood an electric lamp post just in front of their house casting its yellowish light on the metalled road. Countless interminable insects whizzing around the bulb and their split shadows hovering around the platform of the lamp-post always evoked a strange feeling in his heart. He shifted his gaze and tramped along the road.

Chinmay stood stock-still for a moment at their gateway. A jumbled noise was coming from the interior. He got into the bed room where Jayram's sister-in-law was sitting in a sulky mood. All around her, squatted Jayram's mother and sisters. He noticed her untidy and unfurled hair at a little distance. She rolled her flowing hair muttering something indistinctly. She cast her look viciously, a fierce malice was gleaming in them.

"Who are you ? Why are you so much sore at us ?" Jayram's mother supplicatingly asked her with folded hands.

"I am the presiding deity of your house who has not been properly worshipped for a number of days. Why should I remain in this terrible mess ? I went neglected for which you have to pay a heavy price for the dereliction of duty." She threatened them gnashing her teeth.

"All merciful mother ! don't be cross with us. From this day on, we must worship you according to shastric edicts." They all prostrated on the ground.

"Don't take this as her silly babbling. Be on your guard. She is no other than our presiding deity. The Goddess has come over her and no more your sister-in-law." Jayram's mother warned them.

Jayram observed her abnormality from a distance. He never gave credence to absurdity and bawled out, "Baseless, I don't believe this hearsay that a woman can ever be possessed by some goddess. You people believe and are easily duped as you are all steeped in superstitions." The other members seemed to ridicule his rational approach to the issue.

His mother immediately shut his mouth with her hand indicating him to be totally silent.

"What should I do in this baffling situations, please tell me ?" Jayram asked his mother finding him in a sticky position.

"Go with Chinmay to some exorcist. I know one Mohammedan exorcist, who lives somewhere at the station bazaar and can do something to rid her from this evil spell."

They paused a little while thoughtfully and then went off.

The exorcist got down from the rickshaw and stood immovable at the entrance pressing his right nostril with his finger for a moment and then entered the inner compartment.

"Bring some red china rose and a brand new earthen pitcher from the market. I shall put that evil spirit into that pitcher and bury it in the ground."

The exorcist had long matted hair on his back. He ran his hand across it and then took out a pouch containing tobacco from his pocket. He rolled some tobacco with lime on his palm and tucked it in his mouth.

He nudged them and said, "Hurry up, please".

They fetched all the necessary things from the market as required by the exorcist. Jayram was profusely sweating. He looked disgusted and said. "Collecting all these sundries was such a palaver, I would never do it again". Chinmay pressed his hand to relax him.

Whiff of incense and resin permeated the room. Chinmay came out as his eyes began to smart and he felt himself suffocated. He observed the ongoing action of the exorcist from the threshold. Towards the last part of the Puja he peremptorily commanded the woman to hold a copper vessel on her head and drew a line near the threshold with flour and some other assorted things like red china rose, vermilion etc. The woman rushed upto that spot and fell unconscious.

Their horror now laced with fear. Her entire body went

rigid. All bustled about the room when her unconscious body was carried and placed on a bedstead. Somebody arranged her tousled hair and splashed cold water on her face.

Jayram stared at the exorcist and asked questioning the integrity of his magic power, "Will she come to her normalcy?"

"Definitely. I am not a charlatan. I have dispelled that evil spirit and it will no more bother her." The exorcist said with his usual aplomb.

Her husband knew that she was amazingly resilient and she will get over it in a few days. She will recuperate her mental health if not slated by family members. The exorcist had stowed the earthen pitcher beneath the ground and the spirit remained captive in that dungeon.

Jayram's father hailed from Bihar Province. When he was a school going child, his mother accidentally died of pneumonia. His father married again, a choleric lady who often fell out over some trifling matters. She was haughty and for no reason treated the children with an iron hand. In that chaotic situation, Jayram's father could not fare well in the H.S.C. Examination. His step-mother took him to be a trashy and unproductive. As he was a constant eye-sore to her, she cut down the expenditure of his education virtually creating a financial barricade all around him.

On that fateful day, when he was preparing himself to appear at the examination second time, his step-mother sensed his audacity and came out of her bed room. "You son of a stinking bitch, how do you venture to do the same thing without caring a fig for my repeated warnings ?"

She flew into a rage, snatched his books from his hands and threw them into a gutter. Jayram's father saw a swarm of glow-worms floating before his eyes. His father, a silent onlooker, did not come to his rescue. Then he deserted his home, worked in some book-binding shop, scrubbed dishes in hotels, tutored small children to earn a pittance and at night took shelter on the verandah of a deserted building. Many loathed his acrid stench of his destitution and he became an object of mercy. He was down-and-out and wandered here and there to seek a fortune. He turned a globe-trotter. Fortune did not smile upon him. He did every thing mechanically, knocked on every door but no door opened wide to give him an entry in this unfriendly world.

Finally he came to Odisha and settled at Baripada. A civil contractor gave him shelter and engaged him in his work. He gave him a helping hand. The protector was happy with his work. He gave his only daughter in marriage to him. As he had grown old, he entrusted the young man with all the responsibility. His devotion to work placed him on a firm footing.

Nobody questioned him about his caste. From some reliable sources, it was known that he was born in a cobbler family. At the beginning, his neighbouring people treated him as an outsider but as the days rolled on, his modest behaviour won their heart and they did not cudgel their brains as to his antecedents or whereabouts. His past history was buried in oblivion.

The meteoric rise of Jayram's father was enviable. His sufferings in the past equipped him with a daring spirit and he strode on with an iron-will to achieve his desired goal – to establish his family on a solid ground. When his children were not old enough to stand on their feet, unfortunately he died of heart attack. His untiring work at the work-site had an effect on his health. He died but left no viable savings to sustain his family. Jayram's mother did not lose her mental stability. She took the bull by the horns. She inherited this characteristic trait from her father. With dogged determination and undaunted zeal, she tried to get through this sudden disaster. She procured a stitching machine at a low price. The people, acquainted with her, extended their sympathetic hands and as her charge was very reasonable, she got orders from a number of people. Her sedulous effort to earn a living was crowned with success. However, they survived, otherwise they would have to roam with a begging bowl.

"Let's go to my bed room", Jayram dragged chinmay's hand. He drew a chair for him and said, "If you get to the root of all these turmoils, I hold my mother and sisters solely accountable for that. My mother could have instructed her to do the household chore in a soft voice, cajoling her into agreeing to do the work. She is sometimes authoritarian and no daughter-in-law has that forbearance to tolerate the domineering attitude. All mothers-in-law have been indoctrinated from their early age that a daughter-in-law must stoop and she is expected to carry out orders without scruples at the cost of her freedom. They grow up with this idea. This matriarchy, mother being the head of the family is an anachronism today and no more in vogue. That is despised by daughters-in-law at present as they don't like highhandedness, this overbearing attitude to bully them. They will no longer be subservient to their mothers-in-law to remain in perpetual servitude. We are in an epoch of massive change. The bondage of women must, ofcourse, go."

Chinmay wiped sweat from his face with a handkerchief and said, "These are all social evils deeply embedded in our mind. They should be eliminated."

Jayram's elder sister Ruby entered the room and said, "I overheard your conversation. Don't blame us injudiciously as you both are oversympathetic to that woman. Do you think there would be fire without smoke ? Do you think that woman is quite guiltless and we are always found at fault ?"

"Don't butt in while we are having some pleasantries". Jayram grew a little irritated.

"No, we must seek a solution. Now it is expedient to arrange your marriage soon. Some people have sent their daughters' horoscopes for matching. My mother thinks after marriage the problem will be lessened to a certain extent". Rubi was assertive.

"No, I won't marry. It would be like adding fuel to the fire". Jayram said impatiently.

"Do you find any wrong in marriage ? If the girl is sober and sociable and knows how to pay respect to others there would be no trouble". Rubi tried to heal the mental wound of her brother.

"No, you can't say with certainty. I would say marriage is a game of chance. If you are lucky enough, you may get a good girl, otherwise she may put a slur on your family. She would remain a permanent stigma which can't be erased so easily. When we get a girl who is diametrically opposite of your ideals and temperament, we can't cope with, although we are always compromising. People say 'marriages are settled in heaven'. It is a wrong conception because it is made by earthlings. They say because there is no alternative, no option other than compromise with unfavourable circumstances". Chinmay discoursed gazing up at Rubi.
"So you say that we always compromise. We live our lives on compromise ?" Rubi asked sceptically.

"No doubt, we invite miseries if we don't compromise. It is made bilaterally. What I mean, we compromise with each other. Life speeds off in this manner albeit we stumble frequently while going along that uneven path".

"But your wife Maya complains as both of you are uncompromising. You are an amateur and passionate writer. You depict and analyze the character of man and woman in your writing. If one observes your practical life, one may think you a pseudo-moralist. You preach something, do something else. Your actions are at variance with your words." Rubi tried to injure his ego.

"Yes, I do admit. But remember that I am not an exception. I too have lacunas and short comings. When we are in the sub-human stage, we are steeped in ignorance which is the root cause of all evils. Attaining human stage, we do everything that is humanly possible not harming the ego of others. Proper development of personality must be our ultimate aim. Lopsided development is of no use to us.

From birth till death, we go through different phases of life. We pick up truth and after assimilation, we try to practise it in our personal life. We can't say how far it would be practicable. This much I can say, try to be 'humane', there is no harm at all".

"You have started to preach us sermons", Rubi grinned.

"Whatever you say, I won't mind. There should be a reciprocation between husband and wife nourishing each other. They are like co-workers. So a rapproachment is to be established.

I ascribe less importance to afflictions. My strong conviction is that my body suffers but my soul remains detached. I feel a sense of detachment from what is happening around me."

"I interrupt you. Why do you mention soul here?" Rubi grew inquisitive. She tried to make her Conversation not to be stilted.

"I am not a platitudinarian, So don't take it a philosophical prank. I recall an accident occurred a few years back. I was going on my bicycle to bring some fruits. Unfortunately an untrained tempo driver knocked my cycle from behind. I lost my balance and fell headlong on the railway line. For a moment, I could not understand what happened to me, remained for the nonce in a dazed state when a young man rushed to me and dragged my hands to make me stand straight. I ran my hand on all sides of my body and found that my left palm and knees have been bruised and some blood was welling out from the wound. The fruit-seller, I am acquainted with, came running with band-aids and immediately stuck them on my wounds. At that moment I experienced pain in a lesser degree though the wounds were smarting and painful. I said to myself, "Your material body has been injured but it has not touched your soul. It remained unscathed". A strange feeling crept into my mind and I became least concerned about my injury".

Chinmay asked for a glass of water and drank it. Then he continued, " I am narrating another intriguing fact which remains in my mind till today. Once I was in a state of meditation sitting cross-legged on the floor. A pangolin came flying and hovered with buzzing sound over my right thigh. As I was in the initial state of meditation, I came to my senses and opened my eyes. The bee on the spur of the moment landed on my thigh and then it burrowed deep into my skin. It went deeper and penetrated the deep fascia. I could easily fend that bee off.

But I was curious enough to feel the reaction of soul. It was a rare opportunity to go through that experience. I immediately shot up from my material plane to a higher plane (spiritual plane) I became totally indifferent to pain. Then I descended and came to the physical plane. The bee was still there trying to go deeper. I felt excruciating pain and blood was trickling from the wound. I squeezed the wound and the bee died there. I was really horrified. With great difficulty I removed it from the wound as it firmly implanted itself in that fleshy hole. It healed up but the scar was still there on my right thigh".

For some house work Rubi left her seat reluctantly. Jayram spun the chair to face Chinmay directly and asked, "I accept your philosophy halfheartedly. Would you tell me the reason why you often remain in an abnormal state?"

"This happens when I am absorbed in writing. A writer creates his own world. He lives on a higher plane. He speaks his own language. The people around him can't understand him. I am often forced to come down from that higher plane to talk with the people. Once you are on a higher plane, you don't want to come down to the physical plane. You want to lounge about there for a prolonged period, you experience a rare pleasure, an unadulterated pleasure and pleasure only.

There is neither remorse nor repentance nor any illusions and delusions which generally confound us in this materialistic world".

All were in a bedlam. There was an edgy calm in their house. A hush descended over the family. Everybody was moving and doing things silently. The crux of the problem was the unruly daughter-in-law. The consensus of opinion in their family was to send her to her parental house for a few months. Jayram's elder brother was tight-lipped as his meddling in this matter would invite a vitriolic attack on him, accusing him of shielding his refractory wife. His sisters warned him not to visit his father-in-law's house on the sly and keep a tryst with his wife. They were under the impression that he was under his wife's thumb. She wore the breeches and her husband waltzed dictated by his wife. They chortled with glee thinking over her wretched life in the parental house segregated from husband. She would now taste the bitter fruit of banishment and drift away afar for she would not find a safe mooring any where, a cloistered existence.

Though Chinmay had tried to aver her innocence, he dreaded their counter-attack. It would be judicious to remain silent, he thought.

It was past midnight. Chinmay came out of their house. He gazed up at the open sky. Encircled by a hazy beam the pale moon had risen and a few blinking stars in that circle seemed to brood over the distressing condition of humanbeings. There were some high rise office buildings to the left side of Jayram's house and in their congealed shadow, the silhouette of his sister-in-law remained crouched scattering her flowing tresses, stalking to pounce upon her enemies.

As he trudged homewards, a kennel of stray dogs were brawling over some leftover foods by the road side thrown by a marriage party. A weaker one admitting its defeat in that sparring match scuttled off limping with its hind legs and disappeared into the dark alley. To the left, in the vicinity of a mosque, a liquor-shop was still crowded at that dead hour of night. A middleaged man of swarthy complexion, the owner of the shop, was shouting over the din of the crowd to serve the customers roasted brain, egg roll and mutton flourishing his hands to the waiters. He had worn a gold chain and it was ostentatiously swinging on his striped shirt. Outside the shop, on a cemented floor, two to three persons lay sprawled being inebriated and they would lie spread-eagled there till morning with slavering mouth inviting a swarm of flies to feast on them. They lay slap-happy being quite indifferent to their surroundings. The pungent smell of liquor was floating in the air. Chinmay stopped breathing till he passed across that spot. He felt himself rat-arsed when he inhaled that air. It was nauseating and he stepped down a nearby tank to wash his face. Then he headed on towards his home.

TWO

"Have you ever read the Ramayan written by Krittibas, a devout poet of Bengal. Of course it has been written in Bengali. Do you know Bengali ?" asked Chinmay's maternal grand-father when he was twelve-year old and studying in class seven.

His grand-father's idea was that a 'Vidyarthi must have known that language other than Odia. The old man handed him that holy scripture and said, "Read out from the beginning, absorbing, indeed".

He touched his forehead with folded hands and sat cross-legged before Chinmay. His grand-mother overheard their conversation and came out of the worshipping room. She sat a few steps away on the fleecy coat of an antelope, a sacred asan and kept gazing at Chinmay, full of veneration. Chinmay, was, no doubt, in a very embarrassing situation. He flicked through the book, saw Ram and Sita sitting on a royal throne with a sceptre over their heads, at the first page of the book. He withdrew his attention and looked witlessly at his grand-parents.

"What's the matter" ? asked his grand-father.

"I... I don't know Bengali". He drawled.

"O, it doesn't matter, my son. Learn that language. Then you will read the Mahabharat by Kasi Das, another devout poet of Bengal. Besides this, I have kept eighteen Puranas in store for you. When you grow up, you will read those holy scriptures".

His grand parents lived in a remote village, surrounded by a vast stretch of paddy fields and to its eastern side, flowed a rivulet which, after meandering a long distance, merged with the river Budhabalang. There were a few houses clustered together, some scattered at a little distance, all peasants who toiled through thick and thin to earn their moderate living. On a festive occasion, they would participate in this get-together and share the pleasure of rejoicings. They would exchange their ideas regarding various aspects of the function and bat around to celebrate the festival more pompously the next year.

When crops of wide variety grew abundantly on all sides of the village, it looked like a small island fenced by a green belt. There was a riot of greenness everywhere. His aesthetic sense sprouted right from his adolescence stage. The ripples of the flowing river, the ceaseless chirping of birds, the serenity of lush green forest, the sweet aroma of blooming flowers in different seasons, the picturesque sight of clouds, the soothing effect of the moon beam, the rustling of green foliage always had a meaningful message to him. During holidays, he would slip to that village to enjoy the tranquil beauty of nature. He would ramble through the green fields, to be lost in its bountiful profusion and entranced solitude and he was thrilled with infinite rapture.

Back to town, he bought a booklet containing alphabets of three languages i.e., Odia, Bengali and Hindi arrayed in a systematic way. He explored the nuances of the language.It was a sort of self-taught booklet which enabled him to identify the letters of Bengali and thereby read vigorously whatever the book or magazine came to his hand.

His grandfather suffered a lot in his youthful days. He was then a married man but not in the good books of his father. He was very often assaulted by his father as his brothers instigated the old man to bring him to book. The grand old man had earned fame for his notoriety. If he found his servants slackened in farm work or if he found them disobedient, he would tie them to a coconut tree with a rope and flog them mercilessly till they admitted their faults.

Without getting a frail support from any one,Chinmay's grand father's patience ran out and eventually he fled from his house to save his skin. He took shelter on the branches of some trees at night remaining vigilant being scared of his aggressive opponent. Nobody could recognize him as he went unshaven and untrimmed for months. Then the wandering monk went on a pilgrimage. His father-in-law, of course, hunted every conceivable place to trace him out. For about two years he remained absconded. At last he was found out at 'Ananda Bazaar', Puri, when he was eating offerings of Lord Jagannath seated in the midst of itinerant beggars. His long mop of hair and bearded chin kept him unrecognizable. He was dragged to a saloon and tidied up. But his misfortune did not end there. Long before he had been forced by his brothers to sign an agreement paper not to claim his ancestral property in the future. In the nick of time his brother-in-law came to save his bacon and with much strenuous effort in some way he settled him there. In his last days his father was repentant for his past deeds but it was unproductive, for the sins he committed were unpardonable.

Chinmay's grand father had never that spunk to revolt against his father. He remained meek and mild all through his life. The undeniable truth is God-fearing and devout persons suffer a crushing defeat in their struggle for existence.

His was a mud-built house with a thatched roof. It was a large one and could accommodate a big family. There was no other person except a maid-servant and two farm workers, very faithful and obedient to their master. The old grand parents depended on them for every household work. In the early morning the workers would go to the fields holding a sal or neem twig in their mouth and drive the bullocks towards work-site while brushing their teeth.

In winter, they collected dried faggots to burn them in a make-shift hearth to protect them from cold and drove the mosquitoes from the cow-shed. At night they lay around it enjoying a comfortable sleep.

The land which Chinmay's grandfather inherited was at first barren and unyielding, full of gravels. He made it arable and the sylvan goddess granted him a boon. He reaped a bumper crop that year. He began lending paddy to the needy and poor on some little interest. They repaid it double the next year. Chinmay's grand mother, a sagacious lady, was at the root of this rise to prosperity.

His grandmother's nephew (brother's son) Gandharva alias Gandhia often visited their country home accompanied by his wife when he got bored in town life. They had also a small patch of land in that village which he offered to some cultivator on share-cropping. The cultivator, after harvest, carried those crops to their house on his own bullock-cart and stored them up in their granary.

The winter was the suitable time for Gandhia's visit. He stayed in his own house which was at a walkable distance from his aunt's. Towards the last part of the night when it was still dark, he left his bed, brushed his teeth and hurried to his aunt's house. From the doorway he announced his presence and the servants who were gossiping among themselves sitting by the fire place, rushed to the door, removed the latch and opened the door wide to let him in. They greeted him and made him sit on a cot. Then he would instruct a servant boy to bring out a fowl from the coop. He peeled off its skin, dressed it well smearing it with spices dropping some amount of mustard oil. Placing a cooking-pot on burning fire, he would stir it with a ladle and wait until the curry was ready releasing a very appetizing smell. After that he put down the cooking pot by the fire place and gave away some meat on leaf-plates to the servants awaiting it. His aunt or uncle never touched fowl as it might desecrate their customary sanctity. Sometimes he borrowed somebody's bicycle and visited the local market, jostling through the crowd to buy a big chunk of pork though he knew he could not eat it alone. After eating his fill, he saved some for his dinner. His wife squabbled as she loathed his avarice for pork. He chuckled and persuaded her to taste once its gravy-soup with assurance that she would never forget it in her life time.

Half a kilometre away from his house, there were some milkmen living with their families keeping a herd of cows and buffaloes. They were pikey. Selling milk and curd was their chief occupation. They wandered around the neighbouring villages selling milk and ghee although wrangling sometimes arose regarding its purity.

One morning Gandhia was eating fried rice sitting on a cot in his courtyard. A milkmaid entered his compound pushing open the bamboo gate aside. Gandhia raised his head and kept looking at her with unblinking eyes. She placed the milkcan on the ground and asked, "Where is your wife? She asked me to bring her milk every day. I have come for that". "Can you hear me!" Gandhia called his wife. "The milkmaid has come".

His wife was busy separating the chaff from rice with a winnowing fan. She came out and smiled.

"I thought perhaps you have forgotten my words. All right. You now pour one litre of milk into this bottle". She handed the bottle to the milkmaid.

Gandhia's wife threw a few drops of milk on the ground to ascertain its purity. Then she fixed her gaze at the milkmaid and said, "You have mixed water in your milk, you see how it looks", She sounded grumpy.

The milkmaid pouted and said, "No sister, the milk would be like that as my cow gave birth to a calf a few days back. Why should I mix water when I sell it to a respectable lady".

"Listen. I am too born of a cultivator's family. We had

three milch cows in our shed which I used to milk every day. I can easily know what is what?" Gandhia's wife rebutted.

"Sister, you drink it today and curse me the next morning. I won't give you impure milk as money is not every thing. For a trifling fault, I can't show you my face any other day".

The milkmaid poured the milk into the bottle, lifted the milkcan on her head and turned to go at a leisurely pace.

Gandhia heard every word of the milkmaid and watched her swan-like gait. She was really well-built and her symmetrical body could entice even an old man. From the moment they met he was completely smitten by her. He remained under a spell for some moments and his eyes followed her till she disappeared in the next curve of the road. He shifted his gaze to the skeleton-like body of his wife and sighed.

The next morning Gandhia slipped into his dress and ran the comb through his hair standing before a mirror hung by a nail on the wall. His wife threw a glance at him and asked, "Where are you going?"

Gandhia scanned his face and put the comb in a niche and said, "Don't you see I am going on a morning walk. It is not proper to ask a person as to his destination when he is about to go somewhere". He was growing sore but curbed his resentment.

"If you find time, please go on a round to that milkmaid's house and watch what she is doing. We won't buy impure milk by paying a handful of money".

Gandhia laughed inside and shook his head. Now his wife herself showed him the way to reach his destination. He thought and laughed inaudibly. His mind began to stray to that milkmaid.

Gandhia had seen her house but never been a casual visitor. There was a well of laterite stones at a corner of their homestead land and it was fortified by a green fence. The cows and buffaloes had been sheltered under the roof of a shack where they were masticating hay from troughs tethered with ropes. The milkmaid was busy in sweeping away the dung from the floor and she was unconcerned about his sudden arrival. Gandhia hawked to draw her attention.

The milkmaid put down the broom and raised her head. She smiled. Gandhia too smiled back and tried to read the expression of her podgy face.

When she was swabbing the floor of the cowshed, she bent low and she did not know her boobs had been exposed to a vulnerable point. Like flies buzzing around the rotten things, Gandhia cast a covert glance at her and was caught with a lasso.

She drew his attention to her and said, "Master, you see this bucket. It is empty and I am milking the cows in your presence."

She untied the calf for some minutes. It sucked the teats of its mother and then she tied it to a nearby pole. The calf, sticking out its tongue, licked the frothy milk stuck to its mouth. She put the bucket on a small table and began to pour milk into a bottle.

"Now you see for yourself the quality of milk. I won't cheat any customer as we think them our goddess Lakshmi".

With a grin, she handed him the milk bottle.

He laughed in his mind and spoke out, "Yes, nobody can challenge the purity of your milk. If you maintain this, then…"

Her husband suddenly appeared on the scene carrying grass in a sack. He unloaded it from his shoulder, smiled and saluted him.

"I could not supply adequate fodder to our cattle, master. I have been to the river bank to mow the grass with a sickle. I was unmindful while stuffing the sack. I had a hair's-breadth escape from snake-bite as it lay hidden under the thick grass".

"Is it ?" his wife stood aghast and looked at her husband with dilated pupils. She shuddered with fear as if a venomous snake lay coiled up under some trough ready to snap at her leg in her unguarded moments.

Her husband left in haste for some urgent work. Gandhia was unwilling to leave the place so soon. Now the venom of that snake sparkled in his eyes. He turned to her and said, " I don't know your name nor your children either. But you see, I have talked so much time discussing so many things".

"Oh, that doesn't matter. I am Manjula but my pet name is Manju and everybody calls me by that name".

"What a beautiful name ! Manju….. Manju"- he repeated several times.

"Where are your children ?"

"I have one child, master, playing over there". She pointed to the place with her eyes.

"One child only, very good. His mouth tickled and he licked her voluptuous body with his eyes and said in jest, "Mother of one child, that is, of course, very good. Don't go further. You will rather go downhill making your body fragile and unattractive". He cackled in mischievous delight for he knew she would not be able to catch the purport of his saying.

She blushed and lowered her eyes. The trickster took her to be a moron but she was not born yesterday. Rather this dim-witted could not latch on to a woman's sixth sense.

How blockhead he is ! She pitied him for his foolhardiness.

Her husband was cuckolded. She was famished for so many days burning with irresistible passion. She felt herself randy and wanted to gratify her turbulent and riotous lust by a virile and goatish he-man which was long-repressed due to lack of opportunity. She found in Gandhia that real hunk who could fulfil all her desires.

Gandhia lingered a little on some pleas and then walked out through the gate. The milkmaid gazed at his receding image letting a deep sigh, and uttered in a low key 'coward'.

Chinmay appeared at the H.S.C. Examination. He fared

well and was confident that he would come out successful. A long vacation and no work to be occupied with. While in the humdrum of town life, he felt himself cooped up and breathless. He sought unspoilt calmness of the countryside to be relieved from this restlessness. The dingy room of his home could not provide him with that privilege.

He got off the bicycle and leaned it against a wall. His grand mother by that time was about to scurry to the river to have her bath. She was glad at his arrival and told him to wait at home till she came back after finishing her bathing.

He put his bag on a table and took out a framed picture of Lord Krishna. He wiped its surface with his handkerchief and handed her the picture of the Lord.

"Granny, you are a devotee of Lord Krishna, I know. Yesterday, when I was hanging around the market place, I caught sight of this picture, Krishna posing with a twist of head, waist and legs holding a flute in his hand. What a splendid picture ! granny. Do you like it ?"

She kept gazing at the picture reverentially and said, "Yes, my dear. Today I must hang it in our worshipping room. Most of the pictures of gods and goddesses are moth eaten. I have to replace some".

"You please sprinkle anti-termite. Otherwise in a year or two, it will be eaten away and only the glass cover will remain".

His grandmother went inside the kitchen to serve him breakfast.

"There is a cot in the backyard. Sit there and eat your breakfast". Then she pushed the postern open wide and stepped into the backyard.

A soothing breeze began to blow through the door. Chinmay ensconced himself by a pucca well onto the right side and close to it, a jasmine plant had been entwined with the branches of a pomegranate tree. The whole backyard was charged with the sweet fragrance of white tulip.

After breakfast he lay on the cot resting his head on a bolster. The moment his head touched the pillow, he fell asleep. A jarring voice disturbed his peaceful sleep. He turned his head and saw his uncle Gandhia coming. To him he was a bumpkin and an object of scorn. The moment he saw him, he wanted to break away. But Gandhia did not give him a chance to get out of his hold. He clutched his hand and made him sit longer on the cot.

"Chinmay dear, I am really expecting your arrival as your exam is now over. Here in this place I get bored finding no suitable companion. How many hours can you idle away twiddling your thumbs at home?"

"Yes, one can't deny that fact. A humanbeing needs a pleasant engagement. If he lazes, he becomes mentally sick".

"But if I go somewhere to have chitchat or kill time by playing cards, your aunty vehementally opposes me. Does she think that I should rot at home ?"

"She too does not want to be left alone. She hardly visits neighbouring houses. So if she finds you absent at home, should she talk to your pussy cat?"

Gandhia stared at Chinmay in despair. He found no one to take pity on him, to share his woes. Even this young boy gave him the slip and supported his aunty, not uttering a single word in his favour. He reached out for his handkerchief in the pocket and wiped sweat from his face.

"All right you take rest, I will see you later on".

He set right his crumpled shirt, walked steadily to the jasmine plant to gather some flowers. He plucked the buds which were not yet bloomed to wreathe a garland.

Two village maids came hastily to the well with brass pitchers on their waist. The older one tied a rope to a bucket and began to draw water to fill up the pitchers. They had no such outfits to cover the bust, only the skirt of the sari had been thrown on their shoulders to keep their modesty. Gandhia astutely cast a sneaky look at those girls ogling their half naked bodies and began to pluck flowers though his pockets had already been stuffed. He was keen to enjoy virgin beauty which still remained unexplored and unsung. The village maids sniffed something in the air, exchanged their looks and took to their heels homeward as soon as possible.

In the afternoon, Chinmay went to the river to have a stroll along its sandy bed. Some farm labourers, after finishing their work, were bathing. They were quite familiar with him and they greeted him with a smiling face. Their unalloyed love warmed the cockles of his heart. When the evening deepened, he came back home.

"Where is my granny ?" he asked his grandfather".

"Where she would be, she must be in the kitchen".

His grandmother had put a frying pan on the hearth, busy in making cakes. When she saw him, she gestured to him to sit by her side. Then his grandfather also went in to assist his wife.

"I know you are very fond of cakes. You just nibble one and tell me how it tastes". She handed him a stuffed cake with her oily hand.

"It tastes nice, granny, give me some more".

She served five cakes on a plate and beamed a smile at him.

"Do you know Baura's wife died today as that village nurse mishandled the delivery?" She asked her husband turning to him.

"How could I know ? You have eyes in the back of your head. Now stop your preamble and tell me how did it happen ?"

"The child had a leg presentation. Everybody says it is a sign of good fortune. But one can't know how critical it is to deliver a child, that too in an abnormal position". His grandmother said in a sad note while holding an unfried cake on her palm.

"I know, granny, how painful it is to deliver a baby".

Chinmay grew enthusiastic.

The old lady was startled.

She took her eyes off the frying pan and looked at chinmay with curiosity.

"What do you know about delivery, my child ?" She asked with a grin.

"It is beyond my imagination how a woman withstands such a terrible pain. Do you know, granny, the doctors incise the belly first and then take out the living child and put it on a diaper. After that they stitch the belly with the help of a thread and the wound is healed up" said Chinmay seriously.

His grandparents broke into a guffaw enjoying his ignorance.

Gandhia stopped visiting his aunt (father's sister) since that last meeting with Chinmay. A clandestine relation developed with that milkmaid. He did not even blink nor was he upset by barbed words though some hurled bawdy remarks as to his liaison with that woman. They found them in a compromising position canoodling each other, amatorily exploring each others' bodies when her husband went on some errand. For love has flood-gates that, when once open, sweep reason aside.

Chinmay saw his grandmother ill-humoured. She was blithely unaware of the trouble that her nephew had caused.

"I don't know what all the fuss is about?" She asked Chinmay, looking injured and disgusted.

"Granny, tongues are wagging, you can't dismiss the rumour as arrant nonsense. You should not apportion blame to others. One can adduce several proofs to explain his contemptible activities. Do you know gossips get busy and your next door neighbour has spilled the beans?"

His grandmother fell silent for a while. She went haywire. She seemed to be talking to herself. "Whom should I blame? His lot is like that. His wife has been suffering from rheumatism since long. Her rickety body can't give him that pleasure that a young man yearns for", she offered a lame excuse.

The poor woman was, no doubt, in a befuddled state.

Chinmay looked at her gaunt face with a caring attitude.

"Have patience, granny, keep your chin up. If you lose your nerve, the situation will not change."

"I know, dear, This fellow stained our image bringing disgrace to our family reputation. What remedy I have to cure love-sickness ?" She shrank within.

Chinmay was in a lather. He blurted out, "This is not love, granny, simply insolence. He will pay for his promiscuity. There is nothing creditable in being a street-Romeo, people will only laugh in their sleeve. Our enemies are there to gloat over his humiliation".

She was thoughtful and sought an escape. She staggered on her feet and retreated to the worshipping room. Seated on an asan, she closed her eyes. Though she was illiterate, she could recite many lines from the holy scriptures. She started to chant some lines from the great epic Mahabharat:

"The topic of the Mahabharat is as sweet as nectar, Kashi Das says those who are virtuous, they listen to it....".

THREE

The next morning a middle-aged man appeared at the door and made obeisance at the feet of Chinmay's grandfather. He was still burly and broadshouldered in his early fifties.

"Do you know Fatoo ? He was once our cartman and helped me a lot in cultivation work". His grandfather asked turning to him.

"Yes, I recognize him though his hair has turned grey in a few years. His daring spirit to face a ferocious tiger is really unforgettable. I still laugh when he, with a lantern and cudgel, lurched forward from his seat and gave a chase and the tiger disappeared in the bush. It is really a chilling reminder".

It was a time when Chinmay would accompany his grandparents to visit the temple of Lord Shiva once a year on Shivaratri. It was at a distance of about twenty kilometres from their village. It was a festival enjoyed by a large number of people coming from a long distance. The path leading through the deep forest to the temple was rough and full of ridges. The forest was so perilous that a man could not dare go even in broad daylight. There were tigers, wolves and such other savage animals and a man could get to his destination overcoming all these dangers.

Every year on the day of Shivaratri, the people of the villages and urban areas would throng around the temple and feel proud to have a darshan of Lord Shiva.

Chinmay's grand parents and their neighbours, eager to visit the temple, made preparation for the journey a day before the festival. They took with them the rice and vegetables for cooking at their halting place and instructed the cartman to get the cart ready for the strenuous journey. The cartman spread straw overlaid by a blanket making it a cushion.

Just after the sunset, a caravan of bullock carts rattled along the unmettalled road. An arched dome had been erected closing both sides of the cart by a bamboo curtain. Only the front part and the rear remained open where sat the cartman with a staff in his hand to drive the bullocks. A lantern hung by a rope from the roof was casting a flickering light as the glass had been speckled with soot. There were some spots in the forest which were retreats of savage beasts. A long line of carts trailing behind one another suddenly stopped to the utter astonishment of the passengers. The tinkling sound of the bells also ceased.

Chinmay and his grandparents were seated on the foremost bullock cart. Fatoo, the cartman, urged the bullocks to go forward by poking the staff at their flanks but they did not move an inch. They craned their necks upwards with dilated eyes. A fierce terror was sparkling in them.

With a lightning speed, a tiger sprinted across the road and disappeared behind a bush. It was obvious that the tiger being terrified skulked itself in the thicket but its strategy to attack could not be comprehended.

Fatoo immediately got down from the cart and told Chinmay's grandfather that the tiger had not run away but stalked somewhere under the cover of that thick bush, ready to pounce upon them.

Other cart drivers by that time gathered near him with their lanterns. A fear loomed large in their hearts. Nobody ventured to move forward. Fatoo, the dare-devil, signalled others to keep quiet and alone moved to a bush with a lantern and a cudgel in his hands, dicing with death. He guessed where the tiger could have taken its refuge and threw some stones aiming at that spot. To their utter dismay the monster stirred the bush like a violent gust of wind and wagging its tail with menacing deliberation emerged. Its eyes shone like burning embers when the light fell on them. The tiger was dumbfounded seeing such a large number of people. Preparing himself for head-on fight, Fatoo with all his might, flung the cudgel at the tiger. It planted a heavy blow right on its head and in a flash the tiger disappeared into the interior of the jungle.

An old man got down from his cart and came to Fatoo. "Well done my boy, well done, you have shown a blithe disregard for danger", he smacked on Fatoo's back. "It is indeed an act of chivalry and we are proud of that" the old man said flourishing his hands, "And you see how the tiger darted away parring like a pussy cat".

"It was our sheer good luck that the tiger did not turn back to avenge, otherwise the situation would have been something grave". A tribes man threw a sagacious remark from behind.

"Don't waste your time in an ineffectual discussion, rather the quicker we flee away from this place, the better". Chinmay's grandfather warned them in apprehension.

To beat a hasty retreat all went back to their carts and the journey resumed. After going some distance, Chinmay tapped the cart man's back from behind indicating him to halt near a hillock and he got down there. His body began to ache by continuous jolt. He kept on walking on foot by the side of the cart. The spire of the temple now loomed over the tree tops and a faint uproar came floating from a distance.

By dawn, the journey came to an end. The cart creaked to a halt and the drivers unyoked the bullocks near a giant banyan tree and tied them to some protruded roots. They put up their tents there and tidied up their belongings in an orderly fashion. Some went to fetch water from the river, a few steps away from that place. The bank was steep and the path leading to the river was slippery. Moreover on either side of the path the people sat on their haunches behind some shrub to empty their bowels. There were a few Simuli trees here and there overladen with bright flowers and their offshoots seemed to be wrapped with red flames. Some after bathing in the river prostrated on the ground and crawled towards the temple clad with a loin cloth round their waists. A group of chanters came singing in a chorus the sacred name of Krishna and a person collected some coins from the devotees. All around was an air of gaiety and the people were excited with glee draped in festive finery.

Before evening set in, the devotees spread mats or carpets on the ground and filled the earthen lamps with oil. They arrayed the lamps in a line, lighted them and sat on the asan, quite absorbed in meditation on Lord Shiva. They went on fasting till the grand lamp would be lifted to the spire of the temple announcing its termination. Then the whole area reverberated with the blowing of conch-shells, again and again, proclaiming the end of the festival.

On their return journey, Chinmay occupied the rear seat for sightseeing. As the path was dangerous, his grandfather instructed his companions to go along a roundabout route which was safer however it might consume more time to reach home. On the way Chinmay saw an enormous bull gazing vacantly at the caravan of the carts. He laughed inwardly when he recalled a ludicrous incident, his combat with a bull.

He was returning home after a pleasant stroll by the bank of the river. A bulky bull had stood on the ridge of a field, unconcern of anybody's presence. Close to the field, a deep tank was there and its slope was too slippery to step down. The bull stood just on its brink, lowering its head, sniffing something on the ground. Chinmay was to make detour as the path on the ridge was blocked by such a huge animal. He tiptoed to the bull and stood behind it, unnoticed. Caught by a sudden freak, he gave a speedy thrust on its back. The bull lost its balance and plummeted into the water.

It swam across to another side and tried utmost to ascend the slope. To make a fun he pushed its head. It again drifted to deeper region. Exhausted, it remained standing in the water. It stared at Chinmay with utter helplessness. He stepped down and pushed the bull from behind and it clambered up the steep slope with its hooves and was thus rescued. From that day whenever or wherever it came upon him, it used to run away without any reason.

In winter, the villagers harvested their crops and stored them in the granary. For a few months, they did not have to toil for their daily bread.

A group of villagers came to Chinmay when he was basking in the warm sunshine sitting on a cot.

"This year we would invite a famous opera party to enact their play consecutively for five nights. The impresario wants one night's advance for confirmation. Be a shareholder in our venture". An elderly man accosted him with a receipt book in his hand. Chinmay's face brightened up, "That's a good idea, but how much I have to pay ?"

"We want one hundred share holders. Each one is required to pay three hundred rupees. They demand thirty thousand rupees a night. So we have to raise that amount to manage the show".

"You may enlist my name but give me a few days' time for I have not that amount at present".

Chinmay was a little bit reluctant at the beginning. He was a student, not an earner. He was to ask his grand parents for that. His face did not register that much willingness.

The committee decided to stage the plays in a broad field near the village school which could accommodate such a large gathering.

"Please do me a favour. Would you give three hundred rupees to our village committee ? We have booked an opera party and they are shortly arriving at our place". Chinmay informed his grand father after lunch.

"Three hundred rupees ?" His grandfather knitted his forehead.

"Yes, the committee will go through the balance-sheet and they have made a promise to refund the money after the show".

The old man walked into his bedroom. It was completely dark, no inlet to admit light and air into the room. He lighted a lamp and opened an old wooden almirah. He drew a tin box out where he usually kept his money and other valuable documents. He pulled out a wad of notes and began to count it in the dim light of the lamp. He counted the notes several times for he had no desire to hand over such a big amount.

Chinmay was observing from a distance, standing at the door. He went in and said, "Grandfather, don't count it any more. As you are in vacillation, we will gain no profit. You pay my examination fees and that too with a murmur. So I never fare well in examination".

It was conspicuous that the old man did not want to part with his hard-earned money. He handed over the money much against his wish and asked, "Will they pay back?" Chinmay's grandfather, a scrape-penny, was always suspicious that somebody might appropriate his money fraudulently.

"If they don't, I will repay it," Chinmay made a pledge.

He was sulky and began to think himself guilty tangled with this unpleasant situation.

A week later, two trucks came booming and unloaded chairs, bamboo poles, tarpaulins, painted screens, bundles of ropes and other accessories in the centre of the field. The village-urchins ran squealing with delight and moved around the piles with wonder in their eyes. They carried on their work day and night and atlast it came to a completion.

The workers did not go to the fields. Visiting a relative was postponed. The children stopped going to school, even cooking and other household chores were delayed. All were jubilant and excited over the presence of this famous Opera party.

The duty had been distributed among the share holders. They went to their assigned seats and breezily started selling tickets from forenoon.

At the front gate, emblazoned in bold letters on a canvas the name of the opera party. 'TULSI GANA NATYA'. Before evening, the people coming from various parts clustered together before the gate and rollicked. The crowd scattered in all directions, even beyond the field.

There was only one gate, the front gate for entrance and exit. The volunteers were always alert and vigilant as the intruders might hoodwink them and get into the audience seats by scooping up the flaps of the tent.

The gate opened at the scheduled time. There was a terrific rush at the entrance, crushing one another. Chinmay came along with his friends, trying to get in struggling through the crowd. As it was not a biting cold, he had thrown a shawl on his shoulder with an idea that he might need it to wrap himself towards the last part of the night. But he did not know he would be caught in a stampede. He was almost carried and thrown away, sandwiched. For a moment, in that stupefied state, he could not know what happened to him. Now he fought only to save his neck, trampled by so many persons, savagely thrusting and overrunning him. When he came to himself, he found his shawl pillaged by some marauder who always sought such chance finding people in his most distressing condition.

The auditorium was overcrowded. Finding no seat, some people stood at the outer fringe of the audience and witnessed the play spellbound.

Chinmay was clammy with sweat. He could not know where his friends were gone and where they were seated. The bright lights blinded him and he could have only a hazy vision of the stage and the people seated all around it. With his shawl gone, he became least interested and felt restive to linger there. He came out through the gate. The open air made him less tense. Before he left home, his grandmother had inserted a ten-rupee note into his pocket and said, "You are a male person, you should not go out empty handed". He searched his pocket, that was also gone.

That morning, the sky was transparently bright and the mellow light of the sun made the night watchers more drowsy. The balmy air was so soothing and pleasant that they started snoozing.

In winter, there was no possibility of heavy rainfall. But the weather was unfavourable. Nobody could know the table of fortune would turn in a different direction.

At the approach of twilight, the sky changed to a severe form. Black clouds gathered ominously and there was constant rumbling of thunderbolt flitting from one end to other. The wind blew in a tremendous speed. At first dripping and then followed by a heavy downpour. The gale seemed to blow up the tent.

Chinmay mustered up the courage to see the situation. He held an umbrella over his head and walked boldly against the wind. Sometimes it threatened to topple the umbrella though he tightened his grip on the handle. When he neared a pond skirted by a footpath, the sky exploded, the thunderbolt fell just in front of him ripping and half-burning a palm tree which stood by the edge of the pond. Then and there Chinmay flopped back on the ground, unconscious.

One of the members of the committee was following him from a little distance. He heard the splitting sound of the thunderbolt and saw Chinmay fall flat on the ground. He rushed to the spot and sprinkled water on his face. He slowly came to his sense and stood on his feet. When he went to a torpor, his grip loosened and the umbrella flew away blown by the wind. It remained stuck to a thorny bush. He collected the umbrella and both hastened towards the school field.

The rain had ceased.

The booking counter had been brightened by a petromax

light, hissing at the centre of a table. The space in front of the counter was crowded by a large gathering of people. The money was refunded.

In another room, a wrangling was going on.

"You see, we are not responsible for this natural calamity", the manager Mr. Chunu took up a defensive role, "You have given words to pay us fifteen thousand rupees. I am a manager, not the owner of the party. You tell me what explanation I would give to my owner under such circumstances ? " He looked excited and stern. His temper had been frayed.

The village Sarpanch who was the pro tem president of the committee and spearheaded the show seemed utterly dejected. He turned to the manager and said apologetically. "Yes, I do agree. But we too have incurred a heavy loss. It cannot be compensated by any means. After all, we are human-beings. The members are unanimously agreed to pay you five thousand rupees – at best the cost of the food and I, on behalf of the committee, entreat you to be satisfied with that".

The president concluded with cordiality and the other members nodded their heads in agreement.

Mr. Chunu saw him downcast and grew compassionate. Finally he agreed to split the difference.

It was really an ominous night. The boys' hostel was at a distance of one hundred metres from the school, near a primary health centre. There were about fifty students residing in that hostel. As the Sundays were the village market day, most of the students had gone there. During this stormy rain, they took shelter under some thatched roof and could not come to the hostel. It was not in their knowledge that half of the hostel's roof had been blown away. The other half caved in and the mud walls collapsed all of a sudden burying six students when they were busy in their studies. Somebody's legs, somebody's head only revealed that they were under the debris of walls lying unconscious or dead. When the broken pieces of walls were removed, it was seen that they were all unconscious. There was no telephone booth nor any provision for x-ray examination in the health centre. So the village volunteers had to wait till morning. One student was seriously injured urinating blood only. His kidneys had been badly damaged. The doctors and nurses of that primary health centre thoroughly examined him and administered medicines and injections. He was lying flat resting his head in the lap of a teacher. His entire body was smarting inwardly wanting constant fanning. His parents were hopeless. Two hours lapsed in this way having no tangible results. At last the boy stared at his teacher's face and said in a choked voice "Sir, I am going, please forgive my faults if I have any". He muffled half way and breathed his last. The teacher fondly caressed him and closed his eyes. Their last dregs of hope vanished so terribly.

The next morning they hired a van and removed the injured patients to the head quarters hospital.

FOUR

Jayram was teaching English in some local college not so far from his place. He would take some bus sharply at 9 a.m. and come back in the evening. This irksome two hours' journey made him exhausted and he took rest at home, unwilling to go somewhere. He did not budge though his mother and sisters persuaded him many a time to get married but he gave a wide berth to their whims taking some vague pleas. His cousin had a piece of homestead land by the side of a huge tank fallen unutilized for so many years. He was a man without a sou for which he could not build a house there. But Jayram was a visionary. He won over him giving him an idea that it could be converted into a gold mines. He assured him that he would get a lump sum if he handed over the land to be fully exploited.

Jayram took a big amount of loan from the bank and began to construct shop rooms on a top-notch plan. It was by the side of the main road having a mega commercial value.

When the construction work was going on, he came to Chinmay, full of expectation.

"Chinmay, I am in a bit of a jam, Could you lend me five thousand rupees for cement ? Otherwise the work would be left undone".

As it was an auspicious day. Goddess Lakshmi was being worshipped in every household. Chinmay's wife remained busy arranging things for the Puja. She would be tight-fisted on those days.

Chinmay was hesitant to withdraw money while his

friend was in a financial predicament. So being compelled he went with him to a local bank to make a withdrawal.

Jayram put the money in his pocket and said, "Fine, you need not worry for money. I will repay it in a very short time". Then he waved his hand and went off.

Chinmay removed all the books from the shelf, all covered with dust. He cleared it and kept them in his book shelf. In one corner of the room, there were heaps of books, all written by him. His wife Maya finished her Puja and came with a dish in her hand.

"Eat the offerings of Goddess Lakshmi" she said. She could not swallow her anger and pointing at the stack of books she said in disgust, "Why do you write books without any profit. It is not rewarding nor it is a money-making business. My children would have been starved if you had not your paternal property. You toil day and night but all come to naught".

Chinmay heard silently and after a brief pause replied, "It is not my profession, Maya, but obsession. I contributed something however insignificant it may be".

She made a wry face and said, "Then you go on writing. You are a raving mad but remember, I won't allow wastage of money this way. You have made this room messy piling all sorts of refuse. My children could have studied here comfortably or it could be converted into a guest room but you have cluttered it with rubbish-heap. Can't you keep it spick and span ?" She had a fetish for cleanliness. She fulminated and stormed out of the room.

Chinmay strolled towards the market. The publisher and distributor Mr. Harishankar was awfully busy in publishing a magazine for he had given words to the chief editor to complete the work within a week. Chinmay saw his motor bike perked by the side of the press and was glad that he could meet him in his chamber. Mr. Harishankar had sat on his moving leather chair facing an oval table where a news paper and some magazines had been kept. He was keen on the get-up of the magazine and thoroughly scanned its pages for his satisfaction. Chinmay walked in. There were some chairs arranged in a semi-circle for the visitors and he drew one for him. Mr. Harishankar put aside the magazines and looked up at him, smiling.

"Welcome Mr. Chaudhury, perhaps you have forgotten me. Since a long time, I have been expecting your arrival. But you did not turn up to our press. I am at your service at all times."

"No, Mr. Harishankar, I was very busy and did not find time to see you. I am writing a new one under the title "Doubtful Blessings" at present. So I…"

"Very well Mr. Chaudhury. You see I have sent three hundred books to different book stalls of our town but a few have been sold. You know they are hundred percent business men. They grumble to store novel or fiction as the people scarcely buy those books, whereas key books are sold like hot cakes".

He took out a cigarette packet and a match box from the drawer, drew one and stroke the butt end on a match box few times absentmindedly and then lit the cigarette. He puffed for a few seconds and blew the smoke through his nostrils. When it reached its fag end, he threw it on the ground and trampled it under his shoes. Then he continued, "Take five hundred today, the outstanding dues, the next time. I coaxed the stall keepers to give them more commission if they sell off the books in a month".

Mr. Harishankar pulled a wad of notes from his pocket and pushed it towards Chinmay over the table.

Without counting, Chinmay kept the bundle in his pocket and stood up.

Mr. Harishankar stared at the wall clock and gestured to him to sit down.

"Have a cup of tea Mr. Chaudhury, before you leave" he turned to the door and shouted at the bearer.

"My call-bell is out of order as it has been constantly mishandled by my press men. Any how I am pulling on well Mr. Chaudhury, I don't covet for more".

"You see Mr. Harishankar, I always foster an idea to subscribe something to literature. Books are like cornucopia of good ideas. They fritter away money on salacious cinema and opera show, spend lavishly on wine and woman, but they are disinclined to buy a readable book". Chinmay looked irritated.

"It's a fact Mr. Chaudhury. In this computer age, people will no longer buy a book. They will read from the computer. Nobody will come to our press to get his book printed. The system will be like that". Mr. Harishankar's face seemed to be overcast with disappointment.

"I have been discouraged for this reason. Educated people come to my door and I lend them knowledgeable books to read. But after some months when I ask them regarding their progress, I get a negative reply. They flick through the books and keep them on the teapoy only for a show. They are lotus-eaters and spend their time in merry making. Even the people in teaching lines don't spare time for reading, so busy they are".

Mr. Harishankar drank the remaining tea at a draught and said, "Don't be disheartened my friend. Go ahead. If a single person will read your book, then it would yield some results".

"Yes, I too think like that. I never write under a magic spell nor I am in a world of fantasy. In this 'give-and-take' world. You must contribute some worthreading to be remembered, it is definitely worth a king's ransom".

Mr. Harishankar stood up and walked upto the window for a breath of fresh air. He saw people running amuck yelling in a high pitch. He could not understand the reason of that uproar. A gun-shot reverberated in the air, then booming followed in quick succession one after another. One student and two civilians were gunned down. Without warning, the trigger-happy police started firing into the crowd. Then pointing the muzzle upwards they fired into the air. Their motive was now to terrorise the people at gun point. They were frightened by fussilade of bullets and driven back to the main market where they stood defiant to watch the action of the police force. The barbarians chased them and mercilessly struck them with cudgel and rifle butts. The road leading to the main market was dotted by blood. Then the belligerent force got into a large van and drove off.

When the battle field was completely evacuated, the people hiding behind the temple, building and betel shop came out in trepidation. As soon as the van drove off, they hurtled to the spot. Two were shot dead lying in a pool of blood, another injured severely panting for breath. His friends carried him home and laid him down on a mattress. His shirt and trousers were wet with blood oozing out of the bullet wound. He shrieked with unbearable pain. He wanted a drink of water. His mother held a tumbler near his mouth. He drank a little. His mouth remained agape and the water flowed down his cheeks. Then his body convulsed with a violent spasm and lay still.

It was a blood-bath.

From query Mr. Harishankar and Chinmay came to know the reason of the pandemonium.

Mr. Nayak was the owner of a stationery shop, at a ear-shot from traffic squares. A squabble arose between him and the Weights and Measures department regarding taxation imposed by the government. Mr. Nayak and some shopkeepers jointly opposed the arbitrary taxation of the authorities. One by one crowded the place to see the fun. Some humiliated them. Some pushed and smacked the officials. Some pelted them with rotten eggs. The public rained stones on them. They sent for the police force offering an excuse that their lives were at stake. The force entered the scene and the public were put to rout. The mob threw stones at the police and it was rebounded by brutal assault. They showed their vindictiveness by persecuting the innocent people. Life of three persons were snuffed out by this senseless shooting.

The public raided the Office of Weights and Measures department, the stronghold of the authority. All the locks were battered and they dashed into the office. The important papers and documents were put to fire. They overturned the chairs and tables and broke the glass sashes of the windows into pieces. They poured petrol over the broken pieces of furniture and set fire to it with a demonic furore.

The main roads were barricaded by wooden logs. They heaped all the thrown-out rubber tubes on the centre of the roads and set fire to it with wild excitement.

A red alert was announced over night. The government ordered a total clampdown on public demonstrations.

The town fell into somnolence. With arms and ammunition, the police patrolled the strategic places prying the goons intent on sabotaging national property. The roads were deserted. Only a pack of stray dogs were seen scampering here and there. The people were kept confined to one place. At night, in brief snatches of their sleep, they hearkened the clack, clack sound of the coming and receding foot steps of the police, trailed off into silence.

A posse of reporters moved round the town on motor bikes to report the latest news. The whole area appeared gloomy and desolate.

The next morning, a troop of police came marching from the court premises with bold steps, all armed with lathis and rifles. A sergeant-major was leading them striding like a mustang and he was beating the road right and left with a cudgel, twirling his mustachio by his left hand challenging the public.

"You son of rogues, dare not come out,
Keep away, keep away, you pack of downright rascals".
With fiendish grimace, he whacked the ground with his boots. Chinmay's next door neighbour Banchha, a sweeper,

was watching the police force standing on his verandah. He was overdrunk with homemade country liquor. He ran his hand through his receding hair and cast his blood-shot eyes at the police. Suddenly he stood at attention position clicking his feet and saluted. He remained in that position till the police marched towards the temple of Goddess Ambika. The womenfolk remained indoors. They peeped through the windows and saw the marching of the police. A scabby dog, scared by the police, rushed straight to a neighbouring house. The owner of the house drove it out. Several people came from their house and stood on the road peering into the distance with a frightful look.

"How insolent they are ! They think themselves government. The town has changed to a burial ground and they have fatuously made it. They need to be paid for their hubris", stated an old man.

"What can we do, brother ? These are the bad days and we are forced to live in that mess. The sooner we go, the better", conceded a hoary person.

"What is our fault, uncle. We had been to the market to buy our necessaries. When we heard the uproar, we went there to observe the situation. If the officials of Weights & Measures had some dissension with the shopkeepers, they could have decided it in a cool brain. But they were impatient people. They called the police and now you see the outcome". A young hippy donning printed shirt and loose pajamas protested flourishing his hands. He was going to launch into an angry tirade but somebody deflated him.

"What a lot of things we saw in our life. The innocent are destined to be punished. A single death is a tragedy, a million deaths is a statistic," a grey-haired gentleman remarked. "The real culprits took to their heels. We warn the young mass not to go to a troubled spot. But they take amiss our well-meant advice". Some people in that small gathering nodded their heads.

"Those civilians and that young man had no link with

this muddled affairs. They opened fire and three innocent were shot to death and you call it their destiny". A young man gave a counter statement.

"We want to live peacefully without fear of reprisal from the police. But they have created a havoc. You elders seek redress but the authority is non-compliant. They are like two parallel lines. How do you expect a settlement ? When two elephants fight, the grass will suffer", a professor teaching at a University commented.

"That old man Ramakanta, what he was and where is his son now after he got an appointment in the rank of a sub-inspector.

They are nothing but thugs or cut-throats. They take bribes and brag of their wealth. Is this the way to maintain law and order?" The face of a control dealer twisted into a grimace.

"Don't call him old man, uncle, call him senior citizen". A young man said with humility.

All enjoyed his euphemism.

After this harrowing incident, the people were overwhelmed with grief. Over some days, they debated among themselves the pros and cons of this woeful matter. Some condemned the haughtiness of the authorities, some assigned fault to shopkeepers.

Shops remained closed for an indefinite period. The people were in great difficulty to procure their essential things. Restoration of law and order was a sinequanon for keeping peace in the town. Actions speak louder than words. The administrative authority was in a tight corner to take a decision on that contentious issue. Both sides reached an impasse. The people were happy when they heard the police officials responsible for this tragedy were fired from their service, some transferred to another district.

Time sped on. There was renewal of life since peace came back to the town.

FIVE

Chinmay's father was serving in the Collectorate. His honesty and integrity was above board. After his retirement, he engaged himself in cultivation and Chinmay was happy in lending him a helping hand.

His two younger brothers were staying in their working place with their families. Chinmay had done his graduation but he was hesitant to be a service holder. At leisure he wrote books and his writing won plaudits from educated circles.

One fine morning his father felt a dull aching pain in his chest which was diagnosed later on by a cardiologist as myocardial infarction. After some days one night he ate his dinner as usual and slept. Next morning he was found dead and nobody could know when he exited this world.

He, being the eldest son, had to perform the funeral rites however confronted with financial stringency. He went to Jayram.

"I am really shocked when I heard the sudden death of your father. How affectionate he was !" Jayram expressed his grief while drawing a chair for him.

"You know my financial position. I have always some inhibition to borrow money from others. Now I think how to get over this present problem". Chinmay could not ask him for money that he had lent him a year ago.

"Are your brothers unwilling to give you financial help ?" Jayram seemed to evade the fact.

"Yes, but that would not manage the mounting expenditure.

It would be a great help if you repay the money in my hard time" said Chinmay with reluctance.

He was awaken from reverie and stuttered, "Money, yes, that I had borrowed some days ago". He posed as if to recall a forgotten chapter and uttered, "Do you think I will run away with your money ? Shall I be absconded from my place for this petty amount ? Keep faith, I shall not weasel out of my words."

(Et. tu ? Jayram ? Then fall Chinmay)

"No, that's not my point. I have not asked you once for repayment nor I have dunned you for the same. My present crisis impels me to ask you for paying back my money".

He looked irritated. How money-centric this world is ! He thought. Chinmay could not recognize his friend at that moment.

Jayram was clearly taking delight in his discomfiture.

"I have not come here to bandy words with you but expecting you to do me a favour. You have blatantly abused my trust. It is the breach of faith that hurt me most," Chinmay said meekly.

Jayram's elder sister overheard their arguments and she called. Chinmay to come to her room.

"I heard everything. My brother borrows money. But when the time comes to repay it, he resorts to some pleas. I know his nature". She was obviously ashamed of his brother's outrageous behaviour.

"Sister, if I had not fallen…"

"I know Chinmay, I know his nature pretty well. Come tomorrow morning and take it from me."

Though other members of his family did not know this fact, he was in a mortification to face them. How selfish and shrewd a man could be ! How could a friend utter these unfriendly words without shame?" It kept rankling his mind all the time.

Jayram was in a financial hitch. When he got money, he farted and relaxed. Why would he think of his miserable plight?

Chinmay came out downhearted. He felt humbled by circumstances.

Though Jayram had been invited, he did not turn up to attend the obsequies.

From that day Chinmay paid perfunctory visit to his house. He would talk very little with him, find a plea to be occupied with some urgent work and then go out.

Chinmay stopped going to him. He did not want to butt his nose into their private afffairs. Three years lapsed in this way. Jayram could not avoid marriage as his mother and sisters almost forced him to get married. They even did not inform Chinmay about this. After so many years of closeness they seemed to give him the cold shoulder.

Chinmay went on keeping information. Jayram's first wife could not stay long in their house. Her sisters-in-law created a hell for her. At last she fled to her parents without their knowledge.

Then he hastily decided to get married to a literate girl, came of a lower middle class family. There was a great disparity of age. Jayram was in his mid fifties whereas the girl was about half of his age. For some months, they spent their married life happily. Again they fell out over some silly matter and nobody was prepared to bury their hatchets. In the mean time Jayram's elder sister Rubi fell seriously ill and died in the hospital. Mishaps followed one after another. His wife remained in a dingy room separated from others where as Jayram himself and the rest of the family lived in the upper storey keeping no relation with her. There was no pity, no remorse on either side. In the late morning Jayram stepped down to the ground floor and handed her twenty rupees to meet the expenditure of her food. Not an exchange of a single word between them and then Jayram went off to his working place.

Up to his retirement his elder brother remained a happy-go-lucky man floating on air without bothering his head about family affairs. He would eat his food silently at home and go out to gossip with friends. His reverie broke when a tiny bird told something in his ears. All the savings and ornaments of his sister Rubi had been whisked away by evil design. Even his cousin who had given his land on good faith to build shop rooms was deceived. Every thing had been done by Jayram's well-devised stratagem.

Jayram's elder brother did not allow the matter to go further. He filed a partition suit in the local court and wanted to teach Jayram a lesson. The civil suit lingered in the court. Jayram sought the help of a lawyer friend with whom Chinmay was well-acquainted. They both went to Jayram's elder brother for a discussion. He greeted them and said, "Brother, I am not a litigant. I want my legitimate share. But before division of my ancestral property, he must produce the money and ornaments of my deceased sister which are now in his possession".

"You see I am your family friend. I am not a pettifogger practising legal Chicanery. As a lawyer my conscience pricks to pocket your money. We lawyers want a case to linger on and that is our profit. Sometimes we make a pact with the lawyer of opponent's party too. So you come to the settlement and withdraw the case". The lawyer explained the intricacies of a case.

"No, unless that rogue bends down on his knees and comes to me for equal division along with money and ornaments".

"Of course. You are his elder brother. Where is the harm if he comes to beg forgiveness for his faults ? You two are growing old. A time will come when both of you will die while the case is under judgment in the court. What benefit you will get if you don't enjoy your property during your life time ?"

"You go to that bastard and drag him to arrive at a decision". He roared.

Chinmay and the lawyer found him set at defiance. Their

request was brushed aside. They went to Jayram. When he heard the scathing words of his brother, he said with excitement, "I know all about his intentions. He says I am a cheat. His forefathers were cheat. All these years had he paid a single pie for maintenance of the family ? But he wants delicacies and fine dress. Who paid the foppish for that ? People will say what I have done for the family. Now that vagrant came to claim his share. Take your share in the Court. Why are you barking before others ? I have heard and seen many. Don't come to preach me sermons". He grouched.

When Chinmay and the lawyer came down to the ground floor and shuffled across the dining room, Jayram's wife came out of the kitchen. She requested them to sit for a while and hear her sad stories.

"You please see my wretched condition. My husband gives me twenty rupees a day. Is that amount sufficient to meet one's household expenditure"? She cried aloud and beat her head on the wall.

They were stunned and could not say anything in her favour. Involvement in somebody's family affairs undoubtedly ensues troubles. It is wise to keep away from that, they thought.

Chinmay and the lawyer came back hiring an auto-rickshaw. On the way he said to Chinmay, "I have been going to their house spending money from my own pocket. I have a link with them. I have never imagined in my wild dreams that there would be a dispute between two brothers. I have seen the elder one loving his younger brother too much but they have now turned sworn enemies to each other. As their well-wisher I tried to draw out a concord between them but they are unshakeable. The ultimate result is that the ill-gotten property would go to somebody's possession".

"Ill-gotten !" exclaimed Chinmay.

The lawyer laid his back to a comfortable position and continued, " Let us get down to brass tacks, you don't know the story behind it. The land on which the building stood, was once in the possession of a Mohammedan rickshaw puller. He sold away his homestead land for abject poverty. Jayram's grandfather bought it for a song and built a small house there. After his death, his son-in-law became the owner of that house. The building which you see at present is its modified form".

"Why did that rickshaw-puller dispose of that land?" His curiosity increased.

"Hunger. When a hungry stomach revolts, one goes to loot something from somewhere and fill it. That rickshaw-puller had half a dozen children. What he earned from hard toil was inadequate to feed them. Having spent half his income on country liquor, he came with the other half. The entire family went half fed for so many days. He prayed to Jayram's grandfather to give him some loan. His loan multiplied to a big amount which he could not repay. Jayram's grandfather took the advantage of his poverty and registered the land".

"I would have remained in the dark if you had not unveiled the secrecy of their landed property. Every thing we do is preordained. Some gains favour, some becomes victim of his own destiny" Chinmay philosophised.

From the day the dispute started, Jayram's mother remained in a phlegmatic resignation. She lived with his eldest son since Jayram separated his own establishment. She had already reached her ripe old age and towards the last part of her life she became somewhat eccentric. She would alert her daughter-in-law and say, "Make the refreshment ready for my children. They will be returning from school. Don't delay, my daughter".

Though some decades had gone by, she had an idea in her mind that her children were still reading in school.

To remain aloof from turmoils, Jayram started to live in a rented house in his service place. He hardly visited his home.

One evening Chinmay had been to sadar market to buy vegetables. A colleague of Jayram accosted him,

"Don't you know Jayram has been down with malarial fever?"

"How could I know ? I have not seen him for a long period. Whenever he comes home, he remains indoors. He stays a day or two, then goes back to his service place".

"If you find time, please go and see his condition". Then he hustled away.

Next morning, Chinmay boarded a bus. He found Jayram sprawled on a string charpoy. He was moaning with severe backache accompanied by high rise of temperature. He had wrapped his body with a blanket, still he was shivering with chill and rigor.

Chinmay sat on the edge of his bed and started pressing his legs and waist as he could not be a passive-witness.

"Have you taken any medicine or not?"

"No"

"Why?"

"I am not willing to take any medicine".

"May I know the reason. This is suicidal".

"What is the use of taking medicine? I have been discarded by my family, even an eye-sore to my wife". Jayram turned his side with difficulty distorting his face and wanted a drink of water.

There was a tea-poy by his bed side with a tumbler on it. Chinmay rose and poured water from an earthen pitcher. He made him sit and held out the tumbler to his mouth. Jayram gulped it down and said", I have no desire to eat food. There are some pieces of loaves in that cupboard but I feel sick to see any food stuff".

"Though I am not a doctor, I am a bit wellversed in Tropical diseases. I have observed your signs and symptoms. It is purely malaria having three stages. Chill, rigor and perspiration. I don't want to go in details. But main symptoms are anorexia, severe body ache, high temperature and then profuse perspiration. When a patient perspires, his temperature subsides and he feels comfort. In no other fever, perspiration gives relief to a patient other than malaria."

"I too have guessed like that".

"But why don't you go home where you can be treated by a good physician? Your wife would be there to attend upon you".

"I won't go back to that hell. Rather I want to die here smitten with fever". Jayram was impassive and stared at the ceiling with a vacant look. His fever-racked body began to tremble with the slightest excitement.

Chinmay put a strip of wet cloth on his forehead.

"Take at least two pieces of loaf before I give you some tablets. Don't take it on empty stomach".

Chinmay went out and came back with medicines. He administered four camoquin tablets with paracetamol at a time and told him to wait till he perspired.

An hour later, Jayram sweated all over and felt himself relieved.

"I will take you back home. Don't budge, face the problems of life with daring spirit". He at last yielded to his importunity and was escorted home with utmost care.

SIX

A couple of boring months passed uneventfully this way. The winter came and the intensity of cold began to increase. A triangular field in front of Chinmay's house got moist in the morning for the constant falling of dew drops. But it could not disturb the sound sleep of street beggars lying barebodied on the ground .A hoard of beggars turned up to this field in late evening, lit up a makeshift hearth to prepare their food by collecting some dried twigs and then they slept there singing romantic songs of films in full throated chorus. They covered their bodies only by a thin sheet of polythene which could barely protect cold. The ground got wet with early morning dew but they lay flat with least cares. Under a bower of a few neem trees, there slept a beggar couple, one on the wheel-chair donated by the government and the other on the bare ground. The beggar woman was in her early thirties and her husband, a polio patient, always remained wheel-chair-bound as his legs were too slender and infirm to move about. The other beggars would lech after her and stole a favourable occasion to crack ugly jokes with her. One morning when she was collecting some twigs a few yards away, one beggar walked over to her and cajoled, "Why do you remain with this ugly, handicapped man to spoil your youth? Come to my shelter .I will give you everything you need". The beggar woman was stone deaf to his pleading .She kept on collecting fuels. The man walked away without getting any response. Then came another. He winked at her and said, "My queen of heart ! don't spend your life wastefully. I will make you a real queen." The beggar woman listened for a few seconds, stood straight and hurled a twig forcefully at him .She was in a mood to pounce at him but restrained her temper. "You worm of the gutter, don't cast your lewd eyes on me and force me to be foul-mouthed. If you are so aroused, go to someone to cool down your passion. Don't you have the slightest respect for your mother and sister? You venture to tell me such filthy words as you think I have no guts to shield my womanhood. Don't show me your shameless face, else I will send you away by some sound beatings". The man retraced his steps and fled away to save his skin.

Every day Chinmay went past them and observed their way of living. The beggar woman used to go from door to door to collect rice and vegetables. Some would offer her boiled rice, some stale curry and leftover foods. She accepted them without grumbling and came back to her husband to feed him. She would massage his body with oil, bathe him with bucketful of water and then comb his hair with great care. Chinmay kept looking at him with enviousness. The beggar was underfed, looked scrawny and emaciated, but what was there in him that his woman was so much inclined to him, he could not make a sense of it.

One early morning when he was going on his usual morning walk, he saw an old man stumbling over a bumper and lost his balance. He fell awkwardly on the road and his walking stick flew to a nearby gutter broken into two pieces. Chinmay rushed to him, erected him from the ground and brushed off the dust from his body. He fumbled through his tears, "I am a high blood pressure patient. Last night my daughter-in-law became aggressive and kept me unfed. My only son who is a medicine specialist in a local hospital dreads his wife and keeps mum although he knows her oppressive nature."

The beggar woman was watching the situation .She came with a stick in her hand, "Uncle, don't be disheartened, here is a stick of my husband .It will help you walk on the road."Chinmay looked at her smiling face and amazed at her sudden response."You are really a good woman with a sympathetic heart for a helpless one. I have not expected such kindness," he admitted spontaneously. The woman continued smiling with a puzzled look.

The field was often frequented by different groups of people .One morning a wandering tribe came with their tents and belongings. They pitched their tents in the middle of the field and tethered their pet animals like monkeys and dogs to some posts outside the tent. Some had kept various types of birds in a cage chattering endlessly. The monkeys displayed their dance baring their teeth and hopped with their hind legs entertaining the passers- by. The children would stand by the roadside, clap their hands and burst into peals of laughter. They threw bananas at them. The monkeys deftly caught them from the mid-air and gobbled up quickly with their hands. The area rang with babble of voices. Outside their tents; they put up a signboard, a name written on it in bold letters 'JAY MATA HERBAL STORE'. They spread out their medicines on tattered and threadbare carpets to draw the attention of the customers. From morn to dust, there would be always a small gathering of people coming from different places. From their eager faces, they could know how artfully they could be tackled. Somebody came to them for toothache, some for rheumatism, some for long standing dyspepsia and so on. Womenfolk also visited them for irregular menstruation, dysmenorrhoea, miscarriage and to redress their barrenness. Somebody would come unobstrusively being secretive about his ailments. When the crowd thinned out and only a few people were left, he would sit on his haunches beside the quack and whisper his chronic problems.

The quack would look at his face with a knowing smile and say, "So you are going through impotency and hasty ejaculation over some months." Then casting a squint look at some live lizards put before him he would say, "These are sand lizards collected from deserts. We fry them in a pan and make a good amount of oil extracting the fat from their bodies. Then we concoct it with some herbs which produces a very good result in curing these obstinate cases. You have to massage your private parts with this oil and take a herbal medicine two times a day. After a few days, you will see its wonderful result."

"How much it would cost?" The man asked with timidity.

"Oh, it is nothing", he pointed to some bottles kept before him. "These are the bottles filled with oil. Fifty grams of bottle would cost seventy rupees. A bottle of one hundred grams costs something more."

The man asked for a bottle containing one hundred grams.

"Very well", the quack fished out a bottle from a tin-box and held it before him.

"There are sixty pills in this bottle. Take two pills a day, morning and evening. It would cover one month. After that you come and let me know its result."

"How much I have to pay for these medicines?"

The quack lapsed into a pensive mood and said rubbing his chin, "I thought over it. I must give you a little concession. Actually is costs more than three hundred. I could have told three hundred and fifty to some other person. But your case is different".

The man paid the amount and put the medicines in a cotton bag. After he rose to his feet, the quack said in a tone of warning, "Stick to my words, do it regularly".

The man seemed to get back his confidence. A smile played on his colourless face. He felt himself rejuvenated as if his receptacle of life was going to be filled to its brim.

The quack patted his shoulder and said with assurance, "I don't back the wrong horse. You must come back with good news."

The man came out through the crowd with a hopeful grin.

After a few days he reappeared with one of his chums. They pushed and shoved the crowd to get to the front.

"Now tell me the result", the quack asked giving himself airs of an expert physician.

"This is not the case of mine. I have come with a friend, suffering from same troubles." He gasped out and his face was beaded with perspiration.

"No worry, my dear. I have got some aphrodisiacs, very efficacious in this case. He will get over this disorder in three months." The second man squatted on the ground and winked at him. "Disorder." The man got confused.

"Yes, disorder." The quack pulled his hand to make him sit by his side and said." You have abused the system in the past. I mean self-abuse (onanism)." Then he said jokingly, "Take care; otherwise you will cut a sorry figure in your conjugal life. It impairs sexual virility and it would be very much humiliating for you to go kaput during love-making."

"You please give me some effective medicines for that."

"Don't fret. I have cured thousands of cases like this. No patient has ever come downhearted till now. I have not heard any bellyaching from any one so far."

"All right. You do what is needful. But how much does it cost?"

"About four hundred rupees".

"What! The cost is bit high. No, no, you take it into consideration."

"You see. I have curtailed one hundred rupees from the actual cost. If I demand so much, no patient will come to me for the second time. Moreover I always consider the financial position of a patient."

Finally the two sides struck a bargain and they paid him three hundred and fifty rupees.

"How long we have to wait for the result?" they asked before leaving.

"After three weeks you come to me. The medicines will act in a gradual process. Don't expect anything overnight". The quack retorted assertively.

It was evening. The field and its vicinities had been illuminated by electric lights. Chinmay was in his study. His wife was loitering in the verandah. She caught a smell of mutton carried on air from the direction of the field. She entered the study and asked Chinmay, "How much money they are earning every day?"

"Who?"

"These nomads".

"Why?"

"Everyday their wives are preparing mutton. It seems they are earning a fortune."

Chinmay said giving a belly laugh, "They earn thousands of rupees by cheating these idiots. God knows what they give as medicines. A number of patients are coming. But the stock of medicine is always inexhaustible."

"Of course they are running a very profitable business". Maya chaffed him further.

"Is it a business? Simple fraud. They are a sort of Physiognomist. From appearance, they can guess the drawbacks of the patients. They are such mugs who can be easily duped by them. They squeeze them dry and take everything tactfully. If somebody comes with failure to snub them, they would be found nowhere. They are the birds of passage, today here and tomorrow there".

"Why don't they go to a physician?"

"Shame. They feel shame to expose themselves to a physician. They are suffering from some awkward diseases which they keep in secrecy. They dither to disclose it before a doctor. But here they are free and frank, feeling no uneasiness to express. Our people are not yet cultured. With the progress of education, their ignorance will be removed."

"How odd-looking their womenfolk are, with short skirt and striped jacket."

"That is their usual outfit at home. They seldom go outside. When they go bedecked, you cannot recognize them."

So you have unmistakably marked everything", Maya gave a giggle.

"What are you getting at? I don't have any interest in them, these god-damned people".

Their conversation was interrupted as somebody opened the gate. They strained their ears, staring at each other.

"I will take a look-see", Maya said. She came to the verandah and hurried back to Chinmay.

"Your friend Jayram and a gentle man have come," so saying she disappeared into the interior.

He greeted them and led them to his drawing room. After they were seated comfortably on the sofa, Chinmay said looking at Jayram, "I know Mr. Ramesh, the principal of your college. Once you have introduced him to me when he had come with his family during car-festival."

"I don't find any time to come as I am hard-pressed by my own job." Mr. Ramesh said regretfully.

"Yes, he is busy in constructing a ladies' hostel near the college," Jayram replied while looking over some magazines placed on a table.

"So what's the purpose of your sudden visit to Baripada, Mr. Ramesh," Chinmay asked eyeing at him.

"Not so specific. I have come to purchase some building materials. Mr. Jayram requested me to accompany him to pay a visit to goddess Jagadhatri at court market. So while coming back, we decided to drop in on you."

"Very well, after a long gap, I happen to have a chance to see you again. All through the year, the people of this town have been worshipping many gods and goddesses. It is always vibrated with an air of festivities. You know the Hindus worship thirty three crores gods and goddesses. Air, water, fire, sky, river, tree, serpent, monkey, all are gods in our eyes. Each person has his own presiding deity. For centuries the heterogeneity of religious practices is going on. Besides that who are zealots, they think their religion the best in the world. They try to establish its superiority over other religions. If it is endangered, they declare jihad or holy war striking terror into the heart of others. Some despise idol worshippers. The worshipper of multiple gods (polytheist) is regarded as pagans who hold no religious belief. On the whole these are all contradictory with each other. Many sanguinary battles have been fought in the past only for this religion. It is still rife and continuing. Actually we do not know the essence – the cardinal virtues of religion. If we initiate ourselves into human religion or humanity, then this strife will end there. This is the deep-seated reason for which communal riots are rampant in the whole world. Of course my opinion may not be appreciated but our attitude should be refined. We cannot hope for universal brotherhood unless we are liberal in our outlook and nurture broadmindedness to other religions. We only shed crocodile tears but no one comes to the forefront to champion the cause. Mr. Ramesh, what's your view?"

"Yes, what you have told is unequivocally correct. But the fact is that they are not tolerant to each other. There is downright hatred among different sects. Presently the political leaders are fanning the fire of sectarianism to gain their own interest. They promise a lot of things in their election manifesto. You must have observed how they persuade the people to vote their party in election campaign. They still follow the 'divide and rule' policy. They win over the minority pledging them extravagant promises. In India, the upper echelons only get benefit whereas the poor class still remains in perpetual darkness. What do the politicians do after election? The tenure of five years is ill-spent in fighting and criticizing others. Because self-interest is uppermost in their mind. Political chicanery and corruption have been revealed at the highest levels. They are not distraught if the country goes to hell. The politicians use some high-flown words to impress others like national integrity, self-sacrifice, peaceful coexistence, secularism, non-aggression, non-alignment, non-violence etc. It is not a child's play to take over the reins of administration. A person who does not know the definition of poverty and born with a silver spoon in mouth, he cannot know its shooting pain. His 'feel good' thoughts are relevant only to the people who live in clover but it does not conform to the people suffering in acute poverty".

"Mr. Ramesh, excuse me as I interrupt you in the middle. The slogan for removal of poverty has been chanted many a time in our country. How long they will recite the empty rhetoric to befool us? The ruling party has given the lower class people enough. They are no longer in grinding wants. It is not a unsolved mystery to understand their aims. Sometimes when I visualize the future of the country, I become increasingly exasperated. After so many years of independence what we have achieved in comparison to other developing countries. The lower class should not rot for ages. They must be upgraded and uplifted. But this is not the proper way adopted by the administrative machinery. They will make them bone-lazy and easy-going. This indolence will encourage them to be lackadaisical and our dreams for prosperity will soon end in a catastrophe. We have suppressed our resentment because we know we have no patron to back us. Our voices have been hushed; cowed by hostile power, as a result we cannot ventilate our fructuous opinions. We can't be agent provocateur to instigate the people to go in a wrong direction. Though it sounds a peroration, a conscious citizen cannot be insensitive to this vital aspect of his country."

Mr. Ramesh listened attentively. Then he cleared his throat and said, "I am also of the same opinion. It is all happening owing to the blunder of history committed in the long past. From the very beginning our country has been going through political strifes. Since the division of this sub-continent, the situation became increasingly muddled and hazardous. The political leaders who took the helm of the country are devoid of farsightedness. Their underestimation in certain matters invited a series of troubles. The neighbouring countries are biding their time till they get the opportunity to take revenge. The border dispute has not been settled yet. It still remains a bone of contention. Regarding Kashmir, it has been a knotty or thorny issue for all the Indians. There are adversaries hovering inside and outside. Our economic progress is intolerable to them. The leaders of the state are parochial and they are always hawk-eyed to keep their throne safe. You see, here two brothers are at daggers drawn with each other on various issues. The same is happening in the wider field also. To establish supremacy they invade the territory of other countries and forcefully occupy them. The possessiveness is innate in their blood and they think it as their birth-right to keep others under their dominance. So in this critical situation unity is of paramount importance to safeguard our sovereignty. Otherwise we would be passive beholders like King Niro who was fiddling while Rome was burning to ashes."

Maya entered the drawing room and served them tea. Mr. Ramesh said waving his hand, "Since I am a hyperacidity patient, I gave up tea completely. Please give it to Mr. Jayram."

Jayram was sitting all along silent. He put the cup aside and said," I am also a blood pressure patient. My digestive system is not going well as tea causes constipation, I fear to take more than two cups, morning and afternoon."

Maya collected the tea cups and went inside.

Mr. Ramesh smiled a little and said," Mr.Chaudhury, I have gone through your book 'Doubtful Blessings' lended by Mr. Jay ram. Mr. Nayak, the main character of the novel touched my heart very much. It is really very fascinating. The tragic end of his life kept me grieving over some days. He was really adventurous who produced consecutively three films spending a huge amount of money. I heard he was fabulously rich. He gave a break to a local youth in his film who rose to fame subsequently and became a stalwart and front –ranking artist in Oriya filmdom. But as ill luck would have it, his film flopped and it did not bring him any profit. The distributors played hide and seek with him. He incurred a heavy amount of loan from different persons which he could not liquidate in a stipulated time. The banks also gave him notice repeatedly to clear up his outstanding dues. As it was mounting, he got totally confused, lost his mental balance and while going along the road leading to Badambadi bus stand, he fell unconscious and his sense could not be revived. Of course I am not cognizant of the full facts".

"Yes, the novel is based on the real life story and I have borrowed this fact from a friend who gave me a brief sketch of his venturesome work. Any way I am glad that you have appreciated the book which lightened my heart a great deal."

Mr. Ramesh said with a parting advice," You go on writing. Don't be depressed. You know many writings of master writers have been rejected but ultimately they have been placed on a high pedestal when the worth of their writing is recognized."

Chinmay listened to him silently.

Mr. Ramesh and Jayram rose from the sofa. Chinmay went with them up to the gate and bade them good bye.

SEVEN

Bhanjpur, a small locality, situated on the outskirts of Baripada was not so congested in those days, To its eastern side; there stood a little railway station built by the former maharaja of Mayurbhanj state. A narrow gauge stretching from Bangriposi to Basta cut across the town and faded away in the distant horizon. A match box train (people say in jest) used to run along that route puffing a column of smoke and sometimes the children raced behind it yelling in sheer delight. While the train was plying thus sluggishly, people could get down and get in with ease as they pleased (according to some former prime minister visited this town a few years back). Then the route was suspended sine die with a possibility of renovation. After waiting for a long time and pushing the authority to come to their heel, the dogged efforts bore fruits and the station wore a change. Some major modifications were made and the narrow gauge was converted into a broad gauge. Again the station resounded with hubbubs of people.

Mounting on a bicycle, Chinmay reached his friend's house which was within walking distance of the railway station. Sushant just wearily plodded home through the rain. He would unfailingly visit his ashram twice a week where a number of devotees of swami Nigamananda would congregate to perform their rituals. Sitting on a chair, he was drying his hair with a towel. Chinmay kept his bicycle aside and knocked on the door.

"Yes, coming," Sushant responded from the interior and unlatched the door.

"Hi Chinmay, how did you come through this rain?"

"Yes, I waited under a shed till the rain ceased. If I drench, I catch a cold very soon," Chinmay replied while sitting on an armchair laid in front of the T.V. set.

Sushant dragged his chair close and said," I had been to Allahabad a couple of weeks ago to attend a religious conference. On my return journey, I faced a humiliating unforeseen trouble."

'What?" Chinmay was taken aback.

Sushant continued," When I alighted from the train at Howrah railway station, I found to my surprise that somebody had pickpocketed me. I was left in the lurch and utterly moneyless. I slapped my brow with my palms in despair. Being at a loss, I came out of the station and sat on a bridge. I attended the conference with full devotion and pious heart but what I have erred that this misfortune befell me, I began to think. I could not hold back my tears. Just at that moment, a hoaryheaded gentleman with an umbrella in his hand was going along that way. He came to me and asked me with some concern." My boy, why are you crying? Please tell me what happened to you?" He besought me with fatherly affection. I was moved and could not hide my feelings. I narrated my sad story. He was overwhelmed with my sudden disaster and led me to his home. We passed many alleys and sub-alleys. You know calcutta city is crisscrossed by many roads. If someone goes into its interior, he would be totally confused. At last the old man led me through the maze of lanes and reached near his wooden gate and tapped it with his umbrella. An old woman came out of the house and opened the gate.

"Listen to me", the old man said to his wife while ushering me into his sitting room. "Some sneak-thief has stolen away his money in his unwary moment. Say, what will he do in this helpless condition?"

His wife gaped at my face and said, "Son, don't be disappointed. We are here to help you. You stay one night and your uncle will escort you to the bus stand the next morning."

I stayed there and accepted their hospitality for one night as I had no alternative. They entertained me with palatable dishes at night and I spent the night with a fitful sleep.

The next morning the old man offered me one hundred and fifty rupees for my bus fare and directed his son to help me sit comfortably in the bus, bound for Baripada. I shed copious tears, on the eve of my departure, overwhelmed with a sense of gratitude.

I took down his address and promised to pay back his money after I got my home. I knew, as a mark of courtesy, he declined to accept my repayment. I was indebted to him for he helped me in my most distressing situation."

"What did you do then?" Chinmay asked, lost in his narrative.

"Yes, two days after I remitted the money in his address in spite of his refusal."

"You have done a very wise thing, Sushant. I don't like to remain as a debtor. Your conscience will prick you every moment, so long you have not repaid your debt. However you are obliged to him not for his monetary help but for his humanity. A few persons in this society are endowed with this quality."

"Yes, at the time of my departure, the old man requested me to visit him once again but I have lost his address. I faintly remember the route and the alleys which lead to his house. Moreover the lanes are so confusing and zigzag that you will be dog-tired to reach your destination. Besides that the relationship also wears off with the passage of time. Don't you agree with me?"

"Definitely".

Then he added, "I have been going through a chain of predicaments since my wife's untimely death. I will tell you a few incidents which are unknown even to my family members. You know I have one son and one daughter. I have already finished my duty by marrying my daughter to a well-placed boy who is now leading a very happy life. Then my son is doing a high salaried job in a reputed company. I have been left on my tod in this house having no obligation to be worried about. The house looks abandoned. The grim silence all around it seems to be oppressive. I am alone and there is no one to give me company. Still I pass my days with happiness. All are well owing to the divine blessings and my steady devotion to my preceptor. When my wife died without premonition, I was left quite despondent. Everything seemed cheerless and I lost my desirability for life I had ever had. It appeared completely meaningless to me. One night in a moment of rashness, I stood on a table, threw a rope over the beam of the roof and made a noose to strangle myself to death. Everything I was doing in a trance being unconcerned to the external surroundings. But when I shot a glance at the roof, I saw a black venomous serpent lying motionless spiralling its lanky body round the beam. It was blood-curdling and immediately I jumped off the table. Sweat began to stream down my body. Several days passed this way. But I was overcome by suicidal tendency which did not leave me a moment. Again I crept out of my bed at dead of night and quaffed a glass of poisonous substances to terminate my life. I thought, the next morning my neighbours will find me dead. I tried to lie down on my bed but my stomach began to retch violently. I pushed open the back door and stepped into the backyard. No sooner did I reach there, than I spewed out everything. I staggered back to my bed and sprawled myself awkwardly. My heart began to throb and the whole body was trembling like a banana leaf. I could not know when I fell to a deep sleep. Late morning I woke up and went to the backyard with an unsteady gait. I stood transfixed what I saw there. There was no trace of my vomitus. The chickens of my neighbour pecked at all the vomiting in the early morning and were strewn dead on the ground. I shuddered but screwed up my courage. Like Lord Clive, I escaped the jaws of death two times. So I thought God desires something different. Now I have reconciled myself with the present situation which was difficult to cope with at the beginning. I got back my enthusiasm to engage myself in spiritual work. Everyday co-disciples are coming to my house for consultation on various matters and they also get relief by my prudent advice. Chinmay, I am sure and certain of one thing. Those who are born today, they must die tomorrow. One cannot avoid inevitability. Moreover death cannot scare me nor I am scared of any fatal mishap. To me, death is nothing but transmigration of soul. Have you not read in the Bhagavat Gita? When a garment is torn or frayed, we shed it and wear a new one. Similarly when this mortal body is worn-out and comes to a state of decrepitude by the infirmities of old age, we cast our worn-out bodies and enter into others which are new (chap II-22). So after knowing these things why should I cry for this transient life? It is just like a bubble floating on the surface of water. Nobody can say when it will burst and vanish. In other words our lamp of life can be blown out by a gust of wind at any moment. But we lament for its transitoriness. As we grow old, death-consciousness also develops with that. We see it in the offing, looming in a menacing form. We get scared and die every second. This generally happens owing to our sheer ignorance. We don't know the existence of body and living in it our disembodied soul. A body dies and goes through the decaying process. The body formed of five elements, mingles with those, wherefrom it has come. But the soul is immortal and it is not subject to mortality. When this realization dawns on somebody, the darkness of ignorance is dispelled. Swami Vivekananda has rightly said citing an oft-quoted line from the Upanishad, "Arise, awake, go on striving till you reach your final goal."

So exert your spirit, ward off phobia of impending danger and keep on going with gusto."

Sushant relapsed into silence and then he said, "Don't mind if I have given a long discourse. It must not sound discordant to you."

"No, no, I have been enlightened by your analysis. You are indeed, a savant in this field. I would rather say you have dissected life in its true form and this undoubtedly gave me a sense of realization for which I got a heart-felt relief. What more can be expected of this stereotyped life. One should follow your thoughts verbatim."

Chinmay was deeply stirred by his life-story.

Sushant went into the store room and brought a packet of biscuits. He offered some to Chinmay and said, "I confided my secrets to you because you are my intimate friend and you won't disclose it to somebody else. Materialistic people with worldly prudence will not believe my philosophy. They may think I have invented a wholly fictitious story about my past. But God only knows how I had gone through my bitter experiences and came out victorious like a phoenix, a fabulous bird that burned itself and rose rejuvenated from its ashes."

Chinmay heard his wonderful experience and said, "Your house seems to me a real ashram having a hallowed atmosphere. It is a sacred place and it seems to have permeated every part of my body with some sanctity. I wish to linger here to get a rare bliss."

"Of course, many persons say this thing. When I was living a lonely life and got fed up. I thought to sell it away and go somewhere else. But my plan became topsy-turvy when a hermit visited me and stayed one night discussing many things about religion. He hailed from Punjab travelling all over India on a pilgrimage. During conversation I expressed my intention to dispose of my homestead land and shift somewhere to get mental peace. Because my wife died in this very house which looked quite desolate to me. The hermit listened heedfully and fell silent. His forehead suddenly creased and he smiled enigmatically. He moped his face and said, "You don't know the importance of this place. About three centuries ago this place was a hermitage of ascetics. An ominous day came when it was completely swept away by a strong gale blowing continuously for three days. Years passed by, a dense forest grew up and it was inhabited by a large number of birds and animals. Infested with snakes, bandicoots and scorpions it came to be unfit for human habitation and there was no abode of humanbeings in its surrounding areas. After a long time, it became thinly populated."

The hermit stopped his narrative and glared at me, "Your land is a part of that sacred place and now you want to sell it up. It is a divine property and you have no right on that. It would be like selling your soul to the devil", he said with heavy sarcasm.

He stayed about a week and taught me some esoteric yogic practices which helped me a lot in moulding my ways of life. He guided to bring a refined change to my middle class mores. I felt as if a reformation came over me and I started my life anew.

Chinmay said with amazement, "You are really fortunate that you came in contact with such a pious man. His guidance made you unstained and inviolable to keep you away from all the lures of this mundane world."

"Yes, a man of amour propre will not go to a low level but there is every possibility of going astray in this degenerated society. Like weather, human nature is also freakish. A few years back I was lucklily escaped from falling in that vile ditch."

"How?"

"I got acquainted with a young wife of a Marwari businessman. They had rented a big building which was just a stone's throw from here. They had two children who used to come to my house to play in our garden. Very often I visited their house with their kids to have a chitchat. They consulted me regarding the health of their children as I had learnt homoeopathy in my college days. The woman was worried as she was growing obese day by day. She was mentally perturbed thinking that she will look like an elderly woman for this obesity.

One day when I was sitting in their house, she said, "Mr. Sushant, I am very much worried as I am accumulating fat in my body. If I go back to my native place Rajasthan, I shall be a laughing-stock among my relatives. You must have known some medicines to reduce the amount of fat in my body."

Her tone was appealing and I was ready to relieve her from this growing anxiety.

She went into the kitchen and brought some fried eatables and served me on a plate. I crunched them one by one. After drinking a glass of water I sank back into a cushion. It was their master bed room, very commodious and there lay a large bedstead at a corner of that room.

"These fried eatables are very moreish, aren't they?" She asked me in a frivolous manner.

"Yes, I am not so faddy about food. You have mixed some fried peanuts with that which is an added taste, no doubt," I replied.

"Do you want some more? She asked me coming close to me.

"No, this is enough." I said looking at her charming face. She was really a beauty.

There was no one in the house. Her children had gone to their school and her husband to his drapery shop. That loneliness made her more courageous and dashing. She almost dragged me to her bed and sprawled herself on it. I sat on the edge of that bedstead keeping a little distance from her. She loosened her sari and exposed her bulging belly. It was like a lump of white sheet of paper heaving up and down. My passion was lolling its tongue but I checked myself. I was too suss a character to fall into that trap.

"You see how much fat has accumulated in my belly." She said baring her private parts.

I hesitated, unsure of what I would say to her.

"Why are you so reluctant? Put your hand on my belly and feel it." She simpered. It was a plea for her to tempt me. She was definitely giving me the come-on.

"Yes. I am watching it. Stomach is a usual place where fat is deposited. A tyre round the belly adds to the beauty of a woman. It makes her more attractive."

To be frank, I had some misgivings at the beginning as to her frivolity. I was indecisive what to do at that moment. I will betray my fidelity if I deviate from my path for this enticement.

I honestly said, "Yes, you have obesity but that can be slimmed down with administration of medicines. Take it regularly and it will be lessened by degrees."

She got up and twisted her body. She yawned raising her hands upwards. I knew it was her inviting indication. But I was anchored to my principles having unswerving loyalty to my life partner. I usually hate to tamper any woman. She was perhaps dubious about my masculinity. She led me to the front door and said," Would you please do me a favour? Please take money from me and purchase the medicines. I must have a perfect shaped figure before leaving to my native place."

She was surprised at my erratic behaviour. She thought," I am shaking a big chunk of meat before his eyes but how can this carnivorous resist his greed ?" She held out a great temptation to me.

However I complied her humble request and came back home. I divulged the matter to my wife. She was wonder-struck. She gazed at me with enlarged eyes and said," I did not have the slightest inkling that she is so much vulgar and nasty. Don't go to her, I warn you." She made me conscious to have my head screwed on the right way.

I was constantly nagged by this thought for a prolonged period. She challenged my manliness. But she recoiled thinking me an outright moron who could not grasp the inner passion of a woman. My wife began to suspect me and was racked by unreasonable doubts. Although I never cast a furtive glance at womenfolk, still she had misgivings about my movements.

Chinmay interfered, "Sushant, I fail to make out why a woman is always haunted by doubts I fall in with your views. I wish to say, "O frailty, O doubt, thy name is woman."

Sushant smiled and said, "The women are a separate class. A fire of suspicion is always burning inflammably in their heart. You must have read the story of king Bhatruhari how he had been beguiled by women. If you go through 'Srungar Sataka' you will get a clear concept of their queer nature. So far as your novel 'Looking through the loophole' is concerned, you have given a vivid picture of human beings, their omission and commission."

"Sushant, you do not know my reading and writing are repulsive to my wife. Whenever she sees I am poring over books or writing, she becomes annoyed."

"Oh, don't mind it. The women are like that. They waste most of their time making banal remarks. But you are utilizing your time in creative writing. That is enough." Sushant put a consoling hand on his shoulder.

"Sushant, I am getting late .I will see you some other day."

He sped off riding on his bicycle.

EIGHT

Gandhia's grandfather Mr. Baladev was a big land lord during monarchical regime. There was a floating rumour that he had a root in Rajasthan. When he was a seven-year-old child, he was coming with his parents to visit lord Jagannath at Puri. It was the time of car festival. The place was choked with a huge congregation of people. Unluckily he was lost in the crowd and his parents could not track him down in spite of their frantic search. They went back with a heavy heart. By the wheel of fortune, the child came to the shelter of Puri's maharaja. He brought him up with care. The child became a robust young man. He was an expert on horseriding and his sincerity in doing some responsible work won the heart of the maharaja. Once the ruler of Mayurbhanj visited Puri on some urgent matter. He came in contact with that young man. Pleased with his skilful horse riding he brought him to his state. He offered the young Baladev a large landed property and looked to his comforts. In course of time he married and four children were born to him, two sons and two daughters. His house was not so distant from the king's palace. The queen gave birth to a son. She could not feed the child from her own breast as there was no secretion of milk from the lactative glands. Mr. Baladev's wife became its wet-nurse and breastfed it. When the child grew adult and inherited the royal throne, he had not forgotten her loving care. He regarded her as his second mother.

Mr. Baladev was the first and foremost man who introduced horse-drawn coach in the town. He made a stable in his backyard and employed some coachmen to look after the horses. People preferred to go on those coaches on a minimum charge. There was also a shed for milking cows close to the stable. A woman was there to take care of them. Every day she would milk the cows and make milk products like cheese, butter, ghee, curd etc.

Mr. Baladev rose to an affluent man and raised his children with care and comforts. Seeing his progress in life, people used to say, just for fun:

'Tut, tut, you vagabond, spoiled brat

Push Babu Baladev's coach being his pet.'

Gandhia was his youngest grandson. For overprotective parents, he became a truant in his school going days. Excessive mollycoddling made him a spoiled child. They gave him indulgence and his juvenile delinquency was overlooked, as a consequence he tirmed out a foppish in his later age. In his halcyon days he would go around the town riding on the horse back. His father died after a few months of his marriage. He lived fast and soon ran through his fortune. The rest of the patrimony was divided between two brothers. Gandhia gave his portion to local cultivators on share-cropping. Within a few years, his monetary condition became worse. The share-croppers took various pleas, like crops failed for draught, excessive rainfall and sometimes by terrible flood. He only tried to keep up appearances. When the unfavorable time came, he sussed out the value of money. He tried to resist himself from self-indulgence which he used to do in the past. His fair-weather friends did not come to sympathise him in his financial crisis. He was not a habitual drunkard but occasionally took to drink to forget his glorious past.

One afternoon he drank excess and came to Chinmay's house with a tottering gait. He thumped on the door of latrine and did not get any response. He thought that it was their front door. Chimney heard the thumping sound and went to the backyard. Gandhia looked at him with drink-sodden eyes and said, "Chinmay dear, I am calling you a dozen times but you did not answer."

"I have fallen asleep. How could I know you have come?"

"Yes, Yes that is true. Where are your wife and children? I cried hoarse and knocked on your front door but nobody came to open it."

"This is not the front door. Why did you come to the backyard? You are thumping the door of our latrine by mistake."

"What! Is it not your front door? I thought ..."

Chinmay felt agitated and snubbed him- "Yes, you are now out of your control. You should not have come to our house in this drunken state. What my wife and children will think about you? May I know the purpose of your sudden visit?"

"Oh, nothing my dear. I thought I have not seen you for a long time. So...."

"You come to our drawing room and rest there."

"No, no, I am comfortable here. Let me sit on this log of wood."

Gandhia sat on the log and took out a bottle of liquor from his trouser pocket.

"Don't think it otherwise, Chinmay. It is not liquor in true sense. You must have come across a word 'Samarasa', the elixir. Even the gods crave for that. It will make you live longer and stay young. Ha.... Ha....I don't want to grow old. I want everlasting youth and enjoy life." Gandhia burst into uncontrollable laughter.

"I could not imagine that you will be addicted to alcohol. Do you know it will tell upon your health? Once habituated, you cannot give up this bad habit. Eventually you will be a hopeless alcoholic".

"No, Chinmay. It is not like your habit to write day and night. I am just drinking to forget my dismal present.

My wife is my life's bitch. I want to remain aloof from her. But where would I go, Chinmay? Please tell me."

"You need not go anywhere. You are doing something which your wife dislikes. Your laziness incites her anger. You have landed property. It is a source of income, no doubt, but you cannot keep body and soul together depending solely on that. Why are you not starting a business? It will add to your income."

"You have given me a right suggestion. I have no such capital at present to start a business. Nowadays landed property is useless. It has no value. A few months ago, I have had a job in a shoe factory. Products are up to the mark but sale is not satisfactory. Salary remained unpaid for a long period. Of course I did not get the push from the management. Being disgusted I quitted the job of my own accord. My drudgery was unproductive although I sweated blood to earn a pittance. I coaxed my wife to sell away her ornaments to help me start a business of my own. But she is quite unwilling to part with that. So my plan did not work out. What can I do in this present situation? Can any one give me a steer on this?"

"You do one thing. Try to sell some portion of your land fallen unyielding. It will bring you a lump sum to start out in business on a small-scale investment."

"Do you think I have not made any attempt to persuade the cultivators? But no body heat a path to my door. It is the labour problem which has scotched all my plan. Cultivators are unwilling to buy extra land as their own land remained unwrought. Over the past five years, there has been a precipitous fall in land sales. A person of hare-brained idea sells his land at giveaway price. I am hard-pressed this month for escalating costs of health care. Would you please lend me five hundred rupees? I will repay it after selling my rice."

"Why are you wavering to sell it now?"

"Don't you know the price of rice has been slumped down? This is not a favourable time. After a month it will rise again."

"All right, take three hundred at the moment. I have spent a good deal in printing my books. So I am unable to give you more than that."

"I understand your difficulty, Chinmay. You spend a lot but do not get that amount in return. Your achievements are something to be proud of. Don't disparage the character of somebody in your writing. We are all victims of the destiny."

Chinmay brought money and handed it to him.

To steer clear of his prattle, he said, "I am occupied with some urgent work. Now you go home and do your work. I have got a few odds and ends to do before evening".

"Yes, I am going, I will repay your money after a month."

"You won't have to pay back. Be relaxed."

There was a barren land about two hundred acres adjacent to Chinmay's homestead land. After division, he got only five dec. which was quite inadequate for his family. He wanted to purchase another five decimal. to add to his own and extend his area. Mr. Rudranarayan, a descendant of royal family was the owner of that land and he planned to sell off his whole assets and go back to Calcutta.

Chinmay was well-acquainted with him. There was a tin-shed at one corner of that vast land. Mr. Rudranaryan used to sit in that shed two times a day, morning and evening. His manager looked after his property and put the accounts register on his table for his perusal.

"Good evening, sir," Chinmay entered and saluted him.

Mr. Rudranaryan was poring over the register. He raised his head and gazed at Chinmay.

"Welcome, Mr. Chaudhury. How are you?"

He motioned him to sit on a chair.

"I am O.K. sir." Chinmay remained silent. He did not want to disturb him as he saw him absorbed in scrutinizing the accounts.

"Yes, tell me about your progress in writing. How far have you gone?" Mr. Rudranarayan asked him still bending his head.

"It is tough for one to get ahead in writing, sir. There are many hurdles to overcome to reach the finishing line". Chinmay said regretfully.

Chinmay was at a loss to take a decision. It would not be proper to query his personal matter. With slight hesitation he asked, "Sir, I heard you want to sell your landed property."

"Yes."

"I need a few decimal, sir."

Mr. Rudranarayan withdrew his eyes from the register and looked at him with curiosity.

"But I know your homestead land is a big one. Why do you want more?"

"Sir, after division, I got a very small piece of land. There is no extra space for gardening which is my favourite hobby. I feel clumsy in that compact area."

Mr. Rudranarayan surveyed his face and said, "Take that portion of land which abuts yours."

"How much have you decided per decimal, sir?"

"Twenty four thousand, But in your case, a bit reduction. Give me twenty two."

"Would you please lessen the amount a little?"

'How much?" he gave an ambiguous smile.

Chinmay was in a flap. He paused for a moment and said.

"I am ready to give eighteen thousand, sir.'

Mr. Rudranarayan said retrospectively, "The land was desolate and it was left untended for so many years, full of thorny plants, making it quite inaccessible. It was a boggy ground and some portion was remaining waterlogged throughout the year. Water lilies and hyacinths were growing in that swampy area. I virtually revivified the land lying in stupor by spending a huge amount of money on a massive clear-up operation. Then levelling of the ground, all are time-consuming and tedious work."

Mr. Rudranarayan stopped and took out a cigarette from his silver case and lighted it gingerly. He puffed out clouds of smoke with a relaxed mood and continued.

"I have not hiked up the price of the land. So twenty four thousand per decimal. is quite reasonable. People are ready to offer me a good price. I am not keen on money. I want to go back to Calcutta after cessation of this irksome task."

Then he smiled at Chinmay and said." You are earning a lot by selling your books. Why are you so cheese-paring to buy a land?"

"Sir, you made me laugh. Selling of books is quite discouraging. I have not yet cleared up the outstanding dues of the press. Books remained unsold in my study to rot. It is simply a mania I have been doting on. A man of sanity will not do this thing. I have no other source of income except my ancestral property. As you know how much one can earn from such sources, you can easily scale my financial stature."

"All right, you come to the Hotel Ambika at an early hour of night. Now I am staying there. Don't get nervous, I will settle the price favourably to your satisfaction."

"Yes, sir, when?"

"Tomorrow."

Mr. Gurucharan, a senior auditor of statistical department, came from Bhubaneswar as Mr. Rudranarayan promised him to offer six decimal. of homestead land, gratis. He was overexcited with this free offer. He would have to spend money only for its registration. Mr. Rudranarayan was his classmate and they had a very cordial relation right from their early schooling days.

Mr. Gurucharan was quite familiar with Chinmay as his younger brother was studying with him.

A little later afternoon, Mr. Gurucharan arrived at Chinmay's house and discussed this matter with him.

"How much did Rudra settle per decimal.?" he asked.

"Twenty two thousand"

"Are you agreed to pay that amount?"

"No, I just bargained and requested him to come down to eighteen thousand."

"What did he say?"

"I was asked to see him in the Hotel Ambika at night. He will resolve the matter there."

Mr. Gurucharan thought for a brief moment and said, "You see, Rudra is a scion of royal family. Money is peanuts for him. He dislikes bargain. Men of royal blood are not mean like us. I hope he will concur with you. I know him intimately from my childhood days. Do you think he does care for this petty amount? He has legal spouse both in India and America. Of course, for aught I know, he is not a womanizer. His American wife is the daughter of a millionaire, a business tycoon and owner of a car-manufacturing factory. Rudra spends lakhs of rupees a month on drinking and luxurious living. Let us go to him and see what fate has kept in store for us."

While going Mr. Gurucharan warned him, "Don't haggle over the price, it may raise his hackles. He will not go back upon his word, I assure you."

Hotel Ambika presented a very spectacular sight looking resplendent in multicoloured lights. They elbowed their way through the crowd of customers. At the counter, they learnt that Mr. Rudranarayan was staying in room no 135, a luxurious suite, always reserved for the effluents.

Mr. Gurucharan stood at the door of his room and knocked.

"Who is there?" The voice sounded like a command.

"I am Gurucharan."

"Oh Gurucharan, why are you standing outside? Please come in," the sternness of voice seemed to be subdued.

Mr. Gurucharan signalled Chinmay to wait for him and entered pushing the door. It banged shut behind him. Half an hour passed.

Chinmay could not know what was going on inside. He was waiting there with feverish excitement.

After sometime Mr. Gurucharan emerged. His face was dry and cheerless. He just fumbled, "Let us go back, I will tell you the matter later on."

He strode out of the hotel as if he was scared by some savage animal from behind.

On the way back home, Chinmay could not help asking him," What's the matter, brother?"

"Don't ask me, I faced a real embarrassing situation there", an effusion of despair was printed on his face.

"How"? Chinamy goggled at him with nervousness apprehending that his efforts were ineffectual on a wild goose chase.

"You know I entered his room. The moment I stepped in, Rudra struggled to get up from his cushion chair. He was eager to shake my hands but miserably slumped down into his chair. He was heavily drunk tonight, not in a state to have a discussion with us. Our plan went off at half-cock. Let us make an effort tomorrow morning." He pouted his lips with disgust that came with recollection of their foundering. His face distinctly mirrowed his disappointment, though he tried fruitlessly to hide his discomposure. Failure had cooled his enthusism.

At 8.30a.m. both Mr. Gurucharan and Chinmay hurried to the Hotel Ambica. The receptionist informed them that Mr. Rudranarayan left for Bhubaneswar half an hour before by his own car and from there he will go to Calcutta by air.

Chinmay felt himself overcome by a strange weariness. They went back without uttering a single word on the way. Mr. Gurucharan and Chinmay stood speechless under a lamp post for a while. The futility was clearly reflected in Mr. Gurucharan's two eloquent eyes. He could not surmise that his mission would be unsuccessful. With resignation he shook his head in despair and said," I am going back, Chinmay. See you later."

NINE

Dr. Behera came of a middleclass family who struggled hard in his school and college days to be a meritorious student having remarkable academic achievement. He knew only way to improve was through perseverance. Overcoming all the hurdles on his way, he rose to fame as a medicine specialist and was posted at Phulbani. His father-in-law wanted him to be posted in some more convenient place where he could earn a lot by private practice. So he insisted him to try for a transfer. But it was a well known fact that without bribe, the higher authorities will not take his appeal into account and his representation will go unnoticed. Dr. Behera made up his mind not to give a single pie to any one nor did he seek the help of a god-father in his case. He strongly refused to accept any suggestion as he was upright and disliked to grease somebody's palm against his principles.

Dr. Behera was Chinmay's close friend who had a penchant for him from his early college days. Chinmay heard that Dr. Behera came to Baripada for his personal work. As morning was the right time, he tramped along the road to see him.

His residence, a two storied building with a garden in the front kept Dr. Behera busy in hoeing the ground for he wanted to plant some flower plants there. It was overgrown with wild plants but he removed them with a spade. Whenever he came to his house, he looked after the garden. He made it spruce for a grand flowerbed sparing some time.

Chinmay found him working in the garden with a hoe in his hand. His body was glistening with sweat. He welcomed Chinmay with a smile and said, "Let me wash my hands and feet. Then we will sit in the drawing room."

He stopped his work and rubbed himself down after a wash.

There was no one in the drawing room. Dr. Behera shut the front door and sat on the sofa. He looked at Chinmay reflectively and unburdened himself stating a sorrowful incident. He slowly uttered with a tinge of dejection.

"I came to Baripada only to solve a complicated problem of my family affairs. You know I am staying single at Phulbani. My wife being the only daughter of her parents is staying here to take care of them. My son, after completion of computer engineering, married a girl of his choice who was once studying with him in college. Of course I had not seen that girl before marriage. I had not the faintest idea that this love affair was going on for a long period. I contacted several persons for his marriage negotiation. One day he suddenly came to me and said that he wanted to marry a girl whom he knew from his college days. He liked her attitude and temperament. Some facts would remain anonymous if he married a girl by arranged marriage. Though wounded by his unpolished behaviour, I did not frustrate him for he would hold me responsible if any untoward incident will happen later on. I was in complete dark what he was planning in the mean time. Without our knowledge, he married her in a temple and after a month came back with his wife.

That afternoon I was sitting as usual on the veranda on a chair. Suddenly a car halted at our gate and from it got down my son and his wife. My reverie broke when I heard the click of the gate and they entered our compound. The girl was in an off-beat dress, quite vulgar and repellent. A man of refined taste and sensibility will not like such highly objectionable outfit. Strange nauseating feelings ran down my spine. A spasm of anger or anxiety, I could not say exactly, came over me and I was shell- shocked. I fell unconscious on that chair. Though my sense was revived, I lost all the charms for my life ever since their intrusion. He is my only son and for him I had a lofty aim and aspiration but that would be shattered so miserably, I could not imagine. I was stung to the quick by his insolent behaviour. My wife asked me many questions when she saw my doleful face. Although I myself was in terrible anguish I did not disclose my feelings. I think she might be suffering from the same agony. As woman is an embodiment of endurance, she was unable to express her heartache though her soul might be crying. There was a conjugal row, now and then, spoiling the peaceful atmosphere of our home. Some months passed this way. The girl was actually bareft of soft feelings and was haughty and despisingly nasty in her outlook and behaviour. When their feud reached an intolerable point, she took a stealthy flight to her parents. They were also shameless and supported their daughter. They could have attempted to bring a mutual understanding between them. Instead they started a divorce case in the court and along with that a compensation suit demanding five lakh rupees. I have already consulted my lawyer. Now my worries are only for my son and I am a bit imbalanced thinking over the consequence of this case. I am now senescent. Sometimes I become so much perturbed that I forget where I have kept my keys and spectacles. I fear, I am going senile. The constant worries are the cause of my diabetes and hypertension. I could not think my children would be the main reason of my displeasure and all sorts of anxieties. So I resigned myself to fate and bound to swallow the bitter pill of life."

Dr. Behera tried to choke back his tears and fell into silence. Chinmay was listening but he knew where the shoe pinches. A man with embittered and agonising experiences can only realize the pain of others. No consolation can give relief to a mentally traumatized man. However he said: "Our time is quite different from present days. I can't accept the theory of generation gap wholeheartedly. Of course I admit the evolutionary changes in man's life but this present generation has transgressed all social norms. A number of factors are responsible for that. This environment is so vicious that they catch the infection of modern society and go astray. They are awfully devoid of foresight. They are merely aping the western culture and do not pick up the basic values of life. This recklessness at the formative period is the major cause of their sorrows. The actual aim of education is character building. But I regret to say that there is no moral education in our curriculum. So character building remains a remote dream for us. Our moral lapses are ignored because nobody gives importance to that. Everybody thinks it as the general 'go' of the world. You see, to what extent our society has been degraded. Rape, murder, arson, suicide, rowdyism have become the order of the day. Bestiality is sporadic and a day will come when it will engulf the entire society. There is no remorse or repentance for their unforgivable offence. The rogues are careless and doing all sorts of nuisance intrepidly although there is a law to restrain their hateful activities. Tougher life long imprisonment or capital punishment is not acting as a deterrent to the would-be offenders. A good advice sounds absurd to them. They are supercilious and do everything whimsically as a result society has gone down to an abysmal depth of debasement. It is obvious that the future of our next generation is full of darkness. If the law-makers turn to law-breakers how could you be optimistic of a drastic change in society? He should be beheaded by a guillotine if somebody tries to ravish a woman. The chastity of woman is now being molested. The moral fabric of society has been torn apart. It is sickening to think over the horrible incidents which are occuring in broad day light every second in our country. The depravation has reached its culmination. Even a small child is not reprieved from that. The public would be jubilant if their genitals would be severed by a sharp razor. White slave traffic is going on uncurbed regardless of measures taken by the government. The bootleggers and criminals are contesting in the election to come to power. You must have read in the newspaper how a girl had been frequently molested by her step-farther. So one must conclude that society is going towards moral devastation."

"What is your suggestion to tackle this present problem?" Dr. Behera asked, looking desperate. "I have been flustered for my wayward son. If anything untoward happens, it would be like, on my part, committing a social suicide.

"I guess, that girl is incorrigible. A broken glass cannot be joined together. Once conjugal life is split up, you cannot bring back the harmony by patching it up by force or persuasion. Regarding alimony, you try to convince them to come down to a lesser amount. Your son has committed a serious blunder and you have to make reparation to them. After finalisation of divorce, you seek a girl of your choice and the matter ends there." His heart melted seeing his grief-stricken face.

After lunch chinmay retired to his bed room and took a nap with a disturbed mind. His wife Maya scrubbed the vessels and kept them in the kitchen. She entered their bed room and shot a glance at him and asked," Have you enlisted our monthly provisions? I have forgotten to mention two important things. You are very fond of cakes. Please bring one kilo of molasses and two kilos of sundried rice. Don't forget to add these to your list. Do you hear me?"

Maya was always overconscious to replenish her store to find all necessary things at hand.

"I have not slept, Maya. I am just tossing in the bed." He got up and said, "Let us go on an outing this afternoon somewhere. I have been mentally disturbed for Dr. Behera's unexpected mishap. Poor fellow……"

"Yes, you have told me the fact. Good or bad comes according to God's dispensation. One cannot infringe the infallible judgement of the destiny."

"That is true. I feel pity for him. What he has not done for his children? They do not understand the grief of their parents. For their wrongful act, parents suffer without their faults."

"I do agree but it is quite absurd to be remorseful. The wretched son is absolutely unfeeling. What his parents can do? Let us be ready. I will dress up myself in a few minutes."

Maya preened her standing before the mirror. She combed her hair and dabbed her upperpart of body by scented talcum powder with a powder –puff, dotted the cream all over her face and scanned her every profile turning this side and that.

Maya had no such good chance to step out of the house. She used to derive much pleasure in doing household works. At the time of festivals, she got a privilege to visit temple with her mother-in-law. Since her death, she didnot like to go anywhere else. For her home sickness, very often, she had been admonished by her friendly neighbours. Chinmay too often criticized her for she unceasingly engaged herself like a busy bee in drudgery of housework.

Their sons were poring over the books in their study and the daughters were tucked up snugly in bed. Leaving the house in their care, they went out.

They went past the Roxy cinema hall, District veterinary centre and Urban cooperative bank. When they reached near a petrol pump, Chinmay's old friend Pradeep got down from his scooter and hailed them.

"Hi, Chinmay, outing? Good, good…."

"Yes, just strolling here and there for relaxation."

"Very good. I am happy to see you together."

He gave an encouraging smile and sped off.

Maya was out on a spree. She felt like floating in the air as a bird got rid of its cage. There was some residential buildings, lining the road. She kept looking at them.

"This is a posh area. There is a scramble to buy plots in this locality. In that headlong rush, quite a number of people got into debt. This is the central place of the town where shopping centres are gradually extending to western side."

"Yes, if our house had been in this place, market and bus-stand would have been within our spitting distance. Going to market means you have to hire an auto calling for an unnecessary expenditure."

Maya's face seemed to be shadowed with displeasure. Chinmay tried to mollify her.

"Maya, money is everything. I am not a blessed one to buy a plot here. Be satisfied with what you have."

Maya harboured a deep resentment against her husband. She despised a man who was mentally impoverished. She could not nourish such a negative thought. She pretended she was not irritated but the expression on her face was a dead giveaway.

"I did not mean that." she reconciled. "Have you reduced to a penury? You are always haunted by an inferiority complex that you are not financially well-off, so what?" She tried to compose his features into a smile.

"Maya, you mean that, but I never mind. I don't feel contrite about my financial condition. I have a plan in my mind to go on an all-India tour. I have a cherished dream to show you some worthseeing places. I don't know what fate has decreed for me." His stoic resignation towards fate set him unruffled by any accusations. A glow of placidity and forbearance was clearly discernible on his face.

"Is it?" Maya pressed her mouth with the skirt of her sari. "How will you get the passage money, my dear? You really made me laugh. You always day-dream, do you not?

When my son will earn a lot, he will definitely take me to all these places. Do you think I repose my hope in you?"

"Maya, luck is not in my favour. I have had hope that all my books will be sold and I shall have a required amount of money to defray the expenses of our journey."

"I don't want to discourage you. You have written a good number of books. They have been piled in a corner of your study. Nowadays nobody is interested to read. All have a hectic business schedule. Where is the time for book reading? Please, don't mind. I dislike wastage of money without fruition."

"Maya, you are mistaken and benighted. To gain something, you have to give someting in return with equal measure. The more vivid you realise sorrow, the more eager you will be to search for that. This is my quest, I would rather say a frantic and incessant quest for life. I am always obsessed with that aim to explore that uncharted land which still remains obscure to mankind. I only want your wholehearted moral support. Then it will bolster my morale and I shall dive deep into that unfathomable ocean in search of that rare gem. Nobody can impede me to have that drive and initiative. I have eschewed all the worldly comforts for my writing. This is the only luxury I cherish in my life which gives me immesurable pleasure. Maya, delete that thought from your mind at this moment. That will rather spoil our happiness. Let us go to that restaurant, over there."

'Balaji Restaurant' had lately been set up and it gained popularity for its delicacies. It was a Chic South Indian restaurant and its cuisine was different from others. South Indians are expert in this field and they know how to prepare relishing food and serve them at the cheapest rate.

Both entered the restaurant. All the tables were occupied by the customers, no empty space for them. A waiter came over to them, "Sir, come to the upper floor. There are a few rooms meant for the family.' He accompanied them and made them sit in a comfortable room.

The floor was dazzling bright and it was set with vitrified tiles. Maya's eyes were flitting all around the room.

"Sir, here is the menu for you. Please select your items."

The waiter placed the menu chart on the table and left.

"Would you eat ' masala dosha' with some chutney, anything you like." Chinmay asked

Maya nodded her head with approval.

In other room, close to theirs, two boys and two girls were sitting face to face by a table. They were eating their refreshments with spoon. The door was wide open and Maya threw a sneaky glance at them. From their gestures and postures, she thought them to be college students. While eating, they were exchanging their pleasantries. She could not hear clearly what they were talking about. She only caught snatches of their conversation. After a romantic interlude, the girls burst into a peal of laughter and the boys also laughed with them baring their teeth.

Maya gave a signal to Chinmay with her eyes.

"Hush ! don't look at them," Chinmay whispered. "You watch them, how frisky and flirtatious they are!"

Lowering his voice he said, "They must have fixed this rendezvous by contacting each other by mobiles. This is the safest place where they can talk freely. Day by day this intimacy will go deeper. Then one day these boys will elope with these girls and inform their parents, "Dear parents, we got married, forgive and forget, don't deprive us of your blessings."

Maya began to giggle enjoying his humour.

Chinmay added: "You look at the dress of these girls. How raunchy and indecent! Have you marked how they have gone beyond a sense of decorum? Their erotic dress is sexually stimulating to men. That is why they feel horny and go crazy to rape them at knife point."

"Do you call this love-making?" Maya asked with repulsion.

"Not at all .This is grossly physical. 'Wham-bam, thank you ma'am.'- a freaky sentimentality having no genuineness. I have also crossed my youthful days, now verging on old age. But I failed to know what love really means. It remained abstruse to me till to this day. Why are you grinning?"

"For nothing. I am just amazed at your deep study in love affairs. Are you a simpleton? I don't think so?"

"Maya, are you trying to belittle me by your blue jokes? Don't defile me that way. I have taken the shelter of god and spend my days with perfect balance in reading and writing. For this reason, I never lose my mental equipoise though I am cumbered off and on by some obstacle in my life. Have you ever read the autobiography of R.K. Narayan 'My Days'? He was a famous novelist and one cannot tear oneself away from reading this book. After his wife's death, he became completely upset. As he was under the spell of writing books, his misery could not affect him. So in my opinion writing is a divine virtue, no doubt."

'Yes, I do agree. But you told me that you are drifting towards old age. I could not accept it. You apparently look old but your mind is still green and full of exuberance, a real Dorian Gray, untouched by the ageing process".

"Why are you so hypocritical, Maya? I am quite normal, nothing more, nothing less. There is an English word, illusion. You are that veritable illusion which I could not fathom its depth yet. Those boys may think us eavesdropper. Let us go as soon as possible. Yes, I have lost my thread of conversation. What do you like to eat now? There are so many palatable things up to your choice. Is the food stuff not appeasing to you?"

Chinmay called the waiter to bring them some pudding. They started eating pudding made of cheese. Chinmay emptied the rest of the water in a tumbler at one gulp and asked, "Would you like to eat something else, salted peanuts spiced with chillies?"

"No, no, this is sufficient." Maya rose up from her seat and went over a washing basin fitted to the wall. She rinsed her mouth with tap water and waited for Chinmay.

After paying the bill, they came out.

"What's our next mission?" Chinmay belched and asked looking at the Roxy cinema hall.

"No, no, let us go home. Our children must be waiting for us." Maya looked visibly worried.

"All right, as you like, but don't fret. I am sure they are quite o.k. there. They are grown-up and they know how to look after their own business."

"I always keep a beady eye on them. You won't understand my fretfulness because you are not their mother."

"Yes, yes I do agree. Like a hen, you have kept your chickens under a safe shelter spreading your wings. Oh, my darling, how affectionate you are !" Chinmay caressed her hand in fun.

"Do you know we are in a public road? Some people may be staring at us with curiosity, don't cut your ugly jokes here."

"Don't remind me. I have not gone beyond decency. Everybody knows here we are husband and wife. No one will think us immodest if we walk hand in hand along this road."

Maya suppressed her laugh by pressing her lips. "You old shameless fellow!" her eyes flashed a mild reproof.

Back home Maya rested a while on the bedstead.

The children were in the drawing room watching the T.V.

After washing his face, Chinmay went to his bed room and saw Maya sitting motionless.

"Why did you not change your dress, Maya?" he asked while searching a bag for shopping.

"I feel tired," Maya replied without a fuss.

"A little walk has exhausted you so much? Look here, I am going to the market. Call to mind what other things we have omitted. Once I come back, I won't go again. You use to forget this and that and pester me later."

"No, no, I have given you a precise list. Have you kept it with you?"

"Yes I have kept it in my pocket."

Chinmay went out.

After returning from shopping errand, Chinmay went in his study and started reading a book.

Maya was busy in the kitchen. After 10.30 she appeared at the threshold of study and asked, "Would you take your food now? I will serve it on the table. Don't delay, please come to the dining room?"

Chinmay came to the dining room and asked, "Have our children finished their eating?"

"Yes, yes, after eating they have fallen asleep."

Maya served bread and dal on a plate for Chinmay and herself sat with fried rice in a small pot.

"Why fried rice, Maya? Don't you feel appetite tonight?"

"I don't know why I have no appetite, a feeling of fullness is there."

"If you don't take anything, your stomach will be distended with gas. It is not good to remain on empty stomach."

"Since we returned from the restaurant, I am not feeling well. My abdomen seems to be bloated with gas" Maya made a wry face.

"Perhaps the restaurant food is not agreeable to you. The drinking water must have carried infection which upset your stomach. It is difficult to get filtered water in hotel and restaurant. The plates and dishes on which they serve food are not thoroughly washed. So it is not a matter of surprise if we would be caught by some infection."

"Finish your eating quickly. I feel drowsy and I won't wait any more. It will take more than an hour to complete my work before retiring to bed."

The whole house fell into complete silence. Only at a distance a few vehicles coming and streaking off with blow of horn split the stillness of night.

Chinmay's sleep was suddenly interrupted by a throaty gurgling sound coming from the bath room. With a start, he got up and went near the bath room. The door was open and Maya, leaning over the washing basin, was spewing out what she had taken a few hours before.

She heard the footstep and turned to Chinmay. Her face was screwed up with retching and she was panting.

"What happened to you?" Chinmay asked with consternation.

She came back staggering supported by the wall.

"I have been to the latrine. I have had five loose motions. My throat also has been badly lacerated from vomiting." She could hardly speak a few words. She gasped with pain and slumped against the wall.

"Did you? It is diarrhoea. You must have caught infection either from food or water. These two are the vehicle of infection. Now two gates are open, diarrhoea and vomiting. It may lead to dehydration. But why did you not tell me as to your suffering?" Her indifference cheesed him off.

"I thought but did it not to break your sleep. You get irritated by the slightest reason, so…"

Chinmay was cross with her for her carelessness. He threw up his hands in horror at her inadvertent attitude.

"If your stomach was not well, why did you take fried rice? How could you think it proper side-stepping your husband while you are suffering? You could have told me beforehand when you felt some uneasiness."

It irked her further and she said with vexation," Let me suffer, I won't care if something terrible happens to me."

She went back tottering to her bed and lay on it as if she was at death's door. This repeated diarrhoea and vomiting precipitated her into a state of depression.

"It is difficult to get medicine at this unearthly hour. Who will open his medicine store at night for me? Of course we should have stored some necessary medicines for common ailments. How do you feel now?"

"Vomiting has stopped but a rumbling, gurgling sound is still there in my abdomen. Profuse jelly-like mucus is also going out with flatus. I feel a griping pain inside my abdomen," she said with moan.

A few minutes after, she again rushed to the latrine. Chinmay was waiting outside.

"The trouble is same or some change has come in your motion?" Chinmay asked when Maya came out of the latrine after washing.

"No, this time there is no faecal matter, only faint yellowish water gushing out with force," Maya uttered with pain grimacing her face.

"Body mechanism is like that. It will excrete all the unwanted things in a natural process. But we should be aware of dehydration. If the water contents in your body will be depleted by ejection through two apertures (anus and mouth), then there is every possibility of dehydration. We have to wait till morning. I shall consult a medicine specialist as soon as possible. Don't worry. Five or six loose motions will not affect your health so badly."

As the day broke, Chinmay ran to the doctor. The clinic was not opened. It was attached to a big medicine store.

The owner of the store was busy in writing down the serial number. On a small card, he scribbled no.6 and handed it to Chinmay. His assistant opened the door of the clinic before the arrival of the doctor. The patients and their relatives came one after another and crowded the place. Arousing a stir in the gathering of people, the doctor got off a car. He went straight to his chamber with a solemn face, radiating dignity, without casting a side glance to any one. One by one went in and came out with their prescriptions in hand. Chinmay was waiting impatiently for his turn. He pushed the door and got in.

The doctor heard him out and said," Oh, it is nothing. It is simply indisposition caused by food poisoning. It is not so severe and you should not bother about it now. Here I have prescribed some medicines which will stop diarrhoea as well as vomiting. For dehydration, she must be feeling weakness. Drop this small pack of powder in one fourth litre of water, shake it well and let her drink five times a day. The next morning she would be quite o.k."

"Sir, what diet is to be given to her?"

"Don't give her any solid food today on any account. Keep her on liquid like barley, sago, and butter milk and at interval small quantity of pear or pomegranate juice. You may give her glucose, if you like. It will help recoup her strength in a short period."

Chinmay gave him an obliging smile, paid him his fees and came out.

With medicines he returned.

After a little wash, Maya was seated on the bedstead. She looked shrivelled and her eyes were puffy and lustreless with dark patches below.

"Why did you take so much time to get back?" Maya asked in a weak voice.

"There was a crowd in the waiting room to see the doctor. I had to push my way through the crowd although I had a serial number. Now have a look at these medicines"

He put them by her side and said, "This one is to be taken in the morning and evening after food, this before going to bed and this packet of powder to be dropped in a tumbler of water. Drink it five times a day and what is more you will be put on liquid diet for one day. Then you will be all right. Do you follow me.?"

"Yes"

"I am more than a little shaken that saline drip might be required for you. But by mercy of god, we have been saved from that ordeal."

She plucked up courage from his words and a faint smile played on her ashen face.

Chinmay said philosophically, "You see, we had been to that restaurant in a happy mood but we did not know a danger was there lurking unforeseen to strike us. I remember the saying of swami Vivekananda relevant in this context written somewhere in my note book. This is no doubt, an eye-opener to us. 'Our difficulty in life is that we are guided by the present and not by the future. What gives us a little pleasure now drags us on to follow it, with the result that we always buy a mass of pain in the future for a little pleasure in the present.' This is the truth and an absolute truth for the whole human society to be remembered.

TEN

Maya put all the shabby clothes in the washing machine and turned the switch on.

"Would you give me your shirts and trousers ? I am not in a position to move from this place. Don't you want them to get washed? How do you wear those squalid dresses for such a long period? Stained with perspiration, your clothes give off a bad smell. I don't like your nasty habit. I feel like vomiting".

Chinmay was in his study. The novel he was writing was not completed yet. It always remained incomplete. An insatiable desire spurred him and he went on to write three more novels in rapid succession. He felt something was still there to be told and analysed. It must be fascinating to be appreciated by all. Like a painter and sculptor he always remained dissatisfied in his own work.

He came out of study and stood leaning against the door panel, a couple of feet away from the washing machine.

Maya bent forward and kept dropping the sullied dresses one by one in the machine. She removed her strand of hair dangling on her forehead by palm and said, "You know. I have to clean up these dresses before I leave for Rahama. Then I would remain busy in other works. No time to sit idle or gossip. Yes, where is your pants and shirts?"

"No worry my dear, I would wash them myself. Right from my student days I have been doing this clean-up operation in a plastic bucket. No machine can clean it so well as my hands do rinsing them in a bucket."

"All right, do as you like. Go to the market this evening. Purchase all those things that I have told you. Mental-note would do nothing. Write it down on a scrap of paper. There are certain things which are not available in that place. I don't want to omit a single item which is quite essential for my grandson."

"Don't worry, I have made a note of those things what you have dictated".

"What my son-in-law and daughter could do? Mother-in-law is a ripe old woman, much senior to us. She remains in her village. Too decrepit to look after her grand-son. So they are unwilling to take her to their service place. Both are service holders. Who is there to take care of the child? No alternative. I must have to go."

"What happened to that maidservant? She was coming regularly to do their household chores".

"Oh, that woman. She comes in the morning and scurries home before evening. My grand-son, quite tender in age, two years only, not grown up yet. There is no one to feed it. Who would be there by its bedside? They are helpless. Hopeless too. That maidservant's husband was working in a temple. It was quite okay till that period. He was transferred to some other temple at Puri. So his wife was compelled to go with him. It is a real difficult task to find a maidservant. Now it has become a headache for us."

"Yes, your presence there is the only solution. They would be free and feel themselves relaxed".

"You don't know how they have been harassed by a number of persons. To seek a maidservant, my son-in-law had gone to his brother-in-law's house. There he found one. She assured him that she would go after harvest time. She asked him to give one thousand rupees in advance. He gave that amount in good faith. Now you guess the result."

"I know. She just pocketed the money. It was a shrewd

move of that woman to hoodwink a simpleton like him. She befooled him with ease. What did he do then ?

"Then he wrung his hands at home. What could he do? Just mislaid his money serving no purpose."

"We all encounter a horrible situation at present. Society has changed a lot. Too difficult to find a reliable person".

"My son-in-law discussed the matter with a colleague. He was sympathetic and agreed to rescue him from this worrying situation. That woman was a divorcee since long. She was working in the house of a wealthy man living in Mumbai. She was fired for shirking. She was forced to come to her native village after two years.

"Then ?"

That woman was looking for a job. That colleague broght her from her village and he gave them full assurance that she will do all the household chores. But she did not do anything. Now I understand why she did lose her shelter in the previous place."

"Actually I don't know all these things", Chinmay said.

"She did nothing. I mean no household chores. A strange woman".

"What?"

"Yes. When she stepped in, my daughter was very much delighted. On that very day, she gave her a new sari and blouse to keep her in good humour. After eating she crouched in a corner and started dozing."

" A really wonderfull woman. She does not know work brings its own relief. He, who is most idle, has most grief."

"My daughter thought perhaps she had not slept last night or long journey had exhausted her too much. The next morning, after breakfast, she washed her utensils, threw them to a corner and began to doze. She remained reticent throughout the day. When she was asked to sweep the house and scrub the vessels, she denied any knowledge of the household work. Thus she remained unresponsive and uncommunicative for the rest of the day. My daughter at last lost her temper. She burst out " You have had all the fun and I have had all the hard work. I have never seen a lazy woman like you. That is why you have been driven out of your house. No husband will keep such an inactive and slothful wife in his home."

"What a woman she is !" Chinmay became irritated.

"Then my son-in-law informed that negotiator. He reprimanded her and felt sorry for putting them to so much troubles. He was the person who had recommended her as a dynamic maidservant. He was the real trouble-maker who landed them into difficulty although he knew her work-shy nature."

"This world is full of strange men and women", Chinmay remarked. "They should not have come as a humanbeing. What I see, nobody could be entrusted with the duty of a housekeeper. Oh Maya ! there are more things in heaven and earth than are dreamt of in your philosophy"

"Now hear the activities of another woman. Before my daughter left for her office, she instructed that woman to feed the child at the right time. She took the full opportunity of her absence. She gobbled up the food meant for the child and fed it a little amount. The child remained half-fed but who was there to watch her activities? Very often, she takes the mobile of my daughter and goes to upstairs. There she rings to her paramour. But that fact remained obscure for so many days. At last it came to light and she was driven out of the house immediately."

"How strange the character of a woman! They blame us that we have not searched a maidservant wholeheartedly. They cannot be convinced. But we have left no stone unturned to find one. Some of her colleagues have found their full-time servants, working day and night. But how we people are beaten to find one in our locality inhabited by so many people of different castes?"

Maya tucked up the skirt of her sari in her waist and said, "Now the situation is quite different. Our Government has made it so. The lower class people are getting all sorts of facilities. They are no more living at the mercy of others. They won't go to your door nor you could wheedle them by your nice talks. In those days they were loyal and grateful but in this altered situation, they have become most ungrateful wretch. Now take a glaring example of my friend's house. A tribal woman is working there. Every day his wife offers her tea and refreshment in the morning. She is kindhearted and gives the woman her discarded saries and blouses. On 'makar sankranti' festivals, she would offer her a new brand sari and blouse. She still grouches. She just scrounges many things from their house. Whenever she falls in some financial difficulty, they voluntarily help her according to their capacity. Could they satisfy her? I would utter a very offensive word, 'ingratitude'. That is in her blood. People of that category always remain disgruntled. You cannot propitiate them by all means, in spite of your best efforts."

Chinmay disliked their ungratefulness. In this present time there is no way out to mend their ways of thoughts. They are a frightful snob. They only lick the feet of moneyed persons. He recalled a famous saying of Samuel Garth " Ingratitude is a weed of every crime. It thrives too fast at first, but fades in time."

Maya cut in and said, "A few months back, our daughter did a very silly thing. She had given advertisement straight in the newspaper seeking a housekeeper. When I heard this, I became horrified. She did not have an idea that they are house-breakers, That would rather enmesh her in a tangle of further troubles. I have heard a lot of things about their exploitation. They are the first rate cut-throats. They never waver to do heinous deeds like rape and murder. They brutally wipe out the lives of the owners and run away with valuables. They are heartless butchers. They uproot the tree under which shade and protection they thrive. How can a house holder dare to keep such a treacherous person in his house ? What is more, our son-in-law and daughter have some taboos. They won't allow a person of lower caste to work in their house and they scrupulously stick to that. It is impossible to fulfil their conditions."

Chinmay got busy in washing his clothes. While washing he said, "I know all these facts. If you adhere to a social taboo, you won't find a single person. The higher caste people are not gravels of road that you can pick up as you fancy. The caste system is going to be totally abolished in this present day social hierarchy."

Maya put all the wet cloths in a basket and squeezed the water out and spread them in the sun. She came back and said, "Now they came to their senses and scrubbed all the plans to keep a maid-servant. They hinge on me. I must help them in their inconvenient time."

Chinmay emptied the bucket and sat on a chair. He wiped his face with a towel and said, "Maya, I won't regret any inconvenience caused by your absence. Rather I am glad that my grand-son would remain in your tender loving care. They have pinned their hopes on you. I will see you go unconcerned."

Maya pulled out a large bag from a steel almirah and kept it on her bedstead. It was difficult to go with such a large bag. She would carry a few necessary things and no more than that. She twisted her body to relax her muscles and went inside the bedroom. She started to fling the bed sheets, pillow covers, handkerchiefs and her sweat-stained blouses into a heap and said, "I will get them cleaned before I leave for Rahama. Two important things I have forgotten. Pure honey and castor-oil are not available in that place. Add these things to your list and go to 'Baidyanath Pranda'. Really I like Rahama. Fresh vegetables and fish are available in plenty in the market. It is a few miles away from Paradeep, a bustling port on the seashore. From early morning there is a rush of fishmongers in the fish market selling variety of fishes. Have you ever tasted 'Khanga'? A seafish which is my favourite. Both husband and wife are fond of fish. My son-in-law used to visit the fish market regularly. They cook delicious food at least three times a week. Go there and relish it."

Maya was exalted and she threw all the dirty clothes one by one into the washing machine with high spirits.

Chinmay was swinging his legs sitting on a chair. He looked at Maya and felt happy seeing her beaming face.

"Last time I had been to that place. Somebody had mentioned the taste of 'Khanga'. Many people say that 'hilsa' and 'khanga' are identical in taste. So with that yen I went to the market with my son-in-law. But unfortunately we found it nowhere. It was the breeding season. The fish monger told us to wait for a month. But I came back after a week," said Chinmay impassively.

"My son-in-law deserves praise for his strenuous journey by train from Rahama to Bhubaneswar. Though he gets used to it, it is very painful and monotonous by bus and it takes about two and half hours to cover the distance. I always try to avoid journey by bus which is overstraining and prefer train to travel comfortably."

"Remember, don't get down somewhere by mistake. Generally an express bus halts for fifteen minutes at Bhadrak bus stand and there you may go to a lavatory. Don't take any junk food on the way. It will rather upset your stomach, "Chinmay made her cautious

"No, no, I rarely take any food of roadside restaurant while travelling to some place. Mostly I take mixture and fried rice with me. A packet of biscuit and some fruits like banana and apple would be always there in my bag."

"Very well."

After dinner, they retired to their bedroom. Silence reigned and in the still hour of midnight, a muted voice emanated. It stirred the core of his heart and he was plagued by a jumble of questions. What was his achievement during his long career? Did it bear any significance? Right from his childhood days, he was a stoic. He had taken pleasure and pain in a similar vein. But what was that evil force which always put him into endless troubles? His opponents were seeking opportunity to stab him on his back. They derived malicious pleasure seeing him in a stressful condition. He was awfully devoid of practical knowledge. That was the problem with him. He was pig-ignorant that this world is full of jealousy. He was expected to be violent to dodge their blows. Years of failure and torture sapped him of his confidence and it undermined his forte. He had a vague hope that some one would be there to share his woes, a soul of sympathetic heart to remove his afflictions. His receptackle of life would be spilled out with love and affections. But his euphoric mood did not last long. When that spell broke he found that he was keeping only cursory relation with others. He was taken as a day-dreamer and his ideas were reckoned as absurd and baseless. Nobody liked his frenzied activity. Everything seemed incompatible to him. His much vaunted sacrifice was not exemplary in this present world. They were under the impression that he was going crazy day by day. They cackled with mischievous delight. The path chosen by him was beset by so many obstacles. He tried to overcome them but he stumbled and fell. Again he exerted himself to move forward. He was tempted to change his stand and veer to another direction. He acquired knowledge to counteract the inimical forces. He learnt that if somebody would try to assault him, he should be equally aggressive to strike him. In this present day society he should be a legpuller, backbiter, wifebeater, deserving all the praise-worthy names. Then why did he forsake the golden path which would have spurred him on to the goal of success? Which was that invisible power which preempted him from going to the wrong path? What was that divine mercy which reinforced his self-confidence and kept him afloat from drowning in that deluge? What was that force which enabled him to regain his strength to hit back at their salvo of criticisms? Who was he who taught him to walk on the sharp edge of the sword? How could he manage to remain immune from the vicious attacks of the external world? Why did he follow His foot prints with single-minded devotion? That was the saddest time in his life which really bothered him and he questioned the Lord about it.

"Lord, you said that once I decided to follow you, you would walk with me all the way. But I have noticed that during the most troublesome times in my life, there is only one set of footprints. I don't understand why when I needed you the most you would leave me."

The Lord replied, "My precious, precious child. I love you and I would never leave you. During your times of trial and suffering, when you see only one set of footprints in the sand, it was then that I carried you."

The all-pervading firmament echoed with the explosion of his subtle thoughts and he slumbered fitfully throughout the night. Time ticked away.

ELVEN

The people of Baripada town experience a queer monsoon. It starts from the second week of June and ends in the third week of September. The south-west monsoon which arises from the Bay of Bengal causes heavy downpour. The soil which has been fissured and seethed with terrible heat sends forth a sweet thrilling scent when the sky is split by thunderclaps followed by torrential rains. Sometimes a dark bank of glowering clouds pour down ice-crystals with scarce rain scattered all over the place. The children break into a run through the lashing wind to gather those ice-crystals and put them in a bucket or tumbler. After a while it coagulates and takes the form of a tapering spike of ice which they hang on bamboo poles simulating stalactites. They spatter the water accumulated in the puddles by the road side, run at full pelt to the river bank through dribbling rain and dive into the lap of the river Budhabalang.

The Similipal hills looming like a giant sentinel over the tree tops in the distant horizon get blurred through frosty rain. But before that the people go through terrific heat. The whirl wind accumulates all the dust and dry leaves and go past the people and then shot up in spirals. The pedestrians rub their eyes filled with dust particles. They get annoyed but there is no escapade from this sweltering heat. They are compelled to stay in this baking oven.

After a midday siesta Chinmay was sitting in his study flipping through an incomplete novel. An auto halted just in front of his gate. He peeped through the window and saw Jayram and his wife getting down.

"What a great surprise ! I am happy to see you together after so many days." Chinmay greeted them while opening the gate. They sat on the sofa. Jayram's eyes darted inquisitively around the room.

"Is not your wife at home?", he asked staring at the interior.

"No, she has been to Rahama to see my grandson".

"How many days she will remain there?"

"That is indefinite. Because my daughter and son-in-law, both are service holders. There is no one to take care of the child. At first my wife was unwilling to go there as I have to go to the hotel during her absence".

"So you are single. Don't you feel lonely in this big house?"

"No, rather it is an advantage to write something undisturbed. Leave it. But you have not told me the purpose of your surprise visit". Chinmay asked, smiling.

"You know my continual friction with my elder brother. He is now vilifying me giving some derogatory statement before my friends. We have become a butt of ridicule among the neighbours".

"That is happening as you are living under the same roof. It is better for you to shift to some other place. There is another small building of your own in the backyard. You shift there and live in peace". Chinmay suggested.

"But I have given it to a business man on rent".

"So what ? Who says to evict that tenant ? You can tell him to rent another house".

"It's a good suggestion. I will do it in a few days". Jayram shook his head.

"It is incumbent on me to warn you that you must keep good relation with your wife. Your mutual conflict gives them a good chance to scoff at you."

"To speak the truth I had been deranged and veered to a wrong route instigated by my mother and sisters. I paid heavy penalty for that. Now I realize my mistake. and ready to face the music." Jayram's face registered repentance for his past follies.

"That is in some way good. Once a man realizes his mistake, he will not tread that path again. I will not countenance you being rude to your wife. She must have come of a good family. If somebody were in her place, the situation would have been something different."

Jayram's wife all along sat mute without giving comment. She interrupted them in the middle and said, "I have forewarned him repeatedly but he did not take a heed to my advice. Now he is getting a taste of his own medicine".

Jayram stared at the floor. He could not raise his face for what he had done previously without qualms.

His wife grinned and said, "Mr. Chinmay, you please say to your friend to give up his shabby habits'."

"What is that?" Chinmay gaped at them.

"He sometimes moves about in a scruffy outfit for which I am quite ashamed of. You know guests come to our house off and on. What impression they will carry of him ? I can't understand why is he so niggardly and finds pleasure donning himself with odious rags ?".

Chinmay thought for a while and said, "It is not for his stinginess. He does something inadvertantly. What I have observed he never gives importance to dress or encourages a luxurious habit right from his childhood days".

Jayram saw his wife's temper tantrums but remained quiet.

He changed the topic and while shaking his legs sitting on the sofa he asked, "Have you completed the novel?"

"No, not yet. I had busied myself with cultivation work. I did not get full time to speed up writing. Moreover my progress is not satisfactory."

"Get it printed as early as possible. If you are in a dearth of money and necessity arises, I shall feel myself honoured to give you some financial help."

"Thanks for your spontaneous generosity. But at present what I have it will make do. Jayram, we have seen a number of people suffering from mental poverty. They have enough but when the question of give and take arises, they recoil and shrink within. That is the real poverty I despise most".

Jayram became thoughtful and lapsed into silence. He rose up from his seat and said, "It is already late Chinmay. I will come some other day".

They bade goodbye and left.

Next morning Chinmay went to the publisher Mr. Harishankar. On the way he accidently met Mr. Goswami. He was running a grocery shop but could not flourish well in that business. Several people came to his shop to buy things on credit but did not turn up to clear up their outstanding dues. As a result he lost money as well as the customers. He closed down his shop with disgust and set up a stall of magazines and newspapers in front of his house.

He became a sannyasi although living a life of a house holder. His ochre robes and a rosary of holy basil hanging from his neck incited reverence in the heart of the people. After a year the number of disciples began to increase. They offered honorarium at the feet of their preceptor in cash or kind. There was no intimidation or arm-twisting when a devotee made an offer of his own accord. Whisper circulated among his disciples that he was completely free from worldly guile and covetousness.

Chinmay was well acquainted with him.

Mr. Goswami held the handle of his bicycle and asked, "Everyday you come and go along this way, but you never pay a visit to my humble abode".

Chinmay looked at his rosary and bearded face for a

moment and said, "Mr. Goswami, I am single and do everything to keep my family going on. Where is the time to go elsewhere?"

Mr. Goswami wrinkled his forehead and became suddenly grave. He closed his eyes half in a meditative posture and said with a grin, "Of course, had anybody been in your place, he would have faced the same trouble. House holders are always in that delicate position, no way to get rid of that bondage".

Mr. Goswami chuckled and added, "If you give importance to a problem, it will appear in a magnified form. People remain under its coercion. That is why I don't give two hoots to any seemingly difficult situation. I know you are a good writer. You are intent to get peace and tranquil atmosphere where you can write without hindrance. Your mental attitude is an open book to me. Keep your bicycle here and come with me".

"Where?"

"To my ashram, not far from this town. Let us go by an auto and plunge in the deluge of perfect peace there".

Chinmay was in a fix. He humbly said, "Mr. Goswami, I have an appointment with Mr. Harishankar, the Publisher of "Janasankha" Press".

"O, you can meet him some other day. But you should not miss this chance which comes to you as a windfall".

Chinmay kept his bicycle on the veranda of the bookstall and came down to the road.

Mr. Goswami was right. It took only twenty minutes by an auto to reach there. It was by the bank of a rivulet protected on all sides by barbed wires. There was a flower garden and behind it stood a temple whose construction work had been completed a few months ago. To the right side of the temple, there was a mango grove and a few coconut saplings had been planted parallel to the barbed wires. A young boy was watering the flower plants drawing water from a well. A calm beauty had pervaded the whole atmosphere. On the other side of the rivulet, there was a vast stretch of paddy fields and beyond that a small hamlet looking hazy from a distance.

"Hrushi, stop your work and bring out two chairs from the store room", Mr. Goswami enjoined the boy.

They sat face to face on chairs. Chinmay took a glance at the temple and asked, "Whom do you worship in this temple?"

"The stone image of my preceptor who is no more in this world. When he was alive, I had been initiated by him. My disciples have been worshipping him as God. I myself had seen him in the form of Lord Vishnu. If I tell this strange episode to someone, he would scarcely believe it".

Chinmay was looking at him with unblinking eyes.

Mr. Goswami's face brightened with a beatific smile and he continued.

"Those days Guruji was staying in his own ashram after a religious tour all over India. It was a full moon night. Everything seemed to be washed by soothing moon light. Guruji was in his own cottage, absorbed in deep meditation. I came out of my room tiptoeing and slowly opened the bamboo door of his cottage. With full caution, I stepped into his room. The moment my eyes fell on him, I was stunned. The whole room was full of sweet aroma redolent with Champak flowers and basil leaves. But where was Guruji? In his place was standing Lord Vishnu raising his right hand in a posture of blessing me. In a trance I prostrated on the ground and went to a torpor. Coming to my sense, I opened my eyes. There sat my Guruji in a lotus posture throwing back a benign smile at me. I was about to utter something when Guruji waved his hand signalling me to keep utter silence. An affectionate smile flickered in his eyes. I was dazed and stood rooted to the ground. At that moment his voice came floating in the air.

"Don't reveal it to anyone. You are really a blessed

one. No mortal being has ever seen the manifestation of Lord Vishnu in me. Guruji's voice was supernatural. With folded palms I made a deep obeisance at his feet and came out".

Chinmay listened to his narrative with rapt attention.

Mr. Goswami straightened his back and said assertively, "All blasphemers and bog standard people do not believe as it sounds incredulous to them. They are wily persons. They go on maligning others and never think anyone trust-worthy".

Mr. Goswami remained thoughtful for a minute and said, "This is the real path which leads one to indescribable peace and happiness. The rich have plenty but have they got happiness in their lives? Be initiated and come to our ashram regularly.The flood of calmness here will sweep away the mental debris floating you Godward".

Chinmay drew his chair closer and asked, "Mr. Goswami, I have something to say in this matter. Some worship Swami Nigamananda, some are devotees of Satya Sai Baba and some Thakur Anukul Chandra. Although the path is same to reach God, why do they think themselves a separate group ? Don't they show favour to their co-disciples whereas they regard others with contempt? I unflatteringly pay respect to all these preceptors but I don't want to have a 'stamp' on my back as a disciple of some Guru creating an impervious barrier to all my sides. In my opinion Guru means who shows to his disciples the path to attain God and salvation from 'three tapas' (three sufferings). The aspirants follow his instructions and ultimately reach their desired goal".

Mr. Goswami listened attentively. He thought that his modus operandi might be wrong. He tried his utterance to be chiselled with shrewdness. He also knew that such type of persons could not be entrapped by snare or jugglery of words. They were as slippery as an eel. So this person too might get through his fingers at any time. He changed his strategy and decided to play his trump card. He knew the ancient story of that goose who was laying gold eggs daily. But that wretched man became impatient and his avarice landed him in a ludicrous ending. To win over him, he said, "It depends upon your willingness. Of course, your case is different. Without initiation you are allowed to visit our ashram whenever you find time. If baffled by worldly complicacies, come to this lap of serenity and forget your mental agonies. Mr. Chinmay, take my word as a guarantee that one day our ashram will become a hub of religious culture as well as an asylum of spititual destitutes and brokenhearted people." Mr. Goswami became vociferous.

He stood on his feet, went to the inner sanctum of the temple and prayed sometime touching his forehead on the ground and then came back to Chinmay.

Chinmay was getting bored for his lingering grandiloquence. Mr. Goswami cast his glance once again at the temple and said, "Let us go back. We should not lounge about here unnecessarily. So don't delay". He was in a hurry to reach home for there was no one to look after his book stall.

Chinmay's house was by the main road at a little distance from the Sadar market. There was a time when a few vehicles would pass along that road at long intervals. During sixty years of independence, the town underwent a sea change.Trade and commerce made progress at breakneck speed. New metalled roads had been constructed to facilitate transport and business. Even the narrow path of alleys were made concrete. Roads were modified and much emphasis was given for their beautification. Vegetables market was shifted to a broad area under the supervision of Municipality authority. Even the train which had been mocked at as 'match box train' underwent a thorough change. The narrow-gauge was transformed into a broad-gauge. The platform and the station area was made wider to accommodate a large body of passengers. To increase the grandeur of the town, parks were protected and taken care of. During six decades a drastic change came over the town. But with the passage of time, things changed. Now houses had mushroomed and the roads had become so much congested that one had to go along the road with much caution. Even the thoroughfare was so thronged by a huge number of people that one had to go through the gathering elbowing others. Nobody needed a telegram to send message to others. Everybody was seen with a mobile in his hand, he might be a betel shopkeeper or a rickshaw-puller.

Chinmay's wife Maya had constant touch with her eldest son-in-law and daughter. They were filled with excitement at the prospect of paying a visit to the goddess Tarini. The trip would be a welcome respite from the pressure of work. Their son-in-law had promised to make a votive offering to the deity. All of them started their journey hiring a van. Half the way they went through jolt, waggling and jostling inside the van. As the boulders were sticking out of the surface of the road, it made the driving more difficult.The pot-holes were more dangerous and when the van bumped along that dusty and rocky track, it seemed to crack their backbones.

At 10.30 'O' clock, they drove through the main entrance to the temple and parked the van at one side of the compound wall. On both sides of the temple, a long row of stalls were there selling variety of items like flowers, coconuts, earthen lamps, framed pictures of the Goddess, fruits, confections, ghee etc. With some fruits and sweetmeats they hurried to the temple. At first they went to a counter where they had to pay honorarium for the offerings. Chinmay's grand-son, a tender boy of three years got his head tonsured by a barber appointed by the temple authority. "Twenty rupees, Sir", the barber charged them after the shaving work was over.

"What? I have already deposited your charge along with the honorarium", Chinmay snapped back.

"No sir, they will not pay me a single pie", the barber started whining.

"Why ? Is it not an injustice to force me this way to pay your charge two times, in two different places?"

"Sir, believe it or not. The temple authority pocket the money and we, poor barbers, are left emptyhanded. We plead for that but our humble prayer goes unheeded". The barber said while putting the blade and scissors into sheath.

"Don't argue", Maya interfered. "Pay him what he said. You are going beyond social niceties".

There was a circular altar at the centre of the floor where the deity had been installed and all around it, at a little distance, a wire gauge had been erected waist high barring the people to barge into the interior. Several Brahmins sitting inside were busy in worshipping while chanting mantras and throwing away peeled bananas at the deity. On the opposite side of the iron gauge, a number of devotees were squatting, waiting patiently to give offerings through their Brahmins. The Brahmins took milk and ghee from the hands of devotees and poured them at the altar along with milky juice of broken coconuts.

Chinmay was watching the Puja, close to him stood Maya.

"We live in a throwaway society. Did you see the wastage of nutritious foods thrown away carelessly rather unprofitably at the altar?" Chinmay remarked exasperatingly.

"You should not have come to this sacred place with an impure and tainted mind. You have no regards to Gods and Goddesses". Maya said brusquely.

"I really burn inside if this multitude of wastage comes to my sight. Devotees all over Odisha and outside send truck-load of coconuts to this place as offerings to the deity. But what do the Brahmins do here and at every religious centre? Do you know how many children are dying every second owing to malnutrition? How many ill-fed, half-starved children could have been nourished by that? Now the Brahmins have made Puja commercialized. Nobody has guts to raise his voice against this profligacy. Think over it. If you uphold the truth, you will be treated as an infidel."

"It is not a wastage. It is our time-honoured custom and tradition. If you go to a place of worship, will you go emptyhanded? Moreover they are house holders. They have also wives and children. Do you think they have no dreams and aspirations? Could they manage their families with such a meagre amount of income? I don't like our one-trekked views". Maya said tartly.

"You see, worship can be done with minimal. Lord Krishna said in the Gita, "If a devotee worships me with an offering of leaves, flowers, fruits and water with Purity of heart, I am appeased." But what do the devotees do at present? To show off their riches, they offer lakhs of rupees to God. They think God will be overpleased with them. You will be startled if you go to Tirupati where the richest God of the world has been worshipped ostentatiously".

"Your remark is below the belt. I don't want to hear all these nasty things. Keep your ideas and philosophy to yourself". Maya flew into a fit of anger.

"All right, you need not listen to me. But remember, the devotees are still steeped in 'avidya' (ignorance). They are yet to be enlightened by the light of knowledge. They are far from rationality, you admit it or not".

After the Puja was over, they all felt pangs of hunger and they got into their van. When the driver was about to start the vehicle, suddenly a youth came to them with a receipt book in his hand. He scribbled down something on a scrap of paper and handed it to the driver. Chinmay craned his neck outside and asked, "What do you want" ?

"Give me ten rupees, sir. You have parked the van on our temple premises. We charge a trivial amount for that".

Chinmay handed him a ten rupee note and asked,

"What are the other ransoms that the devotees are compelled to pay?"

"You sound awkward, sir – you just contributed something for the maintenance of the temple. What is more?" The boy grimaced.

Chinmay burst out instinctively into a monologue,"What the hell they are doing in the name of God? Beggary under the garb of religion! What do they think? Beggars can't be choosers. Be satisfied with what a devotee offers them".

He heaved a sigh. With displeasure, Maya turned her face to other side.

The van picked up speed.

TWELVE

The most distinctive features of Baripada town was its extreme climate. People felt terrible heat in the summer and biting cold in the winter. When the cold season set in, the hands and legs got numb and people shivered under the blanket. In the early morning for brass monkey weather they would be seen getting some warmth by the fire side to activate their bodies.

After some years the severity of cold had been dwindled to a moderate degree. Now the winter lasted only for two months and people required no more than a plain sheet to protect them from cold. It became a topic of discussion among themselves. They recalled the bygone days when they were reluctant to go outside at night in that freezing cold.

It was the fag end of winter. After a few days an early summer will herald its presence.

Chinmay used to go out on his long morning walk in the suburb of the town. That day he went upto Madhuban to warm up his body. When he reached a large field adjacent to Madhuban, he found some workers busy in making a number of thatched huts. A religious conference was going to be held in that place and the devotees expected to come from different regions will stay in those huts during the festival. All over the field, there were long row of straw-thatched cottages, extending from one end to another. The passage being narrow, it would be difficult for the people to move about in a rush. It might be portentous and for no reason he was set upon by an unknown panic. He heaved an ominous sigh and moved homewards. After a fortnight, the place resonated with festive hubbubs. A stream of men, women and children began to flow and soon the place got congested. Its surrounding areas were also brightened by flood-lights. Temporary shops were installed to supply necessary things to the people. The pedlars were hawking their wares to draw the attention of the customers. The children gathering there whined and pressed their parents to buy them toys and coloured balloons. A mike tied to a bamboo pole was belting out old religious songs.

A little later afternoon the devotees were getting ready to celebrate the occasion with great delight. In the mean time, some were making bread on gas oven, some were stitching garland and some arranging the bouquet of aromatic flowers to offer them before the photograph of their revered Guru. Several women were breast feeding their little babies lying indolently on the straw bed.

When the religious ceremony was going with full swing, nobody could have a ghost of an idea that something would go wrong ultimately. Slightest foreboding might have made them alert to escape the impending danger. It was smouldering somewhere. Then a vast cloud of smoke wreathed upwards and in no time shot up a blazing fire. It leaped from one tent to another. It spread so swiftly that it gave them no chance to save their lives. The sinister tongues of fire chased them and burned them to ashes. It was in their unguarded moments, they fell victims to this conflagration. Fortunately a few could escape by a fluke. In half an hour, the place changed to a graveyard. All over the place, there was only burning embers and lying over it incinerated, charred carcasses of human bodies strewn here and there. Seeing no other way out, the terror-stricken people started screaming and running pell-mell to escape the flames but all succumbed to death. In no time the news spread like wild fire in all directions. People began to scurry like a bat out of hell to the spot the moment they got this sad news. A posse of reporters swarmed the place and were buzzing around, trying to get the full information to report this mournful incident. Doctors and nurses from different voluntary organizations flocked to the place to undertake the cases on war-footing. Some efficient physicians of Tata company took a leading role in the treatment of third degree burn cases. A convoy of trucks, full of medicine and clothes, arrived and they put up their Intensive care unit then and there. The treatment went on day and night. The volunteers carried the patients on stretchers to the tent and there the doctors worked tirelessly. They had been plugging away to save their lives.

On that fateful day, Chinmay had been to his country house to supervise his farm work. He was sitting with a companion in a jeep. When it came near Astia and crossed the bridge over the river Budhabalang, they saw a column of smoke spiralling upwards in the sky, the very place where the religious ceremony was being held. They yelled at the driver to drive along the shortest route to get to the spot. It was inconceivable. In their wildest dream, they could not hope to see such a heartrending sight. Virtually the people were in a tumult desperately trying to save their skin. The police cordon prevented the panicky swarms of people from entering the fire devastated area. There was an old lady who could not trace out her son and daughter-in-law. She was awaiting them with bated breath. At last she tried to break into the cordon of policemen to search for them. Chinmay caught her by his hand and dragged her to a safe place. She was delirious and wailed pitifully beating her forehead. "Don't hold me back, my son. I want to die with my son and daughter-in-law. What is the use of living when I saw them burnt alive before my own eyes".

"Have patience, aunty. Let us wait and see whether they are alive or dead. It may be that they have escaped death. We have to wait till the situation calm down".

The old lady sat down on the ground and wept. "Whom should I blame, son? This is my lot. How God could be so merciless to snatch away my son from my lap?"

Chinmay could not hold back his tears. He only consoled the helpless lady to stop crying.

Another gentleman was rolling on the dust, crying bitterly. Suddenly he got up and ran hysterically to jump into the fire. Some people hugged him and carried his half conscious body on their shoulders and laid him on a bed sheet. They sprinkled some water on his face to revive his sense. When he came to himself, he said, "Brother, my wife and children, all have been devoured by fire while they were sitting in the cottage awaiting me to bring them some refreshment. I was just out for some minutes. When I came back...." He burst into a loud cry and then said through sobbing, "What would I explain to my parents? Whom would I show my face, brother? Should I go home with this sullied face?" His lamentable condition moved Chinmay's heart. He felt as if his body would collapse then and there. He felt dizzy, his spirits had been dampened. He buried his head between his knees and wept silently.

It was a spine-chilling sight. When the embers died out, the people gathered all around the carcasses. The young and old alike were consigned to burning flames, twisted and distorted beyond recognition. Roasted by terrible heat, the fat had melted and it smudged the bodies evoking gruesome feelings. Suckling babies were seen carbonized clinging to their mothers' breasts.

Most of them expired later on though treated with utmost care by Intensive Care Unit.

One man having lost his mental balance burst into the I.C.U. and searched something frantically from one end to the other. His eyes were bloodshot and hair unkempt. He grabbed one doctor by the leg and started crying, "Where have you kept my child, doctor? Please, give it back to me".

Then overcome by a sudden paroxysm of despair he put off his shirt and spread it on the ground.

"Here is my begging bowl. Put my child on it. It came to my lap after seven years by the grace of Lord Shiva. Don't turn your face on me doctor. I won't go unless I get back my child".

He collected his crampled shirt, wiped his tears with it and then went tottering without turning back. The doctor felt a plug in his throat and he stood petrified till the man disappeared into the crowd.

The dead bodies were carried to the bank of a rivulet and placed on funeral pyres. Several cartload of firewood were collected and the putrefied bodies were burnt to ashes. When the volunteers felt the shortage of firewood, they arranged kerosene and petrol cans from somewhere. The atmosphere was filled with acrid smell of searing flesh. It was discussed among some people that the rest of the dead bodies were carried by trucks and thrown in the sea.

The ex-chief minister and former Prime minister visited the fire devastated area and were greatly shocked. They could not smother their tears seeing such a horrifying accident of fire ever happened at Baripada. Though indemnity was paid to bereaved families, it was not a considerable amount. It was met with howls of protest from some corner. Money paid by Reliefs-fund could never fulfill the irreparable loss the people suffered by the ghastly accident. It, no doubt, left an unfading psychological scar in their minds. The devotees could not know that it was a lac-house and it would be inflammed in an inauspicious hour and thousands of people would be doomed to be wiped off for ever.

There were some speculations but nobody could ascertain the cause of onset of the fire. It might be due to short circuit of electricity, some believed the bursting of gas cylinder to be the origin of this holocaust. Closure inspection disclosed the fact that some devotees were involved in objectionable activities which polluted the spiritual atmosphere of the place during festival.

Three days later, a scavenger and his wife were seen poking around the heap of ashes and filling their gunny-sack with empty bottles of liquor.

One could not infer the authencity of this fact. The verity still remained in a shrowd of mystery.

THIRTEEN

Gandhia returned from the village market dangling his bag on the handle bar of his bicycle. This year he got a bumper crops. He sold some from his storage and bought a new bicycle. Previously he had to cringe before others for this trifling thing. He himself had seen so many persons not in a mood to lend their bicycle to others. He kept it in the vestibule and went straight to the well. After washing his face and legs, he felt himself refreshed. He put off his dress and drawing a string cot outside slept on it. His wife Lakshmi came with a bolster and placed it below his head. It was an early hour of evening and a cool breeze was blowing from the south. Lying on the cot, Gandhia looked at the vast blue sky. It was studded with a few blinking stars and a crescent moon was ascending the flight of steps of the sky at a leisurely pace. At a distance, a pack of jackals were howling heralding the advent of night.

"Gone asleep?" Lakshmi asked him. Then she shook him by the shoulder.

"No, I have just closed my eyes, I am a bit tired". He turned his side.

"Please wake up. Let us eat our supper".

"Have you done the cooking so early? It is not yet nine. Why are you so hurried tonight?"

"No, I have to scrub the utensils and sleep early. Tomorrow morning is an auspicious hour. I have made up my mind to go to an exorcist for a talisman".

"Why?"

Lakshmi remained silent. She was hesitant to give him a piece of her mind.

Gandhia got slightly irritated.

"I don't want to listen to any of your blarney. Why do you go to different persons and spend money uselessly buying amulets ? You think those charlatans will solve your problem. You have some gynaecological defects and that is why you are incapable of bearing a child. You remained barren for long twelve years bringing forth no progeny of mine. No medicine, no herbal roots can set right this congenital defect. Your machine is out of order, still your are foolishly pining for that".

"Who can say that my system is defective or yours? The other day that midwife came from the 'Women's Welfare Centre'. She heard my problem and advised me to find out the wrong examined by a gynaecologist".

"Oh, your midwife is an expert in this matter. So call her one day and let her thoroughly examine me stripping me stark naked. I won't feel shame to stand before her". Gandhia broke into spate of convulsive laughter.

"Don't try to regale me by your off-colour jokes. You always go to vulgarity. Never take anything seriously. Whether you eat your food or not, I am going to sleep".

"I care a fig, keep my food on the table. I would take it at my convenience".

"So you don't feel hungry. Sleep here and think over your beloved Manju, that milkmaid who has cast a spell on you. Are you not still in that infatuation?" She said in a clipped voice.

"You tease me referring the name of Manju repeatedly. Your cutting words are allergens to me. It grates my nerves. Why do you nag at Manju day and night? Is she a constant eye-sore to you?"

He tried to restrain his voice milder. He did not want

to have a tussle with his wife. On top of it, the neighbour might hear their quarrelling and think them brazenfaced. Gandhia was, of course, a peaceloving man. But Lakshmi's accumulated wrath which had been burning inside her found expression whenever she found a favourable occasion to fall out with him. She derived a satisfaction from mentally torturing him. She wanted to tease him further. by her snide remarks.

"Since the day that milkmaid came to our house, peace is gone. That enchantress has tied you with a chord of enticement. How shameless you are that you have kept relation with that slut, a worm of gutter ! I can't brook this ignominy and humiliation in the society for you. A person having a blot in his character is despised and he has no respect in society. The people of the village gossip many things. Who can shut their mouths? You are solely responsible for breaking the sanctity of our wedded life. Now I hesitate to show my face because of your stained character". Lakshmi reproved him with rancour.

"Who cares for those scandal-mongers ? They make a great fuss about a trifling matter", Gandhia grew excited. "Who else has the guts to defile me like that? I shall cut off his tongue with a chopper".

"Oh, what bravado! Keep that chopper with you. I may need it when I would feel to hack you to pieces. You are tired with me, are you not? That is why you are roaming around the village like a stray bull".

"Hold your stinking tongue, I tell you Lakshmi, otherwise I shall be forced to root it out. Have you gone off your head? Now the kettle is calling the ladle black! You are also a woman of easy virtue.What is there in your body? One cavernous hole and two saggy lump of flesh bobbing up and down, but you are out to vanquish the world. You denied her to fetch you milk because you have a suspicion lurking in your mind that I have a hanky-panky with that milkmaid without any telltale evidence. I am ready to put my hand on your head and swear by that that I have no obscene relation with her. She treats me as her own brother but you womenfolk take a fancy that there must be something inky in that. Suspicion is verily a poison tree which ought to be lopped off before it spreads its offshoots shadowing the ground".

Gandhia became breathless. He wanted to put an end to this verbal combat. But Lakshmi was unyielding. She shot back, "What! If you are not pleased with my appearance, why did you not tell your parents as to your dislikes? Matter ends there. I do admit that I may not be able to give you physical gratification but that does not mean that you will run after a young cow just like a stud bull".

"Come to the point. There is a saying, 'If the milk is available in the market, why should one purchase a cow?" So I never bother about that. My dear Lakshmi, what should I do then? Living a life of sannyasi in the seclusion? You get pleasure seeing me suffering while I toss on my bed with the fire of passion. I have never seen a frigid woman like you in my life, inert and cold from the beginning. When I am out to have that you strike below my belt. You please tell me what steps I should have taken to restrain myself, to mend my culpable ways. It would be rather wise for me to be castrated. There would be no flute that could make Radha dance. Why are you so petulant and rigid to a minor slip? Women are like diapers, they need to be changed occasionally."

"Have you given me the status of wife? I cook your meal, clean your house, scrub your vessels and all the donkey work I have been doing while you sit around doing nothing. What I get in return, just a bite of food to curb my hunger. I am tired of being treated like a slave." Her voice was husky with spite.

Gandhia dreaded that their quarrel might reach a crescendo. Sometimes he cut jokes with her and enjoyed her angrymood. Tired after a gruelling day, the villagers usually went to bed for early sleep. Now the whole village fell in silence. In the stillness of night, a pin-drop could be heard from a distance.

Lakshmi turned to go. But before that she did not forget to throw a spittle of venom at Gandhia.

"From this day on, you must not touch my body with your filthy hands. You are wandering here and there. What infection you may bring to me that I can't say. I wonder how that eunuch,thick-skinned husband stands this while his wife is doing all sorts of nuisance under his very nose? I spit on you and on that vile bitch, that whore who has inveigled you into dancing as she wishes. I care a little if you dance with that nautch to bring name to your family".

Lakshmi could tolerate many things but not this type of teasing and banter. Gandhia was in a tight corner, he could not decide whether he would laugh or weep under such circumstances.

Lakshmi went to her bed on empty stomach. Gandhia could not know how he slept the whole night on that cot.

The food remained untouched.

The next morning Lakshmi took her bath by the well and prepared herself to go for the talisman.

"Hey Mohadeva, hey Tunia", she called aloud their names to make them ready to accompany her. They were two brothers and their house was close to Gandhia's. Only their plot had been separated by a green fence. Gandhia washed his face and entered his bed room.

"Give me some money" Lakshmi asked gruffly,storming into the room.

"I have no money", he replied tersely.

"Oh, when I beg a pice, I am denied forthwith. But when you squander money for that fallen woman, you have no scruples. Now I came to understand that as she is your keep, she has every right on your money. Whereas a legal wife has no say in this matter".

"Why don't you ask your father to send you a coffer to meet your expenses? I don't receive monthly salary like your brother. If I feel any want, I sell away my crops".

"Then how could I go emptyhanded?" Lakshmi pressed her lips in anger.

"I am really tired of hearing your endless litany of complaints. You should have told me beforehand. Yesterday I had been to the market and purchased all the necessary things. There may be a little amount left in my pocket, say five or six rupees. Will that do"?

"No, I require at least fifty rupees".

"Fifty rupees ! then I have to steal that amount from somewhere".

"Why? You ask your keep and she will definitely stuff your pocket with gingling coins".

"Lakshmi, what are you driving at ? Don't make me fly into a fit of rage. You picked a quarrel last night for no reason and the food remained as it was. Only the wastage of money. You don't know how I do manage to eke out a living. Stop hassling me any more".

"Now you realize the value of money. But when you give that wench costly gifts, you become oblivious of your hard-earned money. I don't want to blame you. I only spoke the fact".

"Bravo ! my truthful lady".

"Will you give me or not? I won't hear the fake excuses of a compulsive liar". Her eyes were ablaze with anger. The smouldering discontent inside her began to flare up.

Suddenly a demonic fury possessed her brain. She summoned all her strength and flew at him and pinned him to the bed. He could not dodge her sudden attack. In that wrestling, Gandhia's lungi slipped away and he became buck naked.

"You scoundrel, you whore-monger, I must make you to come to your sense". She roared.

She pressed his eyes forcefully with her claw like fingers sitting astride his chest.

"Oh, Lakshmi, don't press my eyes so hard. I must go blind". Gandhia groaned under her weight.

"Go blind. I won't atone for that. That would be rather a good requital for you. From this day on you won't dare to look at the woman". She looked at his hollow-eyed face. Her hands went limp. A tide of panic rose in her heart and she loosened her grip and drew back. Gandhia was still moaning. Then he tried to sit up with difficulty. His right leg was in an awkward position and it seemed to be fractured by her body's pressure. He stood with a scream of pain muttering filthy abuses to her. He walked limping upto the vestibule and held the handle of the bicycle to go outside. Unawares, while he was descending along the steps with his bicycle, Lakshmi came like a gust of wind and smashed the hind rim with a big stone.

The rim got twisted and certain spokes were also curved making the bicycle practically immovable. With terrible disgust, Gandhia left it there and went on hobbling on his feet to some unknown destination.

Gandhia had become inured to such insult in the past but since marriage he had not suffered so miserably and that too at the hands of a woman. He was mercilessly assaulted and humiliated by his own wife which was quite intolerable. His zest for life faded. The fruitful tree which he had planted so fondly by his own hand had been blighted. At first he had no desire to show his face to any one. But before going to somewhere he should go to Manju who had been always sympathetic in his hard days. She would definitely pull him up from this morass. The person with whom he had only nodding acquaintance, he would show his lip-deep sympathy. He would receive cold welcome there. That man would have no heartfelt desire to clasp him to his bosom to give him a safe shelter. Rather he would think him a burden on his shoulders.

When he got to Manju's house, she herself came out

and slipped her arms around his waist and conducted him to her bed room. Her face became ashy pale when she received him with a throbbing heart.

She was about to serve him refreshment on a plate but Gandhia denied her waving his hand.

"What happened to you? You came with one lungi and a baniyan. Where is your shirt and trousers?"

Manju looked at his pitiable condition with tears rolling down from her eyes.

"Where is the time to wear them? I have been driven out of my house this morning. My nagging wife got sore for no obvious reason. I am quite fed up with her. She is termagant and lacks gumption. If she demands to have an elephant, you have to glean it from somewhere". Gandhia started sobbing.

"You please go there and peel off your tattered clothes".

"No, Manju, this is my rig-out befitting my position. I have been mortally offended by my own wife and now I am worse than a peasant".

"Now eat some refreshment and rest here", Manju handed him a plate full of food.

"Keep it on that tea-poy. Last night I went on empty stomach. This morning I have not yet brushed my teeth". Gandhia hung his head in shame.

"Let me give you a 'sal' twig". Manju brought one from the shelf of a wall.

While eating Gandhia said, "I have lost my honour and prestige. I have no courage to show my face to the villagers. What would they think of me? Speech bulletins of village folk must have circulated like bush fire from house to house. Now they will spit on my face. I can't raise my head even before a village urchin".

"Don't go home. You obliterate her memory from your mind and stay here as long as you like. Here your prestige will be intact. No ruffian will dare to come to my house to frighten you ". She purred.

With food in his stomach, the ugly head of desire raised in his mind. He looked at her amorously and said, "Manju, I don't believe in caste or creed. Had I seen you before, I would have married you ignoring all social taboos. You are like an oasis in the desert of my life. When I see you, my thirst is quenched and my heart is swelled up with ineffable joy. When you caress me with love, all sorts of my pain are removed. Manju, you are really a priceless gem to me. I know, I can't give you anything in return".

Gandhia's voice quivered with emotion.

"One thing I must warn you. Will your husband take me amiss if I stay here?"

"No, he knows our relation. The old haggard closes his eyes on all matters and remains boozed the whole night. He remains confined to his own world. We are completely safe from that side". Manju reassured him.

"I have to go next morning. Because when my wife's anger would be gone, she must send someone in search of me. Fear is always stalking me. She would keep tracks of all my activities. That possibility cannot be ruled out. Pottering about here means I would invite troubles. So let me stay one night. Then I would slink off to some other safe place".

After dinner, Gandhia enjoyed a sound sleep. Manju had kneaded his whole body with mustard oil. When she entered and handed him some betel leaves, his sleep was interrupted. Manju leaned towards him and ran her fingers through his hair. Gandhia remained motionless in an inexpressible sensuous pleasure.

He held her soft hand in his and said, "Manju, being a mother of one child how tempting you are! To me, you are still a virgin endowed with a sweet heart. Moreover you know the art of cooking well. I smacked my lips when I relished it today. But Lakshmi does it listlessly".

Manju lowered her voice and said, "You need not go elsewhere. There is an attick on the roof where I spread boiled paddy to dry up. I will make it clean and you can sleep there most comfortably. Nobody can trace you out there."

Manju laughed coquettishly. Gandhia was amazed at her cunningness.

He fiddled about with her strand of hair for sometime and pulled her closer to his face. He gazed at her large dreamy eyes wistfully and said thrilling, "My dear Manju….. Majula, You are ravishingly beautiful. I am ready to forsake the entire world for your fawn-like eyes. Here I am giving my unconditional love. I believe you will not shun me like a threadbare quilt, over there".

Overjoyed, Manju snuggled by his side.

FOURTEEN

Over some days Chinmay felt quite restless. The recent mishap created a disquiet atmosphere in the town and he wanted to withdraw himself from this emotional turmoil going somewhere off this beaten track.

An old friend, a business magnet of Gopiballavpur, in the province of West Bengal, had invited him to wear on some days in his company. After his father's death, he inherited a sizeable landed property and after much deliberation took on a drapery business on a grand scale. Within ten years, his business flourished and he reached an enviable record of success. He used to give some amount of money to the poor students in charity and donated most generously a big sum for construction of a magnificent Radhakrishna temple on a piece of land which was also once his ancestral property. Many people from far-off places came to visit this temple. There was usually a little rush in the evening hours. The temple resounded with bells and cymbals at the time of arati. The devotees left for home light hearted after prostrating themselves at the altar with deep veneration. On some special festive occasion, the temple authority had provision to give away the offerings to the people. Mr. Sunanda Dev Goswami with whom Chinmay had a close tie, invited all his old friends to this get-together and he distributed clothes among the poor on those days. He was a scion of a respectable family having an image before the public. Every one held him in high esteem.

It was a gala day of Dola Purnima. From early hours of evening, the temple was more crowded than usual by a large number of people. There sat a tall and lean man at the entrance of the inner sanctum with a violin in his lap. All around him a group of chanters and by their side squatted a few persons holding cymbals in their hands. An old man chanted first the holy name of Lord Krishna followed by others. He was in the lead singing very melodiously. The other persons joined them by handclappings.

Their singing in unison accompanied by the mellifluous tune of violin seemed to pour dulcet in the ears of the people. Behind the chanters, were sitting Chinmay and Mr. Sunanda. Although their clappings were not to the tune, they went on waggling their heads. Sunanda's forefathers were great devotees of Lord Krishna and He had been the presiding deity of their family for generations. There was a day when 'vaisnavism' took the undivided Bengal in its fold and the people were completely lost in veneration of Radha and Krishna. It swept the whole countryside echoing in all corners only the holy names of Lord Krishna and propagating brotherhood and non-violence in true vein among the people.

After the Puja, people unclotted and went their separate ways. Only three persons Mr. Sunanda, the violin player and Chinmay remained till the priest shut the door of the temple and left for home.

They came out of the temple premises. The whole area seemed to be painted white by the flood of moon light. After going a few steps, Mr. Sunanda stopped and turned to the violin player, "Meet my friend Chinmay, my college mate and now a promising writer. He has come from Baripada to spend somedays with me". Then he introduced Mr. Udayanarayan to Chinmay, "This gentleman is a violin virtuoso, a worthy disciple of his great guru Mr. Sisirkana Dhar Chaudhury. You don't know his charisma. He has received kudos from so many eminent persons. He is acclaimed as a wizard on playing violin. If he moves the bow across the strings, people start crowding the place to listen to him. Although we will be a bit late for supper tonight, still then let us go to the riverbed by my jeep and sit there to listen to his violin playing in complete silence".

Mr. Udaynarayan gave a pleasing smile and acceded to their request. They got into the jeep parked outside the boundary wall of the temple.

The river Subarnarekha was at a distance of one kilometre from that place. The riverbed was shimmering by the reflection of soothing moonbeam. Upto the distant horizon, everything looked misty and silvery. A couple of ducks were searching fish by dipping their beaks into the water. When they stepped down the bank, they got scared and flew up flapping their wings.

Mr. Sunanda looked in all direction and selected a spot which would be convenient for the recital.

"Let us sit here". He hitched up his trouser above the ankle joint and sat down on the sand. He reclined behind placing his two hands on the sandy bed and said, "Please sit down and listen to Mr. Udaynarayan who will send us to a dreamy world by the mind-blowing tune of the violin and this river bed goes to be vibrated very soon by its melodious note".

They sat down at his bidding. Mr. Udaynarayan set his violin holding it under his chin and ran the bow up and down across the strings like a falcon flies up grazing the water and then suddenly swoops down, similarly he began to weave a flimsy net of spell to lull them.

Chinmay focused his eyes on his fingers. They were slender like drumsticks and were made for him by God to make him a renowned violin player.

He was undoubtedly an artiste of excellence. Chinmay was wandering and fantasized that he would be lost in that dreamland. This is the world where many geniuses go unacknowledged, he thought.

Mr. Udaynarayan stopped playing and put the violin on his lap. He started singing a snatch of Bauls' song:

There rumbles the cloud
My mind becomes disconcerted
My heart becomes restless
There rumbles the cloud…..

He was not so expert in singing as on his violin. Then he lifted the violin again and swerved aside. He caught the tune of that song on the violin and it seemed as if every alphabet was emanating clearly pronounced from its inner cavity.

He ceased his playing and said, "It is getting late. Let us go home. There is enough time to hear me later on".

"Excellent!" Chinmay remarked. "I have never heard such a superb playing on a violin so far".

Mr. Udaynarayan gave an obliged smile and stood up brushing the sand off his clothes. They came back at late hours of night when the mini town had already gone into deep sleep.

The next morning, after they had finished their breakfast, Mr. Sunanda beckoned Chinmay to his sitting room.

"This morning some guests have arrived", he said casually. "I have to provide them room for their rest. Would you feel uneasy to accommodate Mr. Udaynarayan in your room ?"

"No, I won't feel any discomfort to remain with him. Coming in close contact with such a great man, I would rather be glad".

"You are inquisitive. You ask many things to a newly acquainted person. Don't be curious enough to know his family affairs. If he says out of his own accord, that is different. He is a man of Hooghly district, very near to Calcutta. He is a householder having wife and children at home. But he is a wondering monk. He never stays long at any place. After staying some days here, he must move to some other place." Mr. Sunanda gave him sufficient indication.

After lunch, Chinmay and Mr. Udaynarayan sat on their cot and discussed as to the intricacies of violin.

Mr. Udaynarayan broached the subject, "You see, violin is a difficult instrument. You have to stick to it for a long period with patience until it comes under your full control. When I was a tender boy of fifteen years, I learnt playing on violin from a local guru. But he was not so well-conversant in this art. Dissatisfied, I went to Mr. Sisirkana Dhar Chaudhury who taught me the whole gamut of music, from light to classical. To be very frank, it is not my profession but it has become an obsession with me."

He raised the bow of violin and added, "I have two wives, one is at home and the other is always with me. They cannot pull on well with each other, however I try to bring a conciliation between the two. My wife creases her nose in sheer disgust because she thinks that this violin has turned me monomaniac for which I have grown quite indifferent to my household affairs. We are completely opposite to each other in every way. My position is like mythical 'Trishanku' suspended between the heaven and the earth.

She spurns me and remains aloof in her ancestral house. Sometimes I pay visit to her. My children come to me and I fondle them with fatherly affection. My wife turns up her nose and maintains a distance from me. She thinks her life has been spoiled as her parents gave her in marriage to a low-grade worthless person like me- a wastrel. So the gulf between us grew wider and wider and, I have been driven into a corner. "

He leaned his back on a pillow and said, "I have not yet reduced to a grinding poverty. I have some landed property which I have given to a neighbour on share-cropping. I sell away the produce and meet the expenses of my bare necessities".

He got up from his cot and reached for some betel leaves and asked Chinmay to have one.

Chinmay put it in his mouth and said, "I am also interested to learn violin. But my field of work has been expanded to such a limit that I am always occupied with other activities. I find no time to learn it. Even I dreamt once that I was playing on a violin, so obsessed I was then".

Chinmay thought for a while and told him in a suppliant manner, "Would you please accompany me to Baripada? There is a greater scope to display your outstanding skill and people there must greet you with respect".

He looked convinced and came to a compliance.

Mr. Udaynarayan said grinning, "I have heard there is an ancient temple of Lord Jagannath built by the Maharajas of Mayurbhanj. I have never visited that place. But I have a great desire to go there and play violin before the Lord. I cannot prolong my stay here. I will request my host Mr. Sunanda to bid me farewell when this festive occasion would be over."

After their sojourn of three days there, the driver got his jeep ready at the behest of his master to help reach them Baripada town.

Mr. Udaynarayan's only belongings were a violin and a shantiniketani coarse cotton bag with long strap hanging on his shoulder. Keen to reach Baripada, they started at 4.30 am, when it was still dark. Before the onslaught of sun rays they reached home in a pleasant morning.

At the entrance, there was a dome shaped iron gate on which 'madhabi' creepers had sprawled with blooming red flowers.

When the gate clicked, Chinmay's wife and her grand daughter came out to greet them with a welcoming smile.

Mr. Udaynarayan stooped a little and caressed the cheek of the child and said, "What a cute little child, indeed !" He chucked the little girl under the chin and advanced.

Chinmay said laughing, "Yes, she always hugs a Japanese doll and moves about carrying it in her arms. She is at the service of her grandmother and shares the household chores without any murmur, a minikin housewife."

"My sweet mother !" Mr. Udaynarayan fondly patted her back and entered the sitting room.

Chinmay told him to take off his clothes and hang them on wooden hooks. After bathing, both sat on the chairs by the dining table. Chinmay's wife served them refreshment. While eating Mr. Udaynarayan glanced in all direction and asked, "Have you built this house?"

"No, my father. I have only added one room to the front wing of the building for my study. Nowadays it involves a lot of money to construct a house as the cost of essential materials is increasing by leaps and bounds. So for this galloping inflation I left the house without modification. Only at an interval of five or six years, I get it painted by a mason only to retain its beauty."

"I see". Mr. Udaynarayan bent over the saucer and gulped down the food.

Mr. Udaynarayan was going to the backyard to wash his hand. Chinmay called him back and said, "No necessity of going backside. There is a basin fitted to a tap in that corner of the wall, you rinse your mouth there". Then he handed him a towel to wipe his face.

"Now you take rest in this guest room and have a sound sleep. We usually eat our lunch at 2.00 p.m. You may roll on the bed or read newspapers and magazines. I will call you at the right time".

Chinmay went to the kitchen and said to his wife, "He is totally vegetarian. So you need not bother about his food. You cook what you usually do for us". After lunch, Chinmay adjourned to his own bedroom.

A little later afternoon, they went to the temple of Lord Jagannath on foot. But before going to the temple, Chinmay wanted to see Mr. Bharati, who was staying in his own house just to the left side of the temple at a close vicinity to the main road. His father was a former district collector and his elder brother, a reputed physician of the town.

He was in the interior of the house. When he heard the ringing of the call-bell, he came out hurriedly.

"Oh, Mr. Chinmay ! How come this way? Are you all right?"

"Yes, sir".

"Please be seated on the sofa". He gave them an effusive welcome.

Mr. Bharati stared at Mr. Udaynarayan. In his eyes were a little curiosity, a little surprise and a deep felicity.

"Pardon me, sir. Take no offence as I have not yet introduced Mr. Udaynarayan to you. He is an expert on violin. He is a protege of the great violinist Sisirkana Dhar Chaudhury. If you hear his playing by his dexterous fingers, you will be simply amazed".

A shadow of surprise was still imprinted on Mr. Bharati's face. He said, "Please, give me a little time to take out my tape recorder. It is my good fortune that my elder brother has brought it from USA for our family. It is quite reliable and it can record any sound from a distance".

Mr. Bharati went inside and after a little while came with that tape recorder.

He set it before Mr. Udaynarayan and waited. His wife too came wiping her hand with the skirt of her sari.

Mr. Udaynarayan placed his violin at right position and closed his eyes for a moment. Then he began to play with his gifted hand.

He caught a sad note which soared gradually to a high pitch, then it started descending and tapered off to an indistinct tune which went fading in the air.

Mr. Udaynarayan himself remained spellbound. He went on playing for about an hour, closing and opening his eyes.

Mr. Bharati and his wife sat rooted on the sofa and tears began to flow down their cheeks. They had been completely overwhelmed. All gazed at him in mute admiration when he finished his playing.

Mr. Bharati stood and switched on the tape recorder. It immediately released the tune flawlessly thrilling the heart of the listeners.

He was extremely glad and said, "I will make arrangement for you to play your violin before the Lord Jagannath every evening after arati and offerings will be given to you besides your remuneration. You please come the next evening. I will get it settled with the temple authority".

A wave of warm gratitude went through him.

Then he saluted him again and again overflowing with exceeding pleasure.

After a fortnight Mr. Udaynarayan was found nowhere.

Nobody have had an inkling that he would slip away so mysteriously.

Two decades lapsed this way. Still the vestige of his memory remained vibrantly alive in Chinmay's heart. His song and the melody of violin was still ringing in his ears, unspoilt:

> "There rumbles the cloud,
> My mind becomes disconcerted,
> My heart becomes restless……"

Perhaps there was no one in this world to understand his restlessness and pining of heart.

FIFTEEN

One cannot holdback the irresistible movement of the fleeting time. A week passed by. Tears in Lakshmi's eyes dried up waiting a long time for the return of Gandhia. In every house, a conjugal row was a must. That was just a domestic fracas. Since marriage, off and on, they have had numerous bickerings on some trivial matter. They would remain tight-lipped and smoulder with rage. Then after a few days they would resolve their differences and bring back peace. Like other women Lakshmi had also a dream before her marriage. But miseries came one by one. After three years of their married life, Lakshmi felt severe pain due to inflammation of the knee joint which made her completely immobile on her bed. Both of them went to a doctor. He examined her and declared that she was suffering from rheumatism and if not treated properly, it would lead to cardiac troubles. Then for some organic problem in the uterus she remained barren for twelve years. Whenever she happened to come across some child, her heart writhed within and her motherly affection imbued her to take the child in her arms and fondle it to her heart's content. It pained her more when her husband went to a wrong path. She was burning inside for his lascivious nature. At the beginning she kept it under wraps but when Gandhia crossed the limit, she started squabbling on petty matters. Now this open revolt and piquant contradiction landed her in more painful situation. Her manhandling to Gandhia smote her day and night. She liked to remain aloof from the prying eyes of the outside world.

She sent her loyal lieutenants Mohadeva and Tunia to look for him. She had already relinquished any hopes of finding him as they came back in vain. A cowherd boy reported her that he had seen him working in the sugarcane field. Some said that he had seen him bathing in the river. Others confided that he had gone to some distant place to engage himself as a factory worker. This differences of opinion made her believe that no one was authentic. At time she was assailed by a frisson of apprehension that something unforeseen   might happen or he might encounter a fatal incident for his lechery. She warned him many a time as to the disastrous result of loutish manners. Some months ago a ludicrous incident happened in a neighbouring village. A scavenger got infuriated with his nymphomaniac wife. She had a loathsome relation with a man. Her husband was seeking an opportune moment. One night they were caught in the act and when the man was trying desparately to escape, the scavenger caught him by the neck and knocked him to the ground. The man wrestled with all his might to wriggle out his clutches but at last gave in. The scavenger slashed the dick of that paramour by a sharp-edged razor pursuing a vendetta against his adultery.

In the month of November, when the auspicious 'Prathamastami' was being observed in the whole area Lakshmi crouched in a corner of her house in sullen mood. The house looked bleak. She had washed the floor clean and was ready for Puja. She gathered some flowers to offer them to the deity. But all the time her mind wandered to that person whom she hated from the core of her heart. Her attention was diverted when a beggar cried aloud from the courtyard, "Mother, give me some alms".

Lakshmi came out with a handful of rice and dropped them in his begging bowl. The beggar wanted something more. He asked, "Mother, have you not made cakes today?"

"No". Lakshmi replied jarringly.

"Why not mother?"

"I can't give answer to your all questions".

Lakshmi got angry. But she could not force him to leave the place on such auspicious day nor could she snub him.

"Give me some money. The rice alone cannot fill my belly, mother. I have to purchase other things".

Lakshmi came back with a coin and handed it to him.

"Only one rupee, mother?" The man began to grumble.

"I have no change" Lakshmi glowered at him for his effrontery.

"Then you must have a hundred rupee note. You give it to me. I will give the change you want". The beggar posed as if he was going to perform some miracle with the sleight-of-hand. He pulled out a wallet stuffed with coins from his pocket and dropped it on the ground.

"So you are not a beggar. I have read in the newspaper that a beggar in Mumbai city donated a huge amount of money to build a temple there. You people cannot remain without begging. It has become a habit with you".

"I am not a beggar, mother. I am the chaukidar of this area. You have not seen me before but I have come to this village time and again on some urgent business". Her eyes were riveted on him. He seemed an unlikely-looking chaukidar.

She said distastefully, "I have no business with a chaukidar. You may go now".

"A piece of information, mother. Your trusted man Mohadeva told me the other day that whoever gives the information of your missing husband, will be rewarded". There was a mysterious smile at the corner of his lips.

Lakshmi was startled. She could not believe that this chaukidar had come dissembling his real identity in the guise of a beggar.

She assumed a genial expression and asked, "How

could you dig up his hideout ?" Lakshmi was still sceptic as to his information.

"Mother, I have learned some art from my higher officials how to catch a thief from his bolt-hole. I have good relation with a milkman of this locality. One day I extracted the fact when he was under the spell of bhang. Your husband has been closeted in the attick of that milkmaid Manju's house who has given him a shelter. He never comes outside. So nobody is suspious about his staying there".

"Oh my God ! Of course I had a hunch that he must have hidden himself in her house. But people here gave me a wrong idea that he has gone somewhere to seek a job for him". She was really stunned by this disclosure.

Lakshmi looked radianty happy thinking that her husband was still alive and well-protected. She gave the chaukidar twenty rupees as a reward and the man ungrudgingly kept the money in his pocket.

Relaxed, she finished the Puja and waited for Mohadeva to come.

"Auntie, what's the news? Has he turned back"? Mohadeva asked in anxiety.

"No, but I found out his hiding place. He is now staying in that whore's house".

"Is it? How did you come to know about it?"

"The Chaukidar of this area came to me this morning. He informed me about this. It is authentic and can be relied upon".

"Yes, but the woman is artful. Uncle will not turn up unless he is hounded out".

"He has been captivated by the snare of her seductive beauty. So he has completely forgotten about his home. In this ticklish situation, can he be weaned away from the lure of that enchantress?" Lakshmi paused for a moment, radiating a new fear.

"You need not be worried. Very soon she will get bored with him and drive him out".

Lakshmi fretted about Gandhia. Her husband was on the wrong track. She wanted to contrive a design to bring him back from her clutch. Unless he was contrite, he won't come to good path. Over and above, she wanted the presence of a male person at home. The stock of necessary things was going to be exhausted. Of course Tunia was there who was not hesitant to help her in hazardous situation and he was her added strength. The neighbours were also easy to get along with and they will come to her door at her slightest indication.

At the twilight hour of the day when the sun tilted to the western horizon and the earth was going to be immersed in darkness, Lakshmi went to Mohadeva's house with some cakes.

"Please, auntie, come in", Mohadeva's wife greeted her coming to the doorway. She was holding her child in her arms.

Lakshmi handed her the plate and took the child to her bosom. She caressed its cheeks and ran her hand through its curly hair. When she tickled its belly, the child started laughing. Lakshmi sat on the cot with the child in her lap.

Mohadeva's wife came with a cup of tea.

"No, I don't drink in the evening. I have had tea in the morning".

The child was playing hilariously throwing its legs in the air and was busy in sucking the right thumb in its mouth.

"Let me take the child home. It will play there. You have to come only at its feeding time".

"Yes, auntie, without objection. Rather I will be glad to leave it in your tender care. Her father told me the other day that aunty is alone. She will not feel herself companionless if the child plays there".

"Tomorrow I will come to take the child. It is very

difficult to do your household chores carrying the child in your arms. If somebody is there to help you, you feel yourself relieved".

"Yes, auntie. Nobody knows the difficulty in bringing up a child. A male person does not understand this. He claims that he does more work than his wife. But if he is left with childcare along with household chores, he will realize how much burdensome it is".

"Definitely, I also think in the same vein and say this thing to your uncle".

Mohadeva's wife kept the child on a cradle and said, "Once I had been to my parents' house for a few days. Before my departure he said that he will manage things in my absence. The next day he started cooking. The hearth was a bit dumpy and it was smouldering though he supplied dry fuel in it. His eyes smarted. With irascibility, he broke the earthen cookingware into pieces".

Lakshmi laughed. After a long period, she could laugh heartily.

"Daughter, they have no patience".

Mohadeva's wife was younger than Lakshmi by some years. Despite this disparity in age, she used to play pranks with her. She laughed till the tears poured down her face and said, "They get impatient in other work also. You must have that experience, auntie". She pressed her mouth with the skirt of her sari and tittered enjoying her smutty jokes.

She stopped laughing and said, "To live a life of housewife is not so easy and it is a woman who can only realize it. We are born to grin and bear difficulties. Live and let others live in happiness. If a husband is warm-hearted, we are geared up to bear all sorts of troubles with least grumbling. Our service must not go unrecognised as we toil and moil day and night for them."

Lakshmi was delighted. Mohadeva's wife was jovial by nature. She can season her discourse with the salt of humour. She is the real hub of amusing folk song and funny stories. She would unburden one's heavy heart by cutting jokes and referring many examples and anecdotes - a rancanteur indeed.

"Auntie, I assume things have gone well for you as I see a big grin on your face".

"Yes, your uncle had gone absconded. He was lost and found again".

"Where?"

"Where he could be? That milkmaid has kept him in her spell".

"Auntie, she is boastful of her beauty. A woman knows it very well that her beauty can easily entice a man. But how many days one's physical beauty lasts? When it wanes, she is shunned like a withered flower. Wait, his ardour for her will be cooled in a few days.How long one's heady days of youth will go on ? "

The next day Lakshmi came back with the child. She felt a new awakening in her. She was stirred up by a strange exhilaration. She had already done her cooking. There was enough time to play with her. She stretched her legs and made the child sleep on them. She gazed at its sweet face, caught its two delicate hands in her and waved them rhythmically singing a doggerel:

Sleep my crazy child, sleep

The field where the oat grows abundantly, sleep on that.

Then she caught another refrain :

Swing my little elephant, swing

Inflated with air and water

Swing my little elephant swing.....

A waning moon had risen in the sky. At a distance, a flock of herons were squabbling among themselves to have a perch on the branches of a tamarind tree. The village steeped in silence.

Gandhia was tossing in bed waiting for Manju. He overheard their conversation.

"Where is that vagrant? Did that sneak-thief decamp somewhere ?" Manju's husband was overdrunk that night and sore at his wife.

"He has already fallen asleep". Manju replied in a whisper.

"He only knows eating and sleeping with you. Why do you sleep every night with that lecher, that worm of the gutter whereas I have been kept aside?"

"Oh, why are you bellowing to pull one out of sleep? If he hears, what would he think of us?" She bleated out chastising her husband.

"To hell with him, let him think what he likes. Does he think himself a monarch of this area and we are his subjects? I toil day and night but he does not mow a blade of grass. He wants delicious food. How can I supply him with that? I am a poor man. Is it possible to defray his expenses on food and clothings? Tell him to quit my house, other wise… ." He drawled and sank on the cot.

Gandhia grew panicky. If they drive him out, where would he go ? Everybody is perplexed by his own problems. Who will agree to give him a shelter? Manju and her husband maintained him for a long period without expressing their displeasure. He should not hang upon them like a parasite rather he would go somewhere in search of a job. But who will offer a job to a little educated person like him. He will erect a cottage under that tamarind tree. He had still a gold ring on his finger. He will sell it and start a business. He could maintain him with less expenditure. 'No, I would go this morning without making any delay', he said to himself.

Morning came to activate the people. The cocks shrieked out their cock-a-doodle-do. Gandhia got up and finished his toilet. He waited till Manju's husband left his house.

Manju was busy in the cowshed scrapping the floor and tethering the cows. He went to her.

"Manju, I have been toying with the idea of building a cottage under that tamarind tree, over there. I have to stay in your house till the work is completed".

"You must have heard our conversation last night", Manju said while dropping fodder in the trough.

"Yes, what your husband has said is hundred percent correct. I should not take offence of his pungent words. You have not pressed me but I volunteered to stay here. You have helped me in every way. Too much of anything is bad, Manju".

"But how would you be able to find the wherewithal to build a cottage there?" She asked disapproving his sudden whims.

Gandhia held out his hand and said, "There is just one small snag- how to find the money? Here is my gold ring. What will be its use if not now"?

Manju remained silent. She did not want to refrain him from his plan.

With much hardship, Gandhia at last built a one-roomed wee cottage with a small veranda in the front. He even lent his helping hand to the labourers to complete the work. He did his own cooking borrowing some utensils from Manju. Days rolled by.

Lakshmi looked at the distant horizon vacantly with tears welling up in her eyes. How impertinent the man was ! He was now staying in a straw-roofed cottage doing cooking in his own hands, the man who sought her help even for a glass of water.

The inevitable must come to pass. One morning when Gandhia was coming with a bucketful of water drawing from Manju's well, he stumbled over a big stone. He fell miserably on the rugged road. His legs slipped and the craggy edge of the stone hit his right chest. The trauma seemed to have broken his rib-cage. For some moments, he could not breathe normally. He sat up with pain and went to his cottage almost dragging his feet. There he lay motionless on his cot.

Lakshmi made a gallant effort to get the news of his actual condition by deputing Tunia to his cottage. She was dying to hear his news. Lakshmi heard his narrative and became gloomy. She was in a real quandary. When the evening deepened, she locked her doors and sallied forth with Tunia.

The cottage seemed to have sunk into an abyss of sepulchral silence. It was dark inside. Gandhia was groaning in pain. Groping her way, she entered the room.

"Who is there?" Gandhia asked in a muffled voice.

"It is me, Lakshmi".

"Lakshmi, you have come. I can't believe my eyes". He was in mounting astonishment. It seemed unlikely to him.

"Yes, I came when I heard this distressing news".

Gandhia tried to sit up to reach for the lamp but tumbled back on to his cot.

"No, no, what are you doing? I will light the lamp myself. Please, tell me where is the match box?"

"There, in that shelf".

Lakshmi lighted an earthen lamp. Gandhia's face looked pallid and darker in the dim light. How frail he looked ! Her heart sank.

Lakshmi lost her patience. She sat on the edge of the bed and placed her hand on Gandhia's chest.

"O, Lakshmi, I feel terrible pain there".

"Where?"

"On my right rib".

Lakshmi began to caress that tender spot. Tears were welling up in her eyes.

After a little while she asked, "How are you staying in this cottage in such a wretched condition?"

"Lakshmi, I am worse than an animal. So where can I live other than this den? This is the retribution of my sowing wild oats."

Lakshmi put her hand on his mouth. She evinced a strong desire to be reconciled with him.

"Don't tell me like that. I have already borne a lot of suffering". She begged.

"No, Lakshmi. My follies are inexcusable. I have chastised and humiliated you by so many cutting words. But you did not retaliate as you did on that day. I am a drowning man, Lakshmi. Please, restore me to the shore. Do you know, Lakshmi, it is passion, it is my vile desire which prompted me to go to a wrong path. This is the unsavoury truth for which I have messed up my whole life. I reprove God for that. Try to restrain me by your love and affection. Try to desist my steps whenever I am tempted to taste the forbidden fruits – I mean my moral departure. I am that perverted husband who has been reduced to a wreck. Please help me rebuild my life."

She reminisced, at the marriage-altar, Gandhia had been asked to forgive her ten reprehensible mistakes. Now in this reverse situation, she became lenient and harboured no grudge against his myriads of mistakes.

It was a real cry from his heart.

Lakshmi wiped his tears with the hem of her sari and said, "Our hard days are gone. Look at the eastern horizon, how the sun of new hope and aspiration is emerging through dark ominous clouds. Now let us go home".

"I am unable to put my steps, Lakshmi".

"Tunia is there with his brother. They will help you reach our home. Our house will no longer wear a desolate look. After a few months, it will be illuminated by a beatific smile of a baby. It is now growing in my womb". Lakshmi said pointing to her tumescent belly.

"What ! It betrayed my ears". He was buoyed up by the unexpected turn of destiny.

"Yes, my dear. This is the vicissitude of life. Heavenly benediction is completely beyond our knowledge. When He wills, everything is possible".

"Lakshmi, you repaid me double. My dream has been fulfilled at last. Fortune smiled on my face giving me a new lease of life. The turmoil in my heart has been stilled and my anguish is over". Gandhia heaved a sigh of relief.

"This is your real atonement".Lakshmi said with a broad grin.

SIXTEEN

Nobody could think Jayram and his elder brother would be arch-enemy of each other. His sister-in-law was vindictive and she was seeking pleas to whip up their anger to pick a fight with them. She threw all sorts of garbage in Jayram's courtyard which after decomposition emitted an offensive odour. So his wife could not put up with their nit-picking nature. Like volcanic eruption sometimes dispute arose which drew a small crowd of next-door neighbours and they tried to patch it up.

One day after lunch Jayram's sister-in-law threw the leaf-plates and leftover foods in their courtyard. A squabble was in the offing.

When it came to the notice of Jayram's wife, it incensed her.

She swore at her shouting at a high pitch,

" How quarrelsome the woman is ! She could have thrown the garbage in the gutter but our queen won't do that mean work. She is the real pain in the arse. I must throw faeces in their courtyard".

Jayram's sister-in-law was enjoying her nap. When she heard her shrill voice, she woke up and came out of her bed room. With arms akimbo, she stood and exploded, "How dare you say me these foul words? You bitch ! Where is your effeminate husband? I want to settle with him. One word more and see what a good slap you will get". She advanced a few steps gnashing her teeth. They squared up to each other and started shouting.

Jayram came out of his study and stood behind his wife. He did not want to fight back. He said in a meek voice, "Please, don't create a scene here. We have no more patience to quarrel with you. We want to live in peace. Why are you vitiating the atmosphere by taking some pleas? I am ashamed of your combative nature."

"Enough of your modesty. You effeminate, don't preach me sermons. For your foul nature your first wife fled kicking on your buttocks. Fie on you", she spat a spittle on the ground with contempt.

Jayram's nephew had a stationery shop close to their house. He was a pampered child of his parents. He left his studies and gradually became addicted to alcoholism. His parents turned a blind eye to his dissipated life. When he heard this brawling, he flounced out of his shop like a villain of the silver screen. Displaying his macho bravado he thundered, "So you have guts to quarrel with my mother ? You must be taken to task. Have some sound whacks and you come to behave sensibly". That upstart seemed to have taken leave of his senses.

Livid with rage, he lunged at him. He held Jayram in his grip and planted a heavy blow on his nose. Then he belaboured him mercilessly. By his ruthless thrashing his nose and mouth bled profusely. Jayram squeezed the nostrils hopelessly to stop the bleeding. To save his life, he flew back to his room.

Chinmay received this sad news and immediately hurtled to their house. He saw Jayram lying in a semi-dead condition. Without making any delay, he got him admitted in the hospital.

In the casualty ward, there were only two commodious halls meant for the injured patients. Each hall could provide thirty beds, all occupied by patients. Some were lying on the bare ground encompassed by their relatives.

At the centre sat a middle-aged bespectacled doctor

looking over the patients' chart kept on the table and by his side two nurses, one helping the doctor and the other setting the medicines and injections in order of priority in a cupboard.

Chinmay escorted Jayram into the ward with care, followed by his wife and children. He looked round, not a single bed had fallen vacant. It would be unbecoming for Jayram to lie on the floor with other patients.

Chinmay went to the doctor and told him about his disadvantages. The doctor took the matter into account and said, "You please wait for some time. Very soon, the bed in that extreme corner is going to be vacant".

After half an hour, the patient left with his belongings.

Lying on the bed, Jayram felt some relief. The doctor examined him and said, "I have prescribed these medicines and injections. Bring them quickly. There is possibility of sepsis. I will tell the nurse to give him saline provided by the hospital".

Jayram's wife sat by his bed on a chair and ran her hands on his legs.

The two nurses who were in charge of that ward were going to every patient and they were very prompt in their work. After he was given an intravenous injection, he fell into deep sleep.

Chinmay was watching the nurse intently.

"This is an anti-inflammatory injection with some sedatives. It must alleviate his pain", she said smiling at him.

Jayram's wife was too much worried and she kept looking at Chinmay with great anxiety.

Chinmay understood. "No, you should not bother about his condition. He will be all right in two days. Now you go home and do cooking for your children. You should not go on empty stomach".

"What will you do here at night?"

"To keep a watchful eye on your husband, I will eat my food in that eatery inside the hospital campus. I will fetch a mat and pillow from a friend living nearby. Spreading the mat, I will sleep here tonight".

She left hesitatingly. While going away, she turned back to Chinmay with a disappointing look. He waved his hand giving her a sign not to linger there unnecessarily.

Then another doctor came in to follow up the cases, trailing behind him were two persons with buckets of foods. They supplied loaves and milk to the patients according to the list.

As the night deepened, silence prevailed and only the whirring sound of ceiling fans was heard.

The medicines given to him brought a brief respite from the pain. Two days later, Jayram was up and about and after a little sponging with luke warm water Jayram felt much better. He leaned his back on a pillow and began to talk to Chinmay.

"Have you submitted the injury report in the police station?" He asked in a feeble voice.

"Yes, the officer-in-charge of thana sent for your nephew for a preliminary enquiry. That rogue returned late at night. Your brother also had gone with him. The officer had been squared for his acquittal".

Jayram remained grave. Chinmay said in a depressed tone, "What have you not done for your nephew ? You brought him up with utmost care. You bore all the expenses for his studies. When he grew adult, he totally forgot your sacrifice".

"I think it my duty, not sacrifice. The boy was not a wicked previously but his doting parents made him so. They slurred over his obnoxious activities for which he wilted in the company of bad friends. They are now reaping the consequence when he comes drunken at night and abuses them with foul language".

"The neighbours are coming but your brother did not turn up to see you. Not a whit of sense. What a ungrateful wretch he is ! The injury report submitted in the police station against his son made his blood boil."

Jayram sat up and kept the pillow on his lap. His wife handed him a cup of tea with some salty biscuits.

"I have already started a civil suit in the court to stake my claim on property. I will see to it after my recovery".

Jayram said while sipping tea.

"Your constant tension owing to family affairs is the sole cause of your hypertension. Don't take raw salt, rather it would aggravate your condition". Chinmay warned him.

"Yes, I am always careful about that".

"You do one thing. Ask some important persons to sit for a compromise at your home. You call your elder brother to have a mutual understanding. Because he blames you that it is you who is not agreed to arrive at an amicable settlement".

Jayram laughed and said, "Is it? He always casts aspersions on me. This time you must be present there and see what he is doing. He has objections to everything. He puts forward some odd conditions for which one will be irritated and come to an impasse". Jayram creased his forehead with indignation.

"You see, your father has left a large home-stead land which is worth crores of rupees at its present value. If it is not partitioned, complicacies will creep in and the greedy persons of ulterior motive will try to grab some portion of it by unfair means. So sooner the partition, the better."

"Yes, it will be a bulwark against a rainy day. Let me see what can be done this time". Jayram seemed to have decided to do something worthwhile in his mind.

"Your nephew has been spoiled. His liver is now in a very precarious condition. If it is diagnosed liver cirrhosis, there is least possibility of recovery. Doctors advise your nephew to give up drinking for its deleterious effect but that rang hollow in his ears. He spent his life with gay abandon. He is galloping headlong towards disaster. Moreover if you do not enjoy this property when you are alive, what is its value after your death? While your dissension continues over this property, your nephew will die a premature death. You too have grown old. Nobody can say when the summon will come from the other world. So get it settled as soon as possible".

"You know, Chinmay, my sister-in-law is quite aggressive, a despicable virago. Whenever a dispute starts, she is always in the forefront. If I go to my brother for an agreement, she will laugh at me and I will meet with square refusal".

"Oh, don't be serious. He is your elder brother. If you yield to him, it will pacify his anger. He still retains the memory of your childhood days how he used to fondle you with brotherly affection. So you should take a cut and dried decision in a cool mind not to be penitent later on".

After convalescence, Jayram remained confined some days at home.

Chinmay was a regular visitor. Jayram's restlessness of mind was considerably lessened for his presence. As he was kept on balanced diet, he got back his normal health.

He had sufficient reason to be apprehensive for the future as his high blood pressure seemed to him a cliffhanger. To keep him fit, he consulted a physician and took medicine regularly. Chinmay advised him to take some light exercise. He listened to him with his wonted attention.

One night Chinmay was sitting with him on a sofa. Jayram was turning over the pages of a magazine 'India today'. The T.V. was on. He tossed the magazine aside and changed the channel. He was a good critic and a lover of old classical songs. An old song of Lata came floating with a plaintive note:

> If you give me your sorrow
> I will absorb it in my heart
> And give you peace in return……

Suddenly he was caught by a fancy and said, "I have heard this song several times. But is there any sympathetic heart who can realize your sorrows and give you solace in return? Is there any noble soul who will feel pity for your deplorable condition? Truly speaking, I am in quest of that soul and I shall be waiting for eternity to get lost in that cataclysm of selfless love".

Jayram was overwhelmed with emotion. Perhaps there was some void in his heart which he wanted to be fulfilled.

Chinmay watched him and said, "Jayram, human life is teeming with problems. You cannot have a good riddance unless you overcome them. You may be worn out but you have to run keeping pace with this world. To us, progress is life, regress is death. You cannot turn back or budge a step.

Don't expect anything from others in return. Expectation is another name of desire. If you have no desire, sorrow is gone.

Throughout our lives we have been baying at the moon with no tangible results. This futility is the major cause of our unhappiness. So defeatism must be removed from our mind. Then you can have that rare bliss for which a sage or sannyasi goes in austerity for years.

One thing you must remember: We lead a hectic life. Day and night we go on trotting to gain something. That relentless pursuit does not end there. In this rat-race we look forward to gaining something more. We slog on although the outcome of our frantic efforts turn out to be abortive at long last. This endless craving for earthly gain bears an uncanny resemblance to the will o'-the wisp which lurks at a distance to lure us. We have been chasing for ages to obtain it and our best period of life is thus wasted on trivialities".

Over a month, Chinmay stopped going to his house and was absorbed in writing.

At 3.30a.m. suddenly the land phone began to ring.

Startled, Chinmay got up. He could not expect a phone call at such an unusual hour.

"Uncle, I had admitted my father in the hospital. He left us half an hour ago".

"How"? Chinmay fumbled.

"He felt terrible chest pain at night. You know he is a high blood pressure patient. For about a fortnight, he did not take medicine although we insist him ..."

The phone went dead at the other end.

Chinmay was not surprised. He knew his friend. He tried to guess the possible reasons of this unanticipated death. There must be some misunderstanding between husband and wife. Jayram must have refrained from taking highblood pressure pills. It was self-rejection-suicidal.

Towards the last part of the night, when the darkness was languishly dispelled by the rising of the sun, he rushed to have a last look at the missing face of his old friend who was laid on a bier ready to be cremated. His nostrils had been stuffed with cotton and he seemed to have slept peacefully with a serene face never to rise again to confront the problem-ridden world.

SEVENTEEN

Chinmay had given his second daughter Nayana in marriage to an engineer. All his relatives praised him for his humble disposition. He was living with his parents and two unmarried sisters at Rourkela. It was his service place. He had two daughters, the elder one was eight years old and the younger one was a tender girl of five years. They were studying in an English medium school. On holidays, they invariably paid visit to Baripada with their mother to spend some days in the company of their grandparents.

In her own handwriting, the elder one had written some questions in a note book like :

"Do the lower animals and creatures dream like humanbeings? If in India we go directly making a tunnel through the centre of the earth, at which country we will arrive? If the earth stops revolving around the sun, what will happen to us? Why do our eyes wink? Etc."

His grand-daughter read out the questions and asked him to answer them. Although these questions could not be rejected outright as vague and baseless, it indicated her inquisitiveness and she passed for a precocious child.

Chinmay obviously failed to answer them. The Child rolled with laughter and laughed at his ignorance. He also joined her laughter.

He patted her cheek lightly and became thoughtful. His granddaughter was, no doubt, intelligent and she must shine in the future.

In the afternoon they played with their rubber ball

running here and there in the backyard. Sitting on a chair, Chinmay cheered them and enjoyed their playing.

At noon, the sun blazed all over the place. So exchanging their toys, they usually played indoors.

They demanded various knick-knacks like glass bangles, bindi, celluloid hair clips, balloon etc. and they were overjoyed to possess these tawdry things.

The elder one would say, "Nana, are you sore at us? A granddaughter demands like that".

"No, no, my dear, please tell me, what other things I will buy for you?"

"No, this will do at the moment", she would reply.

They were fond of cold drink. Chinmay would fetch a big bottle and distribute it between two sisters.

In the early morning, he would ask his granddaughters, "What would you like to eat today, my dear?"

"Mutton, nana", they would shout in unison.

When the holidays were going to end, they would remain in a sulky mood. For a day or two they would not eat properly. Then the day of departure would come. They packed their things in a bag and left for the bus stand. Chinmay would accompany them upto the stand, make them sit comfortably and finally wave his hand bidding them farewell. They could not smother their tears at the parting time. Chinmay too would not turn back to see them departing.

Back home, Chinmay would sit silently in the drawing room. His wife was disconsolate after their departure. Heaving a deep sigh she would ask, "Did they find seat in the bus ?"

"Yes".

Then she would muse over their daily activities and do her household chores absentmindedly. The floor had been bestrewn with toys here and there in the drawing room. Chinmay would say, "Remove them and keep them in a safe place. When they would come back the next time, they would play with them".

He got dejected if those toys came to his sight. The more he saw, the more was his heartache.

Rourkela is a growing industrial city. Since the steel plant is set up, the city is facing population explosion. The traffic is always seething with people and vehicles, jammed nose to tail. In the rush hour, a pedestrian feels difficulty to walk along the pavements also. Everybody is fed up to the back teeth for the sound hazards and humdrums of city life. At night, the sky above the steel plant looks crimson from a distance. In every industrial city, there is threatening of atmospheric pollution. In spite of all these hazards, people like to live in a town or city being enticed by its superficial beauty.

Chinmay's son-in-law Paritosh was living in a rented house in the Western sector of the town. Neither he nor his parents were free from modern vices. They had blown a lot of money on hootch. Addiction to alcohol had become a way for them. Previously they were teetotaler but when they kept going to the clubs, they came in contact with the affluent. At that time they were occasionally taking drinks. In course of time it became a habit with them.

Every Sun day was a festive day at their home. Luxury induced Paritosh to incur a loan. He was soon encumbered by a heavy amount of debt. He began to lose his mental stability.

Several times Paritosh persuaded Nayana to accompany them to the club. But Nayana avoided him taking some pleas. She was getting bored with their way of living. It was alien to her nature and an anathema to her sober temperament.

Her mother-in-law Mrs. Sekhar thought herself a modern woman and liked to lead a carefree and unbridled life. She had a distaste for her conservative nature. To her, smoking and drinking is a sign of aristocracy and ultimate status symbol. She seethed with discontent when Nayana became a mother of two daughters, one after another. She had expected a grandson but her daughter-in-law put her on the foil.

Very often she exploded, "Nayana, I tried to upgrade you to our level but you remain unchanged as because you have come from a lower middle class family". Then she added sneeringly, "Yours is below our status. Adamancy is latent in your blood. Your base inheritance has made you intractable. So you won't come to heel. I have committed a blunder having a matrimonial tie with your family".

Once in a women's conference, Mrs Sekhar launched a bitter denunciatory harangue against the imbecility of the people: Our country is hard-up only for the sluggardly people of society. They are the riff-raff who resort to dacoity, burglary, shop-lifting and all sorts of hooliganism for thier existence. They are   the scum of the earth, off-scourings of humanity. This unprogressive attitude has kept them at bay from the mainstream of India.

They got political freedom but economic independence is far from them. For centuries, India has been fostering a philosophy 'happy poverty' (to remain cheerful in wants) for which people have reached rock-bottom.

This antiquated, mouldy idealism has utterly emasculated the nation, unleashing the ugliness of stunted thoughts and half-baked ideas.

The progress of the country has been thwarted for conservative age-old ideas. Now the time has come to exert the people to be dynamic and farsighted to boost it.

A little later afternoon, Nayana had been to the market for shopping. Mrs. Sekhar was in her bed room. She switched on the television and reclined her back on a pillow. Every evening she was accustomed to see her favourite Hindi serial. Her two daughters also came in and sat by her side.

"Mother, Nayana bhavi (sister-in-law) has gone shopping. She may return late as she has a lot of things to purchase before her confinement. Let us go to the kitchen and get food ready for the dinner".

"Let her come back. Don't you see I am watching my favourite serial?" Mrs. Sekhar retorted with an edge in her voice.

"Mother, she must have been tired. You know she is parturient. The gynaecologist has already given the expected date of delivery. After a fortnight or so, she is to be admitted in the steel plant hospital".

Mrs. Sekhar took her eyes off the television and cast a stern look at her elder daughter and launched into a diatribe, "Remember, if she delivers a female child this time, I won't go to the hospital. Let her manage everything by her own. She may send for her parents to come here at the time of delivery. I am unrelenting in this matter, you know".

She was cross and focused her eyes again on the television screen.

The elder daughter Nira loved her sister-in-law. But her mother did not like her sympathetic attitude. She cited many examples how her sister-in-law had been selfish and refractory to her inlaws. Though any injustice was intolerable to Nira, she was biddable and could not raise her voice in a mother-dominated home.

One late night, Nayana felt a dull pain in her abdomen. She went to the lavatory. There she saw exudation of amniotic fluid from her uterus. She became nervous as she had not experienced it before. She was hastily admitted in the steel plant hospital. There the doctor examined her and said, "Your uterus has been ruptured. The fluid is coming out through that aperture. The child is also in an abnormal presentation. If the birth passage becomes dry, it is too difficult to deliver a child".

Towards the last part of the night, with much strain, she delivered a steel-born female child. It had to be operated with forceps.

Early in the morning Nayana felt herself lonely and helpless. After receiving this sad news, nobody from her family turned up at the hospital. There was no one to chuck away the blood-soaked clothes. She was extremely weak and a thin stream of watery blood was still oozing out from her uterus. She knew her inlaws would not show their faces at this critical hour. But her husband ! What she had not sacrificed for him? So it was abundantly clear that his affection was only skin-deep and their relation had been a charade. His absence at this grave hour could not be thought of. It was, no doubt, a matter of life or death. After delivery, a woman gets rebirth. Though she had been left high and dry in this vulnerability, that selfish monster remained callous and unresponsive to her plight.They were humanbeings in appearance but worse than a beast. A deep anguish began to torment her all the time.

With much difficulty, she leaned her back against the panel of the cot. The nurses were shuffling across the ward with saline and injections in their hands. She looked at the entrance reflectively.

There stood her two daughters to ascertain themselves where their mother could be. A fellow neighbour was standing with them.

Her elder daughter came running and hugged her. She started sobbing. Nayana looked ruefully at her face and asked, "How did you come to the hospital alone?"

She pointed at the man and said, "Mother, Dadi (paternal grand mother) did not allow us to come. But when she was in her bath room, we quickly sneaked out with this man".

"Done well. But what was your father doing when you left home?"

"He was getting ready to go to his office, mother".

"So he could find time to go to his office. How self-centred, heartless bugger he is! And she has been wearing out herself for this brute". Here in this hospital, she had been left stranded with no money in her purse. She began to weep.

A middleaged male nurse came to her bed and asked, "Why are you crying, my child? What is your father's name ? Where have you come from?"

Nayana narrated her woeful incident.

"I know your father. I also belong to the same town. Have patience. I will make some arrangement for your departure to home town".

The next morning the man came with a hired van and said, "Daughter, get in with your children. I have already booked our tickets. Let us go to the bus stand. I am prepared to go out on a limb to reach your home-town."

The bus that shuttles between Rourkela and Puri had halted on the stand. They all got into the bus and sat on their seats. At the scheduled time, the driver honked the horn and the bus started.

The man took down the phone number of her father and held up the mobile to his ears.

"Yes, I am Mr. Sahu, speaking from Rourkela. Mr. Chaudhury, Yesterday, your daughter gave birth to a dead child. Her husband and inlaws did not turn up to the hospital to take her back. I am constrained to accompany her upto Baripada in such precarious condition. The bus will not enter the town, it goes by –pass. So you must be present at Murgabadi square to escort us. Most probably it would arrive at 3.30a.m. or thereabouts. The rest is after I meet you".

It was a wintry night. A shaft of cold wind was blowing shivering them in cold. At a distance, a jackal began to howl giving a foreboding sign. Everything had been veiled with dark. The place had been faintly lighted by a starry sky. A luminous star in the eastern horizon was just winking at them. Murgabadi seemed to be immersed in complete silence.

Chinmay and his wife were seated on a slab of stone awaiting their arrival. Every time a vehicle went past them, they peered through the dark to identify it. They grew impatient. It was now 4.30 a.m. His wife chastised him that he had given his daughter to a devil without thinking the pros and cons of her future. Chinmay lowered his head wearing sack cloth and ashes. That was, no doubt, a serious faux pas, he bitterly regretted to have stomached. Over a period of ten years, every now and then, it had been gnawing at him. His gullibility landed him in this misery for which he will remain guilt-ridden till his death.

At last, Rourkela-Puri express pulled to a halt. First alighted their grand daughters and then her mother and the gentleman.

Although they were half-fed all the day, the granddaughters were elated at the first sight of their grandparents. They almost threw them in their arms and said, "Nana, we have come".

Chinmay's visage went dry seeing their pale and drawn face. The children could not understand how grave the situation had been. When they saw their grandparents, their worries were gone. Finding a sanctuary in their protective lap, smile reappeared in their bleached faces.

It was an unusual hour. To find a tempo was not so easy. At last they found one and hired it at a double rate as they had to reach home anyhow.

Mr. Sahu was in a rush to get home. Chinmay appealed him to stay and eat breakfast before leaving.

"You are a big-hearted man Mr. Sahu. I am really indebted to you for you have escorted my daughter safe and sound."

Mr. Sahu paused for a moment and said, "Mr. Chaudhury, I did everything possible to help them. It is all God's desire that I would rescue her from the despairing situation. I don't know what would have happened to her if she had been left uncared in that state. How inhuman and heartless they are ! "

Then he saluted and left.

Next day at forenoon somebody shook the chain of the door vigorously.

"Yes, I am coming", Chinmay responded from the interior of the house.

Lo ! Mr. Harishankar was standing outside the door.

"What a good day! Mr. Harishankar, please come in". Chinmay was overjoyed.

Mr. Harishankar kept his leather bag on the table and asked solicitously, "I have not seen you for a long period. I thought perhaps you have busied yourself in writing something. Not visited my press even once during this time. What's the reason Mr. Chinmay?"

"Quite significant, Mr. Harishankar. I have lost one of my old friends. Then I have been mentally upset for a recent mishap of my daughter which came as a terrible blow to me. I have not yet found out the solution. Any way you please tell me the purpose of your sudden visit".

"I came to give you some amount of money which I got by selling your books. Your two novels 'Looking through the loophole' and 'Doubtful blessings' have gained popularity. Your last novel 'Doubtful blessings' has been selected and adjudged by a panel of juries to be awarded. This is the culmination of your hard efforts and I congratulate you for your grand success."

"Thank you, Mr. Harishankar. I have not thought it will find a place in the heart of the readers. Their appreciation is my reward. I am glad that at long last my labour has yielded some fruits".

"Definitely. Sincerity never goes unrewarded. You have devoted yourself heart and soul to writing. Everybody must appreciate it".

"Mr. Harishankar, I wonder when I think over the writing of great writers. Writing is a strenuous work. Everybody will admit it. Those who have written volumes of books, they know how hard the work is. They never concede defeat. They strain themselves for months and years to give something to literature. I recall one stanza of the famous poet Longfellow which really inspires me when I feel some mental fatigue. That has been etched on my memory giving me an intellectual stimulation."

> The heights of great men reached and kept
> Were not attained by sudden flight
> But they, while their companions slept,
> Were toiling upward in the night.

Mr. Harishankar was listening attentively. He had a receptive mind. After recitation he said, "Mr. Chaudhury, I have been thrilled. I think the poet Longfellow had deep realization about unremitting efforts of the great men. People worship them for their inborn creative faculty. We pay tribute to them".

"Yes, but look at the present time how a drastic change came over the readers. They don't like serious reading. It must be a pas time for them. Commercial writings or pornography have occupied the market. They don't have pangs of conscience that this ribaldry would deprave the younger generation. Those writers know well the recent tendency of the readers. Writing has become commercialised in recent years and their publishers sell millions of books. People praise them although it has no enduring value. I don't encourage fake morality. I spend a lot of money to print my books. But those remain unsold. I am not stingy while I spend money for my children. But can I do injustice to my brainchild? I could have written erotica with blatant vulgarity to gain cheap popularity. There are still some readers who are fond of time-honoured writings. And they believe in that. My heart burns and sometimes I feel to wage a head-on fight with those commercial writers."

Maya entered and served tea in a crockery. She remained standing.

"Why one cup, Mrs. Chaudhury?"

"He never drinks tea. He thinks tea and coffee are the causes of all stomach troubles. One thing Mr. Harishankar, my husband has written a number of books. But what is its value? Rather he should utilize that time in a profitable work. Moreover he does not get back his money what he spends in printing those books. He only burns the candle at both ends".

Mr. Harishankar laughed and said, "Your views sound absolutely preposterous. I am not agreed with you, Mrs. Chaudhury. A writer may not be rewarded at the moment but a day comes when everybody realizes his merit. Most of the writers do not get honour during their life time. I recall one line of a poet who says : 'Fame is a food which dead-man eats.' So there is no such weighty reason to be disheartened". A note of deep respect rang in his voice.

Maya collected the tea cup and went in.

Chinmay looked at Mr. Harishankar and added "I recall one incident. A few months back, I had been to Cuttack for publication of my books. My Professor Mr. Abhayananda lives there. He is a retired Professor of Philosophy and a celebrated writer of India. I went with him to some publishers with whom he has a close link. He introduced me to them. When he put forth the matter, they budged."

"Sir, ours is a big publishing house. We have kept books worth about fifty lakhs whch bring us no such considerable profit although we have already given an eye-catching advertisement to draw the customers. There are a few book lovers who come to us to buy books from our stall. We manage our organization by selling test papers, magazines and key books. If we publish Mr. Chinmay's, it will remain unsold. We run business only to get a profit, if not, then what will be the benefit of tiring ourselves."

"So I had to come with disappointment. Mr. Harishankar, the world is not yet prepared to accept us. A day will come when there would be an intellectual cul-de-sac."

"It is a fact, Mr. Chaudhury." He concurred. " I also encounter the same problems." Mr. Harishankar became brokenhearted thinking the future of his publishing house.

Chinmay continued, "We are averse to reading because we are only qualified not educated. There is a wide and glaring discrepancy between the two. Education has a broad and significant meaning. A man of wisdom or true knowledge is called educated. But who only gets degrees or certificates, he or she is called qualified. Their knowledge is limited. They are only confined to textual learning. They cannot go beyond that. Parrot-wise they learn it by rote. What more can be expected of them?" The profundities of his statement and analytical precision opened up a new vista to one's preacquired bookish knowledge.

Mr. Harishankar took out a bundle of notes from his leather bag. "It is fifteen hundred rupees in toto. Please count it".

He handed it and said, "It does not signify as an incendiary remark nor it sounds bunkum. You have spoken out what is truth at present. The so-called educated feel shame to admit their hollowness. They are puffed-up with their academic achievement giving an affected air of knowledgeable person. They are very tactful in covering up their insipience. I really feel very much disappointed when I come across such shallow braggarts. You cannot fathom them as they remain hidden behind that facade."

He stood on his feet to leave for home. Chinmay went upto the gate and bade him goodbye.

In the month of April, the scourge of heat waxed to an intolerable limit. The soft breeze which was blowing in the morning changed to loo at noon. The living creatures sought a cold shelter to be relieved from its relentless torture. Advent of monsoon was still afar and people kept looking at the sky with eagerness expecting a good shower of rain.

Rumbling of a tractor along the unmetalled road woke

Chinmay. Over some days he remained in a downcast mood for his ill-fated daughter Nayana. She had been forsaken without any valid reason. His brain got confused whenever he thought about the destiny of his daughter. Paritosh asked him over phone as to her health but his parents did not want to keep any relation with her. As the daughter-in-law fled without their knowledge and permission, they were resolved not to take her back.

Maya did not fancy the idea of leaving her daughter in the lurch. There in her father-in-law's house where she was being treated with open hostility was a veritable hell. Nayana was an educated girl. She would find a job anywhere to maintain her children. They had not thought their daughter's marriage would end in such a disaster. They gave a huge amount of money in dowry but all was a complete fiasco.

Maya came with her languid gait and put a plate of parched rice on the tea-poy. Then she sat at a distance on a sofa and said, "Nayana has got a part-time job in a call centre. They will give her two thousand at present. If they will be satisfied in her work, the monthly emolument may increase to three thousand."

"She has done right. I have no objection if she earns a little amount to meet her expenditure". Chinmay said while eating. Then he added, "I had been to that astrologer three days back. He calculated her horoscope and said that her stars are not at all favourable. She is star-crossed. The position of Saturn in the eighth house has created all these troubles. She would have a strained relation with her husband and inlaws. Even a suit may be filed in the court to take a legal action against them".

"Did he not tell you as to its redress?"

"Yes, the astrologer fished out two stones from a drawer. He kept those on the table and identified one as sapphire and the other as moon stone. He picked them to his left palm and rolled them by his right hand. He said with confirmation that if somebody wears them on his fingers with silver rings, there will be no threat of predicament".

"Then what did you say?"

"You see, I cease to believe these astrologers and their prediction. They may say some balderdash to win over the customers. Those two stones will cost ten thousand rupees. When I said, if these stones will not work, I will return them, he became grave. The straight, logical bargain of mine saddened him and he sank into a chair in gloomy silence.

"Then ?"

"I know, this is simply nonsense, just bullshitting. I don't want to have an argy-bargy with the astrologer".

Maya's face looked darker than before. She had a hope that an astrologer could pave a way for them. But he foiled their expectation. Getting annoyed she asked, "Why did you go to the astrologer then?"

"Because it is you who prompted me to do so. I always act according to my conscience. If I had not gone to him, you would have reproached me and thought me inactive".

"So you hold me responsible for that. But when I urge you repeatedly to go to that exorcist living at village Dukra, you turn your face. Do you know he is an exorcist of some fame in that area? He makes impossible possible by his extraordinary power?"

"No, how do you know him?"

"I am always over-wrought about her future. I learnt from a reliable source that this exorcist is working miracles and many despondent people have been benefitted. There is always a rush at his door to meet him, a much sought-after man. Let us go to Dukra and see what he can do for us".

"Maya, don't rash to a conclusion. You always invite troubles for this. I know these charlatans. They say some gobbledygook to cheat people. They can know from one's face that he is in trouble and is ready to do anything. They take the opportunity of helplessness of others. They play their trump card and win over them".

"You don't want to go anywhere. Because you know you have to spend a handful of money. It is your stinginess for which you are unwilling to go to him". Maya's eyes were brimming with tears.

Chinmay did not want to stir up a hornet's nest. So he said, "Yes, I am ready to accompany you. But fix a day for our visit".

"He has fixed two days, i.e. Tuesday and Saturday for the people to meet him. I have decided to go to him on coming Tuesday, the sooner, the better".

"All right, as you say". Chinmay said with a nonchallant shrug.

The next Tuesday in the early morning, they started for the bus-stand. Nayana also went with them as the exorcist might ask her about her father-in-law's house. They got into a bus plying between Baripada and Udala.

By 10.30a.m. the bus halted at Dukra bus stand. The village where the exorcist was living was five kilometres away from that place. As there was no privilege of going by a vehicle, they plodded in dire straits. Scorched and exhausted, they at last reached the village.

To the right side of the entrance, just in front of the main door, there was a dome-shaped shrine where clay made elephants and horses had been installed. Their bodies had been smeared all over with sandle paste and vermilion. Over them, some devotees had thrown a few garlands of china rose. Some incense sticks were burning before the images emitting a sweet fragrance.

Fortunately there was a small group of people at his door awaiting their turn to go inside.

An assistant of the exorcist helped them push through the crowd.

Where the slope started to go into the interior of the

compound, there stood a mango tree. A string cot had been laid down there meant for some important people to take rest. There were four big earthen pitchers kept on sands for supply of cold water to the thirsty people. A young man was seated on the cot before their arrival. His appearance looked sunken and pale and he was waving a plastic fan to give him comfort. Chinmay sat on the edge of the cot and asked him the purpose of his visit. The man moved to one corner of the cot to give him a wider space to sit on and tried to smile. He seemed to be down in the dumps and said in a wounded tone, "This is my third visit to this place. The exorcist assured me each time that I must scrape through the problem but ultimately it was of no avail. Let me see what would be the outcome this time. It is my last-ditch attempt. If I fail, I would not turn up again." Chinmay remained silent thinking that it would be indescent to ask him about his personal problems. He did not know what his wife and Nayana were doing inside the dingy room. After one hour, they emerged through the crowd. They came to him and showed him a piece of paper where Nayana had noted down the required items meant for the Puja. He hunched over the list : one black fowl, two horns of a goat, one egg, two ducks, a half-burnt wood of a creamatorium and some other sundries. Before their departure, the exorcist handed Maya a bone of a human skull to be buried beneath the ground at a grave yard at dead of the night when nobody would be present there. They came back with hopefulness.

Everybody was fast asleep. Only wide awake were Chinmay and his wife waiting to go on stealth to the graveyard.

The path slopped down to a rivulet, full of throny bushes. With a torch and a crowbar in their hands, they groped the way through darkness. It was a dwelling place of poisonous snakes like crates and cobras. But they stepped down intrepidly braving the oncoming adversity. A murmuring rivulet with shallow water, a little wider than a drain, full of fetid garbage was flowing beside the graveyard. They crossed it by the ford and reached the other bank. A jackal was busy in eating a decayed body of a bird. It was scared by human presence and kept looking at them from a safe distance. When the light fell on its eyes, they glowed like embers. Then it disappeared into the dark.

Maya was holding the crowbar. Chinmay switched on the torch and moved the shaft of the light to find a suitable place. Maya dug out the earth and kept the bone in that ditch. Then they covered the hole with turf of grass and left the place. Back home, Chinmay tried to sleep. His eyes drooped but sleep did not come to him. He spent the entire night tossing on his bed.

The next Tuesday had been scheduled to visit the exorcist once again with all the requisites for Puja. Chinmay was to collect them.

On Sunday morning he went to the village market mounting on his bicycle.

He knew a place at the corner of the market where the fowls were usually sold. He bought a small one at a high rate and put it in his bag.

But there was no trace of ducks. He asked a betel shopkeeper, "Brother, where are the ducks available? I know they come every Sunday to sell them".

"Yes, for extreme heat, they stopped coming. But I know the place where ducks are available in plenty".

"Please, give me the precise address".

"From this railway crossing you have to turn to the left side. A narrow road leads to that place. The distance is about eight kilometres from here".

"Thank you".

After railway crossing, there was no other way except that road. He went straight and arrived there. Beside the road, there was a thatched shade where a number of ducks were quacking, protected by wire-guaze.

An old man came out of the shade and asked, "What do you want, sir?"

"Two ducks".

"For the feast, sir".

"Yes".

The man weighed two ducks fastening their legs with a rope and said, "Give me one hundred and fifty rupees, sir".

"Here it is".

The man counted the notes one by one and kept the bundle carefully in the fold of his dhoti.

On the appointed day, Chinmay got ready to go to the bus-stand. Maya and Nayana went with him. The exorcist had reassured his wife that he must bring a reconciliation by his occult power.

When they stepped out of their house, a group of people, carrying a deadbody on a bamboo stretcher were going to the cremation ground. Several mourners were following them. A young man was going ahead throwing coins and fried rice on the ground. At a brief pause they were shouting, 'The name of Lord Ram is truth, The name of Hari is truth'.

Maya said, "It's a good sign. We must come out successful".

They caught the same bus and arrived at Dukra bus-stand. Though it was early part of forenoon, the wind was burning hot. Chinmay stood and looked at the distant village in despair. It was too difficult to cover five kilometres on foot. But he gathered courage to go onwards.

After much physical strain, they reached there. Chinmay sat on a slab in the shade of that mango tree. He waved his hand allowing them to go to the exorcist. They went in. After a little while, Chinmay himself entered the room to see what was going on there. The room was filled with smoke and hot breathing as so many persons had huddled together to place their oblation.

Maya was seated on an asan before the exorcist and

squatted by her side Nayana. With his signal, she took out the egg first from her bag and handed it to him. He smashed it on the ground and threw it to the deity who was completely covered with a red sheet and installed on a wooden pedestal.

Then Maya handed him the fowl and ducks one by one. He signalled his assistant to keep them in his care and said, "I will sacrifice the fowl and ducks at the altar of the deity at midnight. It will be done unnoticed". He went on intoning mantras which sounded quite jargon.

Chinmay could stay no longer inside that room. He felt breathless. He came out and went round the embankment of a large tank which was in front of his house.
Fifty to sixty ducks were swimming there resounding the tank with their quacking sounds. He was disillusioned and came to realise the practical joke played by the man.

So that charlatan had kept these ducks and fowls without sacrificing them to the deity. It was clear that sacrifice was just a phoney show to cheat the people. His jaw dropped.

On his return journey, Chinmay was completely worn out. He handed the umbrella to his wife and told them to walk briskly holding it over their heads. He was a wee bit behind them. On the way while walking he recollected a story of sacrifice when a General of the army handed the container of water to a soldier although he himself was extremely thirsty. The soldier slaked his thirst and gave it back to the General. By that time he was moribund and breathed his last desiccated by awful thirst. He felt invigorated when he remembered a few lines of Robert Frost which were deeply imprinted in his memory. His mind received a tremendous fillip and the purport of the song toughened him up :

> 'The woods are lovely, dark and deep
> But I have promises to keep,
> And miles to go before I sleep
> And miles to go before I sleep.'

There was still a difficult path before him to traverse.

That will be a real test of his mettle. While going along the furrowed track, straining his every nerve, he felt his confidence deflating and ebbing away. He walked on and on. The beads of perspiration dripping from his forehead blurred his vision. It got accumulated and began to flow down his cheeks. He heard the galloping sound of his heart. There were some lapses of heartbeat. His pulse was rapid and he proceeded almost dragging his feet and hoped to catch them in a jiffy. The man who had gone through years of bitter travails, he would not give in.

He was hell-bent and even prepared to go to inferno for the sake of his daughter. His wife turned back. He was walking several yards behind them. The distance began to increase. She shouted at him to keep pace with them. He saw her beckoning him to go near. But his legs were not under his control. He was shagged out after all that distance. The blaze of the sun fell directly on his head. Then he felt a splitting headache. A cold shiver ran down his spine. The loo went past him seething his entire body. Heat pouring from all sides brought him to a state of near-collapse. He fell flat on his face and rolled on the ground.

Maya halted and turned back again. "Where is your father, Nayana? Oh, God ! He has fallen down on the dusty ground. Run Nayana, run".

They ran towards him.

"Nayana, hold his head carefully and I his legs".

She let out a deep heart-rending cry hoping some one to come to their rescue. She had never shrieked so pitifully in her life. Two persons of road side house came running and carried the unconscious body to their house. They hired a van and laid him on a cushion to get him admitted in Sadar hospital, Baripada.

On the way Maya sprinkled water on his face and wiped it with her apron. Then casting a piteous look at him, she pasted a strip of wet cloth on his forehead. After some minutes,

Chinmay slowly opened his eyes. He could not remember anything. Only the faces of his old friends flashed before his eyes. 'Hello Mr. Harishanker, how are you?' Mr. Harishankar stood by his bed with a smiling face and said, "Mr. Chaudhury, do you know you have been given the national award this year?" He could see the angry face of his wife who was scolding him for no reason. With bloodshot eyes he stared at his wife and muttered, "No, no, I have no debt. I have repaid it all".

Then a golden gate opened and his friends came out to greet him, "You lazy fellow, we have come early. Why are you so late? Don't tarry."

Maya saw a faint gleam of hope when Chinmay opened his eyes. In her life, she had seen many deaths and knew its surest sign. Chinmay's face was deathly pale. He uttered something punctuating in his feeble voice, "I have kept nothing, no sizeable bank balance. But I have collected some worthreading books. Please distribute them among my children. That is the only assets I have garnered in my life".

His body writhed in pain. A weird smile flickered across his face.

Maya sat petrified. She started weeping. From the depths of her palpitating heart, welled up an earnest prayer. "Oh, merciful God ! be not unfair to us. Have pity on him. Don't snatch him so ungraciously from me. He is mine. He shall be mine for many existences, mine for ever."

She cradled his head tenderly in her arms and gazed at his waned face.

"What are you saying?" She asked nervously.

His voice had been tapered off to an inaudible whisper. Maya put her ear close to his mouth. She heard him mumbling, "The time has come, give me my last supper".

DREAM PEDDLERS

by

Dr L.K. Singh Babu

PREFACE

Many a time I think how the omnipotent God has created this cosmos – this vast universe where many things are happening beyond our knowledge. At every moment there occurs a change. He has given us his own form and intellect. It is an undeniable truth that human being is one of His strange creations. Sometimes I ponder over the fact how deftly He has given a final touch and how much time He has taken to create all these things. I really wonder when I behold His exquisitely beautiful workmanship. I sit in stunned silence and deliberate in my mind has He chosen our mother Earth as the best planet where all types of living beings frolick day and night to enhance its beauty. It is beyond my ken whether any living being exists in other planets or these innumerable stars, suns and nebulae have been created only to decorate this boundless sky. All these thoughts jumble my mind and I puzzle out to arrive at a conclusion. I squeal with delight whenever I think deeply over His work that He has done with surgical precision.

Human beings dream. This is also a sublime largess of God. I don't know whether lower beings dream like us. Dreams, thoughts and visions are inseparable part of our life. Some dreams augur well, some very awesome results.

Man is always influenced by environment –the surroundings where he lives in. From his nascent stage, he aspires many things, undergoes make –believe and heroworship stages.

His ambitions, his hopes and aspirations – all are

unlimited. He strives. He dreams to materialise – to fulfill all his desired things. He always trots to gain something more. His endless cravings for earthly gain bears an uncanny resemblance to the will-o'-wisp which lurks at a distance to lure him. He frantically chases to obtain it. His relentless pursuit may turn into a utter fiasco but he must slog on to achieve his desired goal.

Our unfulfilled desires which remain in our subconscious mind reflect in our dreams. We are all, more or less, dream peddlers. Under inescapable circumstances we lead a hectic life and are flogged behind to join the rat-race. It is our sole raisondetre and we accede to that.

Life is undoubtedly a curious and hard combinations of odd situations. So far as ' Dream Peddlers' is concerned, I would like to say candidly, this novel is neither the prototype nor the blue print of my life. But there is a distinct touch of autobiography as I am inextricably linked with all these events.

We are agog when our cherished desires – our dreams are fulfilled. Tom, Dick and Harry are not exception to that. 'Dream Peddlers' apparently looks a combination of different chapters depicting the character of different persons but actually it is a seamless novel and the protagonist Sambit is omnipresent at every page of this book.

I don't know how far I am successful in painting the fortitude and foibles of human character in its most natural colours. I hope it would be gripping and engaging to most of my readers.

To sum up I would like to cite Paulo Coelho who says, "Some books make us dream, other bring us face to face with reality but what matters most to the author is the honesty with which the book is written."

Dr. L.K. Singh Babu

ONE

From the time Sambit was a small boy, he knew that he wanted to be a scholar. Although he had a natural flair for it, he neither had a frail support nor did he get a shot in the arm from his family.

When the Second World War began he was born as the first child of his parents. There was no rejoicing on his birth and it was observed perfunctorily. There was always a dearth of money and his father sought refuge in various excuses to get rid of his domestic problems. As Sambit grew older, he found himself more and more encumbered by poverty. In winter, he had no such warm dresses to protect him from biting cold. Quite naive and inexperienced as he was and unfamiliar with the ways of the world, he sometimes became the butt of everyone's jokes. When his playmates were romping about being dressed up with festive finery, he would cast a furtive glance at his own dress, threadbare and worn-out, he felt mortified but he had to remain satisfied with that sullied rags. He never dreamed of savouring gourmet food nor did he want to indulge himself in opulence.

He was born sick and his parents had faint hope that he would hardly bear the brunt of sickness. He was a spoil-sport and a whimpering child who always wanted to satisfy his whims by pestering his mother.

But after some years, his health miraculously improved. Though not robust, he was in trim and he had all the earmarks of an egghead student.

When he was a school going child, he used to sit in the

morning under a mango tree at the backyard of their house and its shady retreat being his favourite place to study, he would sit there reading books and listening to the chirping of various birds.

One morning when he was eating his breakfast being oblivious of his surroundings, the dead body of a sparrow fell on his plate. Startled, Sambit looked around but could not detect anyone who could play such a nasty trick on him. He thought perhaps it slipped from the beak of a predatory bird. Just a few feet above his head, perched on the branch of that mango tree, his cousin Hrushi broke into a guffaw.

'How palatable food I offered you' so saying, he spat a spittle on the ground and got down with a thud from the tree.

He put his hand on Sambit's shoulder and said, 'Let us go to that triangular field to fly kites. Two days ago I sharpened the cord with powdered glass and mixed it with glue. It is as sharp as a razor. Then throwing his hands with much bravado he said, "You watch how my kite would fly menacingly and sever the strings of other kites, one after another."

Then he ran with excitement to his study and fetched some kites of different colours. It was his most cherished belongings and he was always puffed with pride while displaying them before his playmates.

On many occasions Hrushi became the cause of his ire umpteen times. The decayed body of the bird was nauseating. He gulped back his tears and was miffed at Hrushi for his misdemeanour.

In those days kite flying was not only a consuming interest with the children but also the adults were full of beans and they took active part in kite flying matches. In the afternoon they would step out to some open field with their kites. Some climbing over the roof terrace remained riveted on kite flying till the sky was enveloped with darkness. It was a pleasant pastime for them. They get very much excited, if they cut the kites of opponents.

When the severed kite floated away dancing in the wind, the children started yelling and they ran after it to grasp the trophy. If the string became entangled with the branches of some tree, then there would be a competition to tug it with the help of a long bamboo pole.

Sambit was living with a large family. A maidservant had been engaged to do the household chores. As it was tedious to scrub all the cooking wares and utensils, leaf plates and cups were used to ease the work. During lunch and dinner, there would be a little uproar till they retired to their living rooms.

Sometimes at the dead of night, Sambit's sleep was interrupted when he overheard the sobbing of his aunt. He cocked his ears but could not understand anything. All the members were early risers. In the morning when he cast a sneaky glance at his aunt, he found her in a gloomy mood. Her puffy eyes were still smudged with tears. While tidying up the room, she was muttering something under her breath in an accusing tone.

"What the hell the man has done for us, squandering money for that bloody bitch and her children. Is this lousy thatched house fit for human habitation? None can live in a dump like this. A building could have been built here which he spent lavishly for that concubine. One day we will wind up in the gutter. We are doomed to live in this wretched condition. We have been cooped up in this grotty room to die in suffocation".

There was a kitchen at the rear end of the house having one window to let in light and air. Even by day time it was faintly lighted. As it was not a well-lit room, the women of the house used to cook there with grumbles. Sometimes the firewood brought from their farm house was damp and it was a strenuous job to fire up the hearth. It smouldered endlessly, stinging their eyes. They complained that their vision got blurry due to this acrid smoke.

In the mercurial days of his childhood Sambit was very naïve. In later years when he grew up to an adult the curtain of mystery lifted and he could understand what had been a conundrum to him all these years.

It was quite evident that his aunt was seething inwardly for she loathed her husband's philandering nature and this wound became gangrenous in the course of time.

In his childhood days Sambit was a loner. Some cousin sneered at him as a ragamuffin. His uncle was doing some job in the court. When he returned from his office, his pockets were heavy with coins. Every afternoon his children would accompany him to some sweet stall. While going on the way, they looked back to ascertain if they were followed by somebody. They fondly held his hand and were on cloud nine. They thought this privilege was exclusively meant for them and they were quite unwilling to share it with others. Sambit followed them halfway but when he came to know that they were in a mood to elude him, he veered to another direction.

They spotted him from a distance, exchanged their glances and got into the sweet stall. Sambit was very strait-laced and he never badgered his uncle to buy anything.

His uncle sired one son and one daughter by his mistress. Very often they paid a visit to their house. Though his aunt was aflame inwardly she never gave them a lukewarm welcome. They too never felt themselves downgraded and slighted.

Daughter was like a silent weight upon the heart of her parents. When the daughter became nubile, his uncle went to the house of prospective bride grooms and finalised the matter. The daughter got married but as ill luck would have it, after a couple of years she became a widow. She lost her protection and her in-laws were quite reluctant to give her a shelter. Being deprived of her hearth and home, she became destitute.

Her father made every effort to settle her down to a steady job to earn her daily bread. Fortune favoured her at length and she found a job in some primary school.

In the early morning when the mellowed sunlight began to bleach darkness, his aunt would get ready for cooking and later Sambit's mother joined her too. His aunt would always like to chop vegetables with a serrated knife. While putting the chopped onions in a separate plate, she would say, "Keep an eye on the broiling rice, I have to bathe the children as they must be tidied up before school time".

The aunt started massaging their bodies with mustard oil. The children were always scared of this because of its pungent smell and they did not allow her to smear their faces with this oil as it smarted their eyes. But the aunt was hard-nosed and she would not spare them for any pleas. She would drag them one by one and thoroughly massaged their bodies while they tried to wriggle out from her clutch. She poured a bucketful of water over their heads and then rubbed their bodies dry with a frayed towel.

"Your uncle has brought this oil from jail. The prisoners have pressed it out from the oilseeds with the help of a mill-stone. Pure mustard oil. Your eyes are smarting for that", the aunt would say dispassionately. It was her daily chore and she found pleasure in bathing the children and doing drudgery of household work. She was a workaholic and for this reason her face had been wizened and hands became calloused. It was a tad painful for the soft skin of the children. She would play the role of a bai, soaping their bodies (whatever soap came to her hand), rinsing off the suds from their faces, combing their hair carefully and serving their usual lunch by 9.30 sharp.

Though it was not so evident at the beginning but in course of time there started a discord, actuated by selfish motives in their family.

"No one has got that guts to compete on an equal footing

with my children. They will pass the exam with flying colours and become an exemplary to be followed by others", the aunt would proudly say strutting around the verandah. She wanted to jab others by her barbed comments. Sambit's mother never retorted and she would keep mum although she disliked her sooty attitude.

At night when dinner would be served, most of the children were found asleep. During study hours, they used to sit on a mat keeping a speckled lantern in their front. As the night deepened, they felt drowsy, their eyes drooped and they fell into deep sleep. Their mothers shoved them by their shoulder to rouse them from sleep and made them sit to take their food. They rubbed their eyes and began to gulp down their food. As their eyes still remained half-closed, some unknowingly dipped their fingers in the dish of others.

The aunt balked at the idea of living so many years in a joint family. Very often she expressed her discontentment about the gullibility and imprudence of her husband as the bulk of his income was spent in maintenance of the family. With that money they could have built a beautiful house. The children could have been nourished with nutritious food. But her husband, being heedless to the future, wasted all that he earned by slogging. He would have made headway had he cared a little about the wise counsel of his wife. He was not putty in her hands. He was too tough to be led by the nose. So all her efforts to bring him to the right track fizzled out.

"My children scoff their food with the least grumbling. Here in this joint family preparation of yummy dishes is not possible. So during vacation they go to my parental house to relish some delicious food and there they feel themselves satisfied. They no longer like this awful stuff", she tutted with aversion.

One of the aunts was very avid in preparation of pickles. There were some lemon plants and mango trees at the back side of their house. When the mango blossomed, the air was permeated with a sweet scent and a honey-like fluid exuded from them. At the advent of summer, the trees became overladen with fruits. Seeing these succulent mangoes, the children could not resist their greed and they hurled stones at them. There was no one to watch their activities. Their mouth slavered and they plucked them which were hanging just above their heads. After slicing them into pieces they daubed them with salt and chillies. If it came to the notice of some aunt, she would shout and the children would take to their heels.

"You spoiled brat ! You little monster! What a gargantuan appetite you have! Not a single mango will remain on these trees if you strip them naked this way". She would gesticulate wildly and shower abuses on them.

One elderly aunt prepared pickles from lemon and mango with much care and preserved them in separate glass jars. She concocted them with different spices and poured mustard oil inside the jar up to its brim. She kept them in the inner yard near a holy basil plant which had been reared up on a pedestal. Under the scorching heat of the sun, the mango and lemon inside the jar started sizzling and though tightly screwed by lids, they sent forth a very appetising scent. The children stood at a distance greedily looking at them but they never ventured to taste the pickles by uncorking the bottles.

There was a plum tree on the left side of their house which was protected all around by a green fence. The trespassers knew when the plums began to ripe. They turned yellowish and fell down on the ground when a sudden gust of wind swept through its thorny branches. The boys of surrounding areas knew its taste. They could no longer curb their greed and broke through the fence in the off-guarded moments of the owner. The plums were strewn all over the ground. They chewed them to their fill with satisfaction. Before the owner rushed to that place, they would retreat to a safe distance.

Downtown Baripada, there was M.K.C. High School set up by the then Maharajas of Mayurbhanj. It had reached a crowning point of fame during the monarchical regime. Most of the teachers were hand-picked and they had remarkable academic achievement. They were the top echelons of the educational field who poured their heart and soul for the progress of education in their district. Under their tutelage, some students soared to the acme of fame in the whole province and their performance still remained commendable and exemplary to be followed by the younger generation.

At a little distance from the main school building there was a thatched house known as 'Pakistan block'. It comprised six rooms meant for the lower classes. During the rainy season when it rained heavily, some boys would collect a bamboo pole from somewhere and make holes in the thatched roof with its pointed tip. A portion of the roof would cave in and the whole room would become flooded with rain water. It was a funny game and they played their mischief in the absence of their teachers. To show them more pitiable, they made them drenched to their skin and hurried to the headmaster to draw his sympathetic attention. Then the bell would toll declaring half holiday due to inclement weather. Through heavy rain, the boys would run to their homes with yells and whoops of joy covering their heads with their shirts.

Interschool football match was another great attraction for the public. Not only hoipolloi but also the important persons of the town thronged to see the football match. They jostled and shoved others to stand in the front to cheer up their favourite players. For the sake of entertainment of the public, some boys dressed themselves with tattered clothes and acted like street beggars moving in the middle of the medley of crowds. Some carried fried peanuts and chana-jor-garam in a small hamper peddled among the people hawking their toothsome in a loud voice. Some acted like Diogenes, the Greek philosopher, moving around the field holding a lantern in his hand. Some, attired in the dress of a rickshaw puller suddenly emerged from the crowd.

If any team won in the match, then the supporters went nuts. There were wild screams from the spectators and they entered the play field by breaking the police cordon, threw up their shoes and slippers in the air rejoicing their victory. The whole field resounded with the clamour of the people. The winner team was cock-a-hoop greeted by mobs of excited fans.

When the crowd began to disperse, Sambit came out and stood beneath a flower tree known as Nageswar which was rare of its kind because it bore such a sweet scented flower that the whole atmosphere would be charged with its ambrosial fragrance. When the tree came into flower many passersby stood under it to inhale its sweet aroma. Surrounded by the petals, there was a diminutive phallus in the centre of the flower and just above its head, there was a canopy like petal simulating a serpent's hood, very pleasing to look at.

As he turned to go, he came upon his friend Nrusingha. "Hi, Sambit! Would you go to the science room tomorrow?"
"Why?"

"Don't you know the school is distributing milk freely to the boys. All would go there to stand in a queue awaiting their turn".

"Is it cow's milk or something else?"

"Not natural milk but it is in a powdered form supplied by the U.S. government to poor and underdeveloped countries. Tons of milk powder packed in huge tins are supplied to our country everyday. You will see yourself how the peons of our school are diluting powdered milk with water and supplying one glass to each boy as directed by the headmaster".

"Nrusingha, have you ever tasted it?"
"Yes".

Nrusingha turned his nose up and said, "It is not so agreeable. I don't like its odour. Our government is supplying this junk in the name of nutrition. We are now in an economic funk. So the young and old alike of our country are suffering from malnutrition".

Attending drill class was compulsory for all the boys of the school. Shirkers, if found guilty, were heavily penalised by the drill teacher Braja Sir. He was a middle-aged man with a broad forehead and his hair was trimmed short like an athlete.

There was not an ounce of fat in his body and he always stood and walked without bending his body forward. In his youthful days he was an excellent football player and he earned fame in the whole province. He was given a red-carpet welcome by the connoisseurs of football games. If somebody stood hunchbacked before him, he would pull his hair and smack his back affectionately. In the drill class he would be transformed into a spritely young man. Though he was generous and kind hearted, still the boys held him in awe. Under his guidance and supervision, the high school football team became unbeatable and won accolades for its super performance in interschool football matches.

His contribution to 'Baripada Football Association' was laudable. He laid its foundation on solid ground. Many famed football matches were held in Baripada stadium and they defeated many tough opponents and remained invincible. His juvenile spirit infused a new vigour and enthusiasm into the heart of the players. One of the players for his superior skill and uncommon adroitness drew his attention. He guided him wholeheartedly to be a first rate scorer and singled him out as the only player who was as terrific as hurricane to score ball into goal post with right precision. He struck fear into the hearts of opponent players and for him 'Baripada Football Team' achieved phenomenal success. He walked away with many prizes. Braja sir was so much swayed by his skillfulness that later on he gave his daughter in marriage with that young man.

Drill classes were scheduled to be held every Saturday in the morning.

Once Brajasundar sir was on leave. So the headmaster assigned that duty to Harekrishna sir in his absence. He was a corpulent man and remained unusually grave while teaching in the class. He never cut jokes with others. For such a dour and humourless person, drill class inevitably resulted in ludicrous failure.

A huge table was usually laid in one corner of the field on which the teacher stood and gave demonstrations of physical exercises. Keeping tune with him the boys did all the exercise, according to his direction. When Harekrishna sir demonstrated, it sent the boys in fits of laughter. He could not make head or tail of their sudden guffaw. He thought there must be some wrong with him. He lowered his head and caught a fleeting glimpse of his body. It was out of his knowledge that the zip of the trouser was unlocked. He immediately drew up the zipper and was saved from an embarrassing situation. He took a little time to get back his composure. When the headmaster, a strict disciplinarian, overheard the uproarious laughter of the boys, he went to the playground to pry the fact and suspended the drill class.

After some days the car festival came with all its glamour. It was one of the greatest festivals of Baripada town and people came from far and near to have a darshan of Lord Jagannath. Elaborate preparation was made for the smooth management of the festival. As poor sanitary conditions were the root cause of health hazards, top priority was given to that important matter, so that nobody would succumb to infectious diseases. Water and food, being its vehicles, owners of hotels and restaurants were made sensible of cleanliness.

Due to the large gathering of people, water got polluted first. As most of the people were not health conscious, they easily fell prey to these fatal diseases. To keep the environment clean, the health department took some drastic measures.

Stagnant water in canals and gutters was the breeding ground of the mosquitoes and flies. So they innovated a new operating system in sewerage to drain out polluted water. D.D.T. and bleaching powder were sprinkled all over the town. Provisional health centres were set up in strategic places. All the entries and exits were well-guarded to prevent the carriers from crossing the threshold of the town. It was announced in the loudspeakers to keep the food and food materials in perfect healthy condition.

Despite all these stringent precautions, providence had kept something in store for them. When a few stray cases of Cholera were traced out, the health department became alert and gave preventive injections to check the onslaught of the disease.

Throngs of people started coming and they halted outside the town where the concerned department administered them prophylactic antibiotics and injections. In Spite of all these efforts, calamity swooped over the town. A vengeful nemesis descended upon them and took a heavy toll of lives. Gradually it spread its vicious tentacles and people were caught in swirling vortex of terror. Over some days it continued to plague the town. As the Cholera ward was spilled over with the patients, there was no space for new ones. Patients admitted later were forced to sleep on the open verandah.

There were pilgrims everywhere. Gandhi Park, verandah of schools and colleges, church yard and court premises sheltered this vast multitude. Within a few days, Cholera thinned out the crowd.

When the health inspector with a group of nurses visited M.K.C. High School, Sambit was present in the classroom. There were some boys who were very afraid of injections. They sought an opportune moment to run away from their class to escape from this danger. So the class teacher instructed the peon to latch all the rear doors and posted himself at the front door to keep him on his toes. Basant, one of Sambit's classmates, was very frightened to see them. When the inspector with his convoy entered the class, his blood ran cold and he made a bolt for the door. His silly act came to the notice of the teacher and he enjoined Sambit and two other fellow students to give him a chase. Basant ran like the wind. Fear quickened his speed. There were some banyan trees and rows of shops outside the school campus. It was too difficult to catch him on the serpentine path. At last he vanished behind some grocery and stationery shops.

Basant's father was a band-master during the British regime. At the advent of independence, he retired from his service. He had two sons, Basant and Hemant. Although they were Bengalis, they could speak Oriya fluently. Basant's mother was a well-behaved and warm-hearted woman. Once she had fed Sambit with her own hand when he was suffering from scabies on his fingers. She had swathed him with affections. The intimacy between the two families had grown deeper. Sambit's father was tutoring those two brothers. After the band-master left Baripada and went to Calcutta with his family, Basant remained alone to continue his studies. He resided with an acquainted family at the vicinity of 'Ajad talkies' (now Jagadhatri talkies) for some years till he appeared at the matriculation examination. Then he was lost in oblivion.

After two decades he came back to Baripada with his wife. He was now a police inspector deputed for some important official duty. He came straight to Sambit's house and that reunion made both of them very delighted. They were ushered into the living room. Basant gulped down some refreshment hurriedly and left for the police station. He was always fidgety. He felt an itchy impatience for which he could not sit silently in one place. His wife was a mousy-looking woman but very soon she came over her uneasy feelings. She watched a tailoring machine which had been kept at the corner of the room. She walked over it and scrutinised its different parts. Then she turned to Sambit and said, "The machine is not running smoothly. It will work excellently if it is washed with Kerosene. Bring one litre of Kerosene. Your machine will be quite okay".

"Do you know how to repair a stitching machine?" Sambit asked.

She smiled a little and replied, "Ofcourse, some years back I was an employee of Usha Company in Bombay. There I learned machinery work exhaustively, especially how to assemble different parts without flaw".

"Oh, I see. Are you still working? "

"No, no, soon after marriage, I resigned from my job and came to Cuttack to live with my husband".

She sat on a charpoy and said, "There is no defect in your machine and does not require overhauling".

Sambit became thoughtful for a moment and said, "All the machines are like that. If it remains unused and untended, it becomes rusty. At present no one is stitching with that machine. So naturally it is not in up and running condition".

"Yes, after thorough washing and greasing, it will work as good as new one".

That evening she unscrewed all the parts of the machine and dipped them in kerosene.

She drew the attention of Sambit and said, "Let the rust be dissolved. Next morning I will rub it clean with a ragged towel".

She was self-effacing and a down-to-earth woman with no pretensions. She had an ovular face. Her eloquent eyes and red dot on forehead presented an appearance of Mother Durga.

During their sojourn at Baripada, Sambit asked Basant about his parents.

He threw a reflective glance at him and said, "Over some years I became indispensable to my father. Two years back my father died a peaceful death. I have never seen him bed-ridden.

On the night of Guru Purnima, he ate his dinner as usual, and asked my mother to hand him his Bhagavad Gita which he always keeps beside his pillow. Then he slept quietly. Every morning my mother would wake him up. But that morning he did not get up in spite of my mother's hefty shove. She started crying. We all hastened to his bedroom. We could not ascertain the time of his death. We found the Bhagavad Gita still lying on his chest".

Taking a little pause he added, "My father was a great devotee of Lord Jagannath. So I built a temple in front of my house and installed them there. Puja is being done every day. A few devotees too come to the temple and chant the name of god".

"What about Hemant, your younger brother?"

"He is serving under the Board of Secondary Education. The names that you see on high school certificates are all written by him. His handwriting is nonpareil. It is a god-gifted quality".

Basant continued, "Do you know how much I love him? My father's pension was a measly amount. It is quite inadequate to maintain a family. My father was very worried about Hemant. I had to spend oodles of money for his higher education. Soon after his appointment in service, my parents urged me for his marriage. I fulfilled all their desires. My father was a linchpin of our family. After his death, all the troubles let loose. At the instigation of his wife, Hemant separated his establishment. My mother's partiality is also a cause of this separation. We have no such landed property nor any stable assets to be divided. The house we live in was built with my hard-earned money. So there was no question of litigation over this issue. My doting mother and his nagging wife became instrumental to cause this cleavage between us. Now he is living in a rented house with my mother. He hardly visits us. I don't want to keep any relation with him".

Basant became very emotional. He tried to chock back his tears.

"Basant, think logically. So long a person is unmarried, his relation with family members is quite okay. The moment he is tied with a wed-lock, he becomes self-centred and craves for material gain. Hemant is not an exception. There is no botheration as you two brothers have separate establishment".

Basant stayed only two days. He requested Sambit to step in their house at his convenient time and left Baripada for good.

Five years lapsed this way. Sambit had to go to Cuttack on some urgent work. Sanchita, his daughter's friend, was working in the statistical department which was a stone's throw from the bus stand. He knew her address. But during office hours she would not be found at home. Her husband, working as an assistant tahsildar in the Tahasil office would come back in late hours of evening. So he decided to go to her office.

Sanchita and her husband Barun, whenever they found a brief respite from their official work, would visit Baripada and stay a few days in Sambit's house.

Sambit had to wait till the closing hours of the office. Then both of them went to their rented house by a rickshaw. Sanchita phoned her husband and he arrived with some snacks.

"Barun, if you have no engagement, let us go to my friend's house at Mahanadi Vihar."

Barun got the scooter ready and they drove away.

Basant's wife could not expect his sudden arrival. She drew her vail and said, "I did not believe that one day you would come to our house. Is everything at home okay? Her voice was tremulous with joy.

"Where is Basant? Sambit asked.

"He has gone to his office. It is now his arrival time".

Basant alighted from his jeep. With a smiling face he said, "I came to know of your arrival over the phone".

"Have you given them any refreshment?" Basant asked his wife.

"No, no, we have had snacks half an hour ago. No room in our stomach, my dear," Sambit humbly denied.

Basant led them to his Jagannath temple built in the front yard. Marigold flowers and holy basil leaves were strewn all over the altar. Balaram, Jagannath and goddess Subhadra were all wreathed with garlands of flowers. The temple, though not so big, stood on a hallowed ground. The place was calm and quiet. He was enthralled by the spiritual atmosphere of the place.

"Excuse me, Basant, Barun is occupied with some work at home. It is rather getting late".

Basant and his wife came outside to see them off.

"We look forward to seeing you again", they complimented. Sambit gave Basant a friendly pat on his shoulder and bade them goodbye.

TWO

The percentage of educated people is very low in two districts, Mayurbhanj and Keonjhar. Scheduled caste and scheduled tribe constitute the major portion of population. They were primitive people and once they were foraging in the woods in search of food. They live in racial and religious segregation. They lead a simple life free from modern amenities. They have their own way of life and keep a distance from the elites of society. Very few of them have their own land but most of them earn their daily bread as labourers. There was a time when they were completely deprived of visiting any temple. Racial discrimination causes a bitter discontentment in their mind and they are treated as untouchables by the people of higher caste. Time changed. But their social status remained the same. Due to acute unemployment problems sometimes they spend their days unfed and unclad. They are regarded as unprivileged and backward. So there is a great disparity between upper echelons and downtrodden of society. This discrimination isolated them to a separate class and they embraced Christianity without second thoughts.

When they were tossed aside by the higher class, the Christian missionaries hugged them with love and affection. The Charitable trust of foreign countries used to supply a huge amount of money to promote the missionary work. As they were backed by financial support, they worked with full alacrity. They convinced the people as to its superiority over other religions. They were imbued with the thought that it was the only religion which could redeem them from sin. They revived their self-confidence. They began to think that conversion to this religion will surely place them in a respectable position in society. They gave them financial help for their children's education. They supplied food, dress and medicines to the poverty-ridden people. They went to the remote corner of the villages and made them understand the merit of Christianity. They put up tents in the centre of their locality and invited them to listen to the religious songs for their edification.

"O sinners! Why do you go to the path of sin
Who will redeem you other than Christ
Keep your eyes and ears always keen
That opens the door of heaven what we mean".

The missionaries converted quite a number of native people to Christianity within a few years. There was an antagonistic group who opposed them openly. They could not stomach the spread of Christianity in their region. The resentment smouldering in their hearts fanned the fire of fanaticism among people. It gradually reared its ugly head. After much deliberation, they decided to take some measures to check its spread and vowed revenge for their audacity perpetrated on their religion. They warned the missionaries time and again not to trick the biddable people creating a chaotic situation in their peaceful area. But their warning was of no avail. They did not have a premonition of a hush-hush plan of adversaries. At the witching hour of night, a religious person who championed this cause was stabbed to death. The assassin and his henchmen absconded in the darkness of night.

T.C. Francis, hailing from Switzerland some years back, was entrusted with missionary work. He was a short- statured man with a goatee beard. After his arrival, he organised the workers and zealously pursued the missionary work. He was a jovial man and mixed freely with the native people. He learned their language which helped him to interact with aboriginals.

T.C. Francis was also a good football player. He became a coach and encouraged the tribal children to take part in games and sports. His wife and two tender children would also accompany him whenever he went for some missionary work. Mrs. Francis, a loving wife, worked with full cooperation with her husband. She was a slender woman with curly hair and two luminous blue eyes. She was a bit taller than her husband. Her faltering conversation with the native women made them laugh and her speech-impediment was a matter of gossip in their circle. When she would visit them, she would carry packets of biscuits and chocolates and distribute them among the children. The moment she stepped out of the jeep, they would come running and rally round her. She would fondly caress them and kiss their cheeks without hesitation.

Very often Mrs. Francis would enter their kitchen and observe the methods of their cooking. Watered rice and greens was their staple food. She was bowled over how they could maintain such sound health with that poor diet. Malnutrition was meaningless to them. Mrs. Francis became thoughtful. After independence people got make-believe political freedom but real economic one was far away from them. Though tribal people were not well-off, they were free from worries and anxieties which usually baffle people living in ivory towers. She was charmed by their hospitality. Some women would offer her country rum which she politely denied. The sight of naked children haunted her mind but she knew that she could not remove their poverty nor could she fulfil all their wants. They would go to the town in search of work. If not employed, they would come back home empty-handed. While coming on the way, they would sing in a falsetto their folk song.
"O loving one ! would you accompany me to bazaar
I would buy you glass bangles and coloured ribbons.
O loving one ! Do you want sweet scented flowers?
You will fix them in your chignon

O my darling of heart! I will buy you silver earrings
That will dangle and kiss your delicate cheeks.
O my shy beloved! Would you wait at the cottage door
I will come with all your Cherished dreams.
Don't look at the stranger but me alone
Else I would go crazy and be woebegone".

The church situated in the heart of the town was a favourite haunt of the Christian. It had been built on a vast land donated by the then Maharaja. A land for the cemetery was also given to them which was a glaring example of his generosity. The land in the possession of the church was virtually a grass land which was manicured by an English man who kept the churchyard spick and span. He was slightly lame and his right hand had been amputated for some blood poisoning (septicemia) . Mr. Francis had a very friendly relation with him and he visited the church twice a week as he was preoccupied with some other urgent work.

It was also a childhood haunt of Sambit and he often visited this place for its calm atmosphere. Mr. Francis would give him an effusive welcome when he happened to see him on Sunday's mass prayer. The relationship between them grew deep-seated.

One day in a chilly morning Mr. Francis dropped in unexpectedly. Sambit was going to eat his breakfast. When he heard the ringing of a call-bell, he unlatched the door. There stood Mr. Francis with a smiling face. He shook his hand and said apologetically, " I am extremely sorry Mr. Sambit. I don't want to disturb you. I have convened a meeting of workers this morning. So while passing along this road I thought to drop in on you".

Sambit led him to his sitting room and said, "I am rather glad to see you after a long time. Over some days I was thinking about you. You are as busy as a bee, a live-wire who stirs a lazy man like me".

Mr. Francis gave a radiant smile and said, "Work means worship. Through work I feel the angelic touch of God. In my opinion we ought to work throughout our lifetime. If we sit idle and misuse our time our body and mind get rusty. I am engaged in social work and I will remain so to the end of my days. My only wish is to die in harness".

Mr. Francis started to give a lively discourse. In the meantime a valet entered the sitting room and served them breakfast on the table. They chatted about many things over breakfast.

Mr. Francis puffed a cigarette and asked, "While entering your sitting room, I noticed a picture of Mother Mary hanging on the wall. Are you a devotee of Mother Mary?"

"Ofcourse, she is an epitome of universal motherhood. You see how the child Jesus has nestled against its mother. One must admit that she is an embodiment of perfect motherhood. And what to speak of Jesus Christ who sacrificed his life for the whole human race. Even at the time of crucifixion, he forgave his executioners- 'O Lord! Forgive them, for they know not what they do'. What a forgiving heart he had!"

Mr. Francis stared at him with unblinking eyes and said, "Don't take me amiss Mr. Sambit. You worship different gods and goddesses. Some are made of clay or wood, some are of stone. What benefit do you get in worshipping these lifeless things? Is there any logic?"

Sambit cleared his throat and said, "We worship them because they are the true image of gods and goddesses. An aspirant tries to merge with Him through that image. While worshipping he practically beholds no stone or wood. He sees only His infinite form which is quite invisible to gross eyes. It is he who is blessed with eyes of wisdom can see Him as I am seeing you face to face. So we worship His stone or wooden image which is incomprehensible to others. To attain infinite, you have to go through His finite form. A real devotee or a man of wisdom can see Him and feel His existence in a minuscule sand. The ultimate aim of an aspirant is to be united with Him. Then he gets salvation which means he is totally liberated from the cycle of birth".

Mr. Francis ambiguously nodded his head and asked, "Well, Mr. Sambit, do you believe in the existence of God?"

Sambit's face wreathed in a smile and he explained "Mr. Francis, nobody has given a conclusive statement so far. We want only a monosyllabic reply- yes or no. Once a wise saint admonished his disciple, "You don't believe in the existence of God. If you are unable to see the sun in cloudy weather, will you say that there is no sun in the sky".

But one thing is convincing that if there is no God, then why these sages, monks, saints and hermits are worshipping Him aimlessly? Why these swamis, saraswatis, Paramhansas are making obeisance to Him? Do you think they have no sense at all? Falsehood can not stand for so many years. People cannot be hoodwinked so easily by hoaxers or tricksters. There are so many wise and intelligent people who can defy or challenge them. Even scientists believe in His existence.

Then a more complicated question will arise in our mind. Who is the creator of this vast universe? Whether God or it is a chance product. Whether a tree is evolved from a seed or a seed brings forth a tree. When there is a creation, there must be a creator. So there are certain things which are undoubtedly beyond our knowledge. Humans are rational beings. Some day or other they must arrive at a conclusive decision. And we have to wait till that time.

It may sound invidious but I must say one thing. Don't impose your own ideas or views upon others. If you try to vindicate the supremacy of your religion, you will be despised as a fanatic or religious zealot. Your supercilious attitude will be disliked by all. Many a sanguinary battle have been fought in the past for this cause having no fruitful result.

You see Mr. Francis, I am not a tub-thumper. When I

was studying in Sambalpur, I used to go to a local church every Sunday. I had a close nexus with the father of that Church. He was out and out an altruist and tolerant to other religions. After the mass prayer, he would say in denouement of his speech, 'Don't look at other religions with contemptuous eyes. As all the rivers merge themselves with the seas and lose their identity eventually, similarly we will amalgamate ourselves as brothers and sisters under universal fatherhood of God. There must not be any wall of distinction which thwarts us to be integrated. If we make it possible, then the kingdom of God will not be far from us. I have never come across a more magnanimous person like him".

Mr. Francis listened attentively. Then he said, "I concur with your views, Mr. Sambit, you have given me some constructive suggestions which are empirical to be followed. Henceforth I shall take cautious steps not to invite any trouble in future".

He stood on his feet to bid him goodbye. The jeep had been parked by the roadside. He climbed into the jeep and drove away.

A few days later Sambit saw him selling books putting up a temporary stall in front of the court premises. There were some followers singing religious songs in a stentorian voice. Sambit went past them. When his eyes met Mr. Francis, his face brightened with a winsome smile.

He was in a stew over a problem of communal animosity and was accused of stoking up religious hatred in that region.

The fateful night came after two days. When he was asleep with his wife and two children, the homicides came with a heinous motive.

It was a sultry night. A van had been parked in one corner of the churchyard. Mr. Francis sweated profusely and the air was suffocating. He decided to sleep outside, in the open air instead of his living room. While sleeping inside the van, he tossed restlessly. The oppressive heat robbed him of his sleep. He reminisced about the cool balmy air of his homeland. He gently patted the back of his children to send them to sleep. His wife had slept on the other side of the children. Then the sleep came at a sedate pace. His eyes became heavy and he crashed out.

He had a scary nightmare.

There was a heavy snowfall. Mr. Francis was at the foot of the mountain. His aim was to reach its summit. A group of mountaineers came and he joined them. They all started climbing. The weather got worse on each leg of his expedition. The flakes of snow came floating in the freezing wind.

His feet got numb. He looked down and saw a doddery old man following him a few feet below. He peered through the frosty wind. The old man waved his hands and shouted something at the pith of his voice. But his screams were drowned by the roar of the wind. Now he recognized that old man. He was his father who was forewarning him not to climb further. He made him aware that an avalanche was coming from above. But he was determined to put his steps on the summit of the mountain. That was his ultimate aim. He did not attach any importance to his warning. His father turned a raving mad. His heart was filled with an icy-terror. He shouted at the top of his voice again and again. 'Francis, stop climbing, don't you see the avalanche is coming'. Francis did not stop. Though completely tuckered out, he clambered up higher and higher with his frozen feet. He looked up. What he saw was blood-curdling. The avalanche swept him away in a flash and he was buried.

The next morning four charred bodies were found inside the burnt van. They were incinerated alive in reprisal for assassination of a religious leader of a rival group.

- THREE –

Dr. Bhavani Shankar heard everything in detail and told Sambit, "This is a common case with all the women. The first delivery of your wife is normal. I think it is probably secondary infertility which deters further conception. Take your wife to S.C.B. Medical College. There we will meet the gynaecology professor Dr. Mitra. Without thorough testing I cannot say anything".

Sambit went to Cuttack with his wife and there they stayed in a friend's house.

Dr. Bhavani was one of his close friends and he was an assistant professor in the gynaecology department of S.C.B. Medical College. Both of them went to Dr. Mitra's clinic for consultation.

He examined Aparna and after it was over he called them and said, "It is not at all a serious problem. She is only to go through a genuine D.N.C. but before that I must see the report of her endometrium secretion".

He scribbled some pathological testing on a prescription paper and handed it to Sambit.

"Bring me these reports as early as possible" he said as a pressing need.

Dr. Amiya Kar was an M.D. in pathology and he had a clinic just before the entrance of S.C.B. Medical college Sambit went to him, with his wife.

He greeted Sambit and asked, "May I know you sir? Where have you come from?"

"I am from Baripada". He handed him the prescription paper and the testing to be done.

"O I see. I am from Karanjia, so we belong to the same district".

"Do you know Biplab Sahu? He is my collegemate".

Dr. Amiya looked at his face and said, "Is it? He is my intimate friend. Both of us were studying in high school".

After a pathological examination, he said to Sambit, "Please give me two hundred and fifty rupees, not more than that, the cost of the solution only. There is no provision to test her endometrium secretion in my laboratory. You have to go to my pathology professor who is most reliable in this case. Moreover I have to count the number and motility of the spermatozoon in your semen which is also essential to determine its causative factors".

Then they went to the pathology department accompanied by Dr. Amiya Kar.

There the professor asked him the purpose of his sudden visit.

Dr. Kar grinned and said, "Sir, my friend Sambit will stay a few days at Cuttack. He wants a report of his wife's endometrium secretion at the earliest".

The professor gestured to Aparna to go inside the laboratory. After half an hour, she came out tidying up her sari.

"Don't be worried about Amiya. You will get the report in the evening positively", the professor assured them.

After they came outside, Dr. Amiya said, "Sambit, you see how helpful my professor is! To get such a report one is to wait at least a fortnight. My professor is really overly sympathetic to you".

After D.N.C. (Dilatation and curettage) Aparna became a bit feeble. Dr. Bhabani advised her to take bedrest for a few days. Their five-year-old daughter Mita had deep affection for her mother and seeing her debilitated condition she sobbed and began to caress her body sitting on the edge of her bed.

Aparna gradually recuperated her health. One day she said to her husband, "Here in this place my mind has been cramped. Let us go to Puri to have a darshan of Lord Jagannath. There we will stay some days in our uncle's house. I will feel myself pepped up in the temperate climate of Puri".

Sambit's uncle (maternal) was living in Markandeshwar lane, very close to the temple. Fifty years ago, his father Mr. Padmacharan was the manager of Puri temple employed by the then Gajapati Maharaja. The homestead land where he had built a two storied building was also donated by him. He was in the good books of Maharaja and he was extremely pleased with him for his efficient management of the temple. Once he asked Mr. Padmacharan to choose a place of his liking where he could live comfortably. He humbly said, "His highness! I want to stay near my lord. I shall leave my mortal body while gazing at the 'Nila Chakra'. Satisfied with his reply, the then Gajapati allotted that piece of land for his residential purpose.

Mr. Padmacharan had one son and one daughter. He named his son Jagannath and his daughter Subhadra.

Before their departure, Dr. Bhavani's wife requested them to bring her Prasad (offerings) of Lord Jagannath. She was in an advanced stage of pregnancy and her desire must be fulfilled. She was very fond of cakes prepared from rice and molasses.

Though Sambit had visited Puri several times, he had no knowledge about the exact location of his uncle's house. He asked a rickshaw-puller if he knew Mr. Padmacharan. He replied with confidence, "Is there any person in Puri town who does not know Mr. Padmacharan? He is now dead but once he was the manager of this great temple. Sit on my rickshaw and you will reach your destination safe and sound".

His uncle and aunt were overjoyed at their visit.

In the month of December, vegetables were available in plenty. All around the temple, the vendors of vegetables were hawking a variety of vegetables. After he came out of the temple, he saw a stack of cauliflowers, atop each other, selling at a very low price. Some were so big and decent that he could not resist himself from buying two cauliflowers. His aunt fried them and served them with puffed rice.

Subhadra was residing in Dottatota, half kilometre away from them. She came in the morning and asked Sambit, "Would you like to go to the temple of Sri Lokanath with your wife"?

"I have never visited this temple, aunty. Let me hire two rickshaws. I don't know how much fare they demand".

"No, no, I will bargain with them. They demand much more from the outsiders".

In the meantime Reba, Subhadra's daughter, turned up and she was also eager to accompany them.

They all got ready and made a trip to Sri Lokanath.

Sambit's rickshaw reached first. The moment he got down, he was surrounded by a group of Brahmins as a carcass is besieged by the vultures. Some started to pull his shirt, some dragged his hands. An altercation sparked off among them.

Subhadra arrived by that time. She observed this hullabaloo and yelled at them, "You uncultured Brahmins! It is unbecoming to you to act so indecently. Why are you making such a nuisance?"

Subhadra was exasperated by their crude behaviour.

All the Brahmins knew her well and paid her respect.

When that hurly-burly was over, Subhadra approached a Brahmin who knew Sambit's ancestors.

The Brahmin reeled off his family tree and asked his name, zodiac etc. Then he performed the Puja according to shastric directives.

In the afternoon they awoke from their nap. They got refreshed and went to the sea shore to promenade along the beach.

Sambit looked at the distant horizon where the sky mingled with the vast expansion of water. The roseate glow of the sun was shimmering the rolling waves of the sea. He saw a fishing canoe come waggling and rose up on the crest of waves. The next moment it disappeared behind the heaving waves of the sea. It seemed as if the canoe suddenly capsized and met its watery grave. There were some big boats anchored in the deep sea. Some children and elderly men and women were bathing and they were carried to the shore by the sweep of surging waves.

Sambit and others sat on the sandy bed not far from the shore.

Mita walked along the shore and tried to collect the surf in her itsy-bitsy palms. Reba plodded side by side to keep an eye on her playful activities.

Aparna dropped her slippers on the sand and sat on them. A man selling puffed rice and a packet of salted peanuts went past them and hollered to draw their attention.

Sambit was about to call him but Aparna objected.

"Don't buy these awful foods. Dust particles are falling on them blown by the wind. They don't keep their food in a healthy condition. Flies sit on them which are the infectious agents of various diseases. Don't give my child that nasty thing."

A Marwari old man came with his family members after bathing in the sea. He had worn a white dhoti and a white banian. His obese wife was following him with her daughters-in-law and grandchildren. The sarees clung to their bodies exposed their big bosom and revealed the outlines of their obesity. Water was dribbling down their bodies. A Brahmin Priest and his assistant were standing at a little distance awaiting them. The assistant holding a tethered calf instructed them to stand in a line and told them to come one after another. The calf was very frolicsome and it was skittish to run away from his hands. The Priest told the old man to grasp the tail of the calf. It got so irritated that it dragged the Marwari to some distance. Then came the turn of his wife. She gripped its tail tightly and was about to fall headlong as the calf hauled her away to a sand dune. After all the members were dragged like this, the priest sprinkled holy water on their heads intoning some mantras.

The religious rituals being over, the priest told the old man to give him five hundred rupees as his fees.

He assured them that they will not be doomed to hell as they had given a cow in charity to a Brahmin. Gift of a cow is one of the best charitable deeds and they were saved from all the hardships and suffering of the nether world.

Sambit made his wife observant to watch all the activities of the Brahmin priest and how he fleeced the Marwaris in the name of religion.

In the twilight hours they came back home. Uncle Jagannath was seated at the threshold of the Kitchen absorbed in reading a newspaper. When he heard the sound of the footsteps, he raised his head and tossed the paper aside.

Sambit changed his dress and sat beside him.

"Would you like something to eat?" his uncle asked, smiling at him. "I think you all must be very hungry".

Sambit smiled back and said, "No uncle, I will just snack on potato chips and a little amount of puffed rice".

His aunt emerged from the kitchen and handed her husband a cup of tea and some biscuits.

Uncle Jagannath began to sip tea and said, "I don't eat anything other than this in the evening. This is my ideal snacks".

Sambit narrated the amusing episode of that priest to his uncle .

He began to laugh and said, "You see, this place is full of sand. Practically there is no such lucrative source of income to meet their expenditure. But the priestly class and their hangers-on are in an advantageous position. They earn a good deal of money by any possible means. Some of them are millionaires. You cannot know from their outward appearance how rich they are. They are accursed people. The more they grab money, the more is their craving. Sometimes the devotees coming from a long distance feel themselves monetarily tortured. They start to hate their money-grubbing motive. There are a few among them who are not so rapacious but most of them are omnivorous. Once a pilgrim falls into their clutches, they would squeeze him dry. Sometimes brawl also starts between two parties. There is no end to their covetousness".

Sambit butt in, "Uncle, the other day I encountered an embarrassing situation while entering the temple.

A Brahmin flung a garland of flowers around my neck and said, "You are a great devotee of Lord Jagannath. Give me ten rupees as my honorarium".

I was startled and asked him, "How could you know that I am a great devotee?"

"It is beyond your knowledge. I actually know who you are", the Brahmin said in a convincing tone.

Then I instantly removed the garland and put it on his neck in a trice.

'Now give me twenty rupees as my honorarium', I demanded.

He was flabbergasted at my strange behaviour and disappeared in the crowd.

Uncle Jagannath exploded into a guffaw. After a pause he said, "Many incidents are occurring in broad daylight. There are many things which I should not disclose".

"Yes, I do agree. But God should make those piggish conscious of their nefarious design. It is always repulsive. Their devotion dies out and consequently they become atheist. People will abhor them as blasphemers of Gods".

Uncle Jagannath listened silently.

Sambit continued, "Do you know I was once caught in a stampede in my previous visit?

I could not recall but it was an auspicious day. The congregation of devotees was more than usual as Shankaracharya was to visit the temple that day. I had stood just in front of the temple watching the coming and going of the people. A relative of mine suddenly appeared. I did not intend to go inside the temple. But he insisted that I should have a darshan of Lord Jagannath.

"No, no, I am not willing to go inside pushing the crowd. Let me stand here and have His darshan from this 'Garuda stambha".

I just gave him a wishy-washy explanation.

"Come with me. You won't face any trouble there".

He gave me assurance and I yielded.

Jostling our way through the milling crowds, we entered the temple. When I was in the sanctum sanctorum, I overheard that Shankaracharya was coming. I did not know where he was nor did I have a view of him. Then I noticed that people shoved one another remorselessly to get closer to him. Who could not resist that mighty push screamed to save his life. Some were flailing around for their own survival. Many of the old and infirm fell on the ground crushed by the throng of people. A commotion arose in the crowd. Just like surging waves, people rushed to me and I was literally squeezed. Some inhumanly trod on my feet and I was nearly trampled to death. But that relative rescued me from that stampede. He escorted me through a narrow path behind the altar and we emerged from that tunnel. What a nuisance! It made my hackles rise. Was it unknown to Shankaracharya that he would be instrumental in causing such a pandemonium? There I recalled an educational story.

A musk-deer could not know where a sweet scent was coming from. It wandered throughout the forest in search of that source. At last it discovered that it was its musk-secreting gland of the navel which was emitting such a sweet fragrance.

God is omnipresent. Still we search for Him in the temple, church and mosque.

Once a saint sprawled on the floor of a temple, spreading his legs towards the deity. The priest came and abused him, "What a stupid man you are! Don't you know you have dishonoured God by stretching your legs unmannerly towards the altar. It shows your blithe disregard".

The saint did not change his sleeping position. He humbly asked, "His holiness, please tell me to which side I am to stretch my legs?"

The priest got irritated. His red, mottled face showed his fury.

"No, no, don't disgrace my God further. Can't you stretch your legs either to the north or south?"

"O you think God does not exist in that direction".

A forgiving smile flashed across the saint's face. Uncle Jagannath fell in with his views.

Aparna was a woman of sunny disposition. She wanted to do some sightseeing for mental relaxation.

"Aparna, do you want to visit a very interesting place in this locality?" asked Sambit after his breakfast.

"Yes, I will get ready in a very short time. Wait patiently in the sitting room", Aparna said while daubing her face with nivea cream.

"I have not seen that place. The temple of Chaitanya is really worth seeing which was built in memory of that great saint.

He had visited Puri during the reign of Pratap Rudradeva, the then king of Odisha. He was profoundly influenced by him. Sri Chaitanya made a great stir in the religious world and propagated Vaishnavism and due to patronization of the king it spread through the length and breadth of Odisha. All being entranced, chanted the name of God."

Aparna had no time to listen to that glorious history. But she was interested to know more about Sri Chaitanya, a committed preacher of vaishnaism.

"I will tell you about his life later on. It is no doubt an absorbing story", Sambit said while dressing up Mita.

"It is not so distant. We can go to that place on foot. But for Mita, we have to hire a rickshaw".

"Mita, go to your father, He will help you in putting on your shoes".

Aparna stood preening herself in front of the mirror.

Sambit peeped through the curtains to see if she was ready.

"You invariably take a lot of time to doll yourself up. All

women are alike. I grow impatient and brook no delay". Sambit was pissed off for this lengthy wait.

"Why are you so hurried? Then you go alone".

She was hacked off for his burst of restiveness.

"No, no, we won't doddle there for a long time. We must come back before lunch, because aunty will be waiting for us".

Arati had been completed by the time they reached the temple. The incense sticks were burning which permeated the inner sanctum of the temple with a pleasant smell. Sri Gauranga with his close disciples were being worshipped there.

Aparna became enamoured of the temple and its calm environment. The place looked very idyllic and she was completely floored by its beauty.

Mita was sauntering about the temple while her parents stood rooted to the floor and their eyes were glued to the beautiful image of Sri Gauranga.

Mita was unable to control the urge of urination. She pissed in her jean pants. It came to the notice of the caretaker. He came to Sambit and exploded.

"Have you not noticed the warning graffiti on the entrance wall of the temple. You have to pay a fine of five hundred rupees as your daughter has desecrated the temple."

Sambit heard his upbraiding. It incensed him. He protested vehemently, "Who the hell do you think you are! The sanctity cannot be restored by a piddling amount of fine. What does a tender child know about purity? Can you hold back your natural urge? I won't give you a single pie for your irrational and absurd demand. You have gone beyond your perimeter. You Brahmins have made the religion a commercial property. Let your authority come to me. I will see what is what after confrontation.

Aparna intervened, "You go out of your head if you get annoyed. Let them do what they like. I don't give two hoots what they are saying".

Aparna held her daughter's hand and walked away. Before leaving, Sambit threw a stern look at the caretaker. He was cowed and retreated into the interior of the temple.

Back home, Sambit sat in a gloomy mood. The misconduct and unethical behaviour of that Brahmin continued to rankle his mind. He felt a sudden flash of anger and a repugnance to the Brahmin class and their interpretation of religion. He was resolute to repudiate their superstitious ideas and beliefs. When he came back to his cool, he remembered the request of Dr. Bhavani's wife.

The next morning, they went to Anandabazar. It was echoing with the din of the people. Sambit saw a man who was selling only gruel, kept in a large earthen pitcher, raw pepper floating on its surface. The man offered him a little amount of gruel in his palm to be tasted.

"Not so good", Sambit grimaced looking at Aparna.

"Let us go to the temple and approach a Brahmin to give us Prasad of Jagannath", Sambit said while pulling the hand of Aparna.

They bought a variety of Prasad. By that time uncle Jagannath was coming in their direction.

He surveyed the different items of Prasad and pushed his hand in one of the earthen pitchers. In a huff he rushed to the Brahmin and growled, "You unscrupulous! Why did you give them stale Prasad?" There was a smack of bitterness in his tone. "Give them fresh ones".

The next day they came back to cuttack.

Dr. Bhavani's wife accepted Prasad impassively without registration of gratitude in her face. She always looked downcast as if she had been bereaved by the death of some close relative.

Once during a casual conversation Sambit asked, "Dr. Bhavani, don't take offence if I ask you one thing. Why does your wife look so depressed?"

Dr. Bhavani replied in a muffled voice, "I too dislike her

despondent mood. So I keep a distance from her. She is a kill-joy".

After a year, Dr. Bhavani was deputed by the government to go to Arabian countries. There he remained for more than five years. For his overstay, he had to give a satisfactory explanation to the government.

Coming back to India, he constructed a beautiful building at Mahanadi Vihar. While living in that house, he had been affected by some fatal disease. He went to his heavenly abode leaving his family to mourn over his death.

FOUR

Dr. Ghanashyam, a retired professor of psychology, decided to spend his last days at Baripada, in his sister's house. Some years back when his brother-in-law was alive, he was always welcomed with love and affection. At that time his nephews were studying in college. Dr. Ghanashyam was a bachelor and there was no one to depend upon him. Very often he used to give them financial help for which they could get higher education and thereby they prospered in their lives.

One afternoon when Sambit had gone shopping to the market, he ran into Dr. Ghanashyam. He saluted him and asked, "Sir, why are you buying all these vegetables?"

"I am just a paying guest here", he said laughing. "I can't pay them money. They may feel offended by that. So I purchase something for their family in return."

"Your sister and brother-in-law are dead now. When they were alive, you were treated well. You are now living with your nephews. So the situation is entirely different. One cannot say how long you will get along with them".

Dr. Ghanashyam became thoughtful. A servant boy was following him with a bag full of vegetables. He turned to Sambit and said, "I don't care if any unpleasant thing happens in future".

Then he left.

After a month, their meeting near the college was a providential incident. It was forenoon. He was returning home for his lunch.

"How are you, sir?" Sambit asked solicitously. A shadow

of displeasure was imprinted on his face. He held his hand and said, "What you had told me the other day, it was not at all an exaggeration. Over a month, I have been mistreated for no valid reason. They are quite heedless to my comforts".

"How?"

"You know I take care of their family with utmost sincerity. Every Sunday, besides provisions, I fetch mutton for them. But I am underfed. When I return home after a chit chat with my friends, my nephew's wife serves me a small amount of mutton and vegetables".

His eyes were glistening with tears. He had a lurking hope in some corner of his heart that he would never be neglected by his relatives.

Sambit heard his sad story but he could not do anything as he had no right to poke his nose into their family affairs. So he had no other thing to offer him other than ineffective consolation.

A week passed by. His nephew was a habitual drunkard. Every night he got drunk, picked a quarrel with his wife and started a fisticuffs. He hurled abuses at the top of his voice and his wife shuddered with fear.

Day by day it became intolerable to Dr. Ghanashyam. One night the ruckus exceeded its limit. He was forced to intervene and told his nephew to calm down. As he got sozzled, he was not in a mood to listen to his advice. He flew off the handle and sought a chance to pounce on him.

"Keep your advice to yourself. Don't say anything poppycock". He shouted at him furiously and threw all his books and beddings to the street. Then he booted him out of the room.

Having heard this dislodgement, Mr. Patsani, his ex-student, hastened to the spot. He hired two rickshaws and retrieving his things he loaded one with books and other belongings and by another he brought Dr. Ghanashyam back to his house.

Sambit was in his clinic. When he heard this fact, he became upset and hurried to see his condition. He found him seated on a charpoy absorbed in watching T.V. He was scrubbing his teeth with tobacco and in a brief interval spitting his spittle in a brass spittoon. Mr. Patsani recounted that sad incident.

"I regard him as my own father. So long he is under my shelter, I will look after his comforts. He won't face any problem here". Mr. Patsani was very sympathetic to his teacher.

"It is a very risky affair that you rescued him from such a distressed condition", Sambit heaved a sigh of relief.

Dr. Ghanashyam came from a poor family. He was intelligent and ambitious and fared well in his examination. Though he had a brilliant academic achievement, his father could not afford the expenditure for his higher education in a foreign country. There were so many seekers of bridegrooms who wanted to give their daughter in marriage with a scholar having a bright future. After betrothal, his would-be father-in-law gave his consent to bear all the expenditure of his higher education. Dr. Ghanashyam came out successful and was appointed as a psychology professor in Columbia University. At that time his would-be wife was doing her post graduation in sociology. She had a boyfriend. Love burgeoned between them. They were spotted cavorting in the hotel rooms. Though she had been betrothed to Dr. Ghanashyam, she lost all her fidelity to her fiance. Dr. Ghanashyam came to know of her indulgence in drunken orgies of youth. He informed his father for annulment of their marriage. Nobody could know why he reneged on his agreement. He had implicit faith in her honesty but he was jilted by his fiancée. Her betrayal shocked him so much that he took a vow to remain a bachelor. Many well-wishers exhorted him to marry some other girl but he stuck to his guns on marriage.

In Mr. Patsani's house, Dr. Ghanashyam was living in seclusion. A kind of reclusive life. He had no companion to have a heart to heart talk. It was difficult to idle away the tedium of lonely life. So every evening he would visit Sambit's homoeopathy clinic and sit on a chair till its closing time. Sambit would keep a little amount of tobacco and a bucketful of water in the clinic for his use. It was a meeting place of a few retired persons and they would while away their time talking about a hundred things.

Ghasi, a mixture vendor, had earned fame in that area for special preparation of many tasteful things. Sambit's favourite snack was his 'dahi vada' which Dr. Ghanashyam had never tasted.

One day when Sambit came with a packet of 'dahi vada', Dr. Ghanashyam wanted to taste it. He opened his mouth and Sambit dropped one by one. He gulped down all in a short time and belched loudly.

"Now I understand why you eat this delicious thing regularly". He smacked his lips with satisfaction. Then he said, "Sambit, today your clinic is sparsely visited by the patients. What will you do sitting idle? Rather tell me a story which will be an amusing one." "Sir, are you interested in listening to a ghost story? I have recently read a very intriguing story from 'Illustrated weekly of India' under the caption 'The haunted palaces'. Every week you will find a new one which is awe-inspiring. It is not fictitious. It really happened three decades ago.

Tibet is situated in the lap of nature. All around it there are snow-capped mountains, dense forest, ravines, flora and fauna which have suffused the land with natural beauty. There was an old palace in the northern end of Tibet which was built with granite stones. Five thousand artisans worked day and night. After ten years of ceaseless efforts, the work was finally finished. It was called the 'Summer Palace' of the king. Because the king and his family used to live there to stave off the heat of summer. They had a daughter. When she grew young, her beauty became a topic of discussion. She was exquisitely beautiful to be envied by other girls. A personal attendant of the king was besotted by her ravishing beauty. The princess also wanted to marry him for his pleasing personality. But the king was a drag on the path of their marriage. He was quite reluctant to allow her marriage with a man of low rank. The king hatched a plot to eliminate him to save his honour from such a calumny. It so happened that after a few days the young man was found nowhere. They were successful in erasing the last trace of their daughter's scandalous mistake. Nobody could know what became of him. The princess with the lovelorn heart pined for him. The king arranged her marriage in some other place. No sooner did the bridegroom reach the palace, then the princess swallowed a lethal poison and fell into the deadly jaws of death. Since that day a heart-rending wailing of a woman was heard at dead of the night. All the residents, being mortally terrified, left the palace. But every night that dilapidated palace was haunted by a shadowy figure of a woman crying bitterly splitting the stillness of night."

Sambit stopped his narrative and said, "Sir, although there is no newness in that story, it is really heart-breaking."

At 9 O'clock, Sambit locked the door and got ready to go home. He escorted Dr. Ghanashyam up to the door of Mr. Patsani's house. He focused the shaft of the torch light lest the old man might stumble on the uneven railway lines. Dr. Ghanashyam stepped up the verandah and indicated Sambit to leave him there.

The next afternoon Sambit found him standing under a lamp post.

"Why did you stand there, Sir?" he asked while unlocking the door.

"No, nothing, I was just awaiting your arrival".

Sambit switched on the ceiling fan.

Dr. Ghanashyam whipped his spectacles out of his pocket and wiped it with his handkerchief.

"The story you narrated yesterday is very frightening. I did not stir from my bed at night, even for urination. Ofcourse I have no nyctophobia".

"Why? I don't believe in the existence of ghosts or apparition- no reason to be afraid of non-existent things", Sambit burst into laughter.

Dr. Ghanashyam discreetly changed the subject.

"Well, Sambit, is there any medicine in homoeopathy to relieve the painful swelling of knee-joint?"

"Definitely. But you have to change your dietary habits. You are a non-vegetarian and you regularly eat meat. So uric acid has been deposited in your knee-joint. To keep it in healthy condition, you have to maintain complete abstinence from fatty food. Better eat small fry which would be beneficial in this case?"

"You think I have no idea about diet. Guts to teach me, isn't it?"

It made his hackles rise.

"No sir, my intention is not that. This is only my humble request to keep you healthy. It would be presumptuous of me to comment on this matter". Sambit recoiled.

"All right. Try to find a house for me with an attached bathroom and latrine. If there would be a small piece of land adjacent to the house, I would transform it into my kitchen garden".

"Yes sir, of course there is a solution. I own a piece of homestead land and I could have built a house there according to your liking. But I ran into a snag with my plan. I shelved it as I have no financial capacity. My bank balance is only sixty thousand rupees. It is quite inadequate to complete the work. If you give me some financial help....."

Dr. Ghanashyam chuckled.

"I am ready to help you but if I die- I mean life is full of uncertainties. Death is unpredictable".

"Oh you think you would be a loser then and I would

have all the fun. I never thought in my wildest dream to make capital of your credulity".

Dr. Ghanashyam got a job as a visiting professor of Patna University. He shuttled between Baripada and Patna more frequently now.

One morning Sambit saw him packing dried fish in a polythene bag.

"What are you doing, sir?"

"Some professors of Patna University are very fond of dried fish. They know it is available in plenty at Baripada. So I have to comply with their request".

"Cover it carefully. It gives off a horrible stench. Your co-passengers will get irritated".

Then Dr. Ghanashyam vanished again. He surfaced after a month.

"You were absent for a long period, Sir".

"Yes, I had been to my ancestral house. When I was loafing around Cuttack high court, I accidentally met a lawyer friend. He informed me that I have been deprived of my paternal property by the evil designs of my brothers. Even my name had been erased from all the documents. They want to engulf the whole as they know that I have no heir to inherit my legitimate share. So I had to go to the settlement officer and show him all my certificates where my father's name had been mentioned. How treacherous they are!"

"Sir, what will you do if you get a share?"

"I won't give them a chunk of land".

"Sir, can you do one thing? Try to sell away your share at a reasonable rate. Create a charitable trust in the name of your father. Help the poor children for their education. You will be blessed by the departed soul of your father".

"Let me think it over", Dr. Ghanashyam became unusually grave.

One day he unaccountably disappeared. Perhaps he

disliked staying in somebody's house for a long period. He felt out of his element there.

His whereabouts was unknown. Later on Sambit learnt that he had gone to Cuttack. There he stayed in a hotel. He used to eat his lunch and dinner in his room brought by the hotel boy.

One morning that boy came with his breakfast and knocked on the door. But there was no response. He informed the manager. With the help of the watchman, they broke down the door. Dr. Ghanashyam was found dead. As if sunk in deep sleep, he was lying on his bed. He died in obscurity.

Hearing his eternal rest, some ex-students and acquaintances gathered there. They carried the dead body without further ado to the khannagar cremation ground. Nobody gave him a grand funeral – as he deserved-to such an erudite scholar, such a learned man.

FIVE

Dr Anupam's father Mr. Bimal Mukherjee was a petty clerk in the education department. He had always been a go-getter who had a lofty aim to give his children higher education. His second son Anupam was mediocre. Whenever he found time, he assiduously tutored him and under the tutelage of his father, he passed his exam with gratifying success. At last Mr. Bimal's aspiration was fulfilled and Anupam became a doctor.

Getting an appointment in the Medical department was very hard at that time. So he left home and joined the army in the rank of a captain. But he had no job satisfaction. It was monotonous and he was fed up with the restricted life of the army. After doing his hitch for ten years, he applied for voluntary retirement.

He came to his native place and began his medical practice in the centre of the town. At the outset, many people discouraged him as it was difficult to thrive well when there were so many specialists in the town. So people will prefer to go to them for their treatment. He managed to scrape through this tough competition and all their conjecture proved baseless when he rose to fame within a few months.

Sambit had not seen him before. His meeting with him was just a fluke. He had a good physique with a handsome appearance. When their intimacy grew deeper, he said, "Mr. Sambit, you are a homoeopath, try to imbibe some knowledge in allopathy also. Collect a book on pharmacopeia and delve deep into that. If you don't have fundamental knowledge, you cannot treat the patients".

Both of them moved around the town once in a while for mental relaxation. One day Dr. Mukherjee said, "You don't know how miserable my life is. I am an unfortunate one whose wife had deserted him some years back. She is a medicine specialist and has a roaring practice in Calcutta. My father was then looking for a well-educated bride. He found the mobile phone number of my father-in-law from marriage-bureau and contacted him over the phone. After the two parties came to an agreement, the negotiation was finalised and I married her. But that reception night turned into a fateful night for me. I had a grievous misunderstanding with her. She mopped up the vermilion from her forehead and smashed her bangles as an act of defiance and as soon as the dawn broke, she left for Calcutta. Guess the condition of my parents. We grovelled in shame and became an object of ridicule in our neighbourhood. It hurt my social prestige too. Everybody was watching with interest the going-on in our family.

Under unfavourable circumstances, I was forced to keep a mistress. I became a father of one child also. But every day I am haunted by a fear that my legal wife may come any day and lodge a complaint against me. I have not yet divorced her. For my unlawful act, I may be penalised. Are you acquainted with a good lawyer who can protect me from this punishable offence?"

Dr. Mukherjee's apprehension came true. After six months Dr. Nibedita unexpectedly arrived. She was accompanied by her father and elder brother. Her father was a retired engineer and her brother, an eminent lawyer of Calcutta High Court. They stayed in a hotel and prepared themselves to counteract this illegal marriage.

One fine morning Dr. Nibedita and her father arrived at Sambit's house. They carefully sussed out the situation and concluded that it was Sambit who could bring an amicable settlement with Dr. Mukherjee.

Dr. Nibedita's father was a man of mild disposition. After they were seated comfortably, the old man said, "Mr. Sambit, you are just like my son. I fully confide in you. You have been apprised of all the facts. After the marriage of Nibedita, I renounced all the worldly pleasures and became an anchorite. But this dismissal of marriage perplexed me so much that I lost the stability of my mind. I skipped some important engagement and came with a hope to bring a reunion between them. I am ready to do anything for the happiness of my daughter. I want to dole out lakhs of rupees for a pricey clinic where husband and wife can carry on their practice. But my son-in-law's indifference pained me very much. He knows that we are now staying in a hotel. His conscience did not prick him a little to invite us to his house. After all, he is my son-in-law. I did not hope he could be so hard-hearted".

Sambit did not want to be involved in their personal affairs. But he was deeply moved by the woes of this old man. He said consolingly, "You better approach Dr. Mukherjee. He is not uncompromising. Husband and wife are bound with one another and these ties cannot be snapped so easily. If you fail, I will go to him to bring a reconciliation between the two".

Dr. Mukherjee's mistress Rekha could not withstand the sudden trespass of Dr. Nibedita. If the lady doctor will occupy her place, she will be thrown out and displaced from her permanent shelter. She felt pangs of jealousy. She carried her child in her arms and went doddering to Dr. Mukherjee's clinic. She stormed into his room and got aggressive. She began to shout and made a rumpus.

"Your wife Nibedita has come to be united with you. I no longer hold any value to you. I have no objection if you live with her. But I am going. Don't try to hold me back. I am forced to leave my child in your care. Have a good time with your doctor wife".

Her lips pouted and she started to cry. Then she thrust

the baby into his arms, hitched her sari above her knees and ran off like a crazy woman through an alley.

Dr. Mukherjee became dumbfounded for some moments. He had not seen her combative nature before. He was on the horns of a dilemma. He closed the clinic and went home with his child.

Dr. Nibedita was not a woman to eat humble pie. She went to Dr. Prasad, a close friend of Dr. Mukherjee, to tell him everything. Sambit was also present there. They discussed to take some constructive measures to redress her problem and readjust their lives.

Dr. Mukherjee had turned down her request. She was inhumanly rebuffed and that fire of humiliation was still burning in her heart.

Dr. Prasad said, "But we are unable to comprehend why this serious misunderstanding arose on that reception night". He was at a loss and stared at her face to read her inner feelings.

Dr. Nibedita was discomfited and her woeful eyes flicked a little. She took out a handkerchief from her vanity bag and mopped her face.

It was conspicuous that she was hesitant to explain.

After pausing a little she said, "It is possible when the couple leads a sexual life for some days or months. They must come to understand each other and at that time the better-half would have no objection to gratify her husband as he desires. But obscenity may inhibit the sexual urge of his wife and she may revolt against his objectionable demand. In that case sex drive must not be channelled into some despicable way".

Dr. Nibedita stopped there. Her top secret remained inarticulate.

She said with deliberate hesitation, "You see I am also a doctor. Our medical ethics says to disclose everything. But that is so repulsive and obscene..." Then curling her lip she said, "I just don't like him, that's all".

"Yes, go on. Why are you shilly-shallying? Please be explicit".

Dr. Prasad prodded her to spew out everything.

"So you all are eager to hear that thing from a woman". She blushed to the tip of her ears and paused to heighten their curiosity.

"No, no doctor Sahiba. We are anxious to know the actual facts. Why are you so cagey? It shattered your dreams, aspirations and all that a woman desires. Don't take umbrage at our comment".

There was a wounded expression on her face. Dr. Nibedita took a deep breath and answered, "There is not an iota of doubt that Dr. Mukherjee is a downright debauchee(fellator), needless to say a despicable sexual pervert. Don't expect something more overt than this", she said acidly.

This conveyed a lot.

Dr. Prasad and Sambit glanced at each other. There was an exchange of meaningful looks.

Over some days there was no wrangling, no fuss over this issue.

Sambit did not know what happened to them in that brief interlude.

He went to Dr. Mukherjee's clinic.

The doctor offered him a cushion chair. That day he looked more relaxed than usual. Sambit was inquisitive.

Dr. Mukherjee looked at his questioning face and said, "Three days ago they left for Calcutta".

"How was it possible? How could you solve that complicated matter? It was too difficult to handle that situation. It is an achievement, no doubt".

"By God's grace, somehow I managed to cut that Gordian knot. I wore her down with my cajolery.

That evening Nibedita was alone in the hotel. I tiptoed to her and gripped her feet desperately. I appealed to her, "Please forgive your unfortunate husband. I rest my complete faith on you who can lift me from this morass. The mishap which happened in our life is preordained. I am in a moribund state. It is you who can resuscitate me".

"After so many days I got an auricular proof of your love. It struck the soft chord of my heart".

A forgiving smile began to play on her face. I was in a prostrate position. She lifted me affectionately with her hands and planted a kiss on my cheek.

She said in a mournful tone, "Now you are scot-free. Go and enjoy your life".

It seemed to me as if I heard a plaintive cry of a wounded animal in the woods".

Dr. Prasad was amply relieved when Sambit narrated how Dr. Mukherjee came to terms with his wife.

He was lost in thought and said lowering his tone, "Human nature is always mysterious. A man cannot be recognized from his outward appearance. It is tiresome to find out his actual nature as he keeps his deepest secret strictly in concealment. It will take time to get a composite picture of a man. You will be amazed if you hear about his covert activities.

Many lady patients come to his clinic for abortion. The lady having an attractive body falls victim to his lust. He lessens the charge of abortion who allows him to canoodle her without objection. He is a womaniser but he appears to be a sober and perfect gentleman. Extra marital relations always cause havoc in a family. They play the role of conniving swindlers having no fidelity in their conjugal life. A man of protean character can play hide and seek very well. Dr. Mukherjee is a past master at finding ways to get out of trouble".

Days passed swiftly. Dr. Mukherjee's mistress Rekha conceived again. During her first trimester of pregnancy she began to throw up in the morning. She spewed out everything she ate. She always complained of a queasy stomach. Dr. Mukherjee tried to check the vomiting. But there was no fruition. She was reduced to a skeleton. He was hopeless. He requested Sambit to give her some potent medicine.

"Dr. Mukherjee, I will give her a drug which is highly recommended for the persistent vomiting of pregnancy. "Symphoricarpus racemosus' is very helpful in this case.

"Are there any untoward side effects during gestation period"? Dr. Mukherjee asked with concern.

"No, homoeopathy medicine has no such adverse effect".

Six doses of medicine cured her miraculously. Dr. Mukherjee was agog with excitement seeing its fruitful result.

One day he closed his clinic and said to Sambit, "I am going to S.C.B. Medical College to do my Post-graduation in Gynaecology and obstetrics. Would you practise in my clinic during my absence?"

"No, Dr. Mukherjee, I have my own clinic. I am a popular homoeopath there. I will miss you very much. The only consolation is that the duration of two years will pass away very soon".

After completion of his study, Dr. Mukherjee came back to Baripada.

Some months passed this way. One day he broke the news. "Mr. Sambit, I am going to Bombay shortly to open a clinic there. I have a homestead land near Gandhi Park. Before my departure I want to sell it. I prefer to give it to you at a moderate rate. I only want to get back my principal amount. If you buy it, you will get your money's worth."

"Brother! You made me laugh. Do you think I am a moneyed person? Rather I will look for some good customer".

They were inextricably knotted together and Sambit did not want to untie that bond of friendship.

"Why did you take a sudden decision to leave Baripada? Is there any difficulty here?" Sambit asked him in a wounded tone.

"No, I want to go to Bombay because my elder brother

is there. Moreover I will get a wider field for my practice. It is more lucrative and suits my temperament".

Despite Sambit's repeated request he stood pat with his decision. He left for a greener pasture and bade him god-speed. After a month he went to Bhubaneswar and there he boarded a plane to Bombay.

SIX

Tarun was not the classmate of Sambit. He was his college-mate and two years junior to him. He was a man of medium height and slightly roly-poly right from his boyhood days. As he did not come out successful in his B.A. exam, he dropped out of college with sheer disgust.

His father had a vast landed property. But there was no one to look after it. He had given his land to some cultivators on a co-sharing basis. But he got a paltry amount of paddy in return. So Tarun evicted all co-sharers and tilled the land by hiring some wage-earners. That year he harvested bumper crops. He became a full-fledged cultivator. Though he got an appointment letter as a sub-inspector under 'Central Excise Department', he gave a flippant response to that service. At that time his income from agriculture was more than enough to maintain his household expenditure. He fathered two children, one son and one daughter.

On numerous occasions, Sambit had been invited to his farm house.

One summer the temperature waxed to such a degree that Baripada town became a baking oven for the people. To escape from the fiery heat, Sambit rode on his bicycle and got there before noon.

Both of them caught fish in a nearby tank and fried them for lunch.

After the midday meal, they sat on a string cot.

In the course of conversation Tarun said, "Now a dispute has started among my brothers. After my father's death, they want to take their individual share of the landed property. Mine will be about five acres. I am thinking about how I will manage my family after division. I have decided to go back to Baripada. Before that I will give my land to a farmer. On condition, he will supply me some sacks of rice for my yearly consumption".

Moving a little to the edge of the cot Sambit said, "I have always regretted the mistake that you have committed in the past. Why did you forgo that government service? Secondly you have started cultivation in a joint family. One day it will be divided among your brothers. Some years ago I had advised you to be admitted in Homeopathy College of Baripada. You could have earned money being a homoeopath. But you did not listen to me. There is no way out. Shift your family to Baripada. There I will plan what can be done for you".

There was a non-banking establishment near 'Jagadhatri Talkies' namely 'Ananda Paribar'. It was set up by Mr. Ananda Shankar to engage the unemployed youth. For its expansion, he opened a number of branches in different places even outside Odisha.

Sambit had been on good terms with Mr. Ananda Shankar. He was an openhearted man. When Sambit told him about Tarun's financial woes, he laughed and said, "Your friend has run into a snag. I have agreed to appoint him as the administrative officer of our organisation. But according to the by-laws of our establishment he has to deposit four thousand rupees as caution money. Though I am a founder-member, I can not deviate from the rules and regulations incorporated in our by-laws."

A week later, Sambit paid him that amount. One month passed this way. Purnima, Tarun's wife got impatient for the delay of his appointment. She pressed Sambit to speed up the process.

"We should not impugn the integrity of Mr. Anand

Shankar. Don't be worried about that. If he does not appoint him, I shall pay back your money".

One afternoon, Sambit accosted Mr. Ananda, "Why do you make unnecessary delays, brother? Tarun's wife has lost faith in me. I assured her that Mr. Ananda will never go back on his word. Please appoint him as early as possible. You must be as good as your word".

After some days, Tarun joined 'Ananda Paribar'. He observed that most of the branch-managers were corrupt to the hilt and they had pocketed a major portion of deposited money. Though Mr. Ananda knew this embezzlement, he did not take drastic steps to check their malpractice. Lakhs of rupees had been misappropriated with the connivance of Mr. Ananda. The customers totally stopped deposition of money and demanded to get back their principal amount. It gave the organisers a scare. Some branch-managers made off to unknown places. Droves of customers came with wild frenzy and threatened to murder Mr. Anand. He skipped out to Tatanagar to save his skin. They locked the doors and shuttered the windows of the office. They mobbed them wherever they went.

The police conducted a thorough inquiry and the truth started to unravel.

Mr. Ananda was arrested from his hide-out. After a trial, he was found guilty and he was sentenced to three years imprisonment.

Tarun was not in collusion with others. When the police made an undercover investigation, they found him punctilious and completely unimpeachable. He never strayed from the path of financial probity. They exonerated him from all charges of corruption.

After three years' stint in that organisation, Tarun lost his job.

His harvest from agricultural land was quite insufficient, still he sold bulk of the paddy to meet his daily expenses. Sambit arranged a few private tuition to supplement his income. It was difficult to keep body and soul together with that piddling amount of money.

Tarun used to go to the market in the late hours of evening. He would keep worm-eaten brinjals separately and buy them dirt-cheap haggling with the vegetable vendors. He scrimped on food being crushed by his grinding poverty.

He was a picky eater. But his pecuniary position was so wretched that he could not afford that delicious food. His wife would save some vegetable curry, the cold remnants of lunch, for their dinner. The food was always poor in quality and the children whined for some palatable dishes.

Purnima was reluctant to do household chores. She would spread herself on a mattress to watch T.V., a couch potato who pestered her husband to do this and that.

An unforgiving wrath grew in her heart and Tarun became her eye-sore day by day. Everyday he would scrub all the cooking wares and utensils and then wash them with tap water. She would bid him to make tea for her while lying on her cosy bed. He was at her constant beck and call and totally dominated by his wife.

Many a time Sambit chastised her not to treat her husband as a servant.

One day she turned truculent. She threw a piping hot cup of tea at her husband and shrieked.

"Let him do all the household chores. My father really lacks foresight. How did he give me marriage with this vagrant? He gads about without any purpose. Doing nothing and spending his time gossiping with the menials of Radhamohan temple".

She glared at him indignantly and became more virulent, unleashing a barrage of insults.

"You shameless vagabond ! Let your hands and legs be putrefied. Let them fall into pieces. I pray to God to be a widow soon. What is the worth of living such a useless life? I have been embittered seeing your face. Be off at once from my sight", she rapped out an unsavoury vilification.

Sambit could not swallow such filthy abuse. Her raw deal upset him. He tried to simmer her down and get to her work.

"Why do you chew him out in his hard times? You always tick him off for no reason. God has given you a beautiful appearance. But why are your utterances so mucky? Every Monday you go to the temple of Lord Shiva. Do you want to show off your devotion to neighbours? Husband is virtually a real god to a wife. Unless you worship him in your heart, your devoutness is meaningless. God blesses that woman who is endowed with unswerving love and devotion to her husband".

That evening Radhamohan temple was not so crowded. Sambit and Tarun sat on the marble floor. A whiff of incense came wafting in the air. It was their usual place for tittle-tattle.

"Have you heard about the mysterious death of my second sister-in-law? Tarun broached the subject.

"No, how did it happen?"

"The mishap occurred lately. You know my father-in-law was looking for a bridegroom. They belong to Calcutta and that young man is practising law in Calcutta High Court. When I accompanied my father-in-law to finalise the matter, I had a talk with that young man. I disliked his superficial manner. I had a hunch in my mind that it would be an ill-assorted match. I counselled my father-in-law to cancel that negotiation. But he took my warning amiss. He thought I am envious of him as I am jobless whereas he is a reputed lawyer of Calcutta High Court.

After marriage some months passed uneventfully. The lawyer would commute to the court in the morning and come back home in the evening. He would eat his snacks hurriedly and then go out without talking to his wife.

He will come with lots of things at night. He would pull out gold ornaments and bundles of currency notes from his bag and spread them on the floor, count them one by one and put all these things in the locker of an almirah. One night my sister-in-law, awakening from her sleep, asked him what he was doing. He was alarmed as he was unaware of her wakefulness. He immediately stashed those things to avoid her questioning look. Her curiosity ratcheted up and it became the cause of her death. He was apparently a lawyer in the eyes of society but he was a first rate burglar. His mind dwelt on the fact that his wife would be a major stumbling block and she might tip off the police about his secret activities. So she must be stamped out.

She met her quirk of fate very soon. One morning her husband prepared tea in his own hand. He talked with a ladida manner and served her a cup with affected love. After she drank half, her head reeled violently. The cup fell from her hand and she dropped dead then and there".

"What did your father-in-law do then?"

"Nothing. When he went to Calcutta to find out the reasons for his daughter's sudden death, the in-laws shammed to be grieved over the loss of their beautiful daughter-in-law. He was deluded by their lies that she died of heart failure".

"How selfish and callous they are!"

Sambit was beside himself with rage after hearing this sad news.

"Tarun, do you remember an old adage? Marriage is like a chewing gum, sweet in the beginning, sticky in the end. So don't revel in the temporary happiness of married life".

"Yes, every moment I experience that thing in my own life. In my heady days of youth, my wife was very loyal. She stood by me in weal and woe. Now my bad time has arrived. She does not share my woes. She has turned a deep-dyed selfish".

"Don't you know the nature of women which is

categorically true? Woman is a delicate harp. One must know how to tune it. Then one can get the finest melodies if one knows the secret of tuning it. So be on your guard".

"But my dear! Though I am in abysmally poor condition, I wallow in a make-believe world. A dark labyrinth is yawning to engulf me. Come what may", Tarun shrugged his shoulders.

The next evening Tarun was impeccably dressed in dhoti and silken Punjabi which made him look dapper.

"Where are you going Tarun? I think you have an engagement somewhere. You look fantastic in that dress".

Yes, I am going to attend a marriage reception. Come with me. I won't enjoy the party if I go alone".

"Brother, how can I go uninvited?"

"But how am I going uninvited?"

Tarun burst into laughter.

"If somebody comes to know that you are not an invitee, then....?" You may be put to shame as a gate crasher.

"I pooh-pooh your idea. Is it possible to recognize one in the midst of so many invitees? Who has guts enough to cross-question a person? He may belong to the bride groom's party and vice versa".

Then he became thoughtful and said, "I do agree, it is not courtesy to go uninvited. One cannot be so brazen-faced. But what can I do? I have been masticating tasteless food for so many days. Will not the scent of delicious food whet my appetite? So what's the harm if I have a bite of palatable food there?"

Tarun was always helpful. If the electric heater became inoperative, he would be called in, if the thatched roof gave in, he would be called in, if the mud wall collapsed due to heavy rainfall, he would be always at your service. He would arrive without delay. No botheration. You will stop worrying if he was present.

One forenoon, his son came running to Sambit's house.

He was gasping for breath. Sambit told him to come in. But he stood stock-still at the threshold.

He said in a faltering tone, "Uncle, excuse me for I have no time to sit here. Please come to our house and see how my father narrowly escaped death".

Sambit's heart leaped for a moment. In excitement he asked, "What happened to him? Is he severely injured? Don't confuse me".

"My father was cooking with the electric heater. In a frenzy of rage my mother gave him a thrust. He fell head-first down the floor pathetically. What would have happened to him had he fallen on the burning heater".

With dismay, Sambit slipped into his dress and hurtled to their house. Purnima was seated on her bed. She looked grumpy.

"You don't have a jot of sense. How could you do this inhuman act?" Sambit demanded.

"I have done the right thing. Do you know I am carrying my third child? Why did that bugger put his seed in me? Let me see how he would feed my children," she fumed.

She was not repentant a bit for her volatile temperament.

"You are on the wrong track. Is he only responsible for this and you are quite innocent? You two are equally blame-worthy. Don't point an accusing finger at him".

"I got into a hassle with my husband for this. So I am getting ready for abortion. My two children are half-fed. Can he shoulder the burden of a third child? Over and above I have two grown-up children. What impression would they have if I beget a child at this age? Please save me from this imminent danger".

Seeing her cornered, Sambit came to her rescue and went to the nursing home of Dr. Prasad.

"Would you do me a favour, sir?"

"What?"

"Sir, my friend's wife faces an awkward situation. It is

her first trimester of pregnancy. She is a mother of two children and wants no more issues. Their financial position is not at all stable. They can't foot the bill for abortion but they are willing to give your minimum charge".

Dr. Prasad gave a compassionate smile.

"Let her get admitted to my nursing home. Tell them not to delay any longer, otherwise it will go to a more complicated state as well as the mother will face a dire consequence".

"Okay sir".

Purnima braced herself for this ordeal. A cabin was allotted to her. A nurse inserted the laminaria tent into her genitals. It gradually swelled and dilated the cervix. She groaned with pain although it was not so excruciating.

"Your friend's wife is oversensitive. One must feel pain at the beginning. No gain without pain", Dr. Prasad said jokingly.

After curettage and thorough washing of the uterus, she was laid on a bed.

The doctor advised her to rest for a short period. At the onset of the evening, she went home escorted by her husband.

Tarun's relationship with his wife was on the skids. A wide gulf yawned between the two. Most of his time he wandered here and there to escape from the turmoils of family life. His peripatetic life made him sleep invariably on the verandah of Radhamohan temple at night. He was in grips of poverty and during his hard days there was no one to give him solace. He knew that he was predestined to rot in abject poverty, to wriggle in lingering death. He spent his days in semi-starvation and became jaded by the harsh realities of life. He wanted to go away from the rough and tumble world of selfishness. The constant nagging of his wife caused him to reach the end of his tether.

As he was a Brahmin by caste, he was usually invited to attend the obsequies. Once on such an occasion he went to

Bhoogudakota which was at a distance of two kilometres from Baripada town.

Summer had withered the earth. It was midday. With much strain he covered that distance on foot. After eating his fill, he sought a place to rest. He sat on the verandah and leaned his back against a wall. The sumptuous meal made him drowsy. He fell into a sound sleep from which he will never wake-up.

SEVEN

Suranath was studying in Badasahi high school. When he got admitted into M.P.C. College, he came closer to Sambit. He was a lovely young man of medium height having flabby muscles. All liked him for his scintillating personality. He did not stay in the college hostel nor in any recognized mess. He hired a single room of a large building having all the basic amenities.

As it was in the vicinity of temple Ambika, Sambit visited him frequently. They had a greater liking for history than for any other subject.

Sura had collected quite a number of history books.

One fine morning they were engrossed in conversation.

"Sura, what is your opinion about history? It is simply a memory work. You are required only to memorise the incidents and reproduce them in the exam. Isn't it?"

"No brother. You have not defined it precisely. It plays a significant role in human lives. You will be well versed in many things right from the prehistoric period. This is a written record of important incidents that have happened since the dawn of civilization. Everybody must admit that it is a subject of great importance which enlightens us regarding the culture, nation, society, people and their development in various fields. Without history, you will remain in the gloom of ignorance."

After graduation, Sura went to Vani Vihar to do his post-graduation in history. Then he conquered P.S.C. and was appointed as a lecturer in Jeypore college.

Sambit went to Jeypore to face an interview for

teachership. There he stayed in a woodland lodge. While hanging around the market, he came upon Prof. Radhakanta Mishra who was teaching him in college. Both of them stood in a stand still position. Prof. Mishra gazed at his face and said, "You are Sambit. You have come from Baripada. Am I correct?"

Sambit laughed and asked, "How could you remember me after a long period? Even you have not forgotten my name also".

Prof. Mishra's face beamed with ineffable joy.

"Let us go to my residence. We will have a talk there". He was staying at a little distance from the market, in a government quarter.

"Sir, have you been transferred to Jeypore college?"

"No, no, I am now Inspector of Schools, Koraput – Jeypur Circle and I joined my service a fortnight ago. Why have you come to this place?"

"Sir, I want to pursue a noble profession like teachership. The interview will be held tomorrow".

"What are you doing at present?"

"Practising homoeopathy, Sir".

"You see, there are thirty posts that have fallen vacant in my circle. Teachers are not willing to come to this place. There must be your friends having the requisite qualification. After going back to Baripada, tell them to apply and I will appoint them in different high schools".

"Yes sir".

"Tell me your experience while coming to Jeypore".

"It is a long distance, no doubt. Our Bangriposi range is nothing in comparison to Saloor range. It is so zigzag and perilous that my heart palpitated while crossing over such a long and steep range. It was a nightmarish three hours' journey. On both sides of the road, there is unending dense forest. Even sunshine cannot pass through its thick foliage. I was thrilled seeing its verdant beauty".

"All right. Can't you come prepared within fifteen days? For your information, Jeypore high school is the only A-type high school in the whole district where a post of science teacher has fallen vacant. You will be appointed in a c-type school at present".

"Sir, there is only one impediment. Service in c-type means your seniority will not be counted".

"Don't fret. Come and join BisamCuttack high school. I am here to transfer you to some other place if you feel discomfort there".

The next day candidates appeared one by one at the door of the office. The interview was scheduled to start at 10.30 am. Prof. Mishra came out of the office and offered an apology.

"Although the time is already over, please wait another two hours. Some candidates have not yet arrived. There must be some problem or they must be caught in a traffic-jam."

Only twelve candidates appeared at the interview. The selection committee had to wade through their certificates. They were given assurance that their appointment letter will be dispatched to their respective address very soon.

That evening Sambit went to Suranath's residence. He asked a betel shopkeeper about the exact location of his house. It took half an hour to reach there. He was living with his family in the upper floor of a two storeyed building. At the entrance, a bulb meted out a very dim light. He climbed the stairs and found Suranth absorbed in banging a mridanga (an egg shaped drum) seated on a carpet. Sambit silently stood a few feet away from him.

"What a surprise!" Suranath kept the drum aside and being overjoyed gave him a big hug.

"Your sudden arrival really surprised me", Suranath gave a blissful smile.

"I cannot forget you. Is it possible to efface your memory from my mind?"

The meeting gave them a warm fuzzy feeling.

"May I know the purpose of your visit to this forbidden place?"

"I have come here to attend an interview for teachership".

"Very well, where are you staying in Jeypore town?"

"In a woodland lodge. I am leaving tomorrow morning".

"When will you come next time?"

"Most probably I will not come to join a c-type school. Better to practise homoeopathy in my own place. My income is not that bad".

Serving in different colleges, Suranath came to Baripada as a history reader. There came a dramatic change in his life. Previously he was a teetotaller. In the company of bad friends he grew addicted to alcohol.

One Sunday morning Sambit went to his residence. His wife was busy doing her household work. Seeing him she smiled and ushered him into their sitting room.

He slouched on a sofa and asked, "Where is Sura?"

His wife gestured towards their bedroom.

Sambit glanced at his wrist watch.

"It is now 8.30 am but he is still asleep in his bed?"

"Don't you know his habit? Without imbibing that nectar, he won't retire to his bed".

"I see".

Sambit walked quietly into his bedroom. Suranath was lying supine and snoring loudly. Sambit pushed his hand below the fringe of the mosquito-net and shoved him by his shoulder.

Suranath slowly opened his eyes and shook him off the stupor of intoxication. He yawned sitting on his bed.

Then he staggered over to a pillar and sat leaning against it. He took out a lump of tobacco from a tin pouch and began to scrub his teeth. His eyes were puffy and he looked bleary-eyed.

"How are you?" he asked through his tobacco-smeared mouth.

"Yes, I am fine. I have come for your suggestion. My daughter wants to do her post-graduation in history. I am in a sticky situation whether she would do that in M.P.C. College or in Vani Vihar".

"Don't send her to some other place. Let her do that in M.P.C. College. You have to spend a lot of money for her higher education rather than save it for her marriage".

"My opinion is also the same. You have steered me in the right direction".

Suranath walked over to a washing basin and rinsed his mouth with tap water. His eyes darted in the direction of the kitchen and he asked in an undertone, "Would you please lend me two hundred rupees? My penny-pinching wife gives me only four rupees a day. Brother, I am dying for a pint of liquor".

"I won't give you a single pie to encourage this bad habit. Most of the time you remain in alcoholic stupor. You know I belong to a low-income group. You have no knowledge how I spend my days in constant botheration for my children. Don't expect this amount of a pauper like me. I heard that you tipple everyday with a younger brother of our friend who is much junior to us. Don't you feel ashamed? You are in a prestigious position. What your students will think if their teacher is demeaned to such a level. You have pledged many times by touching the feet of your teacher that you will never touch it. But you did not stick to your promise and became a habitual drunkard. Your breath reeks of alcohol. I am well acquainted with a person who had been an alcoholic for a long forty years. But how could he give up that habit?"

"I too will wean away from that harmful thing, I assure you."

"If you make it possible, it will be your greatest achievement. Turn over a new leaf".

It was a sunny afternoon. Suranath was coming from his quarter riding on his luna moped. It suddenly got inoperative near the college. He remained straddled on the seat. Sambit was on his way to the clinic. He saw him immovable in that position.

"Today you have had an overdose", he made a passing remark.

Suranath did not reply. He only nodded his head.

Some students were coming along that road. They saw him in that helpless condition and guessed that he had been totally crocked.

"Sir, we are pushing your vehicle from behind. You just hold the handle".

They pushed it a few yards. Almost immediately the machine sparked into life and Suranath vroomed away through an alley.

"Do you know his brother-in-law owns a hotel near the hospital. He will go to him to have endless chatter. Both of them will be dead-drunk there". They lambasted him with disregard.

After retirement, Suranath built a house at Ambika Vihar. He was an ardent devotee of literature. He had composed an anthology of poetry, full of humours and often recited them to the pleasure of his friends.

Sambit was also a budding novelist. He requested Suranath to be present in the inaugural ceremony of his latest novel.

Before the ceremony, he strolled to his house. His wife warmly welcomed him and offered him a chair.

"Is Suranath not at home?"

"Yes, he has gone to the latrine. You have not shown up for a long time. You stop visiting us".

"The fact is that I have shifted my family to a new house. I have been swamped with work, constructing a compound wall", Sambit said apologetically.

"Do you know about his recent mishap?"

"No, nobody has informed me. I am out of touch".

"As it was a severe cold, he had sat as usual on a wicker stool before the burning oven. As he got sloshed, he lost his balance and fell directly on the oven. His buttock, thighs and legs were all burnt by the glowing embers – a hair's breadth escape from inevitable death".

Suranath emerged from the latrine wearing a towel around his waist.

"Hi Sambit, I have not seen you for ages. You just see my woeful condition. He hitched up the towel and said in an injured tone, "The burnt portions are not completely healed up. A sticky fluid is still oozing out of the blisters".

He walked over to Sambit and showed him the burnt portions of his body.

"O God, how ghastly ! I am really spooked. I have come to invite you for a literary meeting. But how can you go in this horrible condition?"

"No, I must be present in the inaugural ceremony of your novel. You must have written something worthwhile. Even I am ready to go wearing this dhoti", he oozed confidence.

After some months, Suranath's health was in a precarious condition. He went to S.C.B. Medical College for checking as he was suffering from dropsy as well as deadly liver cirrhosis. He was just fighting a losing battle. He was still his optimistic self. A jovial man as he was, he did not take anything seriously. Eat, drink and be merry was the motto of his life. There was no shadow of displeasure on his face, even in his ailing condition. From cradle to grave he was chirpy. He passed away grinning from ear to ear.

EIGHT

Suraj Saha was born in a business community. As a pet son of his parents, he spent his early youth sleeping on the feather bed. He was born a prince. His forefather's business acumen was commendable and they had amassed sizable wealth for the comfortable living of their successors. Suraj was spendthrift and he fritted away money in the company of bully boys.

While studying in college, he would smack his lips making a sound of lecherous kisses and then yodelling some smutty songs try to draw the attention of the girls. He rubbed shoulders with the street-Romeos and they would make lewd comments while they went past them. He went off the right track for his parents as they slurred over his obnoxious activities. It was undeniably one of the seven wonders how he sailed through his B.A. exam. His father wallowed in money and he had an ambition to engage his son in business, so that he would do his best for its expansion. But Suraj was not interested in racking his brain for this tiresome work. All day long he would wander aimlessly here and there riding on his bike. It was just a fluke that he got an appointment in some aided high school. But actually he was not cut out to be a teacher.

He was pedantic and God knows what and how he taught in the class. Sometimes he would bunk off school on flimsy pretext. He was a sleaze-bag teacher who ingeniously changed his date of birth in matriculation certificate by greasing the palms of the higher officials of the education department.

All through the afternoon the rain was pattering endlessly on the window panes and towards the evening, it ceased with a drizzling. Sambit was in his clinic when Suraj Saha entered quietly. His hair had been ruffled, both cheeks abnormally swollen, eye-lids smudged black- all presented a very funny appearance. Sambit stared at him and surmised that there must be some grievous accident. He became nonplussed, when Suraj, in his muffled tone, narrated his misadventure. He was caught in his unwary moments at the tryst when he had some pleasantries with a girl. His brother lay in ambush seeking a right time, ready to pounce on him. Before Suraj took to his heels, he was grabbed by his neck and the girl's brother gave him some sound thrashing.

"Keep your hands off my sister", he warned.

That was the outcome of his loutish manner. With medicines to alleviate his pain and swelling, he hobbled to his home.

There was no shop in the town from which he had not taken anything on credit. Tea shops, betel shops, and restaurants all welcomed him with the hope that he must clear their outstanding dues. He managed to scrounge these things by putting on airs and graces. He had a patina of wealth.

He sluggishly spent his time blathering in different shops. He would entertain his acquainted persons courteously offering them tea, betel and cigarettes. He would never eat anything alone. Sometimes he would call on his friends to a get-together and throw a grand party for their amusement.

From the beginning his parents disliked his teaching profession. In their assessment, a man cannot prosper in this line. He would earn just a meagre amount of money to curb his pangs of hunger. But consequently he would be reduced to a penury. They had a high hope that their son would get a white-collar job and roll in luxury. He would heighten the prestige of the family. But this prodigal demolished all their hopes.

In earlier days, they winked at his youthful indiscretions. Now they regretted and decided to bind him in a wed-lock.

His notoriety was well known in the neighbouring towns and they were ashamed of his disrepute as they spawned such a son. So they looked for a daughter-in-law from a far-off place. They selected a bride from a well-to-do family who were business tycoons of that area. The nuptial day was fixed and the wedding ceremony was performed with pomp and grandeur.

For some months they led a harmonious conjugal life. But Suraj had a grasshopper mind. His love for his wife was shaky for which he could not perch on that flower.

One evening his wife Nimmi had been to the market to purchase some necessary things. Her eyes popped out of head when she saw him shopping with a good looking girl. Another day she espied him from a distance while talking with a young woman. He hailed a taxi and it screeched to a halt. Both of them got into it and zoomed off from her sight. Nimmi was in the company of her maid-servant. Her face turned pale but she was relieved that the licentious nature of her husband did not come to the notice of her maid-servant. They repaired their home.

Nimmi went straight into the bathroom and washed her hands and feet. Her heart began to palpitate rapidly thinking about her uncertain future. She switched on the ceiling fan. It began to whirr. Her whole body had been drenched with profuse sweat. The cold wind of the fan could not dry it up. She was awfully restless. She was drawn into a vortex of despair.

She had been living under the happy illusion that her married life was a successful one. But her citadel of dreams was smashed into smithereens. It belied her hopes. She had a lingering doubt about his character. She was shell-shocked for her husband's disastrous departure from marital fidelity. She was in a tight corner debating in her mind what steps should be taken after knowing his amatory adventures.

Late in the evening when Suraj returned to his home, he saw his wife in a sullen mood. He silently went to his bedroom to change his dress.

He drew a chair near the dining table and asked, "Nimmi, why are you sitting like a statue? Will you not have your dinner tonight?"

Nimmi did not stir from the sofa nor did she utter a single word.

"Don't you feel well? Let me see".

Suraj went near the sofa and held her in a bear-hug. A searing retort welled up within her. She wrenched her free from his grip.

"I have a terrible headache. You serve your dinner yourself", her temper was starting to fray.

Suraj said with affected love, "I don't get pleasure if I eat alone. I become very glad when you give me your company. You are my treasure-trove which I own by my good luck".

His cajoling words set a fire to her mind.

It raised her hooded fangs.

She said rudely, "What a loving and faithful husband you are! May I ask you how many girls have you bedded before my marriage?"

Her cutting words made him agitated. His whole body began to shake. His mouth was completely dry. This sudden attack forced him on to the defensive. He was at his wit's end to offer an explanation.

"Not a single one. You always make a mountain out of a molehill. Although there is not a bean of truth, You have been racked with doubt. This breeds baseless jealousy. You have strayed from reasoning power and gone crazy". Suraj's speech started stuttering.

"Yes, I must go plumb-crazy. Don't tell me a made-up

story. You rank liar! Can you swear that you have no screw with that girl?"

"Which girl?" Suraj feigned ignorance.

"That girl with whom you were going yesterday on a shopping errand".

"Oh Seema! What a sober and decent girl she is ! She has been enrolled in college. Her father requested me to buy her a dress. So we went to the garment store to select one according to her choice". He tried to parry her enquiries.

"Oh I see. The husband of that vulgar woman also requested you to take his wife for a jolly ride in a taxi for the sake of her recreation, isn't it? I am truly ignorant about your cloak and dagger plan".

"O you are really a fish-wife. A devoted wife hides the fault of her husband. But you always hurl slanderous remarks at me. You will drive me mad, Nimmi".

"Okay. I am not so credulous to be swayed by your fake excuses. I must sever our physical ties although we sleep on the same bed. Don't take the liberty to touch me. My body has been deflowered by a John Duan but I have not lost the sanctity of my mind. It still remained unpolluted as pure as the driven snow. I have put it in the casket of my heart not to be defiled by your stinking touch".

Nimmi went to sleep with a tottering gait and placing a bolster in the middle crashed into bed like a stabbed corpse. Her eyes were brimmed with tears.

Suraj's appetite had already gone. So also his temper. He washed his feet and sat on the bed trying to come back to his composure. It was just a passing phase. This incubus will go away very soon. Time was the best healer. One day she will realise the futility of her arrogance. He consoled his mind.

Nimmi fought with frequent bouts of depression. She lay awake. She switched off the light, still sleep did not come to her eyes.

Suraj pulled his wrapper to cover his body and

whispered, "Would you not turn to me, Nimmi? Please come a little closer. I won't touch your body. But why did you grow suddenly repulsive, even unwilling to talk with me? You rave about some imaginary thing".

"I don't talk with an infidel, a treacherous". Nimmi retorted with a woeful tone. She tried to stifle a sob.

"Please Nimmi, don't blame me like that. You keep me hungry, denying me my biological need. There is some ego-hunger in you. You are a masochist who derives pleasure from inflicting pain on me. I let you do whatever you like. But remember, for this dereliction, you will reap what you have sown. You rebuffed me with disdain and flinched from your duty. Your obstinacy will surely drive me to go to that vile path". He rasped.

"Go wherever you want to go. I don't care if you jump in a flooded river or well. You may go to prostitutes or courtesans, it is all the same to me", she said through clenched teeth.

"But why did you retire to bed on an empty stomach? Why are you so averse to food? You know damn well it really pained me".

"Don't insist on me. I won't take a crumb of food. I am on a crash diet".

Nimmi tucked a thin wrapper around her and resolved not to speak to him again.

The next morning Suraj hurriedly finished his bath and got ready to meet Sambit. He was in dire need of a house.

"Brother, you have a building comprising two quarters. It is untenanted for a long period. I am ready to pay you rent what you deserve. I won't take it rent-free". Suraj appealed.

"Why two quarters?", Sambit could not grasp him.

"You see, my driver will remain in the front part. The back part will be occupied by a senior accountant of Central Cooperative Bank, a close friend of mine. The building is a large one which can easily accommodate two families. You need not be worried about that. I will pay the rent on their behalf".

"I dislike irregular payment. That tees me off".

"No, no, rely on me. Don't be faint-hearted. Full responsibility is mine. You need not have to cringe before the tenants". He seemed to be very earnest.

"All right. You have to keep my one request under oath. Never make it a cheap lovenest or a seedy home". Sambit played a practical joke on him.

Suraj tittered and cleared off.

The senior accountant Mr. Hussan paid his monthly rent regularly. Suraj cleared the rent of the driver which had fallen in arrears for three months. Then he totally stopped payment. Sambit lost track of him. He ran away with fifteen lakhs of cooperative bank's money and holed up in a relative's house. The police could not trace him anywhere. Mr. Hussan was held responsible as an accomplice of Suraj and he had to face trial on fraud charges. It was alleged that both of them were in cahoots with other employees of the bank. At length Mr. Hussan was proved as the key figure of this embezzlement and was cashiered from his job. Suraj had no alternative other than to sell away his costly cars, trucks and other vehicles. He paid the whole amount to the bank which he had appropriated by fraudulence.

Then followed a longstanding legal case of his homestead land. He had been bedevilled by the rival party over a long period. He was, no doubt, a squatter. He had occupied some portion of that land unlawfully which was actually in the possession of a doctor. He had set up a clinic there. To resolve the dispute the doctor agreed to give him three lakh rupees provided he waived his claim but he shrugged off that offer. The high court passed the verdict in favour of the doctor and the land slipped from his hand forever.

Suraj had liaison with Mausumi who was born and brought up in a poor family. She was a vivacious woman but remained unmarried due to acute poverty. She was comely and as fit as a fiddle. She played the role of a conduit and opened the floodgates of love for Suraj. He was swept away by the torrential flow of debauchery. The surfeit of mental torture and conjugal row drove him to a wrong path. His sense of self-respect had been demoted and it was more pronounced when the protracted skirmish came to a head and his steps faltered. He slowly stepped on the path of promiscuity without inhibition. When it escalated into a pitched battle, he grew impatient and exasperated. It vitiated the peaceful atmosphere of their home. But Mausumi extended her sympathetic hand.

Suraj was disinclined to return to the trouble spot. The thought of Nimmi irked him more. How pugnacious lady she was! Better to stay with Mausumi who was quite demure and loyal.

On an auspicious morning Suraj married her in a temple. The wedding was a very low-key affair. He put vermilion on the parting of her hair and flung a garland of flowers round her neck. Mausumi held her husband in high regard and drawing a veil over her head prostrated at his feet.

"You are no longer my mistress but a legally married wife. My days of turmoil are over. We will start our life anew".

They writhed in ecstasy.

After three months Suraj recommenced his love with Seema. She was fantastic in bed. Mausumi was apprised of their romantic entanglement. "Let him come today, I must put an end to his lechery" – she was bent on taking revenge and took a solemn oath to pay him in his own coins.

When Suraj was about to enter his bedroom, Mausumi came out of the kitchen. She was holding a kerosene jar in her right hand. Last night, she had a fitful sleep and her eyes were burning.

"Congratulations, my dear husband. You have hooked a big fish". There was a mocking note in her voice.

"Sometimes you say in riddles. I could not follow you Mausumi".

"You do not know how to fry a fish, so innocent you are. You are quite adept at playing hide and seek but alas, I have no such talent. Don't try to palm me off with your feeble excuse. Have you not planned to ditch me to love somebody else?"

She was awfully cheated. Her impulsive decision to marry him was a colossal mistake. She would not take rest until she had completely destroyed him. Her neck corded in anger. She became an avenging phoenix and gave him no quarter.

In a highly inflammable mood she threw a tantrum, "You womaniser! You fiendish lover of cunnilingus! You cannot give up your nasty habit. You are beyond redemption. Who is that Seema who has infatuated you so much? She seems to have cast a spell over you. You are like a putty in the hands of that slut. I must smack her face and strip her naked to be fucked in broad day light. You sleep with me daily, still your carnal desire remains unfulfilled. You wretched Soondi (of low origin) I will teach you a lifetime lesson".

But Suraj was more alert than her. He gained the upper hand and snatched the jar from her hand. With a quick movement he unscrewed the cap and sprinkled the kerosene all over her body. Then he fished out a match box from his pocket and flung the burning match sticks one after another at her. Her draped body immediately caught fire. In a state of frenzy she lunged at him like a vengeful tigress and hugged him summoning all her strength.

Suraj tried to wriggle out of her vice-like grip but at last gave in.

"If I must die, I will die with you. Do you think you will be escaped", she screamed in agonising pain. She ducked the first few blows but did not budge to fight back.

They wrestled desperately with one another. The sinister tongue of fire licked their bodies and they fell in a heap. ■

NINE

Dr. Kar was a man of medium stature. Though his hair started to turn grey, he maintained excellent health at the age of fifty. He used to walk half a kilometre to reach his clinic on time.

He was a great advocate of a frugal lifestyle. He used to eat frugally in cheap hotels and restaurants. He would take three to four chapatis in his breakfast with a little amount of mixed vegetables. If one hears his opinion, one must shy away from a non-vegetarian diet.

"Mixed vegetables contain all the essential vitamins and minerals. It helps in keeping up sound health. Non-vegetarian diet is a well-spring of all the cardiac troubles. Because fat is deposited in the bloodstream, as a result the percentage of cholesterol rises up. High levels of cholesterol in the blood are thought to increase the risk of arteriosclerosis".

He gives a discourse on diet. The patients are occupied with different work. They are in a hurry to come out of his clinic as soon as possible. They have no patience or time to listen to his well-meaning advice or suggestions. The patients get restive awaiting their turn. If somebody barges into his chamber disregarding the serial number, he does not get annoyed with him. He stops scribbling down prescriptions and turns his eyes to the back wall where 'WAIT WITH PATIENCE' has been written in capital letters. It means nothing to the illiterate people.

He shoots a volley of questions to the patients regarding their whereabouts, what they are doing, whether they have harvested their crops, rainfall in their place, what their children are doing, the name of the important persons they are closely associated with, and so on and so forth.

The patients do not want to hurt his sentiments but feel disgusted.

But Dr. Kar maintains his cool. His mental composure remains unscathed. He minutely examines the patients though it consumes a lot of his valuable time.

Dr. Kar befriended Sambit when he first arrived in his clinic as a patient. Since that time their relationship deepened.

Once Sambit's son suffered from herpes zoster. There were clusters of vesicles or watery blisters on an inflamed base of his chest which was very painful. He advised his son to go to Dr. Kar.

He meticulously examined the affected area with a magnifying glass and asked, "Have you taken any medicine for that?"

"Yes sir".

"Who is that doctor?".

"My father, Sir".

"Is it allopathic or homoeopathic?"

"Allopathic, Sir".

"Why did he give allopathic medicine being a homoeopath?"

"My father knows allopathy as well as homoeopathy".

"A hell of a lot he knows. You are suffering from herpes. Does he know the difference between herpes zoster and herpes simplex?"

"I don't know. It is beyond my knowledge".

"All right. Come after a week. I have to study the regression of the disease. Here I have prescribed a 'herpes' ointment. Apply it externally two times a day".

"Yes Sir".

Dr. Kar's clinic was attached to a big medicine store owned by a Marwari.

One forenoon Sambit had been to that store to purchase some medicines. After that work was over, he entered his clinic.

Dr. Kar was examining a patient who had a number of acne on his face. He had worn a shabby lungi and a threadbare banian.

Before departure he placed his fees on the table. Dr. Kar counted them and asked him, "Do you know my fees?"

The patient was discomfited.

"Yes sir", he gave a shy reply.

"My fee is one hundred rupees. But you have given me eighty, twenty rupees less".

He absentmindedly put his hand in the fold of his lungi. Maybe there was some amount of rupees hiding somewhere and he was to ferret it out.

His words got stuck in his throat. He was looking very pale and drawn.

Dr. Kar looked at his face and said emphatically, "You must pay me the rest of the amount next time, to cover the shortfall. Do you understand?"

"Yes sir".

After the patient had gone, Sambit asked, "Sir, have you studied the financial condition of the patient?"

Dr. Kar said punctuating his voice, "Of course, his dress shows that he belongs to a labour class".

"Yes, that dress indicates that he is poverty-ridden. Perhaps he has no money even to purchase a bus ticket. What is more he may not have a single pie to go to a restaurant or hotel to pay for his victuals, let alone a doctor's fees".

"Yes, I do agree. But the people below the poverty line are utterly selfish. If you engage them in your work, they charge high and work listlessly only to deceive the employer. Sometimes their work is not at all satisfactory. Most of them are shirkers and they idle away their time simply chewing tobacco. As the work is not up to the mark, the employer remains dissatisfied. Brawl starts if you point out their defaults or deliberate negligence. I don't have any sympathy for them".

Dr. Kar looked grave.

"Don't take my comment amiss, sir. I have no intention to refute your statement", Sambit reconciled.

Dr. Kar said in a subdued tone, "Mr. Sambit, I have committed a grievous mistake rather than a blunder in doing specialisation in skin. There are so many branches or options which are more lucrative and you can earn a fortune.

You see how much Dr. Mohanty, a medicine specialist, is earning per month. Take the case of Dr. Das, a gynaecologist, Dr. Sahu, a surgery specialist, Dr. Majhi, a paediatrician – they all have taken well-chosen lines because they are far-sighted. They have made a mint of money, bought luxurious air conditioned cars, built palatial buildings, swanky nursing homes and what not. I am a pauper in comparison to them.``

Dr. Kar's face became overshadowed with disappointment.

Then he stopped talking and took off a wad of notes from his pocket. He handed it to Sambit and said, "Please count them. Let me know how much I have earned this morning ".

After counting Sambit handed it back to him and said, "Six hundred in total".

"Only six hundred?" Dr. Kar recoiled.

"So what? You will earn another six hundred rupees in the evening. So it will amount to twelve hundred rupees per day. This way you will earn thirty six thousand per month excluding your government salary. It may wax provided your luck favours you".

Dr. Kar muttered something inaudible. Perhaps he was not fully convinced by his philosophy.

Sometimes being bored, he wanted to see a film. As the cinema hall was very close to Sambit's house he requested him to buy him a ticket. They would go together to watch the film. He usually preferred a second show, so that his patients would not be harassed during his absence.

His eldest son (he had two sons and no daughter) was very keen to set up a medicine store in the front part of their residential building. At first Dr. Kar was not willing as it was a very bothersome business. He wanted to see him in a good government job but his son disliked his idea of servitude. Dr. Kar could not frown upon the new-fangled ideas of the younger generation.

His wife unexpectedly became bed-ridden. It was diagnosed as lung cancer. Once Dr. Kar told Sambit regretfully that being a doctor he could not know his wife's ailment.

She knew that her days had been numbered. She urged her husband time and again to finalise the marriage negotiation of their eldest son. She had a yen to see her daughter-in-law before going to her last resting place. After the marriage when her daughter-in-law came to make obeisance at her feet, her shrivelled face became radiant and in that morbid state also, a seraphic smile flashed across her face.

After the death of his wife, Dr. Kar lost his interest in medical practice. He incessantly made him busy not to think over this dismal matter. In Spite of that he could not erase the memory of his wife from his mind. While talking with Sambit, he would recount the good qualities of his deceased wife.

"I am very glad that my daughter-in-law has acquired all the attributes of her mother-in-law. She is unassuming and looks after my comforts with utmost sincerity. She is not reluctant to do the household chores. It seems as if she is an embodiment of her mother-in-law."

When he was in a jocund mood, he would cut jokes with Sambit.

"Brother, what shall I do with my phallus? It is in a defunct condition. It is meant only for urination and nothing else".

After some months Sambit met him in his clinic. When

all the patients had left, Dr. Kar rose to his feet and came near Sambit. He clasped him to his bosom and began to cry like a child. Tears coursed down his cheeks. His face fell.

"What happened Dr. Kar? Are you in some trouble? I have never seen you so perturbed".

Dr. Kar wiped his tears and went back to his chair. He cleared his throat and said in a remorseful tone, "I am extremely sorry that I could not inform you regarding the marriage of my second son".

He lifted a bottle of water from the table and took a large gulp. Then he put it back on the table and continued, "Of course I have had no desire to negotiate with them. But my son stood firm in his decision. He made me understand that she is his college-mate and he knows her well. In arranged marriage, both spouses are alien to each other. He would have no iota of idea regarding the nature and character of his would-be wife. The bride's father is a retired professor of English and their social status is also high. So it is undoubtedly a homogeneous match. Previously I had set my face against this negotiation. I withdrew my objection and paved the way for marriage.

After some months a wrangle started between husband and wife on some petty matters. This domestic fracas got worse and worse and at last it culminated in divorce. My son is a field officer in a reputed medicine company. After this sorrowful incident, he fled to Surat. His wife is now staying with her parents. We are just twiddling our thumbs sitting at home. I am unable to understand why their marriage ended in such a disaster. Now my son regretted his impulsiveness of a precipitous marriage".

For a long period Sambit had no link with Dr. Kar. During chitchat with his acquainted persons they told him that Dr. Kar is now hankering for money. What made him so money-minded, Sambit began to think. He was also a man of wisdom, a knowledgeable person who knew that money cannot give one peace and happiness. Had he lost his mental balance? So he protested those persons who cast defamatory remarks at him.

"Who says that he is a money-centric person? What you have told me is a load of bullshit. I don't know who Dr. Kar is. I have an indissoluble bond of friendship with one Dr. Kar who is quite sober and gentle, not at all mercenary.

Sambit stayed more than a year in Bangalore.

The visions of bygone years with Dr. Kar floated before his inward eyes. He knew his mobile number and wanted to get in touch with him. The phone beeped on the other side.

"Hello ! Is Dr. Kar speaking?"

"Yes, may I know you?"

"I am Mr. Sambit, speaking from Bangalore. How are you sir?"

"Quite okay".

"What are you doing at present?"

"The same thing, swatting flies in my clinic".

"I see", Sambit laughed.

"What about your second son?"

Dr. Kar remained silent for a while. Then he replied, "He has gone, gone forever".

TEN

Dr. Hariprasad had been posted in the rank of a captain in the army. Before completion of the term, he applied for voluntary retirement. After seven year's stint in that service, he longed to come back to Odisha. He had no liking for the hackneyed life of the army, their dull daily routine. After much strenuous efforts, he managed to get his relief order and left his service place for good.

At the initial stage, a doctor having a bachelor degree in medical science is beset with many obstacles to expand the field of his treatment. As the specialists gain a stranglehold over the patients, a good number of people go to them. Dr. Prasad took it as a challenge. He put up a clinic at a walkable distance from his rented house and people started coming to him for their treatment.

Close to his house, there was a large swampy area which remained waterlogged throughout the year. It was not fit for habitation.

Dr. Prasad sold his ancestral property and sought a piece of homestead land to build a house there. Housing developments had mushroomed the town in recent years. So it was difficult to get a suitable land according to one's choice. At last he bought a few decimals of that boggy land at a low price.

Construction work continued unceasingly and within six months a building was completed. He shifted from his rented house and began to live on the ground floor. The upper storey was converted into a big nursing home. He executed his work with meticulous care and unflagging energy. He would call in specialists of different branches and they were well paid. The nursing home resonated with babel of people and their relations. Apart from the medicine ward, there was a surgery ward where major operations were done. Attached to that, there was a commodious room where abortion cases were dealt with. It was a good source of income and Dr. Prasad had no qualms for that.

Sambit got acquainted with him when he came with a patient suffering from consumption. He observed the patient and said, "I think he is not affected by tuberculosis. After x-ray it will be confirmed".

Then he asked, "Who is the doctor who has diagnosed it as pulmonary tuberculosis?"

"Dr. Agarwal, sir".

"How long have you taken medicine for that?"

"About a month, sir".

"Yes, I will see blood, sputum and x-ray report. Then I will arrive at the conclusion".

After two hours, Sambit handed him all the reports for his scrutiny.

Dr. Prasad stuck the x-ray film to the machine and observed it for some minutes.

He turned to the patient, "There is no lesion in your lungs (Koch's lesion). This disease is caused by tubercle bacillus known as Mycobacterium tuberculosis. So far as your blood is concerned, there is a very high percentage of eosinophils which causes constant cough and cold. You are not at all a consumptive. I am prescribing some medicines which will definitely cure you from all these symptoms."

Some days later in a formal conversation, Dr. Prasad said, "You are a homoeopath. Why don't you learn allopathy? I will guide you in that line. Intensive study will make you a successful practitioner.

"Yes Sir".

"Dr. Prasad's wife was hospitalised for a third delivery. A cabin was allotted to her. She felt severe pain due to inertia of the cervix. Though medicines and injections were given for delayed labour, there was no sign of dilatation. Dr. Prasad remained a silent onlooker. He repeatedly clenched his fist in despair. He kept looking at Sambit with utter hopelessness. Dr. Prasad was not in favour of C.S. (caesarean section). Sambit came to his rescue and said, "Sir, there are some medicines in homoeopathy which revive labour pain and further progress of labour. It is innocuous and has no adverse effect."

Without waiting for his consent, he rushed to the homoeopathy store and hurried back with the medicine. He dropped ten drops of cimicifuga tincture on her tongue and waited for its result. Within half an hour the false pain was gone and the real pain started. She was conducted to the labour room and there she delivered a male child.

Days passed. When the child was one and half years old, it suffered from dysentery. It was laid on a string cot without a bed sheet so that the stool would directly fall on the ground. It was a serious disease of bowels that made it bleed and pass much more waste than usual. Some advised Dr. Prasad that medicine does not work in this case, rather he should consult an exorcist. Dr. Jatania, a paediatrician of the government hospital, treated the case but to no avail. Eight days elapsed this way, but there was no improvement. At last Dr. Prasad decided to take his son to Cuttack.

One morning Sambit brought a Norilet (Norfloxacin) tablet and ground it to a powdered form with the help of a paperweight. He divided it into four parts and kept each part in a separate pouch.

"What are you doing Mr. Sambit?" asked Dr. Prasad. "I am preparing medicine. It is just like a homoeopathic dose and it will not do any harm to your child".

"No, no, don't give it, please. Norfloxacin should not be given to a child below two years. There is contraindication".

"Risk is mine. I have given it in absolutely minimal dose".

The child was cured miraculously by that medicine which nobody had expected.

The broiling April sun was quite unbearable. Flesh and blood could hardly stand its blazing heat. Grass scorched, wells and ponds got dry. People hung chicks of pampas-stalk to keep off the glaring rays of the sun.

In the afternoon when the rage of the sun scaled down a little, Sambit ambled to Dr. Prasad's house. He had sprawled on his bed covering his body with a cotton wrapper.

"What happened to Dr. Prasad?" Sambit asked his wife.

"He had been down with typhoid fever for the last ten days. Dr. Mohanty has given him medicines. Though the temperature came down, it did not totally subside. Low fever is still there".

"Do you know the medicines administered to him?"

"Yes. Paraoxon (chloramphenicol) and Febrex plus (paracetamol)

"Stop those medicines. I will give him homoeopathic medicines. Many a time Dr. Mohanty poked fun at me that homoeopathy cannot cure typhoid fever. Now he will see the miracles of homoeopathy drugs".

She remained silent.

Their conversation interrupted Dr. Prasad's sleep and he turned his side to Sambit and gave a feeble smile.

"I will be back". Sambit went out.

Dr. Prasad had extreme prostration, great muscular soreness and all his secretions were offensive – breath, stool, urine, sweat etc.

He dropped ten drops of Baptisia mother tincture on his tongue.

"Let him take another ten drops at his bed time. Two times a day, remember it".

The next morning Sambit found him seated on his bed. He was up and about and his face was no more pallid.

"I admit the efficacy of your medicines. Towards the last part of night fever completely left me", Dr. Prasad beamed at Sambit.

"I get maximum satisfaction in curing a patient. The doctor who craves money cannot get that pleasure".

After his recovery, his family left for their native village. Only Dr. Prasad and his cook remained at home.

In the morning, a woman and her daughter arrived at his clinic.

Dr. Prasad made a gesture to the girl to lie on a long bench stretching her legs. Then he made a ballottement test of her uterus and said, "The gestation period is already thirty six weeks. After a few days, your daughter will deliver a child".

"What? Some months back her menstrual period had gone. I don't know how she became parturient so soon".

Dr. Prasad was grave. He looked at the girl and asked, "Your daughter is unmarried. How did she conceive a child?"

"Sir, I am undone. I am looking for that culprit who has spoiled the life of my daughter. I coerced her, coaxed her to speak out the name of that brute but she remained reticent and clammed up in her shell".

"I don't want to probe too deeply into your internal affairs. If you want safe delivery, I would make an arrangement but you have to give me two thousand rupees for this induced abortion".

"Would you please come down a bit, sir?"

"No, no, it is a risky affair. Do you know abortions are illegal".

"All right, somehow I will arrange that amount. But see the safety of my child".

"There is nothing to be worried about. Every day I dispose of a number of cases like this."

Dr. Prasad had not fully recovered his health. He solicited Sambit to help him in management of this delivery.

The patient was laid on the table. She was given I.U.S.I.

(intrauterine saline infusion) to quicken the delivery. Dr. Prasad went to his bedroom to take a rest.

There was a terrible heat inside the room though two ceiling fans were moving rapidly. Sambit felt himself suffocated. To keep a watch over her daughter, the woman was seated crouching in one corner of the room. She had made her hair-do neatly and put kohl round her eyes. Her body construction was enticing and she looked more beautiful in the shining light of the room.

Sambit slipped rubber gloves on his hands, dipped his right middle finger in Savlon lotion and pushed it in her genitals. The girl jerked a little in her subconscious state. He did it in brief intervals for the dilatation of the cervix. He came back to sit on a bench and began to read a book. The woman looked at him with a sly-leer.

She stood up and stepped closer. Giving her body a flirtatious sway, she implored, "Please make a room for me. Let me sit here. There in that poorly lit corner, I feel smothering heat. This place is nearest to the fans. Well sir, has my daughter divulged the name of the offender?"

"Yes, after much persuasion, she blurted the secret out that she is involved in rumpy-pumpy with her tuition master. She is carrying his child. Did you not know about her fornication?"

"Sir, my daughter is studying in class ten. I had to keep a tuition master to guide her. Every day I feed him up on milk and eggs. See, how that ungrateful paid me for my kindness in return".

There was no disturbing sound in the room save a whirr of the fans. The still of the night instilled a sensuous warmth in her body. She moved closer to Sambit and put her hand on his thigh. He was unresponsive. She took it as his silent consent. She went a step further. She began to squeeze his thighs to drive him into a seductive pleasure. Her body squirmed and she threw a lustful look at him. Sambit's heart began to beat faster. She snuggled closer to be conflated with him. Her body odour was provocative, sex stimulating. When her hand began to crawl towards his groin, he pushed her away indignantly and quickly sprang to his feet.

"You sleep on this bench, I am just coming".

He slammed the door shut and went straight to Dr. Prasad.

He banged the door.

"I am Sambit, sir".

Dr. Prasad had not a wink of sleep. He was just tossing about on his bed. The room was unbearably hot. He got up.

"Coming", Dr. Prasad responded.

He pushed open the door to let him in.

"Sir, I faced a very embarrassing situation there. She must be a fallen woman".

"What happened?" Dr. Prasad stared at his face with bulging eyes.

"The woman was sitting in the corner of that room gawking at me. She came to me with a pretence and tried to seduce me. I ignored her sex appeal and bolted out of the room".

Dr. Prasad burst into laughter.

"Why did you not pay attention to her? She was expectant to get something from you but you denied her that pleasure. It is quite inhuman".

"I don't like a woman of easy virtue".

"Have you not heard the story of Arjuna and Urbashi in our great epic the Mahabharata? Lend me your ear to a very engaging story."

Once Arjuna killed a powerful demon who was persistently pestering king Indra. He was highly praised for this act of valour. As a mark of gratitude Indra invited him to heaven, his kingdom. He ordered all the apsaras (celestial nymphs) to be present in the dancing hall and to give a dance recital for his pleasure. Urbashi was a celebrated danseuse of

Indra's court. Arjuna was amazed at her breathtaking display of talents in dancing. He kept gazing at her with unblinking eyes. But Indra misconstrued him. He thought that Arjuna was greatly enamoured of Urvashi. So at night he sent her to his room for his gratification.

Adorning herself with her best finery, Urbashi went to his room and knocked on the door.

Arjuna opened it and stood gaping at her. Her sudden visit in the dead of the night was an enigma to him.

He greeted her with salutation and said, "Mother, please come in. Be seated. I am always at your service".

Urbashi was completely dumbfounded.

She said, "Arjuna! I have not come here to have a chat with you but to appease your sexual hunger. Don't you want to enjoy me? You have been attracted by my enchanting beauty while I was dancing in the hall. Were not your eyes feasting on me? Don't shy away when I am ready to offer you my youthful body for your physical gratification".

"Mother, you have misunderstood me. I was just stupefied with your perpetual beauty which has not been waned by the ravages of time. I am not a sex maniac. I had no amorous thoughts in my mind while I watched your dance."

"But Arjuna my body is burning with wild passions. It has reached feverish heat. You denied my love for what my body yearns for. My ardour has not yet left me. With dejection, I have to go back".

"I am helpless, mother. Please forgive your guilty son".

"Guilty or not guilty – I must curse you as you have spurned my love", she hissed in a towering rage.

"Be an impotent for one year".

With a stamp of her foot, she stormed out of the room.

Dr. Prasad ended his story and asked, "Do you understand its purport?"

"Any proffered love should not be rejected", he made a funny comment.

Dr. Prasad came in contact with a savant who had good command over the Bhagavad Gita and Ramacharita Manasa. Everyday he would come to his clinic and read out a chapter or two and then he would elaborately elucidate its gist. Dr. Prasad was completely entranced by the exegesis of the Bhagavad Gita. It was like a running commentary. As he was immersed in listening to him, his medical practice was greatly hampered. He organised a group of religious persons who would congregate in the evening, intone prayer in sonorous notes and discuss the essence of religious scriptures. Sometimes they would sit in the temple of Lord Shiva, sometimes by the riverside to exchange their views after mass prayer. Dr. Prasad was the focal point around which they all revolved.

Then came a soothsayer. Dr. Prasad was attracted by the power of his augury.

He would go on fast and lie in the temple of Lord Shiva, ask the name and zodiac of the person and foretell his future. People became overwhelmed by his prognostication.

Once accompanied by an official of the sales tax department Dr. Prasad and Sambit paid him a visit.

When the turn of the officer came, he handed him an one rupee coin and holy basil leaves. The foreteller smelt them and asked his name and zodiac.

Then his loud voice was heard.

"You are suffering from chronic knee joint pain. You had been to a distant place for its treatment. No chance of recovery", he croaked.

"A few days ago your jeep somersaulted and you fell in a ditch. Henceforth don't go in any vehicle".

He threw his legs in the air and then spread them on the floor.

The prediction being over, Dr. Prasad asked him, "What is your sickness? Where have you been?"

After hearing his disappointing future, the officer looked

quite washed out. He said in an indistinct voice, "Sir, I had been to Velore. There they diagnosed it as bone cancer".

The soothsayer had earned fame in prophecy. Dr. Prasad was a visionary and he made a pact with him. If they charge at least fifty rupees to each visitor, they would accumulate a big sum. It began to take a concrete shape. Money showered on them like rain drops. With that money the soothsayer built a temple in his native village.

Dr. Prasad was distracted from his real path. Some wellwishers advised him not to be deluded by these pseudo-moralists.

As he was busy with religious work, the number of patients tapered off.

His wife warned him, "You are a doctor, Give priority to your profession first". But Dr. Prasad brushed her advice aside.

Dr. Prasad's fortune was at a low ebb. He disliked the inattentiveness of his son in studies. One day he went berserk and beat him ruthlessly. His wife tore him away from his grip.

"Are you a hard task-master? Don't apply your Spartan method to make him a Pandit overnight. What has been ordained in his fate, nobody can change it", she blustered.

The next morning, Dr. Prasad sneaked away to some unknown place.

His wife became despondent. A trace of bitterness crept into her voice.

"O what a desperado he is! He decamped without any dress. Last night he had worn only a trouser and a dirty banian. What the hell he has done", she wailed, slapping her forehead.

Sambit with a body of sympathisers scoured about all the conceivable places. But their combing operation yielded no result.

After five days Dr. Prasad reappeared. As his practice began to ebb, he tried his hand in other lines. He became a field officer of an Ayurvedic company and boosted it to a high level.

He said to Sambit, "My Ayurvedic Company is a promising one. I travelled to Singapore and Thailand by company's grace. Be an agent, you too will make big bucks".

"No sir, I have no such daydreams. I am practising homoeopathy to keep my body and soul together and never run after a trivial thing like money".

After some months Dr. Prasad shut down his clinic and worked in the World Health Organization.

ELEVEN

Sambit became a flourishing practitioner. Some nit-picker lobbed a satirical remark:

'He who has no way out

Practises homoeopathy without doubt'.

There are a number of allopaths who underestimate homoeopathy. To palliate a disease is not at all a credit of a doctor. To cure a patient is the basic principle of medical science which means total annihilation of the disease. Homoeopathy brings a person from disease to an easeful state. That is why it has become so much popular in the field of treatment.

Three decades ago Sambit had set up a clinic near Jagadhatri talkies which was half kilometre from the centre of the town. The place was not so overcrowded in those days. There were a few grocery and stationery shops, two to three tea-stalls, a cycle repairing shop, a temple of deity surrounded by wild bush and creepers and some residential houses littered here and there. A narrow gauge railway line passed through that place which was in a non-functioning condition. Over a long period people demanded to convert it to a broad gauge but the authority gave a cold shoulder to their petition. The place was calm and quiet as no large number of bus, truck and other vehicles travelled along that route. Only a pack of mangy dogs broke its silence when they got into a frenzy and fought with each other for leftover food thrown by the side of the road. But at 5 O' clock the place would wear a different appearance. It was time for the movie's show. Cinemagoers crowded the place, people parked-up their vehicles beside the cinema hall, peanut sellers and mixture vendors plied their business and the place became resonant with the babel of people.

His clinic was a hub of noisy conversation. Some retired persons would sit there and talk endlessly ranging from personal to political subjects until Sambit closed the door and left for home. The fruit seller Purusottam, the tea-stall holder Bairagi, Ghasi, the vendor of savouries and some rickshaw-pullers would also invariably visit his clinic for some medicines.

Seeing them Sambit would be perked up as he treated them as his own.

"Would you like a cup of tea, sir? Bairagi would say in a supplicating manner. He was very grateful. Once when he was crossing the road after supplying tea to the nearby shopkeepers, an angry bull gored his thigh with one sweep of its horn and he fell headlong on the road.

Sambit treated him free of charge.

One evening Purusottam came with his wife carrying a child in his arms.

"What happened to your child, Purusottam?"

"Sir, I am coming straight from the Headquarter hospital. My son was suffering from diarrhoea. After seven days the doctor told me that it was a hopeless case. Where shall I go sir? My wife advised me to come to you for its treatment", he began to whine.

"Well, tell me the signs and symptoms of the child".

"Watery diarrhoea, green frothy stool with jelly-like mucus, gurgling sound at the time of evacuation. If it is kept in a diaper, after sometime it turns grass green". "All right, you take these medicines and after two days report me as to the condition of the child".

"Sir".

Wheat was not available in his ward. Sambit borrowed a ration card from a local gentleman and bought it from the control shop.

After closing the door of his clinic, he approached a known rickshaw-puller to carry him home with his wheat bag.

He was a regular visitor of his clinic. Sambit was sympathetic to him for his wretched condition. But he charged him high. So he had to go to another rickshaw-puller.

Two days later when Sambit opened his clinic, he found him rolling on the verandah. Sitting by his side, his wife was caressing his stomach.

The woman stood up and said with folded hands, "Sir, last night my husband drank a lot of hooch with chicken roast. After some hours he felt a terrible stomach pain and vomited everything".

"Did you know the day before yesterday your husband charged me high though I offered him medicines without taking a single pie. I was prepared to pay him more than what other rickshaw-pullers usually charge. But he pulled a long face to accept that amount.

"Sir, he is very ungrateful".

Then turning to her husband she chastised him.

"Please forgive him. He is illiterate and does not know how to behave with others". The woman was ashamed of her husband's ingratitude.

"Gulp down this medicine. It will gradually alleviate your pain".

After the pain was lessened to a considerable extent, he rose up from the bench.

"Sir, I feel no pain. I am completely relieved. Please forgive this piss-poor rickshaw-puller".

He made a deep obeisance and departed. Sambit always treated minor cases. If somebody suffered from serious disease, he would advise him to go to the specialists.

"I will make a dreadful mistake if I keep such a patient under my treatment", he was stunningly candid with the patients.

Sufferers of sexual debility remained intentionally to the last. They felt awkward to make their secrecy public. They would tell him about their problems in whispers. Sambit will bring out a notebook from the drawer and jot down their symptoms and the troubles they were suffering from.

Sundays are the days of relaxation. The number of patients is less than usual as people get busy with other work on these days.

Sambit was flipping through a magazine sitting in his clinic.

A car pulled up in front of his clinic. A young man, his wife and an old lady stepped off the car.

After they had taken their seats, the young man introduced himself, "Sir, I am an employee of State Bank of India, Betnoti. We have come disappointed by a good number of doctors. All threw cold water on our hopes".

The old lady chimed in, "The fact is that though my son and daughter-in-law are in good health, they have no issue after five years of marriage. I am waiting for another year. If there is no issue, I will seek another girl for my son".

Then pointing to the daughter-in-law she said, "This girl is unpropitious. She is like a barren tree. What is its utility if it does not bear any fruit". She launched into a tirade against her daughter-in-law.

Sambit listened to her incrimination silently. The young man handed him a roll of prescription paper and pathological reports for his scrutiny.

Sambit perused the reports and looked up at them.

"One very important thing has been omitted. No doctor has advised you in this respect. A test of your semen is to be done. I have to count the number of spermatozoa in your seminal fluid".

He handed the young man a small phial and told him what was to be done.

He dropped a few drops of the fluid on a glass slide and

spread the smear. Then he looked at the slide through the microscope.

He beckoned the youngman to his side and let him look at his sample.

"Observe it minutely. There is not a single spermatozoon in your seminal fluid. What would you conclude from that? You are an educated man. You can understand it easily. It is known as 'azoospermia' which means there is no sperm in your semen. In confirmed azoospermia wife's further investigations are suspended. In case of 'Oligozoospermia' sperm count is less than ten million per m.l. with or without poor sperm motility."

Then he turned to the old lady and said, "Sister, you have been abusing your daughter-in-law for no valid ground. She is quite innocent' She has undergone a lot of hardships, mental agony and harsh criticism for which she is not at all responsible".

The daughter-in-law was sitting immobile on a chair, looking crestfallen. When she heard the defect of her husband, she looked up at the doctor with a flash of surprise in her eyes.

Sambit turned to the old lady and said, "Question of issue does not arise in this case. There is something wrong with your son. It is incurable. Of course there are some allopaths who give specific injections on an experimental basis. It has not yet yielded fruitful results so far".

The old lady bent down her head and began to weep.

One October evening Dr. Prasad invited Sambit to a dinner party. He would throw a party every Sunday where a few important persons would gather and wear on time echoing the dining room with their boisterous conversation. Dr. Prasad was very liberal in serving them costly alcoholic beverages.

Sambit and his friend Mr. Shymal were in a hurry to reach there on time. The sky was sullen and the far-flung stars were overcast with clouds. The threatening thunder clouds were swept away to the south by a strong gale and there was no chance of heavy downpour. They elbowed their way through the traffic-jam. An emergency van went past them wailing and then it receded to a distance.

When they turned to the right side, a cat crossed the road and hid behind a drapery store.

Mr. Shyamal halted there. He held the hand of Sambit and stepped back a few feet.

"What is the matter Mr. Shyamal?" asked Sambit.

"Did you not notice that black cat which crossed under our very nose?"

"Yes, but what is that to us? You cry-baby, why do you get scared at the sight of a harmless creature?"

"Do you know that it is an ill-omen?"

"No, why?"

"Nothing, but you must retrace a few steps if you see a black cat crossing the road".

"I don't give a shit what you think. It is all superstitions, tommy-rot. I throw these absurd ideas overboard."

Mr. Shyamal did not oppose him. He related his own harrowing experiences.

"My daughter had been afflicted round the clock by watery coryza and persistent fever.

For her prolonged sickness, I sought the help of a specialist. After the x-ray and blood test were done, the doctor told me to see him in the evening for the report. While heading for his clinic and going past the temple of Lord Jagannath, a black cat sprinted across the road. It sent a shudder through my body. I only mumbled God's name while going along the road. The doctor gave me the report and warned me that my daughter had been suffering from a fatal disease".

Then Mr. Shyamal swerved to the side of the footpath and gripped Sambit's hand as if he had been scared of some inexplicable reason.

He took a long breath and said, "I can prophesy the result of your dreams also. But that entirely depends on the time, whether you saw it in the first part, second part or last part of the night. Some dreams augur well, some very scary results.

Once I had a dreadful dream in the last part of the night. I got up from my bed at the approach of the daybreak. My heart was palpitating from what I saw in my dream a few minutes before.

I had been to a nearby tank. There I plunged into the water. While flailing about in the tank, my hands and legs became suddenly paralysed. I drowned in the water and died a hapless death there.

A few minutes later my elder brother informed me over the phone that my nephew, a tender child of one and half years, died of measles that morning."

Mr. Shymal continued, "Take a glaring example of a bad dream.

Once I was wandering aimlessly in the forest. A tusker was provoked at my sight. I being a trespasser of his domain, he came waddling to attack me. Before I retreated to a safe distance, he caught me with his trunk and flung me on a rugged ground. Then he trumpeted and disappeared into the forest.

I awoke from my sleep. My whole body had been soaked with sweat. On that very day, one of my close relatives died of a heart attack".

His attention wandered for a moment and he lost the thread of his narrative. His body shook a little stricken by the fear of the unknown. Then he returned to the subject.

"I can cite a number of examples. You may think these are all my fabrications, my baseless fantasies. No. There must be a premonition. Some occurs lately, some in the distant future. But our sense- perception is so stunted, so gross that we are unable to comprehend that uncanny indication, whereas lower animals and birds are capable of foreboding that oncoming disaster.

God has given us a limited power of vision. We cannot go beyond that. What seems abstruse or inscrutable to us, it is crystal-clear to the rishis and sannyasis of yore. The omniscient has bestowed on them this foresight. But we laymen are completely devoid of that extraordinary power".

By the time they reached Dr. Prasad's house, all the guests were waiting expectantly for their arrival. The food was served on the table. The bearer brought six glasses of whisky and put ice-cubes in them. While chewing the chicken roast, they began to sip liquor gingerly.

Mr. Sahani was one of the distinguished guests who had a very corpulent body. He was the superintendent of the Excise department. He alone quaffed half bottle whisky and belched loudly.

Sambit was sitting in one corner of the table. Although the bearer had put a glass of whisky before him, he did not touch it. He was a teetotaller.

Mr. Sahani signalled something to Dr. Prasad with his eyes. Both rose from their seats and went near Sambit.

"Is chicken roast delicious, Mr. Sambit?"

Dr. Prasad asked him with feigned concern.

"Yes Sir, but it is highly spiced".

Mr. Sahani was standing behind his chair. "O God! You have not yet touched the glass".

Mr. Sahani grimaced, "Pooh, can't you finish it in a draught?"

Dr. Prasad lifted the glass from the table, shook it a little and stared at the half-melted ice-cubes.

Mr. Sahani suddenly caught both hands of Sambit with all his strength and Dr. Prasad held up the glass before his mouth.

"Now my good boy! Open your mouth. Let me pour this elixir in your mouth cavity".

"No sir, please excuse me. I never touch any alcoholic beverage. I am miles away from that".

But Dr. Prasad was unyielding. He poured the whole content of the glass in his mouth, though a little amount spilled and flowed down his chest.

Sambit peeled off his wet shirt and banian and put them on his shoulder.

Half an hour later, he laughed loudly without any reason. He held his crumpled shirt and banian in his hand and shuffled across the room staring at Dr. Prasad. He looked at Sambit with an ambiguous smile.

"Sir, my head is reeling, I must fall down".

Sambit sat down on the floor for a moment to gather his strength.

"Suria, where are you? Take Mr. Sambit back home on your bike".

"Yes sir".

When Sambit got home, his wife had already spread his bed on the verandah.

He washed his hands and feet, changed his dress and lay down on his bed.

The liquor in his stomach made him retch. He rushed to the backyard and puked all near a guava tree.

The next morning Mr. Shyamal got ready to go on a trip to Calcutta.

Before Durga Puja, he would go to bring sarees and dresses for all the members of his family. He boarded a bus plying between Baripada and Calcutta. He found a comfortable seat near the dash-board. Before the bus reached Phencoghat, an Andhra truck was coming at full tilt from the opposite direction. The tipsy driver lost his control to save a cow lying on the road. In the blink of an eye, the bus and truck crashed with each other. Mr. Shyamal and the driver were sandwiched in a head-on collision.

■

TWELVE

The stadium field was decorated with flowers and festoons to welcome Swami Chinmayananda Saraswati. He was initiated into the spiritual path by Shivananda Saraswati, his guru. Before his death he nominated him as his successor.

A multitude of devotees congregated there to have a darshan of guru who will visit their place after a long time. It was a rare occasion. A group of volunteers organised this religious conference decentralising the duty to different persons. Bamboo barricades were erected providing seats to ladies and gents separately. White cushions were laid on the dais for the esteemed guests. The volunteers tidied up the stage before their arrival. The front space was given importance to keep it uncluttered.

All were waiting with bated breath. A convoy of cars came to a halt near the reception gate. The lady volunteers with a garland of flowers stood there to receive the guests. A party of drummers were also with them.

Swami Chinmayananda alighted from his car with a blissful smile followed by others. Mr. Prasanna, the chairman of the reception committee, and other members garlanded them. The people, with salutation, accorded them a grand welcome. The ladies blew the conch-shells and the place was resounded with their ululation.

The drummers began to beat their drums with full alacrity and the symbolists concussed their discs keeping tune with them. Then the guests were led to the stage. The people stepped aside with reverence to give them a passage. They were very eager to have a close view of the guru. Swami Chinmayananda lifted his hand in a gesture of blessing while he went past them.

After kindling of lights, the convenor introduced the guests seated on the dais. The President presiding over the conference stood up. He started a very engrossing speech.

My dear brothers and sisters!

You have all congregated here although you have your own business schedule.

You all are eager to listen to some educative and edifying from his mouth which will lead you to the right path. Our revered His Holiness Swami Chinmayanandajee has taken pains to come here from a long distance. He will definitely enlighten us as the people of this modern age are groping in the darkness of nescience.

The aim of his august presence is to guide and teach us how to subdue the beasts of ignorance roaming in jungles of the human mind.

In the Bhagavad Gita Lord Krishna says, "O Arjuna ! as a flame is covered by smoke, mirror by dart and embryo by the amnion, so is knowledge covered by desire.

Knowledge stands covered by this eternal of the wise, known as desire, which is insatiable like fire.

The senses, the mind and the intellect are declared to be its seat, screening the light of Truth through these, it (desire) deludes the embodied soul.

Therefore Arjuna, you must control your senses and kill this evil thing which obstructs jnana (knowledge of the absolute or Nirguna Brahma) and Vignana (knowledge of Sakara Brahma or manifest Divinity).

The senses are said to be greater than the body but greater than the senses is the mind. Greater than the mind is intellect and what is greater than the intellect is He (the self).

Thus Arjuna, knowing that which is higher than the intellect and subduing the mind by reason, kills the enemy in the form of desire that is hard to overcome" (translated by Jayadayal Goyandka)."

Swami Chinmayananda will open our eyes more widely in this respect. Let noble thoughts come to us from every side". Then the President took his seat.

Before Swami Chinmayananda's feet trod this town, Sambit was extremely busy in accommodating a large number of devotees in the high school building. The rooms and verandah were all occupied by them and they ate cooking their food by make-shift hearths.

He and other volunteers stayed in the guest rooms of the cooperative bank to keep a watchful eye on their comforts.

Meeting with Prof. Hrudananda was fortuitous. He did not hope that he would bump into his teacher after a long lapse of time. He came from Cuttack being invited by the committee to join this religious conference. He was a professor in Philosophy when Sambit was studying in college.

"Let us sit in my room. This has been allotted to me as a member of the reception committee".

"Yes sir".

Prof. Hrudananda pulled out a plate and dish from a cupboard and put them on the floor.

"I am very fond of 'ghugni' which I usually eat for breakfast".

Then he poured it on puffed rice and mixed it up.

"Sambit, come and join me".

"No sir, I have had breakfast half an hour before, no room in my stomach".

"No, no, you wash your hands and come to me. I won't eat alone. It would be more tasteful if we eat together".

Sambit transferred a palmful of puffed rice and began to eat.

"Why are you eating this way?" Prof. Hrudananda asked with slight annoyance.

"This is enough, I won't eat more than this".

Prof. Hrudananda fell into silence. Remoteness came into his gaze, summoning visions of bygone years.

"Did you remember the days when we both raised money from charity shows for the 'Philosophic meet' of M.P.C. College?"

"Yes sir, that is unforgettable."

"Here also you slogged day and night for accommodation of devotees. It is too tiresome and tedious. Organization of a conference is not so easy".

"Sir, I am doing my duty and I get pleasure in conducting religious work. It gives me an impetus to go ahead. Except the volunteers, there is no one to look after the devotees. If they feel any discomfort here, it would be a disgrace to our town. They would go back with a bad impression."

"Today is the last day of the conference. Swami Chinmayananda is occupied with lots of important work. He must go back without delay".

"Yes sir".

That afternoon Swami Chinmayananda gave a synopsis of Hindu religion. How it has not lost its glory and rich heritage after so many foreign invasions. No religion in this world has fostered such liberal attitude as Hinduism. It is its uniqueness which has installed it on a high pedestal. It never shows its supremacy nor detestation to other religions.

In the epilogue of his speech, suddenly light went out and there were cat calls made by some rogues in the audience. A few minutes later the light came back and he ended his speech. Then thanksgiving followed. All the guests moved out of the stage after making obeisance at his feet.

Swami Chinmayananda made his way cutting through the crowd escorted by the volunteers.

"Get away, get away," they shouted at the crowd. But the people got more and more frenzied to touch his hallowed feet. Sambit did not want to jostle others. He stood behind them. Some rogues started pushing them mercilessly to make a passage as if they shooed a pack of dogs to go away. In that pell-mell he tried to claw a foothold on the ground but a ruffian gave him a sudden thrust so forcefully that he lost his balance and was hurt by the sharp edge of a bamboo pole. The skin of his arm was badly lacerated and blood started oozing out the wound. Sambit reached for his handkerchief and bandaged it to staunch the flow of blood. He stood rooted helplessly looking at the passing crowd and that was the reward of a volunteer for his hard work. He was given at last the jolt of his life.

THIRTEEN

Mitrabhanu was the son of a divisional superintendent of railway department at Khurda. Mr. Akhilesh managed to get through I.R.S. (Indian Railway Service) and was appointed in a high post. It was the place of his second posting, Agra being his first. He had three sons. The eldest of them was mediocre and he got an appointment in a clerical post. The third one was Manasranjan who had greater inclination to music than any other profession and he learnt it right from his childhood days. The second son Mitrabhanu was assiduous who had been invariably criticised by his friends as bookworm. His early schooling began at the service place of his father. As a tender boy of seven years, he had a great liking to see the train steaming on the railway platform and after resting a little, it departed puffing a column of smoke through its chimneys to some unknown destination. Day and night the people would get in and get out of the compartment with their belongings and yell to their children over the din of the alighting and departing people making them aware not to be lost in that rush. Some seemed to be lackadaisical to go to other platforms by overbridge and they would cross the railway lines looking this side and that with much caution.

The T.T.Cs were seen moving here and there changing from train to train to scrutinise the tickets of the passengers. These scampering glimpses of the railway station would always give him immense pleasure and he would enjoy the ceaseless activities of the station and its peripheries with boyish enthusiasm.

The whistling and panting of engines, the banging of buffers, workers doggedly engaged in coupling, all gave the station an appearance of constant activities.

There was a small colony of shopkeepers around the station to supply travellers with food, biscuits, tea, cigarettes, all doing their brisk business. They knew Mitrabhanu and his father pretty well. Mr. Akhilesh was always held in awe by the shopkeepers and hawkers.

"Little master, please come to my shop", then the shopkeeper handed him a chocolate when he went past his shop.

Some would offer him biscuits and other edible things.

The shopkeeper would uncork the bottle to take out a toffee while Mitrabhanu ran his fingers through his hair standing in front of the shop. He would dart his eyes all around to avoid the notice of the railway employees. He would feel like an excited fly on a spider's web.

He would snatch the toffee and vanish behind the rows of shops. He knew that his father would not like this free offer. Slight mistake would not be overlooked by his parents. One day he was beaten by his mother as he skived off school to watch a football match. If he shirks his studies, he would be taken to task.

When Mitrabhanu was fifteen years old, his favourite hobby was reading story books. He would read them by keeping his textbooks over them to avoid the prying eyes of his parents.

Every day a mobile book stall-keeper would sit at one corner of the platform with a large tin trunk, full of books. While going past him, he would hunch over the box, thumb through a few books and at last holding a book in his hand he would ask, "Would you lend me this book for some days?"

"Why not, sir. I have brought a load of books only for your pleasure. But usually I lend a book only for a week, not longer than that. You have to give two annas for each book".

Then he spread some books on the floor and said, "Here is a chain of books which cater to all tastes like Alice in Wonderland, Sindbad the Sailor, The Adventures of Robin Hood, Gulliver's Travels, Treasure Island, Robinson Crusoe, Don Quixote and some other amusing books. You may skim off any one of them which you like best. You cannot walk out as there is a wide range of books for your entertainment".

He threw one of them at his hand and said, "This is not at all trashy. Read this one first. Then take other books as you fancy. This is my humble suggestion".

"Okay. Here are your two annas".

Mitrabhanu put the coin near his box and turned back.

"You will get worth your price, sir. Come a week after and tell me how you enjoyed that book"- he said grinning.

Mitrabhanu's grandparents were living in their ancestral house at Baripada. He was studying in college then and every summer vacation he would visit his parental house as he liked this place and its environment very much. Just adjacent to their boundary wall, there lived Sambit's uncle (maternal). He was doing his graduation in M.P.C. College and whenever he would get leisure, he would slip away to his uncle's house. Sitting on a cement bench Sambit and Mitrabhanu would get completely engrossed in discussion on various aspects of literature. He was a great devotee of literature and an appreciative listener too.

When Sambit read out a poem, he would listen to him with rapt attention.

"Sambitda, it is an excellent poem. It is so spontaneous and expressive that I remained spellbound. The import of your poem is very heart-touching. The words that you have used in your poem have a metaphorical as well as a literal meaning. I would rather advise you to compose an anthology of poetry. Try to be a poet of high calibre. I shall be very much glad if you become a celebrated writer in future. A poem having no pith will be considered as rubbish and it carries no message to society".

During his stopover at Baripada, they would sit on the same bench and absorb in a long discussion. He would always inspire Sambit to start his poetic life on a higher rung of literary ladder.

Time sped fast. Mitrabhanu remained busy concentrating on his career. He came out with remarkable success in I.P.S. exam and became a high ranking police officer. From the beginning he was deeply religious and after retirement he became a spiritual leader. He toured all over India expounding the essence of Hindu religion. He became famous at home and abroad. He was highly praised in the four corners of the earth.

Sambit had no link with him for donkey's years. He learned that Mitrabhanu was coming to Baripada to preside over the inaugural ceremony of an industrial exhibition. He cycled to that place.

After the meeting was over, Mitrabhanu descended from the stage. It was difficult to meet him breaking through the cordon set up by his disciples.

He was impeded by one of them. He rushed to him and waved his hands in a gesture of denial, "Where are you going? What's your business to meet him?"

It ruffled his feathers. He replied in irritation, "You can't understand my relationship with him. How could you venture to obstruct my way?"

The disciple goggled at his face in bewilderment. Then he moved aside to give him a passage.

"Stay there Mitrabhanu. Let me go near you". He lifted his feet to climb down the stairs. He remained motionless there.

Sambit looked at his deadpan face and said, "I have come to offer you my latest novel. Go through it and let me know your appreciation. Four decades ago, you had inspired me a lot and now you will be very glad to see that it came to fruition."

He took the book in his hand. Throwing a fleeting glance at the get up of the book he said, "Yes, Mr. Sambit. I must go through your book".

Then he walked straight not caring to look at Sambit who was eagerly waiting to have a little talk with him. Perhaps he had totally forgotten his old Sambitda or he might have closed the chapter of their relationship. He was inaccessible and unapproachable. A humble person like Sambit could not reach him.

FOURTEEN

Similipal biosphere is situated at the centre of Mayurbhanj district in Odisha. The biosphere covers a major part of the Eastern Ghat mountain range.

The forest wealth includes various timber, honey, resin, Sabai grass, seasonal fruits, mushrooms etc.

The government of India declared Similipal as the eighth biosphere reserve of India.

The forest wealth of Similipal is abundant. The trees like sal, asan, piasal, dhaw, gambhari, kasi, jamun are found in plenty in the forest. It is a permanent source of natural wealth.

For gradual depletion of forest wealth a meeting was convened by INTACH to save Similipal.

That day the municipality hall, Baripada, was full to its capacity.

Mr. Reddy, Mr. Nair, Mr. Acharya,Dr. Mishra, Dr. Mohanty, all were present in the hall.

Dr. Mishra was the convenor. Dr. Mohanty was the last speaker.

He gave a very emotional speech appealing to the heart of the listeners. He was greatly pained due to rampant destruction of the forest as the conservation of forest is of crucial importance.

Sambit was seated in the front row of the audience. He became speechless. He could not believe what he was hearing.

Dr. Mohanty had bought a homestead land at Bhubaneswar. While the construction work was going on, he managed to pick up a large number of wood planks from the wood-cutters by hole and corner ways.

Two carpenters were busy day and night making doors and windows and other furniture. The forest officials had been bribed and he sent them by truck at dead of the night to Bhubaneswar. His skullduggery was unknown to others. Sambit was amazed at his pretentious behaviour as he shed crocodile tears before the public.

That afternoon, a jeep fitted with a loud speaker announced to attend the settlement camp.

It rained intermittently all night. In the morning it turned to heavy downpour. It sent the people scurrying back into their homes.

By forenoon the clouds rolled away to the south and rain cleared the atmosphere.

Sambit had received an official letter from the settlement camp to attend at the appointed time.

On the other side of the railway lines, close to a high school, a settlement camp had been set up to hear the petition of landowners and other anomalies regarding disputed land.

Riding on his bicycle when he arrived at the camp, he saw his elder brother sitting on his haunches drawing lines on the ground. He seemed perplexed by some knotty problems. Seeing him he turned his face to the other side and did not talk with him. An hour later, they were summoned by the liveried orderly of the officer.

His elder brother Gajendra stood in front of the officer for rejoinder.

"What's your name?" asked the officer.

"Gajendra, sir".

"You don't have a surname?"

"Yes, Gajendra Chauhan".

"Who is Mukunda? What is your relation with him?"

"He is my uncle" (Paternal)

"All right. Both your uncle and aunt are dead now. They

have no descendants. You have appealed for the registration of their landed property in your name. There are other brothers who may stake their claim to this property. Has your uncle done a will in your name or any written document in your favour to inherit his property?"

"No Sir".

"Then how did you put forth such a superficial claim without any authentic documents. Is there any evidence or witness to backup your claim?" There was an authority in his tone.

"I had been looking after them in their last days".

Gajendra's voice began to falter. He looked at the face of the officer sheepishly.

The settlement officer frowned at him disapprovingly.

"Here I am giving you a piece of land on the other side of the railway lines. You enclose that land by a fence tomorrow morning. You fraud! You hoaxer! Get out of this place. I won't see your ugly face again".

Then he turned to the other brothers and asked their identity.

"You are all claimants of this property. Write down your names in this register".

On the way his elder brother was waiting for him. He was nervous and visibly shaken. He was completely demoralised for his act of absurd demand. His plan to capture the property went awry.

Sambit consoled him. "You see, I am not eager for any landed property. I shall never be a claimant of this trivial thing. It may hold any value to you but it is nugatory to me."

Gajendra reached home tramping through the mud. He washed his feet and waved a palm-leaf fan to dry up his sweating body. His wife served him lunch. He had a quick bite, drank a large gulp of water and stood up.

"Why did you leave your food?" his wife asked.

"I have no appetite today".

To avoid her look, he made an exit.

The offensive words of the officer grated his nerve. Anger surged up in his mind.

His two sons were a hopeless mess. The elder one was eccentric and the younger was a good-for-nothing layabout.

They were dandy. Cricket was a passion with the younger son Dicky and he would play with the neighbouring boys till sunset being inattentive to his studies. His father was displeased with that. Dicky turned a deaf ear to his advice. So his father told him that he would wash his hands off him since he acted against his aspiration.

The elder son Ricky was extravagant. Though his father used to give him two hundred rupees a week as his pocket money, he always forced him to give more. If his father denied him, he would fly into a rage and slap him hard.

Gajendra's wife was egoistic, very proud of her ancestry. Her husband was a petty clerk. So she sold him short and sneered at him. She wanted to keep her husband under her thumb.

Day by day as a corollary the situation became unfavourable. His wife utterly neglected him. Invariably he went unfed. He no longer lived in clover.

Dada's hotel was his only shelter during his miserable plight. Gajendra regretted his mistake that he had committed in the past. His sons were foppish. He did all the monkey business for their survival and snatched the property of others by sharp practice. He never shared the woes of his close relatives. He winked at his doting uncle when he was bedridden. He bit the hand which had once fed him with loving care. He had messed up his life but there was no turning back. Now the table of fortune turned hostile to him. On his last legs, Gajendra was confined to bed. There was no one to say a consoling word to him. Even his wife was reluctant to wait upon her husband. He died in comatose.

FIFTEEN

It was a foggy morning. Sambit did not go to his clinic in this lousy weather. It was fit for reading a book. After three hours, tired of staying indoors, he put the book on the table and went out.

He looked at the sombre sky and strolled towards the Gujri market.

He spotted Mr. Bhuyan from a distance. Standing near a bookstall, he was absorbed in reading a book.

Sambit patted his shoulder. Mr. Bhuyan turned to him. "What are you doing Mr. Bhuyan in this foggy weather?"

"Nothing, just killing time. Let us go to the Jubilee library. It is a lonely place and we would have an amusing talk there."

The grassy field inside the campus had been manicured and there were a lot of flower plants on both sides of the metalled road.

"Let us sit on this grass-bed".

Mr. Bhuyan sat cross-legged and pulled Sambit's hand to sit beside him.

"What's your progress in writing?" Sambit asked.

"Yes, my two books have been published in Delhi by a reputable publishing house. I am now writing a book based on the cultural heritage of India".

"Very good. I meet you every day in the market. You are not coming for a longtime. What's the problem with you?"

"It is a serious matter, brother. You know my wife is a science teacher in M.K.C. High School. During H.S.C. exam my wife was one of the invigilators. She saw a boy copying something in his examination paper. He was caught at the spot and the copy was submitted to the centre superintendent.

That evening the guardian of the boy unexpectedly arrived at our house. He was in apprehension that his son would be expelled for this offence. There was no way out to get over this problem. My wife advised him to approach the Centre superintendent as she could do nothing in this matter".

Mr. Bhuyan took a little pause for a while and said, "We offered him snacks and tea but he betrayed us in return. He marked a stack of wood-plank in the corner of our drawing room and, being vengeful, informed the ranger of the forest department.

The next morning they came in a van and seized our wood. They loaded the van and drove away.

"Have you tried to restore them?"

"No, it is no use crying over spilt milk. I am trying to forget that unpleasant incident".

"Listen, one of my friends built a two-storeyed building. He purchased a huge number of wood-planks to make doors and windows. After some days he received a letter of objection from the forest department. He was totally upset, vacillating between hope and despair. He was asked to give a satisfactory explanation for the illegal stack of wood.

I took the responsibility to comply with it. I wrote in that letter that every day the wood-thieves, loading their bicycles with planks, go past my house. If it is unlawful, how do they carry on their business under the nose of guards and foresters? Even the employees of the forest department purchase planks from the wood-cutters. They forget the mote in their own eyes.

Mr. Bhuyan, the more we get slack, the more will be their audacity. We must put up a fight against injustice. That will shake their haughtiness".

Sambit shrugged his shoulders and asked, "How far have you gone in writing that book?"

"There remained a few chapters for its completion. My wife is the one who has brought me down in life. Reading and writing are allergens to her. Had any woman been in her position, she would have inspired her husband. But my wife is made of different elements. She is a dissatisfied soul. She always picks a quarrel for a very trivial matter and remains sulky for a number of days. She has made my life miserable. I have warned her time and again not to disturb me while my mind is riveted on writing something. It is just like the austerities of the monks. Like armour, it protects me from the strafe of outside world. I maintain my sangfroid removing myself from worldly concerns, showing stoic resignation towards my fate. I am inured to pain and suffering".

Mr. Bhuyan stopped there and asked Sambit, "I am unable to understand why God has given me such a venomous snake"? Hatred began to stir in his heart.

Sambit interrupted him and said, "The women belong to a separate species. They are incapable of understanding the intrinsic values of life. Most of them are work-shy and do not utilise their time profitably. Engagement in some work plays a very significant role in maintaining one's mental stability. Those who waste their time lavishly not caring about its consequences, they suffer in the long run.

One can keep calmness of mind by reading good books. But regret to say many educated persons are averse to book reading. These certificate holders hide their shallowness under the veneer of knowledgeable persons. They try to protect their image and feel themselves uppish in the cloak of a learned man. Only to pass in the examination and get a job thereby, they burn the midnight oil, otherwise they spend their time lazing away with others.

Now modern life has become cliché-ridden, dull and dreary, losing the zest for life. Majority of people are rotting in that cesspool, still they are unaware of their meaningful existence.

We visit temple, church, mosque and gurdwara but we have no heartfelt devoutness. Can you tell me how many of them go to the place of worship with a pure heart? How many women pay unflinching devotion to their husband? On the contrary, how many husbands keep their marital fidelity until the last? They pose as though they are very pious but inside they are as black as coal.``

Mr. Bhuyan nodded his head in agreement.

"One of my friends, a mathematician and retired principal of the college, never goes to any temple but he is a genuine votary of religion and not a pseudo-religious like other people.

One day I requested him to accompany me to the temple. But he denied me right away. He explained that if you are honest in your thought and action, what is the use of going to the temple? Visiting a religious place with a tainted mind is not at all rewarding. Better sit at home, help the poor according to your capacity, give assistance to the blind and infirm if you ever come across them and you will definitely get the blessings of God.

So under present circumstances, being unperturbed you go on writing. Sometimes the adverse side of life brings a chain of miseries to the poets and writers but with untiring zeal you have to muddle through these problems.

Do you know Xanthippe, the shrewish wife of Socrates, a celebrated Greek philosopher? Xanthippe means an ill-tempered woman. As there is no alternative, you have to put up with an ill-disposed situation".

Mr. Bhuyan concurred with his views.

The next day Sambit went to Mr. Bhuyan's house to see his garden. He was busy putting a fence around it. Trees like mango, coconut, jamun, bel, jackfruits had been planted in the backyard of his house. There was a well in one corner of his land where some hibiscus plants were swinging in the gentle breeze with brightly coloured flowers.

Mr. Bhuyan turned back and saw Sambit keeping his bicycle beside his gate. He stopped working and welcomed Sambit with a laughing face.

"What are you doing Mr. Bhuyan?"

"Just a physical exercise. You can't get a good labourer to do your work satisfactorily. So I fully utilise my leisure in doing all these things".

Then he washed his hands and feet and said eagerly, "You are my guest, you cannot go home without having lunch with me. The tank near the temple is well- stocked with fish. A fisherman used to catch fish everyday there. I bought a big carp which I cooked for my children. Fortunately you have come to our house by God's grace".

"Do you cook everyday? How could you learn this art of cooking? I must relish your preparation".

"You see Mr. Sambit, women are very egoistic as they know cooking. Without their help, nobody can take a morsel of food. But my case is different.

I never seek the help of others in this work. If my wife goes to school in a hurry, I take the responsibility of cooking and feeding my children. Actually our relationship is just mechanical. We are not living together harmoniously".

"Strange are the ways of life. Stranger is the nature of woman. Why do they come to this world? If they shirk their duty, what is the value of their human life?" Sambit was outraged.

Mr. Bhuyan was in a quandary. He expressed his greatest regret. "It is just like crying in the wilderness. My lot is like that. Neither can I swallow nor can I eject it. I am living in my own world. I want to live in seclusion, not to be disturbed by the cavilling nature of the outsiders. Absorbed in reading and writing I have become unconcerned about the day-to-day happenings of this world. I am doing my worldly duties and nobody can blame me for that. But I awfully failed in my worldly mission. Though I am trying to achieve my final goal, my aspirations remain unfulfilled. I know who has scotched my progress. From my childhood days, I have been living in a make-believe euphoria. But I get consolation when I remember the immortal lines of the Bhagavad Gita.

'With the achievement of placidity of mind, all the sorrows come to an end and the intellect of such a person of tranquil mind soon withdrawing itself from all sides, becomes firmly established in God.'

So I have been dreadfully mistaken. I wake up to the realities of life. My longing for transitory things, craving for knick-knacks, crying for a lollipop gives no complacency to my soul. I will live with my chin up, laughing away the problems of life with gusto.   I will remain composed biding my time to listen to my long-awaited swansong".

After a couple of weeks Sambit was wonder-struck when he heard the sad news of Mr. Bhuyan. His heart began to pound rapidly. He could not believe that he had been arrested by the police and was now in police lock-up. For what offence? Was he enmeshed with some nasty dispute? What was his crime? Did the forest department lodge a case against him?

He hurtled to the police station.

With the permission of the police inspector he met Mr. Bhuyan.

He was kept in a semi-dark room which gave out a very offensive smell. A shadow of disappointment paled his face.

"Why did the police arrest you, Mr. Bhuyan? I must go to a good lawyer to release you on bail. Don't dither to speak out the fact".

Mr. Bhuyan's body stirred a little and he recounted his plight in a choked voice.

"In this scorching heat of summer, I came from my college by bus. It was so jam-packed that I could not find a space even to stand comfortably. Sandwiched by the co-passengers, I alighted at the bus-stand at 2.00 p.m. I had not taken any food till that time.

Back home, I washed my hands and feet to feel refreshed. I was so exhausted that I had no patience even to put off my dress. At that time my wife abused me in her high-pitched voice for a very trifling matter. I told her that there is enough time to do that thing. Now I am terribly hungry and let me take my lunch first. But she was a heartless woman. She did not care whether I took my lunch or starved to death. Many times this type of squabble shattered the peaceful atmosphere of our home. She became truculent. In a fit of anger she tugged my banian and tore it into pieces. A demoniac fury blazed inside me. Something snapped in my brain. I planted a heavy slap on her face. She burst into the kitchen and flung the cooking wares, rice, dal and vegetables curry to the dining room. It was horrible as these things were scattered all around the room. Then in anger she stormed out of the house and lodged a complaint against me in the police station".

Mr. Bhuyan took a brief pause and said with tearful eyes, "I have already reached the end of my patience. I do admit anger is a very vile thing. If somebody is unable to control it, he will undoubtedly create havoc. Arson, rape, murder, molestation are being done when a man goes out of his head. I am a modest and upright man. But when my temper is frayed, I can do any heinous thing which nobody can imagine. In such domestic fracas I usually remain silent and try to retain a shred of my prestige. But my wife is not conscious of that. She goes on raving and ranting without thinking of its consequences. Sometimes I think about abandoning my family and going somewhere to live in peace and happiness. But the tender faces of my children float up before my eyes which compels me to rot permanently here. Can they imagine what I have sacrificed for them?"

Their conversation was interrupted by a police constable. He unlocked the door and said, "Sir, our inspector sahib wants to ask you something".

The inspector was seated on a revolving chair and he was turning over the pages of some registers kept on the table.

Mr. Bhuyan and Sambit stood in front of him. The officer looked very solemn and cast a sneaky glance at them.

"Why standing, be seated on the chair". His voice sounded a little harsh.

Then he turned to Mr. Bhuyan majestically and asked, "Yes, what do you do Mr - ?"

"I am Manoranjan Bhuyan, sir. I teach Political Science in some aided college".

"So teaching is your profession. Don't you teach your students etiquette, how to behave with others?"

Mr. Bhuyan could know the motive of the officer. He remained silent.

The officer whacked the table with his baton and said in a stern voice.

"You wife-beater! Do you know I can send you to jail straightaway".

Mr. Bhuyan was irritated. He burst out. "I care a fig if I am convicted for this minor offence".

Sambit interfered, "Sir, my friend is very gentle and sober. To tell you the truth his wife is quarrelsome and does not pay respect to her husband. Mr. Bhuyan is an international awardee in literature and his contribution is, no doubt, commendable".

The police officer seemed oblivious to his statement. He stood and hitched up his pants. Then he swaggered to the urinal with vexation.

The same constable came to them and whispered, "Our officer is very lenient and kindhearted. Give him at least five hundred rupees. He will acquit you from all charges."

Mr. Bhuyan was extremely irritated. He exploded, "Why?

Have I come with a wallet in my pocket? I won't give him a single pie".

Running his fingers through his hair the constable retraced back to his room.

Mr. Bhuyan remained stubborn. The officer hollered at the constable to bring him a hot cup of tea. His plan to earn some pocket money was gone. Mr. Bhuyan's uprightness took the wind out of his sails.

He gave an undertaking and left the police station with Sambit.

"I never venture to say that women are the gateway to hell. They may wage a crusade against me. This much I can say they must be tolerant and cooperative so that the hand which rocks the cradle will lull the whole world", Sambit philosophised.

BLACK EAGLE BOOKS

www.blackeaglebooks.org
info@blackeaglebooks.org

Black Eagle Books, an independent publisher, was founded as a nonprofit organization in April, 2019. It is our mission to connect and engage the Indian diaspora and the world at large with the best of works of world literature published on a collaborative platform, with special emphasis on foregrounding Contemporary Classics and New Writing.